Published by Darlington Press Australia
darlingtonpress.com

ISBN: 978-0-9873305-7-4

ALSO BY PRUE BATTEN

The Chronicles of Eirie

Book One – *The Stumpwork Robe*
Book Two – *The Last Stitch*
Book Three – *A Thousand Glass Flowers*

PRAISE FOR PRUE BATTEN'S OTHER NOVELS

A Thousand Glass Flowers

'Prue Batten leads the way with elegant adult historic fantasy. The Eirie Chronicles set the bar for modern fantasy authors wanting to tread the fine line between reality and fantasy. A fairy tale for the twenty-first century.'
Saffina Desforges, Kindle UK best-selling author of Sugar & Spice and the Rose Red series

'A sweeping, gorgeously written tale of magic, adventure, intrigue – and the very human power of enduring love. It held me spellbound.'
Anna Elliott, author of The Avalon Trilogy

'A magnificent evocation of a parallel world whose joys and sorrows are our own. Beautifully done.'
Ann Swinfen, author of In Defence of Fantasy

'Gloriously described – I simply put this as the best book I've read this year, possibly in the last five. I have read *G R R Martin's* magical *'A Song Of Ice & Fire'* series and thought nothing could beat it. A Thousand Glass Flowers has, and not one of those precious petals is shattered.'
Amazon.co.uk review

The Stumpwork Robe

'... a master artist's skill in painting with words. This has
been the freshest and most unique reading experience
I've had in many a month of Sundays.'
Amazon.com review

'I read both The Stumpwork Robe and the sequel The Last Stitch.
Prue Batten has talent as a writer – the world she creates is beautiful
and believable. She has cleverly woven Celtic mythology and the lore
of the fae into a semi-medieval world. Her characters are vivid
and engaging, and the plot kept me reading on, wanting
to know where it would go.'
Amazon.com review

The Last Stitch

'The author has created a world that is beautiful, frightening,
very real and very different from our own world.'
Amazon.com review

'Batten's writing retains the dreamlike glow of the folktales
she uses so inventively, and adds a chill and ruthlessness
that make fairytales into nightmares.'
Amazon.com review

Gisborne

BOOK OF PAWNS

Darlington
PRESS

AUSTRALIA

Acknowledgements

To Jane V for her copious research in Northwest England
and North Wales on my behalf and to she and Patricia for reading
and commenting from the very beginning.
To John Hudspith for his editing, his advice and his
wonderfully strengthening wit.

To my husband, Robert, who has faithfully supported
me despite my *affaire* with Guy of Gisborne.

And to Milo for being my muse all of his dog's life. (1997–2012)

AUTHOR'S NOTE

Sir Guy of Gisborne is in essence a legendary character, possibly first mentioned in *Child Ballad #118* but potentially in an even older story. Traditionally he is associated with the legend of Robin Hood but I have chosen to move far from the familiar canon and imagine what might have happened in altered circumstances.

Because Gisborne is linked to the reign of Richard Lionheart, the story I have written takes place at the cusp of the twelfth and thirteenth centuries and I have tried where possible to be faithful to the times. Much commentary and research of the period is contradictory so I have taken whichever fact fitted my narrative most comfortably.

There are other liberties throughout the story – the most obvious being Ysabel of Moncrieff's marital status. With her background, wealth and accomplishments, it is highly unlikely she would be unmarried at the age we find her in the novel. At the very least, she would have an arranged marriage to a wealthy nobleman of some standing. I have chosen to take Ysabel out of the mould for the purposes of the story.

And finally, I have used Julian of Norwich's quote out of its later time frame. It is a beautiful saying and fits the theme of the story.

'I dwell by dale and downe,' quoth Guye,
and I have done many a curst turne;
and he that calles me by my right name
Calles me Guye of good Gysborne.'
Child Ballad #118

'And all shall be well, and all shall be well,
and all manner of thing shall be well.'
Julian of Norwich

CHAPTER ONE

The parchment crackled as it opened and I angled it to the light at the window. *'To Lady Ysabel Moncrieff, my daughter, It is with sadness that I inform you of the death of your loved and adored mother, Alaïs de Cazenay, Lady Moncrieff.'*

The letter was dated two months previous and was signed with my father's name, his seal buried in uncompromising oak gall tinted wax. I glanced at the packet again in the hope there would be more words ... something, anything. But my father had sent no message of comfort or orders for my future and I was bereft.

As the writing blurred and I held hard to the stone windowsill, I thought that in eight weeks my mother had died, been buried and had a mass said for her soul every day whilst I sang, danced, hunted and gamed with my Cazenay cousins and friends in Aquitaine. My heart ached with the poignancy of it all and I wept, the tears blotting the green of my gown.

I drifted around the domain in a dark and distant mood and my cousins could barely touch me in my grief because I adored my mother and had lost my way with no one to show me the path back ... my mother, a beauty and a cousin twice removed from the great Queen Eleanor of Aquitaine. Alaïs deserved to be lauded by the troubadours across the land because Eleanor had thought her a jewel beyond measure and had not been pleased to give the hand of one of her favourite ladies to my father. *He* was Joffrey of Moncrieff, an English Baron of greater ranking and the man who appeared to have forgotten his duty to his child.

I saddled my mare, Khazia, the next day and the groom helped me mount, the gown folds hitched into the girdle that hung at my hips. I wanted to gallop and cry far from the meaningless prattle of the castle confines. I wanted to grieve, rent my clothes if I desired and as soon as I was over the drawbridge, the mare stampeded downhill over stones and round jutting boulders with me caring nothing for her safety or my own. My heart hurt. I had not been able to see my mother for two years nor tell her what she meant to me in her last days. It seemed to me that I had deserted her when she needed her daughter beyond measure.

Khazia snorted and started sideways and through my tears I noticed another mount gaining on my flank, saw a hand reach out to grab my reins. Pressure was brought to bear on the bit and Khazia slowed, shaking her head in protest, the horse alongside matching her pace.

Eventually we stopped and both animals stood heaving whilst I swallowed on my pain and turned to stare at the man who had halted me. He still held my rein but bowed his head slightly and spoke. The resonant tone of his voice burrowed through my hurt and blood thumped through my limbs in consequence.

'Lady Ysabel, I am sorry for your loss but breaking an innocent animal's legs does neither you nor your mother any credit.'

I went to slap his face, a face with strong planes and shadows of tiredness, but he grabbed my wrist, tugged hard so that I had to lean toward him, and then calmly placed my fingers back across the reins. His eyes met mine glance for glance, the air solid and tempestuous, but something in his expression touched my grief and my anger stilled for a moment.

I was sure he felt compassion for me, not pity like the rest of Cazenay society, but a kindred understanding of loss and confusion. The mare blew loudly down her nose and shook herself and I realized this man was right; I had been thoughtless and cruel.

I slid down, my gown still hitched inelegantly high, and he dismounted beside me. He towered above with height and broad shoulders, reminding me how effeminate were the men I had known. I guessed he was older than myself by a year or two, perhaps a little more, and he had a manner that implied he had seen life far more than I.

'I am Guy of Gisborne, Lady, and I am charged to return you to Moncrieff forthwith.'

I gasped as I held out a sweaty hand that he took but did not kiss, holding his dark hair back with the other hand. I was to go home, and my heart so lately broken began to warm and I almost thought I might bear my mother's death after all. Gisborne's palm was dry and cool and something about the way our fingers touched slowed the world around me. A blush warmed my cheeks and I glanced at him from under my lashes, noticing he was intent upon me.

'When, sir? When do we go? I am desperate to return.'

'Tomorrow at cockcrow. They pack your immediate needs now. Your chests will follow.'

I stood looking out over the view of the stony valley with the fierce lapis sky and the river trailing away between ivory cliff walls and brushed falling hair back from my forehead.

He followed my gaze.

'It's not the cool green of England's shores, is it?'

His voice held a degree of sarcasm and as he wiped at his brow, a faint sheen of sweat peeled away under his palm.

He was dressed in leggings and laced leather boots that creased across his ankles and the southern winds blew a linen chemise back hard against his chest. For the first time in recent days I smiled.

'But they write excellent poetry, have delectable food and play at courtly manners like none other.'

His mouth barely curled and yet I could see he was amused.

'I read and I write and yet I believe there's a time and place for it. Things here seem out of balance. Too much sweetness and not enough savoury.'

'Is Moncrieff any better?' I asked. 'It is so long since I have seen it. Eight years, Sir Guy.'

'I am not yet a knight, merely your father's steward.'

'You are a knight because you rescue me from this place and return me to my father. How does he? I miss him.'

'I have only been in your father's service for six months, Lady Ysabel. But in truth I would say he is much aged and your presence may sooth him in his troubles.'

My heart jumped and I grabbed Gisborne's arm. 'What troubles? Is he ill?'

I could see he chose his words carefully but I could decipher nothing beneath what he said.

'He grieves,' he replied.

Tears threatened again. Of course my father would grieve; Alaïs was his light.

'Tomorrow you say? How long will it take us?'

'A month to reach the northerly coast, perhaps a few days to sail to the English coast depending on the seas and then two weeks to ride to Moncrieff.'

As he spoke, he helped me mount, and I brushed away the tears that finally trickled down my cheeks. I was to go home at last. So many times I had craved it, losing my temper with the heat, the affectations of my friends, wanting nothing but the quiet, calm cool of Moncrieff.

Momentarily I wondered why I should want to go home so badly with my mother gone. But then I recalled the dour walls of Moncrieff and the way the building stood proud in the middle of its little lake. The way the water that underlined fens life trickled, rushed and sometimes just stood as reflective as a burnished piece of steel. But more than anything, I realized my mother's heart and soul were still there and I wanted to be close to her.

It was my family's habit from when I was born, to make the arduous journey to Aquitaine once yearly so that Alaïs could enjoy the southern climes and meet with our cousins. My father Joffrey loved Aquitaine and would sink himself deep into his wife's familial society. I sometimes wondered if he preferred it to Moncrieff which is northeast of London, as flat as a trencher and surrounded by the blurred edges of fens and marshes.

I loved my family home and Cazenay equally but if I had a choice, Moncrieff was where I belonged because they say often enough that home is where the heart is. On less damp ground, Moncrieff had valuable fields and its forests were sought after for reputable hunting and I had reveled in the riding, even as a child.

In addition, Moncrieff Castle was considered a well-appointed and comfortable place because my mother filled it with acquisitions from Aquitaine, my father's purse strings always open. But its singular most remarkable claim on my affections was its position in the middle of a lake. My father had the habit of calling my mother his Lady of the Lake after the spirit in the legend of Arthur the King and I loved the mysterious nature of such a title.

When I turned twelve, Mama sent me to Aquitaine to join my Cazenay cousins in the belief the sophistication of the courts would add a sparkle to my charm and the chance of an advantageous liaison. Ensconced in an eyrie-like bastion that hung on the edge of white ravines, I enjoyed the atmosphere, but whilst I became educated in the courtly style, I missed the pale colours of my home – the mystic trees and reed-frilled fens, the forests that wrapped around and whispered legends in my ear and the lake on which the swans and I would float.

Despite such longings, at fifteen I was as polished as I could be and becoming objectionable. By twenty, and still in Aquitaine, I was bored. Worse, I was unmarried. My father had dallied with possible marriage settlements but he had hardly been diligent, losing interest if any complication arose. Meetings with suitors were arranged but no son nor their father would have me because I was sharp, opinionated and as accomplished as all of them at hawking and poetry ... even gambling. Worse, I could shoot a bow better than any of them and I suspect they felt emasculated. So I was every man's best friend but most assuredly not a lover nor likely mother of children and my Papa seemed unworried.

My mother? Ah, she despaired.

'My beautiful Ysabel,' she would say. 'Can you be a little less outspoken, a little more accommodating?'

Each year she would arrive at the beginning of the English winter and she would find her daughter a little more refined. At eighteen, I was concerned when an ague kept her at Moncrieff. At nineteen, I fretted that a further ailment prevented her annual sojourn. At twenty, the hateful messenger's packet arrived and my life changed in the time the heart takes to beat once.

Cazenay's skies did not weep for me as I left. The blinding blue stretched as far as the eye could see and the white cliff walls of southern Aquitaine intensified the glare. I did not cry either but my handmaid, Marais, sniffed until I told her to desist.

'It's like the Holy Land,' Gisborne grumbled as we headed away, by which I presume he meant the heat of the south.

I confess I too was hot and took no time when we halted for a comfort stop, in removing my overgown, rolling it and shoving it in a bag on my saddle. I wore just my kirtle, revealing bare arms as I lifted my hair into a plaited coronet on top of the head away from a sweat coated neck.

'You have been there?' I enquired.

'No,' Gisborne answered. 'But I know it's hot as Hades and it may be part of my plan to...'

Being hot made me testy and so I leaped in.

'Why must all men feel they should go to the Holy Land as a rite of passage. Why is it necessary to kill a Saracen before you can call yourself a man?'

'You do not believe in the Christian fight then?'

'I do not. What right do we have to tramp men of an alternate belief into the ground? It is not something *my* God would ask of His believers. Of that I am sure.'

'Then you think King Henry was wrong?'

'I do and I have no doubt Queen Eleanor thought the same after she saw Jerusalem for herself when she was Louis' consort.'

I pushed back a stray lock of hair and noticed Guy looking at my bare arm.

'In the time I have been at Cazenay,' I continued, 'I have met traveling Saracens who are erudite, great healers and men of learning that make us look like primitives. But what hope do we women have of stopping such madness as a crusade. Men are plain stupid sometimes,' I added with just enough disrespect to make a point.

'As are women with bare arms and uncovered heads who parade before men. Lady, for myself I don't mind. But we have men at arms with us who may not be so couth.'

He expression cooled the air. Nothing like the man I had met yesterday and who had opened a door for me to a new life away from Aquitaine and who had heated my skin like a ray of southern sun.

I sighed with no attempt at concealing my petulance.

'Oh for heavens' sake. I am showing no more than their own mothers and wives show in the fields and I am familiar with half of them – they are Moncrieff men who have known me from the cradle.'

'Without doubt,' he replied in a superior manner. 'But you are nobility and should act accordingly.'

I turned to see if he was serious and God help me he was. His face had not a vestige of a smile. I could not contain myself and burst out laughing.

'My memory of Moncrieff such as it is, is that the nobility create their own rules as they go along. Today's bad taste could be tomorrow's new fashion.' Then I added as an afterthought, 'Rather like a crusade.'

To which his mouth gave a twitch.

'You make your point, Lady Ysabel. But let me say, the attitudes of Aquitaine have been your life for eight years. You may have forgotten what England is like. There is a stiff decorum in the houses of the nobility with whom you will associate. It is best you acclimatize yourself to that fact before you reach Moncrieff. It would not do to upset your father.'

I felt put upon.

'So I have spent eight years learning to be something which will not suit England when I could have been back in Moncrieff being truly happy.'

Our horses jogged a little and conversation became difficult but my calf rubbed against Gisborne's and our stirrups clinked. I pushed my mare apart although I would have been happy to be alongside for a while longer. I tried not to analyse what this man aroused in me and to merely enjoy our jousting. There was sharpness, as if a blade could sigh too close to my neck and the danger thrilled me.

As our horses settled, he commented. 'Perhaps both your parents thought you would marry in Aquitaine and it would thus be time well spent.'

'Marry any of those precious poets?' My voice had lifted and I laughed again. 'Jesu sir, songs and chivalry are all very well but I crave to marry a *man*.'

My mare had jogged ahead again and all I heard from behind was a very low, 'Indeed.'

Thus we debated and discussed for three days on the road and as we talked, I felt I came to know the man a little more each day. The erudition of this mere steward surprised me. He talked of the *Y Cynfeirdd* of Wales and the *Fomoire* of Ireland, legends about people with strange names that I could barely wrap my tongue around. We talked of illuminated manuscripts and I told him of my admiration for the church scribes. In all, I was curious that he knew so much. He even quoted poetry written by Prince Richard during his times in Aquitaine. I was beyond grateful that he kept my grief at bay because I was afraid the weight of it would undo me.

During one of our nightly encampments, Marais and I sat under a canopy the escort had rigged for us. I watched Gisborne moving among the men with assurance and with an air of command that seemed to come naturally. It was not quite dark and being mild, he worked in a chemise, strapping his horse with wads of grass and chatting with the men. He towered over the escort and I could see the width of his shoulder as he dragged the twisted grass over the sweat marks on his mount. Marais muttered about her own saddle sores but I allowed her complaint to drift over me. And then Gisborne turned and our eyes met. His gaze held mine and I could not help my lips curving slightly before I lowered my head and flicked grass seeds from my hem.

But I knew as sure as the moon would rise that night that a thread existed between us. It might be fine and breakable but I still had six weeks left to encourage its strengthening, despite the fact that I mourned a mother. I thought on her and wished I could talk with her about men, about what I might expect and what they might desire. But it was too late and how I regretted it, because that spark as Gisborne and I parried our comment back and forth was a pleasure that had fast become a craving.

The next day I noticed Gisborne had changed the formation of our troupe. He placed two men at arms in the front, two on either side of Marais and myself and he and two others brought up the rear. I looked back at him but he avoided my glance as he gave the order to move out.

What had I done wrong the night before? Perhaps I really did need my mother's aid and experience. I recalled smiling at him as it grew dark but I didn't recollect that I was unladylike or false. And yet now he avoided me as if I were plague-ridden. And I couldn't even see him as he rode behind. I knew he would be watching me, how could he not when our horses were practically nose to rump, but I did not behave in an unseemly fashion. I remained quiet and only spoke intermittently to Marais.

I could barely manage the next two days which proved long and tiresome; I was sick of my own company let alone that of Marais who whinged about her homesickness. How tantalising had been the brief foray into more refined conversation with my escort. Now I just had the whining of my maidservant in my ear like the drone of a mosquito in the middle of a hot summer's night.

Our travelling pace was geared to Marais' equestrian skills which were limited. She rode a wide-girthed and very seasoned mare but I chafed to make speed and Marais' unhappy progress annoyed me. Without her, I would have encouraged the men to make haste and we would have been in Le Havre or Calais in half the time, ready to find a ship and some good weather.

I knew instantly that I must rid myself of her before we reached the coast. She belonged at Cazenay because she would moulder and wither in the dampness of the fens and the shade of the Moncrieff forests. As soon as was politic, I would ask Gisborne to arrange safe return for her and I would continue on unchaperoned.

Occasionally what could have been dreary isolation was leavened by the travellers we encountered – merchants, nobility, men at arms, mercenaries and pilgrims. Travellers were always willing to pass the time and thus we heard that King Henry and Queen Eleanor were in marital dispute again. Henry's amorous adventures with half the beauties of Christendom were assuming the scope of legend and it was the only time I heard Marais' voice lighten as she seized on the libidinous facts.

In truth though, Henry was rumoured to be severely unwell and I privately questioned that he would live to a ripe age. His sons continued to battle around him, with each other and with him, and over it all hung the shadow of dark John and golden Richard. I remembered John as a child in Aquitaine and liked him not one bit. He reminded me of the kind of fiend that would pull the wings off flies. Richard on the other hand had Eleanor's heart and the appearance of a hero. I had no doubt where some of the legend would lie after we were dead and gone.

I posed the question to Gisborne.

'Prince John or Prince Richard? Who would you have as your liege lord?'

He started at my voice, as if he had been sure the new troupe formation should keep me quiet and away from his ears. I twisted around to look back at him and for a bare second he gazed at me and then away as if I smelled of something abhorrent. Lord knows why he should treat me thus and it had gone beyond confusing me to a simmering anger.

'Well?' I prompted, feeling the heat of battle begin to burn. 'Are you afraid to answer? Have you no opinions of your own?' I could be cutting when I was angry. It is not a merit of which I am proud.

He seemed to grow before me, his eyes raking me as good as a thrashing. He had a way of diminishing one by the every act of looking down a rather patrician nose from his excessive height upon the leggy rouncey.

'A liege lord is one to whom I have pledged fealty. In my instance, either man has my loyalty. If Richard becomes King I shall swear allegiance to him. If I am a knight, it is what one does. If Prince John became King, I should do the same. But it is a rhetorical question, Lady Ysabel, as King Henry still lives, his sons are vital and one presumes there is a succession plan.'

Furious with his condescending manner, I kicked my mare into a canter and leaped ahead of the troupe causing Marais to be even more querulous, for Gisborne to swear roundly at which I lifted my lips, and for the troupe to hasten after me.

As before, a horse galloped up from behind, a hand grabbed the reins and that voice said, 'You really are a wilful child, are you not?'

My horse stamped about, pulling away from the gauntleted fingers. 'If you think so, Gisborne, you must be right.'

But inside I chuckled.

You see? Two can play at this game.

But by the time we entered Tours, some two weeks of us irritating each other had escalated to a seriously heated moment. I had walked off on my own through a woodland path to a stream without telling Marais and sat enjoying the pastoral views of fields and sheep and villeins working the land, their holdings little squares of tilled and sown ground like some patchworked cloth. It pleased me to be on my own for I had nothing of solitude these days in which to indulge my memories of my mother. The peace I now garnered was balm to the very roots of my being and I couldn't help a disgruntled sigh when Gisborne strode into my presence.

'If you weren't the daughter of my employer, lady or no, I would lay you over my knee and thrash you for your wilful and ignorant behaviour.' He didn't shout but the words rolled out like stones from a trebuchet. The fury that gave impetus to the words was harnessed in hands that clenched as if round the throat of an assailant.

24

'Are you my keeper?' My voice began to lift. 'Mary Mother, all I want is *peace*. Far from your sour moods and Marais' carping. She clings like poison ivy and you glower like a perpetual thunderstorm. Go away, Gisborne. Leave me. I shall return at my leisure.'

'I *AM* YOUR KEEPER,' he shouted and then lowered his voice and ground the next words out as if he wanted his heel to crush them into the ground. 'I am under orders to bring you home safely to Moncrieff. You will return to the rest of the group now. I will not have Marais weeping as though you are dead and the men searching. Christ, Ysabel, will you grow up?'

I was prepared to admit to a degree of guilt, if only to myself. I had not meant to hurt Marais or even to place the men under any sort of threat. I pushed past my father's steward but could not avoid the last word.

'*Lady* Ysabel, Gisborne. *Lady* Ysabel.'

But the point was his as the velvet voice rumbled behind me.

'You spoiled little bitch.'

It was true. Spoiled indeed. There was no doubting the fact as Marais collapsed upon me like a falling tree and wept far more than the occasion demanded. Her own grief at loss of home and family had become a matter requiring tact and civility as soon as possible.

Marais and myself were settled in a small nunnery in Tours attached to the Abbaye de Saint Julien where it was quiet and befitted my status as a lady of rank. Gisborne turned to go but I placed my hand on his sleeve. He wore a leather tunic as we travelled and the worn hide felt soft and smooth under my fingers, as if it had been worn for many years under untold conditions. It moulded itself to his forearm leaving an impression of muscle and tendon beneath my touch.

'I must ask for your time, sir.' Oh, I was so polite. 'I realise you wish to get to your own hostelry but I must talk with you about Marais. Please?'

He nodded his head and took me by the elbow to a bench near the gate.

'Marais must return to Cazenay. No, please … hear me out. She weeps daily and will never settle in the fens. I think you know this as well as I.'

'Indeed,' he replied. 'She suffers pining sickness beyond what I would have hoped for your companion.'

'Then you must see it is a kindness to return her forthwith. Now that we are in Tours, I am proposing we find a group of pilgrims or merchants heading south. If we cannot find that, then send some of the men back with her.'

His face barely moved and it crossed my mind briefly what a spy he might make, never betraying a single thing in his expression.

'But,' he replied. 'It means you will not have a chaperone and your father…'

'Oh please. You think someone like Marais will be able to protect my innocence between here and England? Guy,' his name slipped out and he shifted as we sat together. 'Guy, do not. Just return her to Aquitaine and me to Moncrieff. It is all I ask. I promise I shall be biddable if you do.'

His mouth quirked and because he appeared to soften, I thought to press my case.

'May I ask you something? Did I offend you on that first day of our travels, that you should avoid talking to me or being near me while we ride?'

He rubbed his hands together and leaned forward, black hair falling over his collar.

'No. I changed the way we rode for safety reasons. As to avoiding you, I felt it was unseemly for us to ride together. You are a lady and I am a mere steward.'

'Oh don't be ridiculous.' I laughed. 'If I know anything at all, it is that you are noble-born. As if it matters. You could be a villein and if I thought you were interesting I would talk to you.'

'Perhaps. But I am your father's employee and charged with your safety. If you remember anything of England, my lady, you will remember that status is everything.'

'Status is nothing but being born on the right side of the blankets,' I scoffed.

He said something then that I would reflect on later, something that was much bigger than I gave it credit for at the time. He stood and paced, his expression revealing deep-seated bitterness. His eyes darkened and in profile he resembled nothing so much as a bird of prey.

'Status,' he said, 'is power.'

CHAPTER TWO

'You must let me come with you. If an escort is to be found for my maidservant, then I am surely entitled to have a say in who they might be.' Gisborne shook his head. 'It is not seemly…'

'For a Lady to go about seeking pilgrims or merchants with her steward? Lord, Sir Gisborne, I think it is more than seemly. You can step two paces behind if it is more appropriate.'

He stood, muttering under his breath as he turned away and my words chased him.

'I beg your pardon, sir, I did not hear what you said.'

'I recall saying something about spoiled and thrashings. Your manner has not improved my mind.'

'Yours is little better.' I sighed. 'All I am asking is the right to find the travellers who could best care for Marais. She has been my companion as much as a maidservant for the eight years I was at Cazenay. It is the least I can do for her. Please?'

He walked to the gate as he answered, his spurs jingling in the tranquil and dove-filled quiet of the forecourt.

'Tomorrow, then. After you have broken your fast. Good day to you, my *lady*.'

I said nothing to Marais about sending her back to Aquitaine. I would not have her disillusioned if we could find no escort of any sort. The following morning after breaking our fast in the refectory with other guests, I told her that Guy of Gisborne would accompany me to the market and that she was to rest. She said something then which bought a smile to my face.

'You watch that Gisborne, my lady. I can see you are smitten with him. But he has a dark streak which will muddy your own waters.'

'Heavens, Marais, what *can* you mean?'

I turned away and looked out to the forecourt where I could see the man standing in the early morning sun. Sometimes I wondered if that stillness was merely a studied attempt at ease – to conceal the fact that he may be heartsore and tired beyond belief. He looked toward me and I hastily stepped behind a pillar as Marais continued.

'He is a man laced with bitterness. You can see it in the back of his eyes and such bitterness can eat away at a man's insides.'

'Oh Marais.' I laughed as if I had not a care in the world. 'Do you think I wish to love him? Jesu, how wrong you are. He merely returns me to my father. Besides, he is too taciturn for me. I like light and life.'

But I lied. I wanted to know so much more about him. The fact that Gisborne's form and face were striking mattered not one speck. Or so I told myself. He had a past of some sort and I wanted to know. Despite being my father's steward, he was indubitably of the nobility and that made him acceptable. I chose to forget the mad, bad and indifferent nobles that littered the past history of the world in which we both moved.

The cobbled streets of Tours took on the semblance of a pilgrim's way for us both. The sun beat down and each inn and church knew of no one heading south immediately. A group of pilgrims had left the day before our arrival, heading toward Marseille in order to find passage to the Holy Land where they planned to walk in the footsteps of Paul. A gathering of merchants was to leave the following week for Toulouse, but I could not leave Marais on her own for that length of time. I sighed and rubbed my aching feet against each other as we sat in the shade of vines at an inn.

'We can't wait a week.' Guy grumbled. 'We risk the closing down of the sailing season as it is. Once summer is over, the winds rise up and the seas become hazardous.' He unlaced his leather surcoat and pulled it off, revealing a chemise that should have been whiter, and looking down at my own clothing I realised we both bore the marks of dusty travel.

Gisborne had walked by my side as we scoured the town for a group in which to safely place Marais. He was a dark presence with a hand at my elbow and I was aware of his effect on people as we moved through the alleys. Women stopped talking to watch him pass and men stepped out of his way. Not feeling remotely humble, I gloried in the attention.

'I'm not afraid of a bit of rough sailing,' I replied. 'And call me Ysabel. This deference is ridiculous.'

'That's not the point,' he said and I wondered if he meant my title or the journey. He signalled to the innkeeper. 'A small flagon please. And two mugs.' He turned back to me. 'It is more to do with your safety than anything. Thank you.' He acknowledged the maid who bought our refreshment and she simpered, her eyes a perfect *come to me* flutter.

I snorted as if her behaviour were laughable, but as Gisborne poured the wine I noticed his hands and shivered. Strong but fine, as if he could as easily handle a *rebec* as a broadsword. He passed me a mug and our fingers brushed as I took it. The sensation burned my flesh and yet as I looked at him raising the mug to his own lips, I doubted he felt a thing.

This remove of his frustrated me. On the one hand he gave the impression of being so secure within himself, so confident, and on the other it implied a barrier, as if he were warning away anyone who might try to get close.

Sometimes his manner intimated calm and it was at those moments the fortress walls looked as if they could be breached but then he would move his head slightly or give a fraction of a glance and the hope of such a thing would die. Many would call him aloof, even arrogant. But in my kinder moments, I did not. I saw a river that was deep, a smooth swathe of shadowed water that on a cool day is so inviting. In my mind I could see myself wading in and then I could hear a roar as round the corner rushed a deadly current that could suck me under…

'Lady Ysabel?'

His voice penetrated my thoughts and I put down my mug, a flush coming to my cheeks.

'I'm sorry. You were saying?'

'What do you wish to do with Marais. It seems she must come with us or stay here until the merchant train leaves for Toulouse.'

'I dread leaving her alone, even if she is at the nunnery…'

'Pardon me, Sir and Lady.' A heavily accented voice as deep as distant thunder spoke to us from the leafy shadows. We turned together. Sitting behind us was a Saracen, his turban a grey as slate colour, his robes the dour and dusty shade of the desert nomad. He had an iron grey, neatly trimmed beard and his eyes were as black as the coals from a fire. A woman of comparable age sat with him, her hair and half her face hidden under the folds of a dust-coloured *hijab*. Hennaed tattoos stained her hands in a filigree pattern and she smiled at me her hazel eyes softening to crinkle at the corners.

'I am Ibrahim and this is my wife Haifa. *Salaam*,' he touched his forehead and his chest and bowed his head. 'I am a doctor from Acre and I am travelling back to my home. I leave at dawn tomorrow and shall be travelling through Toulouse. Is that close to where you wish your friend to go? She is welcome to join my wife and myself.'

I looked at the Saracen woman and found nothing but innate kindness in her eyes. Her hands had not led an idle life and she was Marais' age, I guessed. She smiled and spoke, her voice like warm honey. '*Salaam Alaykum*, Lady. We are quite fluent in the tongue of the English so your friend would not be lonely and I should welcome the company of another woman.'

'*Alaykum as salaam*,' I replied.

Guy's eyes opened a little wider at my response to these travellers. I had learned the Saracen tongue from the itinerants who visited Cazenay and felt an uncommon advantage over him as I thanked Haifa for her kind offer, saying that Marais' younger brother lived in Toulouse and it would be perfect.

'The lady we talk of is not English and only speaks Occitàn.' Guy responded.

Ibrahim rattled off a comment in the tongue of Aquitaine, saying that Marais would be amongst friends and once again, if we wished for her to travel with them she was welcome.

'Thank you,' I returned in the same language. For me the deal was settled.

'Have you men at arms?' Guy had turned fully toward Ibrahim and I could see he was thinking the same thing, that Marais would be accommodated and we could continue on.

'No. We trust in our God to protect us.'

'But there are godless men on the road sir, and I am sure the Lady

Ysabel would never forgive me if I allowed anything to happen to her friend. Would you be adverse to men at arms escorting you? I can provide you with men that I trust from my command.'

Ibrahim grimaced. 'I find escorts attract as much trouble as they deflect. But if you think it will keep your lady friend safe then I cannot object. Perhaps we can eat together to seal our plans?'

Thus it was that Marais' journey was organised. Guy went to the nunnery and retrieved my homesick servant and we all ate together as I introduced her to the suggestion she return to her home. At first she protested, my status and sex requiring her presence she said. But I worked away at her and gently convinced her that I would be safe in the care of the Moncrieff men. Eventually she agreed, more happily than we had hoped, and she and Haifa gossiped in Occitàn about their families, their homes and many other things and it seemed a plan made in heaven. Arrangements were made to meet at dawn at the town gates with our escort and we would watch Marais leave with her new friends. We would take the remaining men at arms and head north.

So it would seem I would now be alone with Guy of Gisborne, except for Wilfred and Harold, the remaining men, and who had known me since I was a little child. When I asked Gisborne later why he had left us with only two, he replied quite forthrightly.

'Ibrahim, Haifa and Marais are elderly folk, not able to defend themselves easily in a difficult situation and no matter what Ibrahim may think about *his* God, the very fact that he and Haifa are Saracens is like to bring down the wrath of the ignorant upon them. Thus it seems a safe measure. We can look after ourselves.'

'She'll be dropping the next one afore I get back.' Wilf answered my question as we trotted along what passed for a road between Tours and Le Mans.

'You make it sound as if she's a ewe popping a lamb,' I laughed.

'She might as well be,' piped up Harry. 'How many's that now, Wilfy-boy?'

'Enough of yer cheek.' Wilf pushed his own horse against Harold's and then turned to speak to me. 'Lady Ysabel, we had thought we'm call the babe Alice, if a girl. After the Lady Alaïs, yer see. She were always good to us.'

'Wilf, that is so kind and I think my mother would be honoured. For myself then and for my mother's memory, I shall hope that a ewe lamb is popped!'

The journey was light-hearted in so many ways except for the dark cloud that hovered on the edge, Guy remaining quiet if watchful. Whether he approved of my repartee with the men, I knew not nor cared, for Wilfred and Harold had picked me off the ground often enough when I was younger and out hunting with my father's entourage. Ponies suited to my size and with personalities larger than a destrier's would buck me off frequently in those days. The men were quite a few years older than myself and bore the pressure of a hard life on their faces. Not for them wines and the warmth of furs. But they bore their social rank with equanimity and were good men.

I had made no real effort to draw Guy into our conversation. The men kept me occupied with their chatter and I minded not at all. It was enough that he rode by my side. His presence and the men's talk filled the air around me, ameliorating the grief for Lady Alaïs that crouched in the back of my mind. In quieter moments, I recalled Gisborne's hand at my elbow, a vague smile on his lips when I did something that amused him, and a quick but enigmatic glance and in my head I had whispered conversations with my mother, telling her these things. There was part of me that considered myself quite pathetic but I went back to the thoughts like a parched man to water.

The sun shone benignly, unlike Aquitaine where everything seemed bleached white. The more northerly we journeyed, the more subtle and beautiful the light became. Forests of flickering shadow and dancing leaf marked the edges of our path and the horses' hooves crunched over a stony way worn into ruts and holes by those who went before us. But we met few travellers. At times it felt as if we were the only living things and then a bird would fly across our path, or a rabbit would hop past. Once a deer stood bathed in sunlight, watching us pass with a twitch of his ears.

But he leaped away as if the Furies were behind.

'To me!' Guy yelled.

Within a staggered heartbeat, the three rounceys surrounded me, Khazia dancing as the rumps of the horses pushed at her. I heard a whistle and an arrow flew past, lodging in a tree. I held tight to the reins with one hand, thanking God for the *misericorde* at my girdle. The metallic sigh that was the unsheathing of swords had already sharpened my anxiety like a whetstone.

Half a dozen felons ran toward us, swords raised, their mouths dark screaming circles as a terrified Khazia tried to spin.

'Stay behind us, Ysabel!'

Guy's voice yelled as he and the men pushed their battle-trained mounts forward. The horses reared, danced sideways, kicked out, even gnashed with their teeth and not once did a sword find a mark, my men's powerful parries deflecting harsh blows. I held Khazia hard between my knees and longed for my own sword as I watched a brigand fall with half a shoulder gone and could not take my eyes away from the spouting blood.

'Ysabel, Ysabel!' Guy screamed. 'Behind!'

I turned in the saddle and saw nothing but a sword lifting, sour breath gushing toward me in a noxious puff. Panic filled my veins with ice, fingers I didn't know were mine pulled the blade from my girdle and threw it end over end into the man's neck, his sword hand dropping its weapon as he tried to pull my knife from his throat. Blood spurted wildly, the attacker groaning with wet gurgles, Khazia shrieking as the man folded under her feet. My head felt as if it were wrapped in a cloud and I thought I would fall on top of the bloody carcass but Harry was by my side grinning.

'Great stroke, milady! You're a born soldier!'

'Harry,' I croaked. 'God, Harry!'

He laughed and turned to fight off the remaining brigands. My three guards pushed forward, slashing until another of the ambushers had fallen. One more collapsed but I kept my eyes on Gisborne's back, unwilling to see the damage my protectors wreaked. Two left, only two, four attackers dead or mortally wounded. The remainder threw down their swords and began to run and Wilfred was behind them, his horse cantering as he drew his sword back in a wide sweep, catching one in the thigh. It was callous butchery and I longed for it to stop.

'Let him go!' I screamed.

But as I shouted, I saw Wilfred arch back, his arms swinging wide, his sword dropping.

'Jesus God,' Guy called to Harry. 'The archer! Pull back, back!'

But Harry's horse reared and an arrow caught it in the neck. It spun around and before Harold could turn it again, another arrow shrieked in from the left and caught my old friend deep in the chest, another in his shoulder and a third in his arm.

'No!'

I spurred Khazia forward across the glade and into the brush, filled with fury and grief. The hidden archer looked up at me as the mare burst through the leaves to tread about, hooves slicing into bone, muscle and sinew. Khazia's shoes bruised and cut as the felon cried out in agony but hatred filled my soul as I screeched at him.

'They were my friends, my friends!'

I threw myself off the horse as the man's eyes stared into a forever horror, frozen in time, his last breath bubbling out in a red froth. I picked up his bow, a short Saracen one of a type I had handled in the past and turned back to Gisborne, but a movement behind him caused me to rip an arrow from the dead archer's quiver with speed, nocking it to let it fly.

Oh God, Gisborne!

'Fall, fall!' I shouted.

He dropped forward without hesitation and my arrow caught the final rogue. The man screamed, a hideous high-pitched wail, reeling from the trees, pulling at the arrow embedded in his eye. It would have been a kindness to kill him but Guy galloped to my side as I leaped onto Khazia's back. He grabbed her reins and pulled me after him and we fled the ambuscade.

'We can't leave them like that. We can't!' I sobbed. 'They were my friends. They have children. Guy, please!' We had stopped some leagues away and our horses' sides puffed in and out like bellows. I sat as if I were a half-empty sack, drooping with shock as the image of Wilfred arching back on his horse, went through my mind over and over again.

'What will happen to them if we leave them? I can't do that. In the name of God I owe them a burial. For their families and for my father.' I wiped a sleeve under my nose and rubbed my hand over my face. As I did, I noticed it was spattered with blood and cried out, holding it away from my body.

Gisborne jumped off his horse.

'Here,' he pulled me down by the waist and held me by the elbow as he passed me a cloth from his saddlebag. 'Hold it and I'll wet it from my flask and you can clean yourself.'

My hand shook as I held the fabric that proved to be a chemise. He placed his palm underneath to support it and I looked up at him as he did so.

'I owe you thanks, Ysabel, for my life.'

His voice barely showed the emotion of what we had just been through. A slight hoarseness, but it's depth smoothed like balm as he rubbed the damp cloth over my hand, removing the blood as tears rolled own my cheeks.

'I'm sorry. I should stop crying but I find I can't.'

'It's shock. You were very brave.' He gave my hand a final wipe, lifted it to his mouth and kissed it. 'Fearless. Wilf and Harry would have been proud.'

'Fearless?' My mouth stretched into a grimace. 'We must go back. I won't go on until we have done our best for them.'

'I don't agree. Wilf and Harry would understand, Ysabel. When you fall in the field of battle, you are lucky if you are buried.'

I took my hand back. 'Then they shall be lucky. If I only give you one order whilst you are my father's steward, it's that we must go back.'

His face hardened and I wished it had not because it was as though every plank of the bridge between us had been axed. I lay my hand over his arm and squeezed.

'Please, I beg you to understand. I am not being presumptuous by saying it is an order but if I have to use my father's name, I shall.

'I do understand, Ysabel. I understand that you have known Wilf and Harry for years and that you shared a life at one point. That you feel for their families. That it is your Christian duty. Don't think I don't understand. But what I *know* is that it will be foolhardy and dangerous.' He left my hand on his arm, his own closing over it. 'You need to remember that for you to die so soon after your mother would inevitably be the death of your father. Think on that.'

I hadn't really thought my demise would affect my father one way or the other because he had been so vaguely affectionate in his treatment of me. Loving when he was with me, but when he was not, I barely heard from him.

'But if my father had fallen, I would hope someone would bury him. If you fell, I would want the same for you.'

He slipped away from my grasp at that point and cupped his hands to give me a leg up into the saddle. He mounted his horse and made no comment at all and I felt chastened. Had I been too personal? I only spoke my mind after all. But I felt vindicated as we turned our horses and headed back the way we had fled.

I wished we had not.

Eight bloody and disfigured men lay in frozen death throes. Eight men who had wanted to kill us and steal everything we had. We had to move through them on foot to find Wilfred and Harold, Gisborne with his sword drawn, me with an arrow nocked into the Saracen bow.

Gisborne's eyes were everywhere and I forbore to talk because we listened to every sound from the forest. Every rustle, every creak and crack. Besides, my breathing was so fast I doubt I could have uttered a word. I had never ever seen human death and the brutality of what lay around us was almost beyond my coping. I took a huge breath and Guy must have heard because he turned and in that one glance that passed between us, I felt fortified. I don't know if he saw the fear in my eyes … panic where my mouth filled with bile and legs waved beneath my gown like strips of ribbon. All *I* saw in that quick glance was support, as if his arms were around me to guide me away from this hell.

But then I tripped and looking down, realised it was the felon Wilf had chased and whose leg he had almost severed, the limb at an obscene angle. I began to vomit until my sides ached and I had nothing left.

'Deep breaths, Ysabel. Take deep breaths. Go to the copse and stay with your back turned until I find them.' Gisborne's fingers closed on my arm and he pulled me away.

I was disgusted with my weakness and shook my head.

'No. This was my idea. Besides, here is Harry.'

He lay in his own blood. He had been stripped to his *braies* and everything he owned had been pulled from him. He had always worn a leather thong around his neck about which he twisted the golden hair of his wife and the white-blonde hair of his daughters in a glorious loveknot. It was an exceptional keepsake and I would have loved to return it to his family. Instead I reached for his hair which lay tangled in the grass, his basinet stolen, and using the sharp edge of the arrow, cut three locks for his family and placed them in the tiny leather purse at my waist. His eyes were wide but it was far too late to close them and I knew I would ever see that look of sadness.

'Here's Wilf,' Guy bent down and rolled the near naked soldier over.

Thanks be to God his eyes were closed and it was obvious he had died instantly from a pierced heart. I cut his hair as well, because they had taken the iron wristlet he wore with his family's names engraved. I remember he had taken that wristlet to the priest at Moncrieff, Brother John, a man of letters, and asked him to scratch the names of his family on it. The priest, only used to a goosequill, had done a remarkable job with the tip of a dagger and Wilf had been so proud, showing it often to any who would look.

'Who has taken everything?' I looked around, my eyes focusing on nothing but leaf and tree, as if that would sustain me.

'The cut-throat band to whom these others belong. They have taken our baggage horse as well, and the men's rounceys and weapons. If we are lucky they will be long gone to whatever hell-hole they call home.' Guy placed his hands under Wilf's armpits and lifted him across his shoulder, laying him over the saddle of his own rouncey.

He tied him on and I could only watch.

'We shall bury them away from here. We passed a stream on the way back and its sides were sandy and we can dig graves more easily. Besides, I think if we are to do this, it is best away from their murderers.'

He was right and I should have thought of it but my mind was sluggish and all I could do once Harry had been tied on board was take the reins of Khazia and lead her

It took us till dusk to bury them, covering them with dirt and stones. We left the graves unmarked for fear they would be opened by greedy passers-by and I was pleased that Guy had settled on a spot below the roots of birches that stood skirted by ferns. The burials barely showed and we were silent as we looked one last time before heading into the gloaming.

'Guy?' I could barely see him as we rode, but he answered.

'Yes?'

'Thank you.'

'I owe you a debt,' he replied.

'You owe me nothing of any sort.' I sensed him slipping away from me. *Don't go.*

'A life debt is just that, and can only be paid up when I have saved your life in return. Until then I am most completely at your service.'

37

He invited no argument and yet I would not be dissuaded.

'I wish you would forget it,' I argued, but he moved the conversation to other things.

'You shoot as well as any of the men. Where did you learn?'

'I hunted at Cazenay. It was the only way one could have a little excitement in a mundane lady's life and I became rather good at it.' A brief image of my disgruntled suitors danced through the macabre events of the day.

'And the Saracen bow?'

'Like the tongue, learned when the Saracen travellers were at Cazenay. I like the bow. It's small and light, better for someone short like me. The long bow is too unwieldy, the crossbow too heavy. Sadly the little bow has a shorter lifespan in our damp climates and doesn't hold together as well as English bows. I like the power in such a small weapon. It could almost be called a woman's bow.'

I heard a chuckle.

'My little archer,' he said softly.

A smile crept onto my own face.

'Where do we go?' I asked.

'We need shelter for this night. Le Mans is too far but if we ride all day tomorrow, by dusk we shall be inside the walls.'

I was glad to think of defensive walls and heavy gates, for today I felt as vulnerable as a fawn amongst wolves.

'There!'

Gisborne's horse moved to my right and Khazia followed without me even twitching the reins. A forester's hut lay in shambles before us, providing a wall and a piece of timber under which we could shelter. I slid from the mare, clutching her mane for support and within moments we had hobbled our mounts so they could graze within reach, a small puddle of water close by. Gisborne would not light a fire in case we attracted interest and I, who already trembled with cold, wrapped my cloak tight around me and nibbled at the stale cheese and bread he passed me. I sipped the water from my flask and then placed a weary head that ached upon my saddle. My heart lay heavy in my chest, its beats marked, limbs knotted beneath as I drew myself into a huddle. As I turned my back against the world, I felt a tear sneaking from my eye, my body shaking as if I froze.

Guy's arm sneaked over my side.

'It is exhaustion and shock, just breathe deep and steady.'

He curled himself around me like a drake's tail-feather, his own warmth seeping into my anxious frame and I found my breath slowing to match his. As I grew more comfortable, my eyes became heavy and it was only as I finally sank into sleep that I realised my hands lay under his and that his thumb stroked over and over across my knuckles.

It was the first time I, Ysabel the virgin, slept with Guy of Gisborne, a chaste event that left me as intact as Marais could have hoped.

CHAPTER THREE

Sometimes when one wakes it's as if ice has been dropped down one's spine but I woke as if I were wrapped in silk and wool. Warm, loose, remembering only the stroking of my knuckles. As I arched my body, I knew he had left me but I felt no fear. Not immediately … and then, like the aforesaid winterfreeze, cold crept over me as I recalled death; Wilfred's, Harold's, my mother's. I sat up with a rush.

'Lady Ysabel, you're awake.' Guy strode into the clearing with the horses. 'I took them to the stream and they drank their fill.'

My breath gushed out. I hadn't realised I held it. But his presence eased the distrait of my memories and I clambered up, folding the cloak he'd laid over me, straightening my gown and re-plaiting my hair in a rough braid.

'Here,' he held out a palm filled with redcurrants. 'They might be a little tart but there is nothing else other than the water. At least *that* is clear and sweet-smelling.'

'Do we leave immediately?'

'As soon as we are saddled.' He shouldered our gear and began tacking the horses.

'I'll be back momentarily,' I muttered and dashed to the stream, taking care of nature, washing my face and hands. When I returned he was mounted and passed my reins over with no comment and I leaped aboard, no leg-up, quite able. But he'd already pushed his own horse on and missed my agility.

Alone. Just he and I. Riding abreast. Silent. I could only think he regretted holding me last night and yet I was so grateful.

'Guy?'

'Yes?'

'Thank you for comforting me last night. I was cold and…' I hesitated, 'so very cold.'

'It is best bodies lie close when it's cold. One body warms the other.'

'Of course.' Huh, of course, I thought wryly. 'Where shall we put up in Le Mans?'

'There is a priory.'

'For me no doubt,' I replied with the taste of tart redcurrant on my tongue. 'And you?'

'An inn close by.'

'I could stay at the inn as well.'

'I think not, Lady.'

Lady? Mary Mother! After yesterday?

I was too tired to argue. All at once I wanted to bathe, find clothes, eat.

'How long from Le Mans to the coast?'

'Another few days.'

His mood had become more removed. Truly a woman would be mad to bother further. I've always disliked sulky men as it implies an arrogant individual used to being indulged. But this man next to me had not been spoiled.

How did I know when he had told me nothing?

Simply, he was my father's steward.

If he'd led a truly privileged life he would never have been a mere servant. And yet I knew he was of noble birth, so why then such a humble position by comparison? I knew I could secure answers at Moncrieff but I have ever been impatient.

I chose my time.

We had been riding by a small rivulet and stopped a few miles from Le Mans. As I dismounted, my foot twisted on a stone and I wrenched my ankle so that it swelled dramatically.

42

'What have you done?'

Gisborne bent to check my foot, my gown folds still hooked up for riding. Without my leave, he scooped me up to carry me to the water, stripping my hose and boot.

'Place your foot in the water. The chill will ease the swelling.'

I stood with him holding my elbow, embarrassed, conscious of the value of nuisance.

'Truly, there is no pain. May we ride on? I wish to get to Le Mans as soon as we can.'

'Can you walk?'

I limped slightly. 'Enough to get me to my mount.'

He sighed as if I were so much trouble, lifted me up and hoisted me back on Khazia, slipping the hose up my leg and placing the boot back on with infinite gentleness. I reached to his hand.

'I'm sorry. This is such a fraught journey. I apologise for being such trouble.'

His attention focussed on placing my foot in the stirrup as if I hadn't even spoken. My father had given him orders … to mind me like a nursemaid. He should be accompanying my father on social occasions and official domain business. Even royal progresses because as a noble of greater ranking, my father had his place at Court. But instead this man smoothed folds and minded a precocious woman.

'Please accept my apologies.' I offered.

'You needn't apologise. Not when you shoot a bow like a trained archer and when you speak the Saracen tongue.' His mouth tipped up. 'You are quite an enigma, Lady Ysabel.'

Me an enigma?

I laughed. 'I shall assume that to be a compliment. Can we go?'

The mood had lightened in the blink of an eye, and as we rode more peaceably I took a breath.

'Guy, why are you my father's steward?'

He rode along without saying anything and then, 'Why are you interested?'

'You know about me, thus I should know a little about you.'

I tried to pose the reply lightly, as if it didn't really matter. Again there was a taut silence, as though he warred with himself about what he should and should not say.

'I needed employment.'

Short and to the point.

'You needed employment? Gracious. Since when do sons of the nobility *need* employment?'

'Again this idea that I am a noble.'

'Deny it then. Tell me that your courtly manners and your education are a product of a lowly upbringing.'

A very small smile appeared and I felt the warmth of it across the breadth between us. 'Honestly Ysabel, you are like a horsefly. Apart from swatting you away, one can't get rid of you until you have your bite.'

'At least I am plain Ysabel now,' I muttered.

If he heard he made no comment. What he did say opened up a discussion that filled the miles left until we reached Le Mans and which left me breathless and filled with sorrow for a man and his mother.

'I am noble born,' he said. 'I am the son of Baron Henry of Gisborne and his lady, Ghislaine. Like yourself, Ysabel, I am an only child.'

'Why aren't you at Gisborne then, helping your father manage his estates at the very least?'

'Because there are no estates left to manage.'

I gasped and pulled my mare to a halt. 'You say?'

He sighed and I could see the story hurt him deeply.

'My father went to the Crusade as a Templar knight. He … renounced his marriage and passed his possessions over to the Church. Admittedly he sought a guarantee that my mother and myself should be housed and some of the monies from the estate should go to our welfare but the Church was so much bigger than my father and a year after he left for Jerusalem, my mother and I were turned off Gisborne. We sought to travel to Anjou to my mother's family, but she caught an ague and died in a small priory near Great Harwich. As for my father, he is still alive I believe; if you call the way he lives a life. Somewhere near Jerusalem, he leads the life of a leper…'

My breath sucked in. 'Guy…'

'He may be aware of his wife's death, I don't know. The Knights Templar seemed to lose interest in him once they had our estates and once my father became a leper. So you see, I have nothing, Ysabel, and yet I am noble born. I am the son of a madman who believed he could secure a passage to Paradise if he joined the Knights Templar and fought in a Holy

War and thanks to him my mother died in ignominious circumstances. My own future is what I make of it. I took employment where I could find it and because I am highborn and educated, I have been the steward for a number of nobles. But I do not stay long with any. I leave whilst I am respected and liked and I work my way back up the chain.'

It seemed I could not stop him. Once he started, it was like a confessional and words flowed from him, dripping in un-camouflaged bitterness. I found I hardly blamed him. It was a sad story and I was not a little afraid of the chill manner with which he told it.

'I said to you once that status is power. Thus I work my way to knighthood. Have no doubt – I shall be knighted and recognised and shall have lands and wealth. And no one, not any single man, shall ever take from me what I see as mine.'

We rode further and my heart sank just a little, for bitterness is a hard nut to crack.

'I would lay bets that this is not what you wished to hear, Lady Ysabel,' he commented. 'But you now know with whom you travel. If it offends you, I apologise. But it is what I am.'

I didn't know how to respond. I had lost my mother but she died in comfort in the magnificent Lady Chamber as they called her room at Moncrieff. I still had my father and he hadn't disavowed himself of me, but not only that, Moncrieff was still our family demesnes. I had led a charmed and spoiled life in Aquitaine where my father's wealth and that of my mother's family meant I wanted for nothing, least of all status. How could I possibly understand what he felt? Every word he spoke had been underlined with wicked irony by church bells clanging on the wind from Le Mans, and I wondered if he had repudiated the Church altogether after being treated so falsely by men of God.

'Those bells are loud,' I said to break the tension but he didn't reply and so against my better judgement I pushed him further. 'Have you never wished to find your father?'

'I know where he is. There is a leper order, the Order of Saint Lazarus outside Jerusalem. It's an Hospitaller order run like the Knights Templar and they care for each other and others who have the illness.'

'Then he is a man to be admired.'

'He had no choice. He was a Templar and he was a leper. It was join the Order or die on the streets of Jerusalem. I feel nothing but disgust for him. He killed my mother.'

'You should forgive him, Guy. He will die a terrible death.'

'He will have monks around him to hear his final confession and give him his rites. He does not need my forgiveness.'

I felt to ask him anything else was to open wounds that he was perhaps trying desperately to heal. Heal and forget?

Somehow I doubted Guy of Gisborne was a man who would ever forget.

To arrive in Le Mans on that day was to learn of a change in the course of history. We had heard rumours on the road of the Plantagenet family wars and thus it was no surprise to hear that King Henry had fallen sick whilst at Le Mans where he had been born. He and Richard were in the middle of a brawl over succession, with Phillip of France siding with Richard. Phillip and Richard attacked the town and feckless, disloyal Henry ordered parts of his birthplace to be burned to stall their invasion. But even a King could not control a wind that changed and caused a massive conflagration, threatening to burn his birthplace utterly. Henry fled, leaving the town to put out its fires and lick its wounds.

He had retired to Chinon but his health failed by the day and he died two days before we arrived at Le Mans. I was surprised the town even thought to ring mourning bells. Guy said such was the power of a King.

'But', said I, 'the King is dead. Long live the King.'

The bells rang with heavy resonance anyway.

It was a relief to me that we had arrived in scorched Le Mans at all because I was exhausted beyond belief: saddle sore, heart sore, tired, dirty and hungry. I should have mourned my former King but I did not. To be frank I cared little and found the smell of burned buildings still lingered in the air, not unlike Henry's memory.

I wondered who could mourn an obsessive man who burned innocents alive to satisfy his need to make a point and overpower a son. Further, I decided that if *any* of his sons wanted to fight to secure their kingship, I cared not at all. I wanted to divest myself of all memories of fighting, of blood and gore and yet I knew that what Gisborne and I had dealt with between Tours and Le Mans would live with me forever.

The Sisters of the Priory Saint Jean were kind and generous, providing hot water and a small oak bath despite the fact that it was late in the evening. The lay sisters had been directed to care for their new guest who obviously had coin to pay her way and I briefly thanked the Lord that Gisborne had lined palms to make it so. The bells of the Priory chimed and despite the fact they marked Vespers, I wondered if they also tolled as a reminder of the deceased monarch. I gave thought to Eleanor, wondering what she felt about her king-husband's death. They always said she loved him despite his despicable treatment of her, what with his florid temper, his loose morals with the fair Rosamunde and others.

I only knew that when *I* fell in love it would be forever and that I would only ever marry a man that I truly loved. Which bought me back to Eleanor, whereupon I decided she would be brokenhearted.

My thoughts also went to Gisborne.

I shrank from the idea of investigating why. Whilst I soaked in the tiny bath in front of the brazier at the priory, I knew he might well be doing the same at his inn. We had arranged to meet after we had broken our fast the next day. The town of course would be in some sort of mourning ordained by the Church, but as long as we could arrange our forward passage, he seemed less than worried.

How he felt about Henry's death, I could only guess. What I suspected was that he would shift the pieces around on the chessboard that was his life, and work out how to move forward and upward. There was a part of me that hoped it would be at Moncrieff but in reality I doubted it. The man had ambition and for all that Moncrieff was a wealthy estate it was not his.

Ah yes, status was all.

The bells rang through the night but I managed to sleep by telling myself they rang for Richard rather than Henry and that there would be a coronation and England would be content and my homecoming would be filled with the excitement of this new reign. But in truth, I was so tired the bells merely rang me to a long and heavy sleep.

The other guests in the dorter had risen and left by the time I woke and dragged on my filthy clothes to make haste to the refectory. The portress of the priory handed me a message and as I ate a slice of fresh bread, I read

Gisborne's words. He wrote with a good hand and I added it to his other attributes. There were stories that even some Kings could not read and write but my father's steward appeared to do both.

He asked that we delay our meeting till midday and that he would collect me from the priory to purchase fresh clothes and supplies. But whilst heavy of leg and low in energy, I had no intention of watching the Sisters follow their daily devotion to God. Such placid, quiet rhythms might have been sustaining but instead I asked for directions to the marketplace.

'Should you venture alone?' The portress asked. 'You are a Lady, it is not seemly.'

'I have no choice, Sister.'

'Two of our Sisters are going to the market to sell our honey. You could go with them.'

'I thank you then. If they would not mind my company perhaps it might be best.' I hastened to the gate to meet my companions.

The town still smelled of food, of smoke, of many bodies moving about daily life. Of cats, dogs and horses. Here and there was evidence of Henry's flame and fire, but with the resilience of all great places, the market continued and the townsfolk found evident joy in it, shouting and laughing … a meeting place to ease the angst of days past.

The Sisters accompanied me as I went from stall to stall. I doubted I would find any clothes ready made for my purpose as bolt upon bolt of fabric lined the more expensive end of the market but then the Sisters plucked at my sleeve and showed me a fine stall on which lay folded garments.

I pulled out a woolen *bliaut*. Like the chemise I found, none would be as good as those that were tailored to my size but the fabric was of decent quality and a serviceable cloak wrapped around the bundle; all that was functional and suited to my journey. The Sisters and I finished our business and they escorted me to the head of the street in which stood Guy's inn. I thought to wait for him, surprise him even, and bid the Sisters adieu with thanks. I would return to the priory anon, I said.

The street was crammed with stone buildings and paved with cobbles that wove and bent away around corners – but not deftly enough to hide two men leaning in toward each other. One was tall, the other unremarkable.

One was Guy of Gisborne.

I pulled back against the wall because there was something about the way they spoke that implied secrets. Gisborne shook his head and the other man grabbed his arm and spoke with unguarded intensity. The midday light caught on a heavy silvered chain hanging around the man's neck, a badge of sorts.

I could see that he had finally snagged Gisborne's attention as he continued to press whatever was his case. Gisborne showed no reaction, merely listened intently, but when the other man stopped talking Guy looked up and saw me.

He frowned and spoke to his companion and then waved his arm and I had no option but to walk forward.

'Lady Ysabel.' He bowed. 'On your own again?'

'Good day.' Some instinct made me want to show the other man there was nothing but a servant-mistress relationship between myself and Guy of Gisborne. 'The Sisters saw me to the top of the street. They helped me make market purchases.'

My eyes swung meaningfully to the shorter man who eyed me with interest.

'Lady Ysabel,' Gisborne said. 'May I present Sir Robert Halsham.'

'My lady.' The silver chain flashed as the man bent over my fingers and the hairs on my neck prickled. He reeked of something untoward.

'I have heard of your father, of course,' he said.

He held onto my hand moments longer than was decent and I withdrew it to grasp the clothes bundle tighter to my chest and looked beyond him.

'We have business, Gisborne. You may have forgotten.'

I swept past them into the inn and heard Halsham mutter. 'Arrogant, but a beauty.'

Gisborne's footsteps sounded behind me. Through the door as I glanced back, I could see Halsham walking along the street whistling and the sussurating sound sent a shiver sliding down my spine.

'So polite, Ysabel.'

'I didn't like him.'

Guy's eyebrows rose. 'A quick assessment, surely.'

'He has an air.'

'He said the same of you.'

'What he thinks of me matters little. What were you doing with him?'

He sat and beckoned to the serving wench who gave him that eye that all maids did. Honestly, it was like an affliction!

'I had business with him,' he said.

'He looks remarkably dishonest. Not at all the kind with whom I imagine my father would do business, I am sure.'

'It wasn't your father's business. It was mine.'

'Huh, I'll bet he has dishonest dealings.'

'Ysabel,' he hissed, his palm slapping the table in front of me, causing heads to turn. 'He has just returned from Jerusalem via Antioch and Malta. In fact he had news of my father. Now are you happy?'

The maid put a tankard of ale in front of me with a wooden platter with a trencher of bread soaked in some fragrant onion and meat juices. She smirked at my chastened expression.

Vile wench!

'Your father. He is well?'

'He is dead.'

'Guy...'

I reached to touch his hand and he flinched.

'It is no matter.'

The topic of his father was thrown out like pigswill. *'Leave it alone'* was the message. Any vestige of care disappeared from his face, wiped as cleanly as if he had washed it with a cloth. His secrets, all of them, were buried so deep inside his soul that I wondered what it would take, or even who, to reveal such.

But his father's death was surely only a fraction of what Halsham had imparted. Patently I could not ask anymore out of respect for the grievous news so I wondered if I could inveigle more detail on the ill-made news bearer.

'Halsham is a knight?'

'Indeed, as the introduction indicated.' Sarcasm fell to the table amongst the breadcrumbs.

'He has fought in the Holy Land?'

'I thought you didn't like him and yet you show inordinate interest in the man. To answer you, he has fought in many places. He is a Free Lancer.'

'Really.' My attention was piqued as I chewed on the bread. 'A mercenary.'

'Yes.'

In an instant I recalled what I thought about chessboards and Guy's future.

'Guy, you don't perchance think to become a Free Lancer yourself?'

He coughed on his food and his eyes opened just a fraction wider and if I knew anything, I would say he dissembled.

'I am your father's steward, Lady Ysabel. That is all you need concern yourself with at this point.'

'Hmm.' I tapped the table with my finger, my eyes meeting his deep blue ones. 'Remember this, Sir Gisborne. Secrets are dangerous.'

We wandered through the town and watched people go about their business. The sun shone and we checked at the livery that our horses were fit and shod ready for an early departure on the morrow and I fed Khazia a crust of my bread. We left Halsham far behind in our perambulations and we talked again of ballads and such which seemed to be Guy's great love. We stopped at a tavern that had trestles in the sun and as I sat back under the pergola over which grapevine threaded, I asked Guy to tell me one of the stories he knew.

'One of the Welsh or Irish ones. You seem to know so many.'

He seemed so relaxed as he sat back, no evidence of the kind of grief that lurked in my heart waiting to jump forth. If I were a cynic, I would have said the news of his father's death released something in him but knew it was pointless to ask. He stretched his long legs out, hands clasped over his middle.

'I shall tell you the one of Finn. Some call him Fionn. It's a good tale.'

I leaned forward and watched him closely as he began to talk.

'I shall tell you how he met his love. Women like that.' His eyes glinted and he grinned, the angular planes of his face shadowed under the dappled light of the pergola.

'Fionn met his glorious and most beautiful wife, Sadhbh, when he was out hunting in the wild forests. The eldritch Fear Doirich had turned her into a deer as punishment after she had turned down his proposal of marriage and she was doomed to wander the forests alone forever, as she never thought to find the love of her life, for who would want a deer to love?'

He looked at me and I smiled back, urging him to continue.

'As a graceful doe, she was grazing one day when Fionn's hounds, Bran and Sceolan, tracked her down. Almost ready to pounce on her and drag her down by the neck, they froze. The two huge hounds had once been human themselves and recognised the magic that surrounded her. Fionn paused with his spear raised and she looked at him with her dark eyes and something great passed between them and he spared her. He set forth back to his lands and was charmed to see that she followed in his footsteps. The minute she placed a hoof on Fionn's estates, she transformed back into a woman and she cried out. Fionn could barely keep his eyes from her, so struck was he by her beauty. He and she fell deeply in love and they married and she was soon with child.'

I guessed he had shortened the tale significantly for the sun was sliding and dusk began to tiptoe close behind and being conscious of his duty, I was sure he would want to escort me back to the priory before dark.

'But the Fear Doirich came to Fionn's home,' he continued, 'and filled with fury that she had not only transformed back to a woman by finding her way to Fionn's lands but also that she had fallen in love and married the King, the evil wight turned her back into a deer. He chased her away into the forests and she quite literally vanished. Fionn, aghast, left his estates and spent seven years searching for her. But to no avail. He was brokenhearted and the only thing that saved his mind was that at the end of the seven years, he found a child, not quite seven, naked, on the enchanted hill called Ben Bulbin. The child had Sadhbh's eyes and he was sure he had found his son whom he named Oisin. Father and son hugged and cried but of the child's mother there was not a sign and Fionn knew then that his great love was lost to him forever. And so he invested his attention in the boy.'

He looked down at his hands at this point and I dare say he thought of his own father and what he had lacked.

'This child grew to become one of the noblest of the Fianna and one of the greatest Irish storytellers.'

He lifted his goblet and drank a mouthful of the ale he had ordered for us both.

'That was wonderful. Where did you learn such marvelous stories?'

'Ah, that would be telling,' he grinned as he stood and stretched. 'Some secrets are meant to be kept!'

I stood as well, knocking his arm not so playfully.

'But let you not forget what I said, Gisborne. Secrets can be dangerous.'

Chapter Four

I prattled away the next day, my voice a counterpoint to the clip-clop of the horses' hooves and the creaking of the saddlery. At one point I chatted so much about Moncrieff and my memories of the place, it was many leagues before I realized Gisborne had said nothing – just quietly allowed my words to drown him. But as my monologue on my memories of Moncrieff drew to a close, he spoke up.

'Moncrieff may not be what you remember, Ysabel.'

I straightened my gown where it had rucked at the top of the stirrup leathers, the creases biting into the flesh of my thighs.

'How so?'

He eased his horse to a halt and I pulled up beside him. 'Eight years is a very long time to have been absent. I have no doubt that when you left for Cazenay, Moncrieff was the absolute epitome of grandeur.'

'It was, as I told you.'

My brow tightened. As though I were about to hear something awkward. His face had such a dark look about it ... not anger, not that. No – solemn was a more apt description, almost as if he had news of a death to impart. I rubbed at my temple.

'Three years ago your mother became ill for the first time. What you don't know is that she remained bed-ridden, never regaining her health.'

'How do you know this?'

The grief that I had pushed away on my own account began to creep forth again. No one had told me my mother had stayed frail. She had only ever written to me with her usual sweetness. My father certainly hadn't seen fit to enlighten me. If I had known I would have traveled back home with undue haste to nurse her. The kind of thing expected from a loving daughter; the kind of thing that might have eased the band of guilt girthed around my chest.

'Come,' said Guy. 'I think we should eat, drink and rest the horses. Rouen is not too far but we shall make better time if we are refreshed. I shall tell you while we sit.'

I went about settling Khazia and sitting on the grass by the road but it was a habitual thing and I barely noticed. Not when my mind filled with images of my glorious mother as a faded, ill woman. The previous night's damp still lay upon the verge, the odd dewdrop sparkling as it caught the daylight. Moisture crept through the folds of my gown, chilling me more than I wished.

'She barely left the Lady Chamber,' Guy continued. 'I know this from Cecilia of Upton…'

'Cecilia! Cecilia is my mother's friend and one of my own godmothers. She has written to me whilst I have been away and said nothing…'

'Your own mother's very good and trusted friend who was prevailed upon by the Lady Alaïs to reveal nothing of any weakness. It was your mother's way of showing her deep love that she didn't want to worry you. Cecilia is still at Moncrieff. Out of loyalty to your mother's memory she stays to keep your father company as best she can and to wait for you. She told me how your mother was the life of the place, how she was loved by all, how she threw herself into everything before she became ill. But mostly she told me how she was your father's backbone.'

Ah, such truths I knew, but as Guy spoke something cold and unpleasant began to crawl down my spine.

'As Lady Alaïs became more frail, your father lost direction. His bailiff struggled on but your father weakened in tandem with your mother. When I was employed as the Baron's steward three months before your mother died, Moncrieff had slid badly. Fields had been left un-tilled, those that had been harrowed were unseeded. Sheep flocks were untended. No wool was gathered for sale. Food crops were reduced. Cecilia had kept as much as she could from your ailing mother in order to spare her but she was a prescient woman, Lady Alaïs, and it was she who urged your father to hire a steward. She had heard of me through Cecilia and must have thought that along with the bailiff, we could keep your father on the straight and narrow.'

'I can hardly believe you.' I jumped up and began to pace, parts of my gown still hitched into my girdle. 'Father would never allow Moncrieff to fall into disrepair. He lived for the glory of the estate, was proud beyond belief.'

But in truth I knew that my father was a weak, disingenuous fool whom everyone loved. As in many marriages, someone like my father was improved by living with the love of his life, that person giving strength where there could conceivably be none.

'He grieves. That is all. When I am come, it will make all the difference.'

There was an imploring note to my voice when perhaps there should have been an assertive tone and I suspect Gisborne understood, because he took my hands in his own and I forced myself to look into his face.

'Oh Mary Mother,' I uttered. 'There is more?'

'I have worked with the bailiff to put things to rights.' He held my hands firmly. 'The land is as it should be. The forests are managed, the hunting stock controlled. The domestic stock is farmed as expected. The castle itself has been thoroughly re-organised and interior and exterior inventories taken.'

'But…' My voice was hollow and I refused the food Gisborne handed me.

'Three years of disorganization has meant three years of drawing on your father's coffers.'

'He is a rich man, one of the Greater Barons. I…'

'*Was* a rich man.' Gisborne's voice was so definite that any hope I might have had vanished completely.

'Was?' I whispered.

'Ysabel, there is little left. The staff of Moncrieff has had to be whittled down considerably. Moncrieff just pays its dues and that is all.'

'But the villagers, how are the villagers surviving?' A knot of panic began to twist. I was not going home to my memories. So much for the contentment I imagined in the reign of Richard.

'We, that is the bailiff and myself, make sure that no one starves.'

'Is there enough to pay *you*?' A new note entered my voice, a bitterness resonating with the life that Guy had lived in his time.

'Enough. You need not fret, those that are there are paid. But Ysabel, the Baron needs someone strong to guide him. Your homecoming is vital.'

I suspected he was not telling me crucial information on my father. Something was missing but I found myself unwilling to unveil any more truths. I was not ready. Instead I asked something else, something that flashed into my mind in an instant and articulated itself before I could hold it back.

'Did my father ask you to fetch me back?'

As I asked, I dared him with the intensity of my gaze. He looked at me long but then scrutinized our joined hands. I felt tears gathering, one rolling down my cheek as he began to answer.

'No. No, it was Cecilia's idea. I agreed with it. Simply, if you do not return then Moncrieff is lost.'

My face must have crumpled, I can't recall, because he took me in his arms and held me while I cried. As the storm passed I stayed still, feeling the warmth and comfort.

And something else.

His lips grazed my temple.

I moved my face and my cheek touched his. An infinitesimal move that sent shocks coursing through my body.

I turned my head slightly so that his mouth brushed the corner of my own and then I tipped my lips to his. We barely met. Air passed between us. But then by mutual consent, more pressure was brought to bear and we kissed long. I kept my eyes closed, pushing Moncrieff to the outer edges of recall by what I did and what I was feeling.

His mouth slid down my neck whilst his hands lifted my hair and I knew, as sure as I knew that my father and Moncrieff would be changed forever, that changes were being wrought in me at the same time. But in the far off reaches of rationality, I wondered just how deep those changes would run.

I hated our time in Rouen.

Khazia tripped in a rabbit hole a league before the town, a ligament in her foreleg damaged and her leg swollen and hot. I was forced to lead her and thus we arrived, both of us, footsore and tired. Gisborne offered me his rouncey but I wouldn't ride. The mare had carried me unstintingly for eight years, it was the least I could do to walk beside her whilst she suffered so. Gisborne joined me leading *his* horse, a petty cavalcade, and we barely spoke although each time his arm rubbed against mine butterflies danced in my belly.

But try as I might to regain the feeling of light and life I had held fleetingly in my heart back down the road, the issue of Moncrieff and my father subsumed everything. For me it felt as if the sun had gone from the world and that a grey pall hung over me. I felt it would not change until I could see Moncrieff for myself.

We took the horses to a livery and I spent time grooming Khazia and making sure the straw she stood on was thick and cushioned her legs from further problems.

'No foot, no 'oss,' I whispered as I gave her the last of the apple-core saved from a windfall Gisborne had scrumped on the road.

'She's a beautiful mare, Ysabel.' Guy stood behind me as I tightened the linen holding a poultice to her leg.

'She is.' I rubbed her between the ears. 'Papa arranged for her to be waiting for me at Cazenay. She's of Barbary blood, fast and fleet and she's only twelve. She would be a good broodmare. Maybe back at Moncrieff. She needs time to mend, Gisborne. I need to poultice her daily.'

'Ysabel, we have no time, you know this.'

'But…'

'We need to rest now. And I shall make sure that Khazia is tended, but you need to realize that this is truly a disaster…'

'I think you make too much of it. Disaster for Khazia surely, but us?'

Guy took me by the arm and led me to an inn. I thought it was a step forward that he didn't just deposit me with more good Sisters for a day and a night of prayers and the confessional. But the fact we had rooms side by side at the hostelry meant little as I went over and over the situation that Guy had revealed earlier. My home was under threat. My father's inestimable wealth had diminished. Guy implied it was because my father grieved for my lady mother but his words lacked conviction and I wondered at the real truth.

We ate a simple meal from one of the booths lining the street, a small game pie and some ale.

'Khazia,' Guy said, 'is a problem.' He flicked pastry flakes from his surcoat and rubbed his hands together to remove the last crumbs.

'I disagree…'

'I know how long it can take a horse to repair from a torn ligament, Ysabel. To push Khazia would be a cruelty.'

I swore to which Guy raised an eyebrow, and I threw the remains of the food to a passing cur where it disappeared in two gulps. 'Khazia needs a day or two, that is all, no longer. She's strong.'

Guy scoffed. 'You've seen the road. She'd be lame in half a league. Be rational.'

'What do you suggest?' I snapped.

'There is a way round this.'

'Tell then, because I'm damned if I can see it. We must wait days, that's all there is to it.'

'No.' He looked down at his hands. 'We can get new horses.'

'What!' The enormity of what he said almost knocked me backward. 'And leave Khazia in Rouen. You jest.'

'No, I don't. We must leave on the morrow so we have no choice. I can see no other way around this.'

I walked away from him but knew he followed close as we headed back to the inn.

'You ask me to do something that hurts, Gisborne. On top of all I have lost and appear to be losing, you ask me to get rid of a horse I have had for eight years, a friend.

'A friend who was not so important that you thought little of what you might do to her by galloping her downhill at Cazenay.'

'You bastard,' I swung round and lifted a hand that he caught in mid-arc, but I shook him off. 'How *dare* you presume to know what I feel for Khazia! That day at Cazenay my mind had slipped sideways with grief for my mother. But I know what I think now and I know that you ask too much.'

'Ysabel,' he lowered his voice and at any other time I might have said he was being solicitous. He opened the door of the hostelry and I passed through. As we climbed the stairs he continued. 'You need to get to Moncrieff and soonest. We have no idea what we might find at the coast with the weather. Above all else that is an imponderable. We can sell Khazia and buy a good horse to get you to the boats quickly. Sell that one in Calais and buy a ride in England. No, no,' he pressed my arm. 'Don't say it. I know what she means to you but it is the only answer.'

I knew he was right if urgency was what propelled us. But it seemed to me that if there had been extreme need for speed before, he had kept it quiet and I could only guess it was for my peace of mind. Since our new understanding he had opened a little about what I would find and now haste stretched my nerves as if I were on the rack. But I was convinced he knew more than he was telling.

'Gisborne,' we stood outside my chamber door. 'What *else* do you know? You ask me to sell Khazia so that we may make haste. It seems there is something behind this, something of import. Have the grace to tell me.'

He leaned across me and I smelt the faint fragrance of leather that hung about him. His hand twitched the door latch and the room was revealed, lit with a brazier in the middle of the floor and a cresset on the wall. 'May I?'

A lady did not invite a man into her chamber and I was no whore. If anyone saw us… I glanced quickly along the corridor but it was deserted and so I nodded my head and almost ran inside as he followed, shutting the door carefully. He moved to a coffer and I sat on a chair a safe distance away with my knees jammed together and my gown strained as tight over my knees as if it were a door barred to the world.

At any other time I would have marveled at his face. I loved the sharp planes, his straight nose, hair that sat on his collar. I tried to seek an answer from his expression but there was nothing and in fact he sat as if he leaned over the chessboard to plan a series of moves without his opponent sizing him up.

Perhaps I am an opponent.

Then again I wondered if I might be a pawn. It seemed to me a woman's life could be legitimately described in such a way – she is offered up as a bride of advantage or perhaps she is offered to the Church. Leastways she is a commodity. In my case, I had been offered up to be sure, but thanks to my less than diligent father, the man who would rather write songs than plan succession, I had managed to keep the pawn on the board.

'Ysabel, what I shall say you won't like. You ask what I know. What I shall tell you is the truth and I ask that you don't hold such truths against me but rather accept that they are inevitably facts you would have found out.'

'You scare me,' my stomach had tightened and I could feel my heartbeat become unnervingly irregular. 'But I will not blame you…'

'This is what I would say. When your mother died, your father sank himself into his cups. In the beginning he kept to himself. Ysabel, please do not cry for I have still more to tell.'

My eyes prickled and perhaps the candle flame caught the sparkle of an unshed tear, but I did not weep. I wished I could sob and wail because my chest was so tight I thought I might not get a breath inside. This is grief, I thought.

Grief. My silly, weak father.

'But then some hunting friends began to call. They took your father out on long expeditions, returning him blind drunk, and then collecting him again the next day and so on. Not so bad you think? Perhaps not, until word began to spread from different demesnes, that games of chance were being played and with large stakes.' He stopped and scrutinized my face.

'Tell me, tell me and be done.' I whispered.

'Your father has staked Moncrieff, Ysabel, and they say that a Baron De Courcey might be the winner.'

'No! No!' I uttered as I jumped up.

'Hush,' he held my arms, making me look at him. 'Hush. You need to get back to Moncrieff and talk with your father, with the bailiff and with the priest.'

'Who is he, this Baron De Courcey?' I shivered and Guy drew me toward the fire.

'A thug. Moneyed, titled and a thug.'

I began to shake and I barely noticed as Gisborne rubbed his hands up and down my arms to engender warmth.

'He shall not have Moncrieff.' I spoke through chattering teeth. 'Over my dead body if necessary, but he shall not have Moncrieff.'

I sat up high on the cot that night barely able to sleep, my arms around my knees, staring into the dark. The candles had long since melted to stubs and the brazier had burned to embers which cracked, sparked and occasionally flared – testament to the breeze that slid under the door from the hallway.

I could barely think of Father. Anger smouldered inside me like the remaining coals of the fire – it would take little to fan it and cause a conflagration.

'My Mother,' I whispered to the dark, a clear vision of her in my mind; honey gold hair bound in pleats and with a filet of twisted silver and gold around her head. She was as beautiful as Eleanor of Aquitaine and my father was lost to her the moment he met her, just as he was now lost without her.

'What do you think of this fool man, Lady Mother? Without you he is a oarless ship, a lost sheep.' My voice became louder and my fingers twisted on the covers. 'I *trusted* him to keep me, to keep *you*. I *trusted* him to keep Moncrieff and now it seems I might be without home or name. He gave no thought to his own flesh and blood, his daughter. Help me, Mama.'

I prayed and thought how ironic it was that the one time Gisborne didn't place me in a religious house for the night was the one night I really needed spiritual support.

'Dear Lord, keep Moncrieff from the hands of the greedy. Let me find my home as I remember it when I return.' My voice crept into the corners of the room and I crossed myself. I wished that I could see my mother sitting in the chair, that she would answer me. But the shadows were ambiguous and I was alone.

Khazia!

A phantom-like silver coat appeared in my mind, white mane blowing back like a bannerol in an Occitán wind. My equine friend and confidante of eight years. Many a time I had ridden out on my own and told her things I would tell no one else, lambasting the quality of proposed husbands, denying the concept of marriage.

Even on this journey I had chatted to her about Guy of Gisborne. I trusted her far more than I trusted Marais and at least Khazia would not gossip. She knew my soul had begun to stir in response to Guy's tinkering, that I fancied myself as a little more than his employer's daughter.

Paramour? The voice that whispered such things lay deep within me and I shuddered. But then why should I not allow him into my deepest heart? I had lost almost everything and had nought but a feckless, untrustworthy father to whom I must return and maybe a home that was no longer mine.

The tears slipped from the corners of my eyes. Gisborne and I had much in common. He had nothing and no one. Neither did I, for what was my father worth? Guy and I should be kindred spirits, united in our travails.

It appears you may have no dowry, Ysabel.

For a man who thinks that status is power, what good would you be?

'Be silent!' I hissed this last to the soul-deep voice. I did not want to know because since my feelings for Gisborne had begun to stir I had cherished this obscure idea, one I only shared with Khazia, that maybe *I* could give him status.

As the daughter of the moneyed Baron Joffrey of Moncrieff, I could give him wealth and a title. My mother and godmother thought well enough of him to encourage his employment. He was considered educated and steady. Why else would he be trusted at my father's shoulder? Despite his apparent emotional state my father would surely see Gisborne as the capable son he never had. Perhaps marriage could be within my grasp after all.

Thus I had daydreamed to my horse and her ears twitched and I remembered now that she snorted loudly.

Derision. That's what she thought.

What man with ambition would want to tie himself to a damsel with nothing? If my father had lost Moncrieff, I would be penniless. Landless. I would no longer be Lady Ysabel of Moncrieff but just plain Ysabel.

'Oh God help me,' I moaned as a likely future stared across the room at me.

I could not bear the thought of Khazia being sold. The horse was the last part of a past life to vanish and it poured acid on an already suppurating wound.

The bells of the Benedictine Abbaye Saint Ouen chimed the hour for Vigils and I shivered as I have ever held the belief that the midnight hour is the witching hour. 'Mary Mother, protect me...' I began and crossed myself again, wondering how I could expect God to right my wrongs. Briefly I thought that if Father had gamed Moncrieff away then I had a choice beyond the road. I could become a *religieuse*. Many noble women did for any number of reasons. They might be unmarried, unloved by their family, of ill-health. They may even have a calling.

Ah, but what they had and it appeared I did not, was a dowry for the Church. Besides, if I were to be honest, the thought of being incarcerated in a House of God was not at all my calling. I could never become a Bride of Christ. As this idea left the way it had entered, a soft tap could be heard on my door.

I jumped up and ran to it, my heart pounding. Inns were all well and good but at least one felt safe in the dorter of a House of God.

'Ysabel,' Guy's voice whispered. 'It is I…'

I flung the door open and dragged him in. 'Are you mad? Everyone shall hear you and I will be seen to be a harlot!'

'Then it is good that we leave in an hour.' He bent and stirred the fire in the brazier and the room warmed in the firelight.

My eyebrows rose. 'An hour? But it is dark.'

'A military troupe leaves for the north and we can travel in their wake with a group of merchants. It will be safe. They go to meet Richard at Calais.'

'But what about Khazia?'

'There is a Comte de Lascalles with whom I have spoken and he was attracted by Khazia's breeding. We agreed a price,' he placed a bag of coin in my hands, 'and he has also traded me a good campaign horse as part of the bargain.'

'Khazia?' I could have wept.

'Will be taken to the Comte's estates as soon as she is able.'

'No! I must see her. I must say farewell.' I threw the bag and it hit his chest. 'How dare you do this without my approval!'

He glared at me, his eyes as cold as iron.

'As I recall, we decided to leave forthwith for Moncrieff. Khazia, like Marais, was a liability.'

'Goodness Guy,' I snarled. 'Shall I become a liability of which you must rid yourself as well?'

'You are frequently a liability, Ysabel.' His voice stroked the hairs on my neck in a frightening manner. 'Here…' He threw a bundle at my feet. 'Whilst I do think you are winsome in your shift…'

I grabbed the blanket off the bed to wrap myself.

'Too late, I am afraid.' He swung his gaze over every inch of my now covered body and there was nothing I liked in that expression. 'And a pretty view it was too. You will be riding a campaign horse and as we are with soldiers, my advice is to dress as a youth. I have leggings and an undershirt and surcoat in the parcel along with boots and a hood. Your dark cloak is unremarkable and as much a man's. It will serve. For what it is worth, Ysabel, it may pay to be dressed thus until we reach Moncrieff and find out what awaits us.'

I hugged the blanket tight, humiliated, wishing I had never thought I could marry him.

'Why? What does it matter if a noblewoman rides to the coast with an escort?'

'I don't know. My gut crawls a little, that is all, and it is better to be cautious. Dress and be downstairs in an hour. I shall have the horses.'

I watched him turn, his back straight, stride long. I would swear he had put me back to where he had me safely positioned before we had sent Marais home… all tenderness gone in the blink of an eye. Thoughts of my little mare must now be pushed aside and I had no option but to trust this man and hope he guarded me with genuine care.

I stared up at the campaign horse – a giant creature of the Apocalypse. Shadows jumped and flickered and thoughts of Moncrieff receded unhappily to the back of my mind whilst I contemplated the mountainous shape in front of me. I sighed as I thought of my little grey mare on whom I could spring bareback if I chose, and I would almost have given in to all my woes if the bristly lips of my mount hadn't brushed over the top of my hand as it lay on the hitching rail. The animal was infinitely gentle and I lifted my eyes to his, what I could see of them in the dark, and would swear he sent me a message back telling me not to concern myself with things I could not change.

Indeed. How you right you are.

Gisborne was nowhere to be seen so I called to the ostler. 'The mounting block, do you have one? Steps?' I indicated the horse. 'To get on?'

He looked me up and down with curiosity and then replied, 'Yes … sir. This way, please.'

With a youth's clothing and my hair diminished to a knot under the hood he assumed I was a male but my voice had obviously thrown him a little. Ah well, no doubt he thought I was partial to men rather than women, my tones more those of a certain type of youth. He indicated the steps and retreated, staring at me as left.

I retrieved the horse and the animal plodded after me with giant hooves that echoed on the cobbles. He seemed resigned to his fate as my ride and I promised him as I gathered the reins, that I would be kind and not heap my sadnesses upon him. He stood patiently as I lifted my foot high up to the stirrup. I have always been supple and managed to spring upward and then clamber astride. What I had not reckoned with was the breadth of his back and I whimpered as I settled, my thighs burning as if they were stretched across the rack.

I clicked my tongue and we moved through the leaping shadows of the torchlit space to the front yard of the livery.

'Ah, Y… Yves. I was wondering where you were. You are ready?' Gisborne's dark shape could barely be seen.

'I am, sir,' I replied gruffly.

We walked passed a flame as I looked at him and his eyes glinted with merriment – something one rarely saw. 'We must make haste. The company will not wait.'

We trotted side by side, my horse the height of his.

'My voice is hardly masculine, Gisborne. How long must I maintain this vocal charade? It rasps my throat.'

'You could not speak at all. Play the mute. What a turn-up that would be.' He laughed and it vibrated through my body, settling its echo in delicious places. He spurred his horse into a canter, scattering itinerant drunkards and street laggards and I urged my mount to keep up.

The horse had a long stride despite his muscle-bound bulk. I could imagine him in battle, dancing away from a sword, kicking out with powerful hind-legs as soldiers advanced upon him with pikes… every movement choreographed in his early training. 'What is the beast's name?'

'He is called Monty. Short for Montaigne.'

He laughed but I knew it was at my expense so I shut my mouth, concentrating on the road.

We approached the city gates as the company of armed men began to ride out, the sight leaving me breathless. Dawn was breaking and the dark shade of night began to weaken as streams of light emerged from the eastern horizon. Weaponry winked, basinets and chainmail flashed, the noise of jingling harness and many metal-shod hooves reverberating above the sound of a waking town. Fifty rows of men rode two by two, the first ten rows carrying pennants in Richard's colours – three golden lions with blue claws and tongues on a red field. Behind the army rode a mounted division of twenty men with black surcoats and an indistinct shield crest but they and Richard's cohorts leaped well ahead of the band of merchants and ourselves who brought up the rear, twelve of us in all.

Our pace did not slacken. We continued at a canter through the bucolic countryside as the dawn light strengthened from grey to oyster. The thundering rhythm startled birds, and people lifted their heads and stared as we passed. In the fields, men stilled their oxen from ploughing and their wives ceased collecting the weeds in sacks or trugs, the seasonal work broken for a moment as they watched and wondered. The rich tilled earth provided a foil to the greener fields close by. I could imagine the scene painstakingly translated on parchment or vellum with a skilled hand laying down colour and then transcribing words that might indicate the seasons or the hours of the day in any month – a scene in a book that Guy would love I was sure.

We had many leagues to cover and I could feel my legs tiring, the inhuman stretch of my thighs across Monty's back threatening to unseat me. Periodically over difficult stretches of the road, when it narrowed or when we approached large traveling groups, we would slow to a walk on the cry of a disembodied voice far ahead. The command would feed back through the ranks and thanking God for the reprieve, I would stand in my stirrups to stretch my legs. Once I even thrust one leg over Monty's wither, jamming my thighs together to try and rest them, but Guy glanced over and frowned and I desisted, groaning as I felt for the stirrup and heard the call to canter on.

The distance we traveled passed in a blur and I lost interest in the surroundings, discomfort tainting everything. When we finally halted at midday, barely a single part of my body was without pain and I dreaded the moment of dismount, knowing that dressed as a young man I must do without Gisborne's strong hands to help me. I gritted my teeth and jumped down, falling against Monty's damp shoulder.

'Can you manage?' Gisborne moved in next to me as I closed my eyes and lay my forehead on the horse's shoulder. His hand reached around my waist as I sagged. 'Ysabel,' he whispered. 'Alright?'

A soldier dressed in the unknown black livery walked past looking for trees against which to relieve himself. He glanced at us with open curiosity, his gaze fixing on Gisborne's enclosing hand.

'It's too loose,' said Guy as his fingers slipped behind Monty's girth. 'Make sure you tighten it before we mount again.' He muttered to the soldier as he turned away. 'Can't find a decent squire for love nor money.'

Love nor money.

The soldier nodded and proceeded to piss in full view against the trunk of an oak. Gisborne turned to me whilst the soldier had his hands full and lifted his eyebrows. His mood seemed lighter to be sure and I wondered if it was because each league we covered we were one league closer to England.

I gave passing thought to the way his moods shifted and whether I could cope with his tortuous mindsets in the long term. But then I cast my mind back to the many kindnesses he had shown me as he was forced to reveal my family's straitened circumstances. I decided that despite his dour and withdrawn moments, despite his callous philosophy of status being power, he *had* shown me respect. And in all honesty, there remained in me the faintest hope that I would find Moncrieff safe and my father happy to have his daughter once again in the fold.

CHAPTER FIVE

Monty's coat became slick with lather despite his astonishing stamina and as I looked between his ears I marveled at the campaign animals in front of me. I could only imagine the courage and steadfastness that rushed through their veins.

We stopped twice more for short rests until the final longed-for halt was called. In flat tussocky land that spread for miles we stopped to make camp. To our right flank was an immense coppice of spindly birches, their leaves the acid green of spring, most in bud and summer not far away. A stream sketched a languid line from its distant source, trickling past our feet to flow to the coast far off. It barely ran and I wondered if every horse would suck it dry.

Guy was close and our eyes met and I could see he felt sympathy for me and what he had put me through with this subterfuge. And yet I understood. The merchants had told of our dangers; that there were brigands and lawless Barons all across this moorland who would think nothing of picking we dozen off. I would have loved to make mention of our own fatal run-in earlier in our travels but Guy's eyes barely flickered to warn me to maintain my charade.

As I looked around, I began to feel some awkwardness, even concern. Clustered in myriad bunches unsaddling horses, tethering, lighting fires, and doing any number of other such necessary things were one hundred and sixty one men. Whilst dressed as a youth, my skin prickled at the thought that I was the only woman amongst such lusty and perhaps unbridled company. I kept my head down, unsaddling Monty, tethering him close to the stream where he could drink his fill and eat. I knotted up some tussocks and dragged them over his body to remove the sweat, concentrating on his spine and girth where he might suffer friction galls on the morrow. I was conscious of Gisborne watching me, knowing he could do nothing to help because I was after all a mere squire. My job was to serve my master and such scrutiny made me blush but I lifted my eyes to his. His mouth twitched, nothing more.

I walked over to his mount and began strapping him, wiping with a smooth motion and settling the animal. I picked up his giant hooves and checked them for stones caught on the edges of the shoes and then retired to sort out the saddlery and make some sort of bedding for us. We had saddles for pillows and our cloaks for warmth and a large saddlecloth each that could be another layer. For the rest, we should have to sleep close to the fire and hope we would be warm because we could hardly lie curled against each other the way we had previously.

I fished in the saddlebags and found bread that had been sliced into thick pieces, some salted pork and a slab of cheese, and was surprised to find my stomach rumbling. The forced pace of the ride had pushed such thoughts far from my head earlier and so I crispened the bread near the coals of the fire, placing slices of the meat with crudely cut cheese onto it so the cheese began to bubble and run. I passed part of the meal to Gisborne as he sat beside me and I began to chew on the other.

One of the merchants, a smart, loud chap with an eye to his own good looks, spoke to Guy.

'You say he's a pretty ordinary squire.' My eyebrows lifted at the comment. 'But the meal smells good enough and your horses are comfortable and your sleeping arrangements settled.'

He passed Gisborne a wine bladder and a swig was taken as the fellow continued. 'Pretty enough fellow too,' his gaze slid over me and it was obvious he couldn't see a woman beneath the clothes, only the body of a youth that he might desire.

'Indeed,' said Gisborne. 'Pretty enough if you like his sort, and capable with it and tied to a maid as beautiful as he in my demesnes.'

My eyebrows rose further and I coughed, reaching for some water.

The merchant seemed disappointed and I thanked God for Gisborne's quick thinking.

'Yes,' said Gisborne. 'He's to account for himself to me on this journey as he got his maid with child before we left, and them both unwed. She'll be dropping the babe just as we are due back. He has a lot to prove apart from how well his oats are sown.'

Stunned at Guy's little history, I shook my head, seeking a way to leave these men for the privacy a woman needs. I moved first to the horses to check them, hoping I could sneak behind and cross to the birch coppice without attracting attention from Gisborne or his dainty merchant friend.

The shadows were long and night barely a breath away. The moon had risen and was lighting the sky to the east whilst the sun had set in the west casting a bronze glow heavenward. What little light there was lit a path amongst the spindle-thin trunks and my feet crunched older leaf fall occasioning a swift scuttle of forest creatures. Ahead was a shrubbery, waist high with dense enough growth to offer a woman privacy and I heard the chuntering of the stream over pebbles and a desperate urge to cool leg aches and wash away dust led me close to the running water.

I stripped off my boots and hose and stepped in, the level reaching my knees, the cold water biting into the inflamed skin, strips of red chafing indicated where the stirrup leathers had rubbed. I splashed my face and drew off the hood, unknotting my hair, feeling the smallest night-breeze finger the strands.

All around crickets and frogs whirred and croaked and the occasional flutter of wings battered the air as a small bird or some insect dipped past. Above the nocturnal sounds, the army vibrated – shouting and laughter, the burble of men's voices, the whinny of horses, the crackle of many fires. I pulled the hose and boots back on and stood to walk back to the camp, hood tugged through belt, twisting and knotting unwilling hair into a tight roll. My mind was far away, thinking on my home and a weak father who had forgotten that trust is all and as I turned past a birch, a hand grabbed me and another covered my mouth so that I was pinioned. A powerful arm encircled my chest like a ring of iron.

'Why, what a hard flat chest you have, milady.'

I struggled against the hand and a familiar voice whispered in my ear.

'Now then, my lady, don't struggle. What do you think the army out there would say if they knew we had a woman of such godly gifts as yours in our midst.'

He laughed softly and I hated him as much again as I did the first time I met him. My hair had fallen down and covered my shoulders and I could hear him sniffing it.

'Your hair smells so fine, Lady Ysabel. So much nicer than the horse and man sweat that has beleaguered me these last days.'

He nuzzled under my hair and kissed my neck and I squirmed and tried to kick but his grip tightened and he laughed – a snicker colder than a winter wind.

'I think we could be such loving friends, Lady Ysabel, don't you? Especially if you don't want your little secret revealed.'

I thrashed my head about but he held me more grimly, his grip over my mouth almost suffocating. I tried to open my jaw to bite his fingers but he clamped ever stronger.

'Don't fight, Lady Ysabel. If you deny me then I shall contrive something terrible against Gisborne out there, maybe even against your father. You wouldn't want that, would you?'

I froze. The man had his own kind of influence and I knew it was no idle threat.

'There, what a good girl you are. That's better. Now, if you move or make a noise when I take my hands away, rest assured I shall indeed cause much suffering to those closest to you. That's it, just hold still whilst I put this here,' he placed a gag across my mouth and pulled it tight as he talked as if to a recalcitrant child. 'Oh what a lovely neck you have. See? That's not so bad, is it? If I just tie your hands like so, we can get down to business.'

He stayed behind me all the time but in my mind I could see his face as he rubbed himself against me and I wanted to scream but could barely articulate a moan.

'Now, now…' he ran a hand down over my shoulder. 'It's going to be…'

The words choked off.

'Halsham,' Gisborne's voice whispered. 'A move and you're dead.'

Another movement behind me and a flick and then Gisborne saying, 'Step away, Ysabel,' as the bonds at my wrists fell apart. With a stroke of a knife in one hand, Gisborne had freed me whilst with the other he held a *misericorde* against Halsham's throat. Moonlight fell between the trees and perhaps it coloured Halsham's face with pallor or maybe he was actually frightened. Whatever the case, I could see a trickle of blood and would not have been adverse to the repulsive throat being slit, ear to ear.

'Halsham,' Gisborne growled, more gutteral and filled with anger than I had yet heard. 'You are a marked man.'

Halsham laughed. He had courage; I would give him that as the blade pressed his skin – courage or blind stupidity.

'You think, Gisborne? Think again. If you hurt me, who do you think shall be the cur? Myself, who marches with Richard's men to London or you, a lowly steward?'

'Enough,' Guy snarled at Halsham and more blood appeared.

'Oh, Gisborne, why trouble yourself for this penniless little has-been? Don't you know? Moncrieff is no longer her father's. Not at all. If you thought to buy yourself some sort of sinecure with the family for services rendered, you're wasting your time.'

I could barely listen to the man and yet...

'What do you mean?' My voice cracked as I dragged the gag away.

'Holy Father, she speaks!' Halsham grinned at me and I was reminded of an image of Beezelbub in an illuminated manuscript I had seen in Aquitaine. 'I mean, Lady Ysabel,' he continued, 'that all you have left now is your title. Your father has ceded the entire domain of Moncrieff to Baron De Courcey in payment of gaming debts.'

He yelped as Gisborne dug the knife ever deeper so that a stream of blood ran down the knight's neck to his chemise. 'Let me go and I shall forget this little event.'

'No! Don't even think of letting him go!' I wanted Halsham's head on a pike.

'Be silent, Ysabel,' Gisborne muttered and then his hand dropped, Halsham's coming up to staunch the flow of blood.

'Wise move, sir. Your future is not with her and I can make or break you, never forget. I shall make you pay for this one day,' he indicated the bloody incision at his neck. 'Have no doubt. But in the meantime you are a man to be used and I can raise you to heights quite beyond a steward. Think on it, dear chap.' He sauntered past me. 'You know, Lady Ysabel, I actually think he just saved me from making a terrible mistake. When

I tup I like to get my money's worth and you, dear lady, have no money.'

He laughed as he left the coppice and I spat after him, whipping round to Gisborne.

'You double dealing bastard! I *trusted* you...' I bundled my hair, yanking the hood over it and went to leave, to saddle Monty and head out on my own but his hand grabbed my arm and he tugged me back.

'Now you know, Ysabel.' He spoke through gritted teeth. 'Isn't it what you wondered? You go back to nothing. Nothing beyond an arranged marriage with a noble or with the Church.'

'Better that than with someone like you.'

I wanted to scratch his face I was so filled with ire.

'I will see you to your father,' he continued. 'If he is no longer master of Moncrieff, I am no longer his steward but I will honour Lady Cecilia's orders.'

'How long have *you* known about Moncrieff?' Tears threatened and I hated my weakness.

'Tonight.'

'Ha!' I mocked, the expletive bouncing around the glade.

'Why would I waste my time escorting you back to Moncrieff if I thought there was nothing for me to go back to?'

But I was not listening, not really, wishing to rant as a release for my hurts.

'You thought you would get money from Cecilia at the very least. And notoriety. You are like Halsham, Gisborne. A user.'

Two hands grabbed my shoulders and shook me.

Tell me I'm wrong then. I want to be wrong.

I could barely see his face and then the moon moved away from the branches and lit his eyes and his reply chilled me and thrilled me at once.

'I thought I could use you, yes. But then other things got in the way.'

'What things, Gisborne? My father's bankruptcy?'

His eyes burned with a terrifying coldness that I shall never forget. He bent his head and pressed his lips hard against my own and then dragged me back to the camp, stepping amongst snoring bodies and pushing me down onto my bedding.

I lay for hours, long after I heard his breathing become regular. I hated myself for being a woman who relied on men. I hated my father for being so damnably weak. I hated my mother for dying. I hated the world and

God and Mary Mother.

But more than anything, I think this night I actually hated Guy of Gisborne.

He reached over my shoulder the next day and hoisted my saddle onto Monty's back and I pulled the girth under the belly and cinched it up. The long hours lying awake through the night had done nothing to ameliorate my feeling for him. The truth was that I doubted him, doubting my own thinking in the process. How could I trust someone who would allow a man who would rape to go free, for that is what Halsham planned – the rape of a woman. The idea that I could ever place myself in *any* man's hands for protection was galling.

But some weakly female part of me wondered if Gisborne might truly feel some sadness for me. That he worried the news about Moncrieff and my father's inexorable weaknesses on top of the death of my mother could tip my emotional state. Perhaps that was why he had fed the known facts to me drip by drip like a mother feeding milk through linen to a sickly child.

But then, I reasoned, if he felt so kindly toward me, why did he let Halsham go? I watched the way his mind worked as he held the knife to Halsham's throat; the way it said yes, then no. I saw his hand fall and Halsham walk away. That was not the move of a man who cared for *my* emotional state. It was the action of a man who weighed consequence and erred on the side of ... what was it again? Ah yes, status and power, two conditions apparently lacking in my own life.

The thoughts chased themselves around in my head and Monty took it upon himself to turn toward the merchants' group and join in as we received the command to move off. Gisborne trotted up beside me but I avoided him with contempt.

And yet I had to be honest with myself.

My heart was breaking.

On so many counts.

My mother, my icon, was dead. I had lost what little love and respect I had for my father. I had lost my home, my fortune, my future. And the final straw had been realizing how I had misjudged Guy of Gisborne.

God, but I was naïve. I had thought there was a heart there, valour. But bring him to a pecuniary choice over a moral choice and his true colours showed. It reminded me of another man of whom I knew, one my mother had talked about. The fellow may have been a man she loved once, I do not know. But he did something shameful, untrustworthy and dishonest, placing his friends, his compatriots and my mother under threat. He had ended by taking his own life, jumping from the battlements of Cazenay. No wonder she had opted for my weakling father.

But to return to Gisborne.

He chose Halsham over me and I would never forget.

I barely noticed the countryside changing. Monty carried me completely in his care. The reins hung loose and I rode in amongst the tangle of my thoughts. My main concern was what I would find at Moncrieff. Who was this Baron De Courcey? I wondered if my father had somehow managed to maintain a share in anything that would give me a roof over my head.

There was a village, Hayrood, a few leagues away from the castle but part of the estate. I recalled an unassuming manorhouse that could suit the purpose; two levels of stone and daub and with a thatched roof and a modest component of chambers. But I could not see De Courcey being so beneficent.

I thought of my mother's things; her jewelry, her Book of Hours, her basket of embroidery threads, her frame and lute. Surely those were my inheritance. I wanted everything. Everything she had owned. Not for its monetary value but because everything was redolent of her spirit, her mind, her heart. Had my father no thought for what these things might mean to Alaïs' daughter? This is what cut into my soul. His apparent disregard for me. This was my father and I hated him more with each step that Monty took.

Every thought built on the previous one and my hands twisted on the pommel of the saddle as tightly as bands of muscle began to tighten around my head. We rode steadily until midday and I noticed not at all. Unaware that Monty had dark sweat stains on his shoulder or that Guy still rode stirrup to stirrup next to me. I would have continued on as all around me halted if Guy's hand had not reached for my reins.

Mary Mother, how many times has he done that in the last few weeks?

I turned to him, I couldn't help it, but I could read nothing there; a statement perhaps of things as they now were. As a penniless dependant, I was at best a tolerated responsibility, at worst a despised nuisance.

'You are frequently a liability, Ysabel.' I could hear his words so coolly delivered.

No situation sat well with me and I preferred not to imagine in detail what it was to him. My state was repugnant and my headache strengthened accordingly.

Dismounting for our midday break, bread and cheese again, I noticed we had reached the coastline and were tracking north along a coast road. The land fell over cliffs and below, waves crashed with rhythmic ferocity against the rocks.

A whisper sounded close to my ear. 'Don't step too close, Lady.'

I shivered. 'Would that be a threat, Halsham?

'Take it any way you like,' Halsham replied. 'I should hate to have to report your death to your father. Where would that leave Gisborne?'

I looked about to see if anyone observed me speaking when I was supposed to be dumb. Reassured, I stared into those calculating eyes.

'What happens to Gisborne is of little concern to me. More to you I would imagine. You and he seem to have tied yourselves to each other like a betrothed couple. As to my father – I doubt that he cares overmuch for me at all. You may do your worst.'

'Halsham.' Gisborne strode between us. 'Do you look for me?' He gave me a quick glance. 'Go about your business. I would like some food before my stomach forgets what my mouth is for.'

As I left I heard Halsham laugh. 'No please or thank you? Why carry this little charade any further? Just hand the chit over to the merchants and let them see your Lady Ysabel to England?'

I didn't hear Gisborne's reply but when I looked back I saw Halsham's face creep into an expression of ridicule as he made some comment in response to whatever was said. They talked a little longer and then I saw Halsham offer his hand, as a knight might do. Gisborne stood immobile for a moment and then returned the clasp and for me, the thread between Gisborne and I stretched thin to breaking.

The afternoon's ride continued at the same pace. For some leagues we had seen the walls of Calais in the distance and it couldn't approach quickly enough. Oh, I had vague plans that I could offload Gisborne and sail to England alone or if necessary, hire a guard. But I had relied on Gisborne to pay for everything till now, believing he used my father's coin. I had nothing and my head felt cleft in two.

Finally the troop halted two by two beneath the gates, Richard's colours fluttering in the seabreeze. Horses stretched their necks, snorted, skirted back and forth on the road. Harnesses jingled and men muttered with tiredness. The Watch hailed us, the gates opened and we moved slowly at a clinking, clattering walk until we merchants brought up the rear and the gates slammed behind us. The army continued on to their temporary quarters and Halsham's troupe, with the smug man at its head, wheeled to the right to I know not where. Nor did I care, wishing that he would drop off the face of the earth.

Gisborne raised his arm to farewell the merchants, wishing them well and calling me to follow him. We walked in single file over narrow cobbled streets toward the smell of the sea, turning underneath an arch and into the rear yard of an inn. Monty halted and I heaved a sigh as I swung over to jump down. Gisborne's legs had taken the strain of his dismount with no problems at all, but my knees folded and I stumbled against the horse as the ostler went to take him from me. I held the reins back. 'No. I would do it myself. Thank you.'

'You don't have…' Gisborne started to say.

'But I do, sir. *He* has been loyal and caring. It is the least I can do. I owe him much.'

'If you must.' He followed me into the stalls and tied up his own horse, unsaddling and grabbing whatever he could to wipe away the sweat.

The ostler watched us, bemused. I could see he was unused to merchants strapping their own mounts. But Monty deserved this and when he was dry and cooled, I made sure he had fresh water and hay and only then did I speak to Gisborne.

'Where is my room. I wish to wash and replace my clothes and then I wish for you to inform me on which boat I am to travel. Other than that, I have nothing else to say.'

I brushed past him and walked swiftly to the entrance of the inn where we were shown to our separate rooms, and as Gisborne moved to walk into my chamber behind me, I slammed the door in his face.

Dirt stained the cloth that had been left for me. The water in the bowl looked as if it had been collected from a moat and I craved a warm scented bath, for my nails to be clean, for my hair to once again fall in a silky swathe. But it was not to be. I turned from the bowl to reach for clean clothes and of course there were none.

A firm knock sounded at the door and Gisborne called. 'Ysabel, open up.

I stayed quite still, wrapped in a rough towel provided by the innkeeper's wife.

'Ysabel, for God's sake grow up and open the damned door.'

Grow up? Grow up, you think?

I grabbed a cover off the bed and threw it around me like a cloak and hauled the door open.

'What? Damn you, Gisborne, what?' My forehead tightened with tiredness and frustration.

He pushed past me, slamming the door behind.

'How dare you enter my chamber,' I hissed. 'What do you think the innkeeper will say?'

'The innkeeper thinks you are my wife and that we have had a dispute because you asked to ride as a man on a man's horse and that I was disgusted with your lack of wifely obedience. If he is listening, I dare say he is smiling. So you can rant and rave as much as you like but you will merely fuel his enjoyment.'

'Your wife! God above!'

'The idea is as unpalatable to me, Lady Ysabel.' He threw a bundle on the bed. 'Now that we have the pleasantries out of the way, we can deal with business. There are some clothes. The innkeeper has a meal for us. When you have completed your toilette, I shall await you down the stair.'

'I am not hungry.'

'God *save* me, Ysabel! We haven't eaten a decent meal for days. It would serve you well to eat and then to sleep because our vessel departs at tide's turn in the morning.'

'All I require from you,' I said as I tilted my chin up, 'is the name of the ship on which I shall sail. Your responsibility to me ends with that.'

'My responsibility ends when I hand you over to your father, his behaviour notwithstanding. Unfortunately for both of us that is still some time hence. Like it or not, it is the way of it.'

Whether I wanted to or not, I looked at the man who stood before me and my stomach curled and rolled. His proximity unsettled me, turning me awry. He reached for the bundle on the bed and shook it out, holding a white linen chemise for my inspection. It was beautifully worked on the hems and must have cost much more than he had in his purse. I looked to the rest of the bundle and gasped. A midnight blue, finely woven *bliaut* draped like a shadow across the edge of the bed, its folds pooling on the floor. A cloak of the same shade but edged in black sable lay underneath and a boot fell to the floor, black kid, more than good enough for traveling.

He pulled the other boot from underneath the bundle and I blushed as I reached for the chemise he offered. Our fingers touched, the slightest glide of one hand over the other. I would swear he left a searing burn behind and I looked up from the closely woven linen. Our eyes met and his were as dark as the *bliaut,* darkening more by the second until he moved and the spell broke.

'I will leave you to dress, my lady.'

He bowed his head as if we had just met and left, the door closing behind him.

My equilibrium rippled and crashed around me.

I had deceived myself.

I wanted to hate Guy of Gisborne but it was far too late for that.

All I could do now was hide my longing and I hated my naivety, my ignorance. Cazenay had not helped me grow at all. It had simply been a rarefied atmosphere whereby men and woman were thrown together to play games of love, games based on the rules of Eleanor's courts – shallow rules, rules that grew like weeds from the words of troubadours' songs and poems. There seemed nothing of reality in my previous life and I felt at sea, utterly.

I grabbed the damp cloth and scrubbed my body again until it reddened, as I wished to be clean when that fine clothing slid over my skin. I placed one nail underneath the others, scraping until they were almost spotless.

I would have loved some perfume, some floral extract … anything to take away the smell of horse and road and the never forgotten odour of death which had stalked alongside us these last weeks. But there was nothing... until I slipped on the first of the clothes and smelled lavender.

Each garment had obviously been stored in a chest with bags of herbs and the fragrance was delicate, engendering a lifting of spirits.

The soft wool of the *bliaut* fell from my breasts and as I reached for the ankle boots, I noticed an emerald and aqua girdle lying in a shy heap. Picking it up, I ran my fingers over goldwork that edged the peacock feather design. It was a glorious piece of Saracen needlework and against the midnight of the gown, it made a statement of wealth and privileged nobility.

How did you manage it, Gisborne? More importantly, why?

With the bowl and cloth, the innkeeper's wife had left a wooden comb and I began to work through my hair, removing tangle after tangle. Oh, it was so dirty, itchy and oily after days on the road, the kind of hair a lady would never have been seen with in Cazenay. A final comb through and I plaited it, twisting the plait loosely atop, resurrecting whatever I could of a style that I remembered but had no looking glass to check.

I would have liked my Cazenay goods, my small but loved collection of jewelry, even my own bone comb – but they were gone. Carried away by our attackers, by Wilf's and Harry's murderers. My stomach growled as I recalled that dreadful moment although less with grief than with emptiness. Time to eat, time to descend the stair.

Time to confront whatever was coming my way.

The gown wafted around my ankles, its folds heavy, flowing with each step. As I negotiated the stair, I grasped the *bliaut* so that I would not fall, progressing slowly, recalling from an ancient past the grace that I had learned at Cazenay. Gisborne stood at the bottom with his back to me but the stair creaked and he turned.

I swear I did not imagine the glance that came scorching up the steps. He held out his hand and I laid my fingers in the palm. It should probably have felt cool against my own because the stair was breezy and dark but in fact a shocking touch vibrated up my arm. My breath sucked in and I held it as he bent his head, drawing my hand upward. The pressure of his lips on my fingers was like a butterfly wingbeat and when he spoke, his voice reached in and touched every secret part of me.

If I was a castle wall, I had been well and truly breached.

CHAPTER SIX

There are times in life when one just wants to forget about concerns and cares – ignore the shouted whisper of caution in the ear. To believe that nothing could ever be wrong and that every dream or fantasy one has ever had is about to be fulfilled. This was such a time.

Gisborne drew me along a passage to a large room at the front of the inn. It glowed with light from cressets and a fire popped and cracked in a modest hearth. A few people sat at benches and trestles and the hubbub eased briefly as we entered – rising again as we sat. The innkeeper placed mugs and a flagon of ale in front of us and I watched Gisborne's hand lift and pour. Even such a simple movement had its effect and part of me sighed with such sadness that we were destined for something other than what might have been. I was unable to speak and the silence between us grew longer and longer. He fiddled with the mug, looking around, never meeting my eyes.

He had kissed my hand so why this apparent indifference?

Ah but think, Ysabel. The kiss was like a butterfly wingbeat. Does that not mean so light as to be devoid of emotion?

I closed my eyes, realizing that I had made something of nothing and to my own detriment. A serving wench placed a rough platter in front of me, filled with a meal from which the most delicate fragrance arose. On its edge sat chunks of steaming bread and the juices of the stew had begun to soak in, casting a fawn stain upon the dough. The sauce was thick and glossy and I could see parsley, onion, and succulent pieces of rabbit and my depression lifted as I took my first mouthful. It was a gift from God. My eyes closed as I chewed, tasting the flavour on my tongue, identifying garlic and thyme. When I opened them again after swallowing, I found Gisborne's gaze upon me.

'Good?'

'Mary Mother, I had forgotten what well-cooked food tastes like.' I sipped the ale, lifting the bread and tearing off a piece with my teeth. 'I'm actually starving.'

'I did tell you we needed feeding,' he said as he tore at the bread himself, dragging it through the fine sauce.

Be polite. Expect nothing.

'I confess you are right.' I said. 'And I think I shall sleep the better because of it.'

'You should have a good sleep tonight. I cannot guarantee our comfort on the boat and the weather does not look good. It may be rough.'

'I'm not worried. I am used to sailing that stretch of water. I did it every year as a child.'

He sipped the ale and topped up my mug. 'And that was how many years ago?'

'Eight.'

'And you have not been aboard a boat since?'

'No, but you are either seaworthy or not and fortuitously I am. It will not be an issue for me.' I loved the sea and I couldn't wait to prove it. 'But Master Gisborne, I would that we talked for a moment on other things...'

He had a habit of turning his head slightly to the side when he was perplexed or assessing a situation. His brows would crease a little. It was that same glance that now met mine and I wondered if he disliked the title I gave him. But it was impossible for me to call him Guy. 'Guy' was a title reserved for a close friend. Whether he fascinated me and had fingers on my heart was immaterial; I could not call him my *close* friend because he had let Halsham go and it stood between us like giant hurdle. Nevertheless, there was a certain propriety to be observed, an etiquette.

'I owe you thanks. My clothes are quite beautiful. Where did you get them.'

'It is the charge laid upon me, Ysabel, to keep you safe and comfortable.

84

Clothes are a part of that.'

'But these are very expensive.' I drew the fabric through my fingers, enjoying the softness of the wool, the fine weave. 'How have you paid?'

'I have funds.'

His voice began to close down, a note to it that advised me to stop now, this instant. I could see if I pursued it I was going to drive a further wedge between us and that was not my purpose. I was tired. Tired of struggling with the depths of emotions that had stretched thin almost to breaking by circumstance these last weeks. In many ways I knew it was Gisborne who had kept me on an even keel on this dreadful journey of realisations. If I looked beyond his arrogance, his misplaced ambition, temper and moodiness, he had been there when I needed support. Which is why I did not pursue the issue of expense and tried another tack instead.

'Well tell me then, *where* did you buy the clothes? For this is quality, the sort we would see in Aquitaine.' I fingered the girdle. 'This is Saracen-made and the gold thread work is very fine.'

'You are astute. It *is* a Saracen piece. The goods all came from the merchants with whom we traveled. They have warehouses here in Calais from where they ship goods to England. Your girdle came from Acre as a matter of fact and the woolen fabric in the gown was woven and dyed in Bruges, the wool no doubt originally from England, the garment itself made here in Calais. As to the chemise and other things, I have no idea. It was a matter of moment to do business. You needed a change of clothes, I could provide them.'

'Then it as I said, thank you.'

I spoke simply and pressed his hand unconsciously. He froze, looking at it, then at the empty jug. Removing my fingers, he picked the jug up and asked the wench for more ale. It wasn't a rebuttal but it had a sense of removal and I blushed with the stupid spontaneity of my action. I suspect he sensed my discomfort because he immediately asked a question that diffused the moment.

'How are you after the journey aboard Monty? Two days on a campaign horse…'

'I know what you are going to say. That it is hard enough for a man let alone a woman. Well, truth? God but I am sore. I swear I thought I would fall down the stair. But Monty was reliable beyond words and I can only think that whomever acquires him will be a lucky man.'

'You did well. None of the merchants suspected you were a woman. Indeed I would that you reverted to your disguise when we are on the boat and in England.'

He fiddled with his knife, the one he had taken from his belt when eating. It had a bone handle that was intricately carved. Irish, I thought.

I must ask…

But his words jumped out at me.

Disguise? Again?

I remembered he had said that once before, as if it were important.

'Why? For what reason?'

My stomach began the slide that was becoming habitual. Gisborne shook his head slightly and I assumed he was not going to be explicit so I pushed.

'Please. If this is something that can affect me, you must say. Tell me. Am I in danger?'

He sighed and shifted, his voice so low it rumbled.

'Danger? Not like the forest where we lost Wilf and Harry. A different sort of danger.'

'What then?'

I was going to England for God's sake, to my home. What danger could there be? I had no inheritance to speak of and was worth nothing to anyone.

'Halsham told me that De Courcey waits for you, Ysabel. From my point of view it's best I get you to England and to your father unrecognized. After that, it is not my concern. But I will not let you fall into De Courcey's hands. Not until you have seen your father.'

'*Halsham* said? And you trust *him*?' I scoffed.

The rapist? God help me.

'In this instance, yes. He had nothing to gain from telling me of De Courcey. And even if it were doubtful intelligence, I would be a fool to ignore it. Your safety is at stake.'

I shivered. 'You scare me.'

He reached across and touched my arm, a small squeeze that he withdrew as swiftly as it was offered.

'I don't mean to. Have you eaten enough? I think we should retire and rest while we can.'

'Yes,' I stood, anxiety beginning to bite. 'But you need to tell me more. I need to know every single thing.'

He placed his hand under my elbow.

'There is not a great deal more to tell.'

But I knew he told an untruth, almost as if he wished no one to hear us. I looked around the room. Men sat drinking, apparently uninterested in us and yet he seemed concerned that we would be overheard. He was an unnaturally cautious man, a characteristic no doubt birthed when he had been turned from his inheritance.

I gave him my hand and he led me from the chamber, up the stair and to my room. All the while my heart pattered as we walked close, our bodies side by side, his hand beneath mine. He pushed open the door and we passed through, he moving to a chair by the window, me taking a seat by the hearth. I pulled the folds of the gown from underneath my feet and fiddled with the hem.

'What else have you to say? Why did you imply danger?'

He sat in the shadows by the window. I couldn't see his expression, whereas I dare say he could see every mood flash across my own face.

'De Courcey is a violent man, Ysabel. For some reason he wants you.'

'How violent?'

'The kind that as a young boy would probably have killed puppies. Ysabel, trust me. In this instance I do know best.'

He was just a dark voice in a corner of shadows.

'Be specific, Gisborne. How violent?'

'God damn you, Ysabel.'

'No,' I almost shouted as I stood up. 'God damn you if you don't tell me.'

He came toward me, a subtly clad figure whose face I would remember all the days of my life. 'Ysabel...'

'Tell me.' This time I yelled.

He was so close and I let his arms slide around me as he pulled me toward his chest, buffering me from his next words. 'He would rape you, Ysabel, if he wanted you. It is what he does. He would kill your father if he wanted to and then attend a banquet immediately after.' I struggled against him but he held tight. 'It – is – what – he – does.'

I sucked in my breath and a little sob followed but I had no tears as I reflected on how much my life had collapsed in a few weeks.

'God…'

He eased me away from his chest. He was infinitely gentle, lifting my face so that I had to look at him, his hands either side of my jaw. The pain I felt as my ruined life rattled around me like a thunderstorm was stupendous, but he was there… as he had been every step of the way, and once again, I let him take the pain away. I lifted my right hand to his and covered it as it lay on my jaw.

There are times in life when one just wants to forget about concerns and cares. To ignore the shouted whisper of caution in the ear…

I tilted my head, closing my eyes. I want to feel every sensation and the intensity sharpened without sight. I said nothing because I was afraid sound would shatter the moment, would make him think twice about what he did.

I tried not to think at all.

His lips moved to my neck and I lifted my shoulder as the delicate touch stirred me. His stubble rubbed at my skin and it should have been uncomfortable but it was a sublime touch – rough and smooth. His hands slid to my shoulders and then down to my arms and I felt the pressure of his fingers as he pulled me harder against him. I turned my head and kissed his chin lightly as I was afraid of being too forward.

I need not have worried. He met me halfway, his hands retracing their journey, leaving a trail of echoes in their wake, cupping the rounded edges of my shoulders in his palms, his thumbs circling before easing away to I knew not where. My eyes remained closed and I could feel the proximity of his body to mine as for a moment there was no sound but for our breathing, the crack of the burning wood in the hearth and the softest creak of leather as Guy moved.

And then he spoke.

'Ysabel,' his voice stroked my backbone, the words so soft. 'Ysabel.'

I dared to open my eyes and as I did, my fingers lifted and touched smooth muscle and bare, warm skin and I knew at once there was no going back.

The hours passed and I confess to not one feeling of profligacy. I would carry the memory of this night to my grave. He would leave me, of that there was no doubt and it was as it must be, but I meanwhile had a treasury of emotion and sensation to draw on whenever life looked as if it would bankrupt me.

As the moon passed across the heavens outside, the trees made intricate designs on the walls of the chamber and still we were silent, our breathing the only sign we were alive and aware. His fingers traced ancient patterns down to the well at the base of my spine and I tried to decipher them as if they were runes that spelled my future. Vaguely I remembered his Irish knife and his love of the Irish ballad and it all fitted together around me so that I stretched with languid ease as he slid over me.

They say the lovers' knot has an unbroken shape in Ireland, that it simply winds in and out, over and under in perpetuity, and that is forever how I remember the intertwining shape of this night of nights as Guy of Gisborne and I, Ysabel of Moncrieff, made love.

Later, as we curled into each other's bodies, I dared to speak. 'I would ask only one thing, Sir Guy.'

'I am not Sir Guy,' his voice rumbled through his chest as I lay my head on it.

'It is semantics,' I replied. 'Knightly behaviour can occur with or without a title. In any case, it's a discussion for another time. But as I said,' I rubbed my cheek against his damp skin. 'I would ask only one thing.' He said nothing and so I presumed he waited. I swallowed and left my head lying still as I did not want to look into his eyes. I was afraid of what I might see and so I launched into a simple plea. 'Don't regret this.'

Once again he did not speak, nothing in reply for so long that my stomach sank to my naked toes. But then his hand stroked the top of my head and all he said was 'Ysabel...' in a faintly chiding way.

I couldn't ask for more. I had no right to. I was a willing participant.

Besides, I thought I knew which way the game would go.

Something warmed my back and as I stretched, my shoulder was gently shaken. Through sleepy lids I could see the sun streaming into the chamber. Guy's voice spoke just loud enough to push the last threads of sleep from my consciousness.

'Ysabel, wake you. It's time to dress and break your fast. The boat leaves in an hour.'

I sat up quickly, dragging the covers over me. To be sure it hardly mattered because he had seen every part of me overnight. But something about daylight and the resumption of our journey made me more coy than I had been in hours past.

'You should have woken me earlier,' I said.

'You were tired and needed to rest. I would that you had your wits about you.'

'Meaning I haven't till now? I am sure you jest.'

His mouth gave the smallest hint of a smile as he turned.

'I shall leave you to dress and meet you down the stair.'

Dressing in men's clothes is a quick business apart from the need to bind my breasts tightly. My hair, more sweat-filled than ever, smoothed easily into a tight knot that I thrust under the hood. I folded the coveted lady's apparel into a neat bundle and placed it in a sack that slung from the shoulder, wrapping the cloak around me because the cold of concern had started to make itself felt and yet it seemed a fine spring morning beyond the walls. Heading for the stair, I clopped down as would any youth of my age. I had every intention of being anything but a woman.

Gisborne waited outside, passing me some bread and dried figs. 'This'll have to do. We need to get aboard the boat immediately.'

'Why?' I asked, noting the bread was fresh and that I was ragingly hungry after last night.

'De Courcey's men are in the town.'

Any lightness of heart disappeared in a moment and my predicament once again stood larger than life in front of me.

'You say? How do you know?'

I stuffed the bread and figs into the small leather purse that hung from my waist and licked lips that had become dry in an instant.

'Halsham.'

His reply was uncompromising and he looked away up the street, his eyes forever roaming shadowy corners as if danger lurked in every crevice. 'He ate with De Courcey last night.'

There was so much I wanted to say about snakes, traitors and more but I desisted and followed hard on his heels as we sped down the darker alleys, winding in and out of shadow, twisting ourselves in amongst the ordinary folk of Calais.

The townspeople moved toward the wharves like water going down a drain, as if all the business of Calais was to be done by the sea. This was a town of trade, of diplomacy and secrets and patently it suited Gisborne, this ready-made camouflage of the populace as we fled to the waterside. I had no time to think, to rationalize and had to rely entirely on his assessment of the situation and as we sped around a corner, he grabbed me, pulling me into a doorway, shoving me behind his darkly clad body so that we were just a deeper shadow amongst many.

'What…'

'Don't speak!'

He reached behind with one hand, grasping my arm, squeezing hard and I sneaked a look around him and saw a small squad of liveried men jog past in formation, following a man mounted on a chestnut gelding. They moved swiftly, too swiftly for me to see the face of the man that led them, but I recalled Halsham's livery. Black with a blood red shield.

Halsham is De Courcey's man.

'Guy,' I whispered, the unsuitability of using his name forgotten. 'Is…'

'De Courcey.'

My head flung round as I tried to glimpse more of this person who must surely be my nemesis. All I could see were broad shoulders and russet hair on a man who sat his horse well. All I could *feel* was the back of an enigmatic man who had loved me last night and whom I had loved back.

The troupe passed from sight, turning a corner, and Gisborne stepped from the shadows.

'Quickly, we must get to the boat and away before he realizes you are gone. If I am right, he makes haste to our inn. Leave your sack behind.'

'But it's the gown and girdle.'

'Life matters more.'

The response was curt as he began to jog and I puffed beside him.

'Does it occur to you that Halsham has betrayed us, Guy?'

But he didn't answer.

The wharf was less than two hundred yards down a steep, cobbled way.

'That's the *nef.* The *Marolingian*,' he pointed.

She was moored alongside the wharf, a mast poking into the midday sky like a marker and from its tip a white pennant fluttered as if to remind one that the breeze waited impatiently to propel the vessel through the water. The crowd had burgeoned even more; perhaps they enjoyed farewelling a departing vessel.

In so many ways the mass of people was much to our advantage. In so many others it signified nuisance as it slowed our escape from the alley. Gisborne set off again, running with speed, dipping and dodging as I sprinted to keep up.

I tried valiantly to tread in his footsteps but the swirling folk pushed and shoved as they went about their business. Soon he was out of sight and my heart hammered. All I could do was set my feet doggedly somewhere in the direction of the docks. Looking above the crowd, I could see the pennant and I swear it waved to me. As if the devil were behind, I shouldered and bullied, calling, 'Let me through. Aside you. Out of the way.'

Sweaty and disheveled, folds of the cloak muddied at the hem, I finally stood quayside. Gisborne was on board scanning the crowd and as he went to yell again, his eyes met mine and I *swear* I saw relief. His eyes closed for less than a second then he was shouting. 'Come *on!*'

I flew up the plank, the captain grabbing me.

'Here Mistress, hide in amongst the hogsheads with Master Guy. The Baron's men are approaching.'

He pushed me down amongst oaken hogs and a sail was pulled across.

'Jack,' he called. 'Cast off! Piotr, cast the stern line. Ailric, pull up the plank. Ready oars.'

The oars were pushed out on the starboard side with a woody clatter.

'Pull!'

The vessel juddered slightly as it moved away from the wharf. The larboard oars pulled again more gently to gain us distance from the wharf.

'Ready port oars... and together, pull!'

The movement changed to a steadier forward motion and I whispered to Gisborne.

'Are we safe?'

'Ssh!'

He bent and looked underneath the sail and I joined him.

'You there, Captain!'

De Courcey's men lined the wharf in their death and blood colours and De Courcey himself stood in front, his chest puffed out as he called, expecting our captain to spring to his attention.

'Aye?' was the shouted reply.

'Have you two passengers aboard? A man and a woman?'

'Do I look as if I take paying passengers?'

The wily captain spat over the side of the vessel toward the wharf and one could be forgiven for thinking he spat at De Courcey.

'But I see'd 'em,' he said craftily. 'They come aboard a half hour back and asked for passage up the coast. Had to tell 'em I was bound for England, not Bruges.'

De Courcey swore and I made fists in silent exultation.

'Hold the boat steady, men,' the captain continued before directing his attention at De Courcey again. 'I'll tell you what I told 'em.'

The boat drifted parallel with the quay but mercifully far enough away to prevent even the most intrepid of De Courcey's men from jumping aboard. De Courcey paced along with us, keeping within earshot, pushing people out of the way. A young boy balanced on the edge of the wharf and but for kind hands that reached for him, would have pitched into the dark depths below.

'I sent 'em to the other wharf,' said the captain lifting his shoulder to indicate a direction to the stern of the *Marolingian*. 'There's a boat there, a sister ship. She's goin' to Ter Streep and I told 'em they could get a barge up the Zwynn to Bruges from there.'

De Courcey swore and Guy snorted softly.

I looked back from under the sail and saw the captain touch his forehead with two fingers. De Courcey had flushed red and turned on his heel. He was a good enough looking man in a ruddy, explosive way. His chin was strong and cleft and his hair, that curious wine shade, lifted in the seabreeze as he turned, his heavy cloak flapping about him. He wasn't as tall as Gisborne but he had a breadth of shoulder that gave him an illusion of extraordinary power. Men backed away from him as he hurried back to his troupe and I would forever be reminded of a King in the making.

Or a kingmaker.

'Oarsmen, pull!' the captain roared and De Courcey looked back over his shoulder. We turned to larboard a little more and then the oarsmen pulled us out into the current and we floated swiftly on the tide, well out of view of the quay.

'Right you two, we need the sail now, keep your heads down until we are well to sea.'

'Thank you, Davey.'

Gisborne reached up and shook the captain's hand.

'Pleasure, Master Guy. Yer know I do it fer Lady Ghislaine. She were good to me when I were at Gisborne.'

The sail was quickly rigged and hoisted by the crew and for the first time for weeks I felt safe. Out in the middle of the sea between England and Normandy no one could touch me. Not my father nor De Courcey. Not even that carbuncle, Halsham. The sea purled under the bow of the *nef*, seabirds wheeled above us and the sun shone. Standing at the gunwhales, staring toward England's shores, Gisborne's hand slid over mine. He gave a small squeeze, subtle and almost invisible, but a support nevertheless.

'Are you afraid?' he asked.

'A little,' I admitted. 'De Courcey looks like a man who is used to getting what he wants.

In truth, whilst I did feel safe here on the *Marolingian*, I was afraid of home. Part of me wanted to flee west when we arrived in England. Head to the wilds of Wales. But I thought of Cecilia and what she had done by sending Gisborne to find me, to warn me of my father's parlous state, of Moncrieff's decline. There was part of me that felt I at least owed her thanks and in person. Otherwise I would not be the person she remembered.

As for my father?

I was confused. If I was a daughter worthy of my mother, I had a duty to see him but my feelings toward him were as ambivalent as his no doubt had been toward me. Why else would he have allowed Moncrieff to slide so badly that De Courcey was able to pick its bones? But more than anything, I wanted and *needed* to see my mother's tomb, to say my own farewells. My mother had been my love and it was inconceivable that I should run from the respect she was owed.

'I would that you continued to view him with caution,' Gisborne said in response to my comment on De Courcey. 'He certainly wouldn't have *your* best interests at heart.'

For a while, we just watched the shipboard activity, the men working as a well-oiled team, the sail now bellying, oars shipped, the cry of sea birds overhead. When I was a little girl, I used to revel in these journeys and the crews with whom we sailed were always kind and patient with me.

They told me tales of merrows and mermaids and I would claim to be a mermaid myself, or a descendant of one. I was afraid of nothing. Not the sea when it turned black as pitch in the middle deeps of this channel, nor when it sharpened its teeth in a gale and gnawed at the sides of the vessels in which we sailed.

The crews would tell me stories and my favourite was the one about the selkie, a lithe creature who shape-changed into a divine woman. A fisherman captured her when she sat on the shore one day as a woman and he hid her selkie's skin which meant she could never return to the sea. She was at his mercy, living a grief-stricken life on land, spending hours standing on the shore, the waves washing away her tears, the wind tearing at her unfettered hair, pulling at her, saying 'Come back, come back to where you belong.'

As with most tales, the ending was bittersweet, the fisherman finally giving the skin back so she could return to her home. But he tried to follow her and inevitably drowned, which is why, said the sailors, that all shipboard men beware the beauties of the sea.

Such were the tales that filled my voyages.

And now I had different tales I wished to be told and touched Gisborne's arm.

'What is the connection between you and Halsham? No, please don't turn away,' I said as he readied himself to walk off. 'You have some sort of history or you and he wouldn't have been so ... tolerant of each other shall we say, over these last few weeks. You let him go when he threatened me with rape. You could by rights have killed him! And when you nicked his throat with the knife *he* could have called for help and had you arrested but he didn't. And when I said he'd betrayed us earlier, you didn't disagree and yet...'

'And yet?'

He looked toward the horizon, away from my scrutiny.

'And yet. Yes. Exactly.'

My God, I felt he should have sworn an oath to call the snake out over it.

'Halsham is…'

'Yes?'

Guy kept looking away as he gave me his answer.

'Halsham is my cousin. His mother and mine were sisters.'

CHAPTER SEVEN

Cousins? He jests!

Whatever he had been going to answer, this was not what I had expected to hear. I thought of Halsham the first time I had met him in Le Mans. A man whose manner had stood the hairs on my neck and who bowed over my hand with a look as licentious and assessing as it was cunning.

'But he looks nothing like you,' I said.

I recalled him standing next to Gisborne in that cobbled street. He had none of Guy's angularity, nor the breadth of shoulder. Why, the man was quite ordinary. Any semblance of strength was an illusion bought on by the cut of his surcoat with the insignia of the Free Lancers.

And his colouring. Where were the fine skin tones that Gisborne might have inherited from his mother? The midnight hair and pale skin and eyes the colour of the sea? Halsham's colouring was as flesh-toned as a babe's. His thinning hair was a mottled brown that would no doubt fade to nothing if he could hold on to it.

'No,' said Guy, continuing to stare across the decks. 'And yet he is the child of my mother's sister.'

The sea hissed along the sides of the vessel as though it mocked this odd revelation. Above us a seabird cried out to underline the ocean's rejection of this claim of kinship. The sun had become lost behind a drifting grey cloud and I shivered slightly in the damp.

'What were the two sisters like?'

I felt that anything I could glean from Gisborne was to my benefit. Such things as hair lifting on my neck didn't happen without reason.

'My mother was...' he stopped and shifted his position, ill at ease.

I laid my hand on his sleeve but he barely reacted, choosing to continue with his gaze resting on a far-off memory on the horizon.

'My mother was a beauty; dark, elegant – with piercing blue eyes that people used to say were fey. As though she could have come from the mists of some strange, enchanted isle. My Aunt Marie-Anne was shorter and equally as dark, but her hair curled wildly whilst my lady mother's was straight. My aunt's eyes were green.'

I recalled Halsham's own; green with a taint of mud.

'His father, then. It must be that his father was fair, surely.'

'Uncle Roget's family came from close by Amiens and he himself was quite fair. He was a mercenary, one of many Henry employed with scutage monies and when Henry landed in Dorset, Roget was amongst the army with a force that came to Henry's notice for its organisation and performance. After the Treaty of Wallingford, the King rewarded Roget with lands and a title near to Wales. Roget reinvented himself as an Englishman and the estate of Cwm Branar became Halsham. Whilst it was a large estate, I think he always envied my father the richness of Gisborne's lands.'

Guy settled into the telling and I let him talk.

'Roget and Marie-Anne caught a deadly pox when Robert was about twelve years old. Roget sickened rapidly and died within the week. Many others died on the estate as it swept through with plague strength. Not long after, Marie Anne died as well and Robert was left an orphan.'

He leaned back against the gunwales and folded his arms across his chest, a defensive position that warned the world away.

'My mother insisted that Robert live with us. The estate returned to the King and monies were paid from Treasury and held in trust for Robert for when he should need such funds. The King obviously held Roget in some esteem and rewarded the son accordingly.'

And wilful arrogance was bred into the son from that moment.

'Did you get on? It is almost as if he must have been your brother.' I tried to envisage twelve year old Robert and... 'How old were you, Guy?'

'He is only a year or two older than myself and thus we had the same education and training. We were taught all the skills a young knight needs, but as to getting on – yes and no. We tolerated each other. Robert adored my mother, Ghislaine, and has never made a secret of the debt he owed her for taking him in, but in so many other ways he is grateful for nothing but what he takes for himself. Yes, he is my cousin, and yes, we lived like brothers, but I have never liked him. Ever.'

'And yet you engage with him and…'

I was almost going to say defer to him but I stopped in time because such a statement would only have demeaned Gisborne and I could not do that. Not after the previous night.

I gazed at him as he continued Robert Halsham's history as if I hadn't spoken. His eyes had no vestige of emotion, unreadable, but his jaw was quite rigid. Such a set spoke volumes and I could only presume every word unleashed a host of memories that he had thought to leave locked in some private room of his mind and that my persistence and perhaps our relative closeness had turned the key.

'Robert left Gisborne when he turned sixteen. He asked my father for his funds and left to join the Free Lancers. He has fought wherever the mercenaries secured contracts and was knighted around the time of Beckett's death; for I would prefer not to think. I know you wonder why I should have anything to do with a man whose principles you don't like, but whilst in the Holy Land he kept an eye on my father, paying money to the Order who cared for him in his last days and arranging for a Christian burial. Whatever I might think of my father for deserting my mother and myself, I suppose I owe Halsham a debt for that at least. It was an honourable thing to do and surprising and I must show some sort of gratitude in return. In addition, he…' Gisborne stopped precipitately as though he didn't want me to know any more.

But I was too quick, some would say precocious.

'And in addition he has offered you position, hasn't he?'

Gisborne finally looked at me. At last he seemed to acknowledge that he hadn't just been speaking to an empty space next to him on the deck.

'My father left for the Holy Land only a month after Robert left Gisborne. In fact they fought side by side at one point which leads me to believe they developed some sort of relationship. Robert was aware the Templars had taken over the care of our estates and by various means he eventually heard that my mother and I had been turned off and that during our attempted journey to our French family, my mother had died. Be under no illusions, Ysabel, he doesn't offer me a position in his army out of love for *me*, or even pity. Strangely for a man such as he, he offers it as payment of a debt to my mother.'

It *was* strange. Halsham had his own agenda and I found it hard to imagine that he felt any kind of debt to Ghislaine of Gisborne but perhaps I was wrong. Maybe he did feel great affection for his aunt. Certainly I would never know and could only take Gisborne's word.

'So you will join the Free Lancers after we return to England?'

'He offers me wealth, Ysabel.'

Status and power, Guy. It's what that bitter side of you craves.

My thoughts were broken by a yell from behind us.

'Ship aft!'

We turned together. In the blurred distance, a sail marked the horizon. A crewman hopped on the rigging and scrambled aloft and eventually his shouts dropped down to the decks of our vessel.

'A *nef*, full sail, sittin' high in the water! Canna see her colours!'

Almost immediately I recalled De Courcey striding along the wharf, that red flash of anger implying that he would move Hell to accomplish his mission. He wanted all of Moncrieff, even the daughter.

'It's De Courcey, I know it.' There was nothing of the lady about the way I grabbed Gisborne's sleeve and dug my nails in. 'If the ship's in full sail and it's sitting high in the water, it means she has no cargo and will catch us easily in this breeze.'

'Now don't take on so, Mistress.' Davey's voice touched us from behind. 'Davey's been known to sail this ditch in a chase many a time in many weathers and none's yet caught him. Besides, there's a bit of a mist coming, look you.'

The grey cloud of earlier had thickened and dropped low, hanging wisps of fog across the wave tops. The vessel astern drifted in and out of view.

'I can sail into a creek from here with my eyes closed.' Davey grinned, his stained teeth showing big gaps between. 'You and the master here need to make secret landfall on English shores and I swear that's exactly what'll happen.'

He began to walk among the crew, speaking softly, and each man went to the hold and heaved a hogshead onto his shoulder.

'What do they do?'

The tone of my voice pitched higher with anxiety. The hogsheads were hefted over the *Marolingian*'s sides, one after another splashing into the sea and bobbing aft.

'Don't fret, Ysabel. They're empty. They were merely subterfuge. Davey has been waiting for us to arrive. It was planned on my journey to Cazenay.'

My mouth dropped open.

'You say? Does this mean then, that you anticipated trouble?'

Guy raised an eyebrow.

'One can't be too cautious and Cecilia had given me to understand that you might become a valuable commodity.'

Holy Mother but I was angry. All this time...

'It didn't occur to you that you might pay me the respect I deserve by telling me this back in Aquitaine? God, Gisborne! How dare you?'

'Oh hush, Ysabel. Don't rant. The crew will think you a harridan. I had no idea what you were like when I met you, whether you were strong, weak, given to hysteria, the manner of a child even.' He grimaced. 'Now I think on it...'

'Stop it.' I punched him in the arm as hard as I could. 'This is my life you play with.'

He had the gall to laugh but became serious in an instant.

'It seemed to me enough that you knew your father was not himself and that Moncrieff suffered in consequence. And besides, you grieved mightily for your mother. As to the complete loss of Moncrieff, as I told you, I didn't know till Halsham mentioned it. If you ask me, I showed a great deal of respect for you.'

'There you are, Mistress.' Davey joined us. 'Already we make extra speed. And we've got a thickening mist that makes us a ghost ship. We can sail northerly whereas they will presume we sail westerly. We'll be right where I want us when we hear waves on the English coast. We'll sail maybe a day or so on until we get close by Great Yarmouth and then I'll signal to shore and one of me mates'll row out and collect you.'

Gisborne gave me a fiendish glance.

'See, he can sail into a creek from here with his eyes closed, Ysabel. All you have to do is trust him.'

I spent time huddled in a corner of the ship, a cloak wrapped round fending off the damp of the ocean. Guy took his share of the watch in the dark hours. Just he, Davey and a skeleton crew of rowers whilst the others yawned, snored and filled the spaces around me with their odour.

If I lay down I could hear the sea hissing past the planks of the *Marolingian*. 'Ysabel,' it whispered, 'Ysabel.'

'What?' I wanted to shout. 'What are you trying to tell me?'

But it just kept repeating *'Ysabel, Ysabel,'* as though I didn't know my own name.

I thought about De Courcey and why he chased me. Father had signed away Moncrieff so my existence should have had no bearing on it one way or the other. Which brought my thoughts back to the beginning again – why did *I* matter to De Courcey?

When I realised the answer, my stomach dropped through the planks to sink to the ocean floor.

How naïve I was to think such an arrangement would be as simple as my father handing over Moncrieff.

Stupid, stupid Ysabel.

My mad, thoughtless, inexorable father had not only given up his estates in payment, I swear that in some way or other, he had given up his daughter like a piece of coin. How, I had no idea but it must surely be answer.

By the Saints! I hate him, how I wish he had died instead of my mother.

I looked back to the time before Gisborne had arrived at Cazenay and I realized how ignorant and immature I had been, how indulged by everyone. I possessed some useless accomplishments but no experience of life or death and no understanding of the grosser side of human nature. Now here I was, swamped by the realities of gambling, deceit and … I thought of Wilfred and Harry … murder. It was the difference, quite simply between Heaven and Hell.

I sighed and turned over. I lay on a bed of mildewed sail and faced one of the wooden ribs of the ship, reaching out a finger to touch it. It was smooth, as slippery as silk except for that mark there, and another. It was too dark to see but I tried to trace them and in my mind, decipher them. My finger went over and round, over and round. That and the sounds of the boat, the creaking of the rigging, the sighing of the wind through the stays and the ever-present *'Ysabel, Ysabel,'* of the water lulled me into an dreamless sleep.

Days passed; me with my circular thoughts, Gisborne working as a member of the crew, the seafog persisting. If I saw him at all, it was as a shape through the mists. He'd be bending to a task, laughing with the crew or in intense discussions with Davey. He would appear and disappear like an enchanted being. Once he glanced up and caught my gaze. There was no smile but our eyes met and held and I took strength from the moment.

Davey had ordered the sail lowered a few hours after the mists enveloped us. All sound was muffled and we could hear nothing of our pursuers. The men took their place at oars that were well greased with seal-oil. Gisborne sat at a larboard oar and when Davey signaled, for no voices were allowed, he pulled with the rest. He half stood, his broad shoulder taking the strain as the oar scooped down into the water and up again. But then the mist drifted across him and he vanished and my heart skipped a beat. It *was* like being on ghost ship, as Davey had said, with shapes dissolving, a silent ambience with only a faint splash as the oars dipped. The water sighed along the planks but there was no other sound. Ghosts from past and present. I wasn't sure if I felt intimidated by the pervasive atmosphere or not.

At one point we heard rhythmic tolling and Davey jumped down to the rowers. He spoke softly but all appeared to hear. 'Larboard oars pull. The rest of yer hold.' The vessel juddered and began to shift away from the sound. The other oarsmen joined in, we moved forward a few lengths, then the larboard oars were stilled for one pull and we straightened again.

Davey joined me at the stern.

'Bell Rocks,' he said.

I knew of Bell Rocks, greedy and hidden beneath a swirl of weed and white water. Death to many a boatsman.

'Another day and a half and we'll be off the coast. We're making good speed.'

My stomach flipped over.

'The other boat?'

Davey tapped his nose.

'Trust Davey, mistress. There's no one can creep about this ditch like me. There's some even call the *Marolingian* magick.' He thumped the mast with his fist. 'I'd stake my life on the fact that they've headed directly across from Calais or maybe even tried to sit the mist out. Either way we've lost 'em. Trust me.'

Trust you indeed. What choice?

That night the same soft sea-song sang me to my sleep. A hand shook my shoulder much later and woke me and I could see a sharper light behind Gisborne as he squatted next to me.

'Ysabel, wake you. We are off the coast at Great Yarmouth.'

I sat up as if a bolt of lightning had struck.

'The other boat?'

It was becoming a litany.

'No sight, as Davey predicted.'

Guy stood and in the daylight that ventured through the mists I could see he had almost grown a beard and that his hair was windblown and knotted. Shadows looped under his eyes and yet his manner betrayed little of his tiredness.

I grabbed his hand.

'Stay a moment. I need to talk.'

He squatted down again and his fingers laced through mine, my heart swelling.

'About what?'

'Moncrieff. What if I don't go home? What if I go somewhere else entirely?'

His hand fell away from mine.

'You would not see your father? Or Cecilia.'

Or my mother, but he didn't say the words.

I could feel my jaw tightening and I grabbed my hair and smoothed it back, twisting it into that all too familiar knot.

'My father? My father whom I believe sees me as some sort of currency? Why would I? I would have been better to stay in Cazenay.'

He gave me a measuring glance and then lowered himself to sit next to me, his back against the rib whose marks had so soothed me.

'In hindsight Cazenay may have been safer, but you are in England now or near enough, and you have unfinished business. Something's awry in Moncrieff. More so than when Cecilia sent me to collect you. How it is connected with you I can only begin to guess but even if De Courcey has assumed the estate, there are things that are rightly yours. Things of your mother's, things in your father's library...'

'My father's *library*?'

A library?

Mother had never mentioned that Father had books. An interest in monastic works certainly and those held by some noble houses, but his own books?

'Ysabel, are you listening?'

Guy nudged me and I nodded.

'My suggestion is this...'

I sighed. I could see it coming...

'We ride as secretly...'

Of course!

'Ysabel!' Guy shook my arm.

'Yes. Secretly to Moncrieff. Even though I am afraid of De Courcey. Even though it seems he wishes to use me in some way, you want me to return to Moncrieff.'

Gisborne frowned at me.

'You've shown immense courage thus far. We can see this through and then I swear when we know what has happened and taken what is yours, we can make a plan and I can see you and your father safe if needs be. To Wales or Ireland, even back to Aquitaine – far from De Courcey.'

'My father can stay at Moncrieff, I care not.' For a moment I thought he would dispute but perhaps he thought of his feelings towards his own father and could see the hypocrisy of argument.

'Yourself then. I shall see you safe.'

I flung myself on him, hugging him.

'You would do that?'

His hand spread across my back, his fingers pressing.

'Of course. I would never leave you defenceless. We can get word to Cecilia and find out what De Courcey has done and then make plans. Once you are safe, I can leave.'

Leave? Leave me? There! There was the truth of it – the game unfolding to the end.

I sat back on my heels, unable to help that I must seem disappointed, disillusioned.

'Ysabel, I...'

'Master Guy?' Davey's voice drifted toward us from amidships. 'Can you come, sir? I need you.'

My face twisted, I know it did. It shouldn't have because I had chanted to myself that I knew which way this was to be played. I thought I was beyond naivety, that even though I found the man suspect after he had let Halsham go, I had knowingly laid myself out for him.

'Go,' I said, pushing him. 'Davey needs you.'

I pulled on my coping face, the new Ysabel who was courageous and could tackle anything. I watched him begin to move away and I swear it was as though someone had taken a sword to my whole body and cleaved it in two. 'Guy,' I called.

He looked back. The strengthening light illuminated lines of dirt and fatigue.

'One thing...'

'Yes?' His head quirked to the side, that quizzical gaze that I had come to know so well.

'I want a bath in Great Yarmouth.'

'Ghosts,' I murmured.

'Your pardon?'

Gisborne turned away from surveying the sea to focus on me. As I observed the state of his hair, his beard and his clothes, I wondered how close to vagabonds we seemed.

'Ghosts,' I repeated. 'We have been ferried by spectres on a ghost ship from Calais to England. It is how it seems. Do you see?'

I pointed in the direction Gisborne had been staring. The mists had returned after a brief and sunlit break at dawn and the *Marolingian*, anchored in the depths of the miasma, was invisible. Of the dory that rowed us to shore there was no sign. It boded well. I felt that if we were so well hidden now, surely we had the advantage in my secret return to Moncrieff. I wouldn't say that my spirits rose but I was just a little less tired.

'What is he? A smuggler?' I asked, referring to Davey.

Gisborne chuckled, a quiet sound muffled by the strands of fog that eked over the water's edge onto land.

'Some say so. For my part, he is a good man and loyal. Steadfast, I would say.'

I detected a note in his voice, as if there were very few in this world that he would trust and Davey was one of them. Trust had been something I had taken for granted all my life, for why should an indulged daughter of a noble house have need to worry about such things? But in these last weeks I had been forced to face the other side of human nature; the side that revealed the worst qualities of men. I turned away from the water, the pebbles crunching under my boot-soles.

'What now, where do we go? It is still days to Moncrieff.'

He pushed on ahead of me, talking back over his shoulder.

'We need food and horses. Davey has organized…'

'How?' I interrupted.

Davey's web of intrigue is even larger than I imagined.

We walked off the shore and onto a thin ribbon of coastal path as Guy continued.

'I sailed to Calais with Davey and thought it expedient to have plans in place for our return. Whilst I travelled into Aquitaine, Davey sailed back to England, organized things and then beat back to await our arrival in Calais.'

The mist had dampened even more, turning to a fine mizzle that dampened our faces and settled on our clothes in a layer of moisture and reminded me of dew on a spider's web. We plodded through the damp coastal grasses and I followed behind Gisborne – if there was one thing I had learned in the past weeks, it was that he knew where he was going. He showed no sign of being tired, his stride determined and long.

'What is the connection between you and Davey?' I asked. 'It must be very strong.'

It was one of the few times he was genuinely forthcoming.

'His family were a part of the Gisborne estate long before I was born. Davey's mother, Ailsa, was my mother's maidservant and was dearly loved. As to Davey's father, he died not long after Davey was born so my mother made sure young Davey was always provided for within the house. But Ailsa sickened with a flux and even though Lady Ghislaine tried valiantly to care for her, seeking all the help she could, it was of little use. I was quite young when my parents buried her and Davey has never forgotten the care. He left not long after, to find his own way. He always felt he and the sea belonged together. But by the same token, he always promised to be of service if ever he could be. He said he had a debt to pay and would pay it over and over out of love and respect for the Gisborne name.'

'A sad story; poignant but heartwarming.'

I also thought it was reminiscent of Halsham's story but would not say so, nor would I credit the latter with any of Davey's apparent qualities.

Gisborne nodded. 'Davey is my friend and shall always be.'

Something about those words gave me the confidence in Gisborne that was so lacking when Halsham hovered in the background of his life, as if deep in his soul he *knew* that good outweighed bad by far, because no matter what, Halsham implied bad to me.

I pushed stray strands of hair from my eyes.

'Where are we bound?'

'Saint Eadgyth's close by.'

'And this has also been arranged by Davey?'

'No, it is familiar to me and I let them know…'

'Ah yes,' I interrupted. 'You let them know we would possibly be coming their way.'

Another religious house.

My sarcasm earned me a hard look.

'Yes,' was all he said.

The mist showed no sign of easing as we trudged on and all I could think of was how constrained I felt. I, who had known freedom and who until a few weeks ago had not a care in the world. The mist pressed in on me as though it represented all my troubles. There were moments where I just wanted to scream against the injustice. I had never been cruel or foul-mouthed and I followed the religious rule so why did I suffer so? It was as if I were a mere speck being tossed around in some fierce wind from here to there. Each new revelation that came my way battered the speck against this barrier and that and I felt pieces of me falling away.

When I had first met Guy of Gisborne, I had thought the worst that could happen was becoming aware of my father's weak-minded perfidy. But now Baron De Courcey stood facing me across the battle-lines.

Is this what a soldier feels as he stares at the opposing forces across the battlefield? Loosening bowels, shaking hands and sweat dampening his palms as he tries to hold his bow more firmly.

I thought back to the moment in the woods when I had nocked that arrow into the fated Saracen bow. As I thought of it, so I drew in a deep breath.

'Ysabel?'

'I'm just tired…' I butted in. 'And wondering why my life has, to this point, become a progress through many, many religious houses.'

Gisborne laughed.

How could he seem so at ease?

'Ah, my Ysabel…'

My Ysabel?

'I suspect that is not what you were thinking at all. But in truth, the houses of the *religieuses* are always trustworthy when we need such secrecy.'

'Saint Eadgyth's?'

'Completely.' He turned and waited for me to catch up. 'See, there it is.'

He stood back and I looked past him, the mist having begun to thin. The weak sunshine drew the vapour up to the heavens as if it had been God's loan to us for just as long as we needed it.

The path joined a pockmarked road that trundled from a far distance, perhaps Great Yarmouth, I know not. Set to the side of the road amongst a coppice of ancient beeches, a small church gleamed palely. Walls extended further and I could only assume they were built around an inner space, perhaps a garden of some sort and that this dainty priory was surrounded by a miniature cloister and cells, perhaps a small frater and kitchen combined, maybe even a communal space where the good Sisters could congregate for contemplation.

'It's so small,' I said.

'There are only eight sisters.'

'Truly? Then how do they survive? What work do they do? Where are their lands, their income?'

'They are a small priory of Benedictines attached to an abbey near Great Yarmouth and they are scribes, doing handsome work for the bigger religious houses and for the nobility. They are self-sufficient materially and spiritually.'

Ah, is that a lesson for us both to learn, Gisborne?

Our path headed downhill and inland a small distance before it met with the road and as we walked, I thought of Ghislaine of Gisborne.

'You rarely speak of your mother,' I dared.

'No.'

'I should think she is worth talking about. You would honour her.'

By God, Ysabel, said this tiny, easily ignored voice in my head, *you may think you're courageous but you're infinitely stupid as well.*

'But,' he stopped, standing deadly still. 'I choose not to. Ysabel, do not ask again. Some doors need to remain shut. This one and the Order of Saint Lazarus are just two.'

We reached a door in the wall and he rang a bell. It was rusty and its rope careworn but the bell's tone was clear. A panel slid back behind a grille and a face surveyed us.

'Sister, I am Guy of Gisborne returned.'

The panel slid shut and the door opened with much rattling of keys. A nun smiled and nodded at us.

'The Prioress expects us,' Guy added. 'I have my companion as was planned and she is in sore need of rest, food and a bath.'

The nun bowed over her hands and then beckoned for me to follow. I took a step and then hesitated.

'What will you do?'

Guy rubbed at the leather of his gauntlets.

'Go to a roadside tavern close by.'

'And?'

It truly was like getting blood from a stone.

'Well, I shall endeavour to have a wash of some sort or even a bath.'

His smile was mischievous if small.

No doubt appalled at the implied intimacy of our discussion, the good nun touched my sleeve, eager to shut the door on this licentious world. I lifted my hand and said, 'A moment please, Sister. I would speak with my escort.'

I turned straight back to Gisborne, my gaze searching his face, fixing on his eyes and daring him to run from my eternal questioning.

'A bath. Of course. But what else will you do? What else have you done in our travelling time while I have been on my knees praying in some chapel or other. No…' I grabbed his arm as he turned away. 'No. Out of respect for our … closeness, I charge you to answer.'

He sighed and his lips tightened.

'I walk about. I talk with the villagers. I manage to secure valuable intelligence.'

'How valuable?'

He stood for a moment and then looked over my head.

'Sister,' he said. 'My friend is ready to accompany you. Ysabel, I shall see you on the morrow.'

Chapter Eight

He turned and walked away, dismissal in the set of his shoulders, and the nun pulled hard on my sleeve so that I had little choice but to follow. Any disquiet at his reticence would have to be shelved in the back of my mind as the door in the wall closed behind me.

A dulcet quiet drifted over us – bees, birds, water trickling somewhere, and silence. Whilst Guy had ensconced me in a number of religious houses, this one had a different air. There were similarities to be sure, but the preciously small nature of the place made me feel as if Mary had taken me in her arms and lifted me to some place beyond strife. The thought I could become a religieuse floated through my mind once again.

I envied these nuns their horarium, each day evenly divided into an ecclesiastical infinity. They prayed for God's grace but expected none and were grateful for everything. They were safe within their cloistered community and I envied them with a passion.

But Ysabel, you could never exist here. Not if your life depended on it.

My heart twisted sharply as the words *'Not if your life depended on it'* resonated. As if some sort of prophecy had crept in the door as the Sister turned to lock it. I watched her heavy brown robe swing. The sun caught on the plain ring on her hand and her toes spread across leather sandals beneath her hems.

The woman's feet made a crunching sound as we moved from the stone flags of the cloister to a graveled path that cut through the neatly trimmed, central herb garden. Only twenty or so steps and we reached another heavy door. The Sister knocked, waited and then knocked twice more before swinging the door open and indicating I should enter. I walked inside with due diffidence, conscious of my dirty clothes and that I may be less than fragrant.

The space was larger than a cell to be sure, but austere. A cot, folded blankets, a straw-stuffed mattress, a stool with a woven rush top, a crucifix. A tallow candle. And a tall thin woman whose face was the image of a heavenly being – ageless and with the purity of a saint imprinted on her features.

'God be with you,' she said by way of preamble. 'You will be taken to your room by Sister Thea where you will find a tub and things you may need. They were organized by Master Gisborne. Of course you are familiar with the horarium…'

The Prioress was perfunctory and to the point and I could see she would invite no comment or question.

'… so you will understand how we divide our day. You will eat with us. We do not know who you are as I required Master Gisborne not to tell us and I would ask that you refrain from engaging with our Sisters. Saint Eadgyth's Priory is a cloistered and quiet community and we prefer to keep the world at the door. You may walk in our garden and orchard but unless you are accompanied by a Sister, I would ask that you do not wander elsewhere in our domain. God keep you.'

She picked up a small hand-bell in hands that were slim, white and heavily veined with blue. The spider's web of her delicate bone structure moved as her fingers rattled the bell. In response, Sister Thea opened the door and stood back for me to pass. But something made me turn back and I caught a glimpse of the Prioress's clear, guileless eyes gazing at me. I smiled and before I could stop myself, my voice, as alien as a man's in that place, drifted over my turned shoulder.

'Thank you,' I said and followed in Sister Thea's determined footsteps.

We proceeded at a measured pace and because the remains of the earlier mists had dissolved, I had time to observe that the walls continued further than I had thought. There was a hedge across the end of the herb garden and through a withied gate I could see the ordered rows of a vegetable garden and the longer pasture and wildflowers that underlay an orchard of trees. Everything around me was touched with an odd luminescence; I would thereafter call it God's Light as it was gentle, soft as light touching a pearl. The fragrance of herb and the sounds of bees again stirred the embers of envy in my troubled soul.

We progressed through the cloister and its west-facing end was hung with roses that were heavy with buds. I was so busy looking at everything, at the carved pillars, at the Roman numerals above various entrances, that I hadn't realized good Sister Thea had led me through a narrow door. Only the change in the ambience, the diminished sounds of the ever-present bees and birds, made me look up. The cell wrapped around us, more sparsely furnished than the Prioress's. A narrow cot, as though it were a child's, sacking laced in a frame; a brown woven blanket, a crucifix hanging on the whitewashed walls. But my eyes rested longest on a cut-down wine-barrel lined with a piece of fine linen and from which steam eddied.

Sister Thea backed out of the room and the door barely clicked, leaving me to walk to the tub to trail my fingers through the hot water. I looked around to the bed and noticed a small folded pile that I had thought might be an extra blanket but on examination proved to more thoughtful largesse. Linen undergarments lay neatly folded and I wondered what the Sisters thought as their work-roughened hands lay them down.

But surely they must wear something similar.

Although I had heard of an abbess who wore rough woven fabric flush against her skin as a form of penance on a daily basis. Ah, not for me scratchy wool and God's forgiveness, I was sure. I sifted through the rest of the folds and found men's hose and a chemise, a clean tunic, a leather belt and a hood of wool that would cover my head and shoulders admirably – and a small pile of folded cloths.

I flushed, thinking on something that had been forgotten as we travelled.

My courses had not appeared in all the time we journeyed, a factor due entirely to the tension of the journey, I was sure. But over the last few days, a vague ache had spread from my lower back and settled in the lowest part of my stomach. In a fever as I remembered the night I lost my valued virginal state, I ripped the filthy clothes from my body and threw them into the corner of the cell.

The water had drops of fragrant oil in it and it lay on my skin so that when I bought my arm to my nose, I was transported to the enclosed garden in Cazenay, a place of summer sun and warm delights, where worry was an anathema and the trials of the world were the stuff of a troubadour's song. It was a garden of petals, pollen and poetry and my mind floated in the memory for a moment.

A coffer was pulled to the side of the tub and there lay a piece of soap, rough to be sure, but smelling sweet and with flower petals embedded deep in the impure block. That such a small place as Saint Eadgyth's could provide me with such a thing was worth a prayer and as I sank below the surface, hair and all, I thanked God.

The water lapped around me, its perfume doing more to lift my spirits than the thought that in a short time I would be clean. I lathered my hair and scrabbled fingers back and forth, scrubbing away dirt from the leagues we had covered and then I sank again below the surface, rinsing, running hands through until every strand squeaked. My skin demanded the same treatment and I took the bar of soap and slipped it everywhere, stripping the sweat and grime and then I lay back to enjoy the last of the water's warmth, twisting my hair and flipping it out over the edge of the tub. But I kept the bar of soap in my palm as its fragrance was a comfort – so valuable a thing, that little sliver of soap.

Valuable.

The word pierced my mind.

Value.

The scales began to fall away from my eyes in much the same manner as the dirt had just sloughed off my skin.

How valuable?

I could see Gisborne backing away from my questions.

And no wonder.

Guy of Gisborne was a spy.

A spy who traded information for wealth. That must surely be how he survived when neither Cecilia nor my father had given him money.

But Ysabel, he provided not just for your safety but for your every need. Does it matter?

I wondered if it did. But then I remembered the constant appearance of his cousin, Halsham, and suddenly it did matter because if information went to Halsham, there was no doubt it was used for ill. I could not see the dishonourable knight using it to push King Richard's cause. Of course not. It would be used to feather Halsham's nest and lift him to a position of status in the eyes of the King until he himself had the position of power that he craved. And Gisborne wove in and out of it all like a masterful gameplayer.

What information is he selling? What does he barter?

I shivered.

The water had chilled and the grime sat on the surface in a slurry of murk. I grabbed a spare strip of linen and stood, wiping goose-pimpled skin, wringing hair out and wrapping it in the strip. The tub lining had an unsightly tidemark and I spared a thought at what the Saint Eadgyth's nuns would need to do to return the linen to its pristine state. The pain in my lower back persisted despite the bath but I was clean, the dirt of my travels gone and I was glad as I pulled on the men's clothing. Underneath the pile lay a wooden comb, an honest little tool carved with simple fingers. Nothing like my own which had a scene of Diana the Huntress and a hound carved into its handle, but honest nevertheless.

Honesty.

I took up the comb and dragged it through the knots as the sweet bell above the Priory rang for Sext, my belly rumbling a base accompaniment.

On leaving the cell, I expected to see the nuns weaving from the garden or the scriptorium to the frater but all was still except for the trailing echoes of the bell. I trod the gravel path in the direction of the refectory, damp hair heavy on my shoulder, but as I looked at the clean edges of my fingernails, I sighed. I should be indulging in this new purged state, stripped of dirt and sweat, but instead the cleanliness jarred with my awakening of earlier. As I began to dwell on likely perfidies, a movement to my side caught my eye and Sister Thea drifted into view, smiling benevolently and indicating I follow.

We moved to the wall on the other side of the garden where the Prioress's room stood under the protection of the colonnaded cloister. As we walked our footsteps echoed in the pristine silence of the place, Sister Thea's leather soles a hard tap, my own boots a softer sound. I glimpsed an open door and saw four desks in rows of two underneath a tall horn-covered window. Sheets of parchment lay on each surface with pots of colour, quills and reed pens and I longed to divert, to stay a moment, to gaze at the richness of the illumination and the skill of the copying. The smell of the inks drifted out but Thea urged me on and within two more paces we reached the kitchen and frater from which a pleasant fragrance of new baked bread eddied. Thea stood back and I entered and seven veiled and wimpled heads lifted.

They were curious, have no doubt, but in less than a blink, six of the seven resumed eating, the Prioress's presence enough for them to observe priory etiquette. I sat next to the Prioress and she passed me a thick crust of the warm bread and a bowl of the pottage. I ate in the curious atmosphere of the room where the only sounds were of fabric rustling as an arm moved, or a muffled cough from an irritated throat, a scrape of a sandal on the stone blocks of the floor. Rough wooden platters were shifted occasionally and wooden beakers filled with water, the sound of the chuckling stream from pitcher to mug like the sound of the purest voice in the choir in this quaint silence.

Odd and intrusive then, when the Prioress said to me, 'Speech can disturb us in our devotions and exercises our resistance to temptation far more than is necessary. I thank you for observing our silences. We do speak but only when required as you will see. When you are finished you may leave us. Our Sisters will work in the gardens or in the scriptorium until None when we would see you in the Chapel.'

The Sisters' heads had lifted at the sound of the Prioress's voice and I watched their eyes swivel from her to me, almost as if they anticipated temptation at its most virulent. When I merely nodded and smiled my acknowledgement of what had passed, I swear there was a tangible sigh of regret in the room. The Prioress stood and the nuns followed in single file like a duck and her babies. I moved in their wake but then headed to the garden paths and thence to the orchard where life seemed less constrained and I could breathe and sigh audibly without guilt.

I wondered if the nuns realized that they had created heaven on earth in their little orchard. Thick pasture and wild flowers dragged at my feet and the trees bent toward me, heavy with the promise of fruits. I dared not pick anything and instead enjoyed the fragrance of the place as I searched for a quiet place to sit and sift through my thoughts. At the end of the orchard pale headstones gleamed and I headed toward them as if the dead and honoured may shed light on a confused mind.

There were not many tombs and they were simply carved. Here a nun's name and a date. There a prioress's with a little more sculpted flourish. But the last drew me to it like a beacon and my heart stopped and I dropped to my knees, my fingers tracing the letters one by one.

'Ghislaine of Gisborne,' it read and the tears sprang to my eyes.

'I know your son, my lady. I have been his charge these last weeks. He has been diligent and chivalrous, you would be…' I stopped as the tears rolled unchecked.

Maybe it was that I spoke to his mother or even just to *a* mother. Maybe it was that all those hurts immured deep inside me were in need of acknowledgement and who better to understand and acknowledge hurt than a mother.

As I knelt by the headstone, my fingers went from tracing the chiseled name to rubbing back and forth over the mound that was her resting place. A path had been scythed, winding around and through the stones, but on the mounds themselves the grass had been shorn like a sheep's fleece. Underneath my palm, the nap was smooth and cool, a little damp from the mizzle. I had a vision of Sister Thea working diligently with a pair of shears at each mound.

My conversation continued, 'I know your nephew as well, my lady; the one you might call Robert or even Rob; the one I call Halsham but whom I would prefer not to acknowledge at all. He has come far, I tell you, but he is suspect. Whilst your son is a man of whom it is possible to be proud, I fear your nephew, who holds *you*, Lady Ghislaine, in the highest esteem, is not.'

I looked around and noticed a branch hanging low from a hawthorn, its leaves a fierce green. There were some chamomile daisies close by and bright blue flowering rosemary and I picked some sprigs of each and joined them with the greenery of the hawthorn, tying everything around with a twine of ivy that clung to the priory wall. Laying the offering against the headstone, I knelt again.

'Your son has all the intellectual breadth of a scholar, Madame, and at any time I feel sure he could make his mark honestly but he struggles with bitterness. Born of the plight that struck you and he and left you homeless; that took his heritage and your life.'

In my mind I could see Guy curling around me in the shelter of the ruined woodsman's hut as I trembled after Wilf's and Harry's deaths. I remembered his breathing and how I sought to slow mine to match his and how his thumbs traced hypnotic and calming circles over my knuckles. My eyes filled but did not spill.

'You see, my lady,' I said. 'I worry. He hitches his cart to Halsham's horse. He chooses deception and cunning instead of...' I stopped and sighed. 'It's what he chooses. It is the way of it.'

I heard the ringing of the bell for None. Looking up, I could see Sister Thea standing at the hedge, an arm raised to shield her eyes from the sun which rested lower in the afternoon sky

'Watch over him, my Lady of Gisborne. Guide him and help him make wise choices. I ask not for me...'

Sister Thea moved toward me and I scrabbled the tears from my cheeks, pushing myself off my knees, the marks of my body now a moulded intaglio on the grass.

I ask not for me.

'... but for him.'

I turned away. A feeling of separation pulled at me. I didn't want to leave, as if in that one moment I had a last found someone who could help me through my confusion. I could hear the rustles as Sister Thea's robe caught against grasping plants, her approach filled with haste and I recognized perturbation in her manner.

She took my sleeve and pulled me behind her at a jogtrot to the cloister, clipping along the colonnade until we reached the chapel door, sidling into the space beyond as the bell's echoes reduced themselves to the overwhelming silence that was Saint Eadgyth's.

Flickering candles along the walls lit the gloom and apart from one narrow arched window in the Norman style and filled with glass, there was little either to commend the architecture or to allow light to enter; but the window was unstained unlike so many of its noble counterparts. It was set high in the wall above the altar and allowed one to observe the moving and changing panoply of the heavens and on this day a small beam of sunshine slipped through and fell in a gleaming path to the simple altar where a brass cross stood flanked with two large candles.

Unlike my soap which had been rendered with a perfumed oil and filled the air with its aroma, the candles were mere tallow and the smell wound through the others within the chapel – of unwashed bodies and woolen robes, of female odour, of bad breath close by. This was a plain priory devoted to God and the simple life. In larger houses and abbeys, I had heard of the escapades of the nuns, of baths, cosmetics, hair feathered across a forehead beneath the wimple, of self-indulgence on an obvious scale. Saint Eadgyth's was different and whilst the odour was not pleasant, it was possible to understand why it existed at all.

Profound quiet thundered around my ears. I could hear my heart beating, could hear the nuns breathing and for a reason I couldn't identify, I felt uneasy. Beside me Thea sat calmly upright on the bench, her eyes fixed on the narrow window. The Prioress knelt directly in front of the altar on a cushion and she too stared at the window. I looked around and realized all the nuns looked upward and I was struck by the beauty of the image, as if they expected God's or the Virgin's love to come streaming down on the strip of sunlight. I had no such faith and wished the meditation was over, whatever prayer they made. I squirmed and took deep breaths, feeling hot crammed between Sister Thea and another whose feet were less than a comforting sight when I looked down.

Sister Thea must have sensed my disquiet because she nudged me gently and nodded to her lap. With one hand she passed me an end of a slim knotted cord. As I watched her in prayer, she closed her eyes and her fingers slid over the other end and at each knot she would pause and her lips would move. I looked at the grubby end she had passed me and ran my fingers over the whipped cord from one knot to the next.

Unaccountably I began to think on a simple prayer.

'Protect Cecilia, Lord,' One knot.

'Protect Marais.' Another knot.

'Protect all those in Cazenay.' Another knot.

'Care for Wilf's and Harry's souls and those of their families.' Another knot.

By this time I had almost reached Thea's hands as she sat blithely pursuing her own devotions. So I slid my fingers to the bottom of the cord again.

'Bless Lady Alaïs, my mother.' A knot.

'Bless the Lady Ghislaine.' Another knot.

I took a breath and stared at the window and as I closed my eyes could only see a pair of storm blue eyes gazing back. I bit my lips and as my fingers slid to the last knot I prayed in the silent way of Saint Eadgyth's – 'Father, bless Guy of Gisborne and protect him.'

A movement in front drew my attention and I opened my eyes to see the Prioress stand, cross herself and turn to walk to the door. The nuns followed two by two, leaving Thea and I to bring up the rear as she slipped the estimable cord and her hands beneath her tunic. I smiled my thanks and she turned away and went toward the frater whilst I went to my cell. The sky had the vivid tinge of dusk about it and I realized how tired I was. Knowing the expectation was that I should attend each devotional – Vespers, Compline, Vigils, Lauds and Prime – before Guy collected me, I resolved to sleep as best I could.

I slept deeply, and at each of the bells I barely reacted to the sound so that Thea's hand would shake me gently. I would roll off the cot, totter after her in the shadows and enter the fusty smelling chapel. At Compline the window showed nothing but a strip of dark against the deep shade of the stone walls and I closed my eyes to doze rather than pray. At Vigils and despite my best intentions, I found myself slumped on Thea's shoulder but she was kind and betrayed no disappointment at my worldly manners.

She passed me her little cord and I followed my self-styled prayer circuit but it led to musing on Guy's face and I gave up and just counted my chilled toes again and again. This was the test and I had failed miserably. There was not a shred of the religious soul in my body and I knew how false it would be to become a nun and that I would do a religious house no favours by my presence … moneyed or otherwise.

At the end of each devotion I would crash back down onto the cot which squeaked and groaned, and freezing cold, I would swaddle myself as tightly as if with a death shroud. Each time, despite the cold and the discomfort, I would fall asleep thinking on my future.

Finally the bell rang for Prime and this time I met Thea in the cloister, feeling guilty at her absurdly pleased expression. At the end of the devotional, we followed the Prioress to the frater and I sat with a huge sigh, an empty platter lying in front of me. But the Prioress once again passed me a piece of crusty, fragrant bread and some cheese and on the table was a pile of polished apples whose red and white stripes were the only colour in the room. For liquid refreshment we had ale – a shock when I expected the spring water of the day before. The light in the room was bright and the air fresh, as if the nuns were excited to begin a new day.

The Prioress led all the women outside and as I followed she met me at the door and crooked her finger. She was a stately woman and we moved along the cloister away from the nuns who had gone to their separate duties.

'Master Gisborne will be here within the hour and Sister Thea will collect you from your cell. I am glad that you have attended our devotions and that you might have found some measure of comfort in prayer because I saw you at Lady Ghislaine's graveside and I noticed in the chapel that you had been weeping.'

How alert you are, Reverend Mother.

'I do not know the connection between you and I do not wish to, but we at Saint Eadgyth's are ever grateful to she and her son. Without the monies that Master Gisborne pays us, it is doubtful that we should continue here quite as comfortably as we do.'

I must have looked surprised because she swiftly counteracted any likely response.

'You did not know? Then I must prevail upon your discretion. It would not do for us to betray Master Gisborne's confidence.'

I nodded.

Gisborne, you come at me always from secret places.

The Reverend Mother scrutinized me and I felt the pressure of her gaze.

'I had thought you were family but I can see by your ignorance of our beneficence that you are not. Let me say this. Lady Ghislaine was someone blessed by God. We loved her in her short time with us. She was dying when she arrived at our door and yet having her here was like having God's Light shining. It is difficult to put into words but when she died she left us all better people. Her son knows this and whilst we did all we could for her and he thinks to repay us, in truth we wished we could have done more and he needs do nothing. Sometimes however, a prioress must take what God provides and in this instance, He provides us with a gratuity. We are in turn, grateful.'

I wanted to say something but was without words. Would she understand if I said that I cared for Lady Ghislaine's son? Would she understand my fear *of* him and *for* him? I remained silent and as if she understood, she indicated my cell.

'There is warm water for you to wash and we have taken your old clothing away. Sister Thea will collect you when Master Gisborne arrives. In the meantime, perhaps you should rest.' She began to turn away, her robes swinging around her. 'And perhaps you might pray.'

With that she left and I knew I wouldn't see her again, but a new dimension had been illuminated and I stored it in my mind to think upon. I washed my face and hands, using what was left of the piece of soap, took the small comb and ran it through hair that was then twisted into a knot and then I sat on the cot, waiting.

But I was never one to wait with ease and jumped up, my limbs busy, my mind busier. I wondered if it was anticipation of what was to come, or perhaps of seeing Gisborne but whatever the issue causing my distrait, I determined not to wait in the cell, but to go back to the bottom of the orchard.

Everything around glittered, the sun spring bright. The headstones glared and I squinted as I read Lady Ghislaine's name. I did not speak this time but noticed a rose lying with my self-styled cluster of the day before. A stunningly folded petal that looked as if it were shaped from fabric, a bud that had almost but not quite opened, as if it were shy of showing what it really was. It was as faded as a copper platter that might have been found in the ancient burial mounds that littered the fields of England. I had never seen a colour like it, almost implausible. Kneeling on the dew-wet grass, I touched it with my finger.

'You have found my mother.'

My heart clanged but far less sweetly than the Priory's bell. It rang with warnings of dangers past and present, of what was to come and I couldn't help the way I jumped.

'You startled me.'

I stood and looked from the rose to him.

'Good morning, Ysabel. Are you rested?'

'Thank you, I am. And yes. As you say, I have found your mother.'

I dared him to speak, to laud her praises as the Prioress had done, but he maintained a silence and I felt prompted to speak again.

'It's a beautiful rose, I have never seen anything like it.'

'Indeed. It is a mere adolescent and grows on the priory wall. It was a cutting from my mother's garden. She found some specimens of wild rose that she loved and blended them. She had thought to carry it to Anjou.'

So she was a gardener.

'It's the colour of old copper.'

I could barely believe that we stood over his mother's grave and blandly discussed elements of botany and reached up with my hand, indicating that he help me off my knees. His palm slid over mine and grasped and he pulled gently.

'It's good to see you this morn, Guy. I confess to feeling at odds and awry with what is to come; your companionship gives me a modicum of strength.'

'A modicum? Then I must try harder.'

He gave me that sideways look and I smiled.

'Already I feel happier. I must tell you that I have failed miserably as a would-be nun. I am altogether too self-indulgent.'

We began to walk and I noticed he didn't look back toward his mother.

'Indeed.' He spoke in a voice that had an almost invisible lilt to it. 'Whilst the doors of the church would no doubt always be open to you, I must say I cannot see you succeeding as a Sister.'

'I can't imagine succeeding at anything right now. I tell you, I've never felt more displaced in my life. A woman in straightened circumstances has little choice. Men are able to pull themselves out of their situations by many means, as you are aware. For women there is the church, marriage or prostitution. None of those appeal and I would prefer to think I am not suited.'

He took my elbow and guided me through the opening in the hedge.

'What would you do if you could cut your own cloth?'

'If I could legitimately do anything I liked, I have always admired the *trobairitz*. Do you know of them?'

'You surprise me. Such a profession! It means lady troubadour, does it not?'

'Why yes, you surprise *me* that you know.'

We had reached the end of the path through the garden and had stepped into the cloister.

'I know something of Aquitaine, Ysabel, and can see the charm of what you would wish. There is freedom for such women that resonates with you, obviously. Perhaps when this is over you can return to Cazenay and pursue such a thing.'

Perhaps I could, but whilst my Cazenay cousins adore the troubadours, they would not wish one of their own to become a travelling poet. They believe in a social hierarchy as much as my father's peers.

I could see Sister Thea at the door to my cell and I turned to Gisborne.

'Excuse me for one moment, I have some things to collect.'

I left him and walked to Thea's side. She gave me a warm smile – as if she recognized the blush on my cheeks from something in her past. We went into the cell, one after the other and she gave me a small sack that I pulled open as she passed me the comb to place in the bottom. She picked up the neatly folded cloths and I thought on the ache that was as pronounced as the previous day, my belly and breasts taut, reminding me of my womanhood. She dipped her head as she placed these on top of the comb and I gathered the bag shut and pulled it over my shoulder but she stayed my hand.

She dug deep into the folds of her robe and pulled a small hemp string free. It was plaited and knotted at intervals and I knew instinctively that she was giving me support. That she had watched me use her own cord and had thought to assist me further.

How kind and how prescient.

I ran my fingers over the plait, stopping at each knot and then reached forward and hugged the nun and I'm sure it was not my imagination that I heard a little intake of delighted breath.

We left in exactly the manner that we had done everything in the last day – Sister Thea at my side as she led Gisborne and I to the gate. We passed the scriptorium and the nuns therein looked up. I would swear one face, younger than the rest, had a look of yearning. I wondered what her thoughts told her; to desist and follow the Path or to think on what might have been if Fate had led her a different way.

As we reached the gate, I turned to Thea and took her hands. I could be silent no longer.

'Thank you, Sister,' I whispered as I squeezed her palms.

She opened the gate with much key rattling and Gisborne passed through as I stood next to her, almost as if I was afraid to proceed.

But Thea gave me the slightest push and said very softly in a voice as sweet as the bell, 'Go kindly, my lady, and God bless. I shall pray for you.'

Before I had time to acknowledge the effort she had made on my behalf, she had shut the gate and locked it.

The walls of the Priory stood at my back and Guy waited in front of me, two horses held. 'Ysabel? Is ought wrong?'

Wrong? God above, where do I begin?

'Nothing that wasn't wrong before, only now a lot closer,' I replied as I took the reins from him and grasped the stirrup.

But he took it away and turned me from the horse's side.

'I swear that as long as I am able, I shall keep you safe. Rely on me.'

Our eyes locked and I wanted so much to believe in his omnipotence. Instead I took the stirrup again and as I mounted, the leather of the saddle creaking, I merely said, 'Thank you. It is appreciated.'

I followed behind, my horse a spritely bay gelding, his ears pricked and his coat sleek and smooth to the touch. As we walked along the road away from the Priory, I heard the bell for Tierce. Hard to believe it was so early in the day and already I felt as if I had been up for hours. I fiddled inside the sleeve of my tunic where I had pushed the hempen string and pulled it out. It was a pretty piece of knotting and weaving. I had a thought that Wilf and Harry would approve as I tied it in a circle and slipped the bracelet over my knuckles to lie on my wrist.

'What is it?' Guy asked.

'A gift from Sister Thea.'

I explained about the devotions and about Thea's own cord.

'She grew fond of you in a short time.'

'Less time to know of my shortcomings. Any longer and I would have received nothing, I can assure you.'

'Ah,' he said as he clicked his horse on. 'You are overly hard.'

You say? Have I changed then? Have I improved?

'What intelligence did you garner whilst I was in the Priory?'

His back straightened, shoulders lifting with tension and I watched as he sank his weight down through his calves into the stirrups.

'Gisborne?' I prompted.

A sigh.

'Nothing of import. Merely that there has been no sign of De Courcey's men on the road we travel.'

'And that is a good thing? Could they not be taking another road entirely and shortcut us on the way?'

'You forget they don't know we sailed to Great Yarmouth, Ysabel. If they sailed to Dover, we are like to arrive in Moncrieff well before them, even if they ride at a gallop upon landing. In principle, you should be able to see Cecilia and your father, make up your mind what you will do and be gone before De Courcey enters the demesnes.'

'And what of Halsham?'

'God, Ysabel!' Guy dragged on his reins and spun his horse to face me, frowning with temper. 'Your questions always raise the issue of trust. You either trust me or you don't. If you don't, then say so. I would rather know on what ground we tread before we proceed further.'

His eyes glared and I shivered in the shade of the trees. Intimidation and an incipient threat hung about but I would not be cowed.

'Trust,' I said, fiddling with Thea's prayer cord. 'I owe you honesty to be sure because we have been as close as a married couple this last few weeks.'

His eyes opened wider and then slitted again.

Ah, yes, that got a reaction.

'There are times when your inability to be open frightens me,' I continued. 'There are times when you slide off on your own that inspire lack of confidence. Your relationship with Halsham sickens me, cousin or no. And yet despite it all, I would have none other but you at my back, Gisborne. All I ask is that you treat me less as a trouble and more as a trusted friend.'

'I could ask the same of you.'

'Trust is earned and I would be less than grateful if I didn't say you had already earned it, but I know you spy…'

His gaze sharpened.

'You spy for money and I fear for myself at such times because spies have enemies.'

Oh how selfish I sounded but I needed to air my concern.

He looked at me long.

'You need have no fear for yourself. I do spy for money as it happens, and have done for a number of years. I am skilled at my job, Ysabel, and would never put your life at risk.'

'Then answer me. Where is Halsham?'

'I imagine with De Courcey.'

'And that doesn't worry you?'

'No, it doesn't. There are some things Halsham doesn't know, and Davey is one. We have an edge and I hope that Fate will let us play it out.'

You hope?

'Is there a chance it may not?'

'Nothing in life is ever certain,' he replied.

I must have looked stricken because he said:

'Please, Ysabel.' He rode his horse next to me and laid his hand on mine. 'Trust me.' He picked my hand up and kissed the inside of my wrist, right over the top of Thea's bracelet and my strength, my determination, folded.

Damn you, Gisborne.

I wanted to be free of this feeling. I wanted to do what must be done and move on. I wanted to leave this life and all that had happened behind.

All of it, Ysabel? You lie to yourself.

I found my fingers curling around his and there beat a moment like that in the room at the inn when he had held me naked against his own body.

'I want to trust you, Guy. Just as I trusted my own mother.' I laughed a mirthless laugh. 'Leastways, as a woman I feel I have little option.'

Our hands were joined across the pommel of my saddle and we sat as still as statues and then, damn him again, he leaned over and kissed me long.

CHAPTER NINE

The journey continued like a roll of thread unwinding and sometimes I despaired of ever seeing the end. There were other times when I never wanted the end to appear as it meant so many things that I couldn't bear to countenance. The first time a familiar landmark appeared, my stomach jolted. The instinct to turn and flee was a powerful one and had me almost undone. Would I have continued on without Gisborne's protection? Somehow I doubted it.

I wondered if his so-called dependability would make me feel safer in this hornet's nest we approached. Such a good question; such an unanswerable question.

At some point the landscape had begun to change into flat, moist fens where our paths meandered between ditches, bogs, rivulets and patches of feathery reeds that towered above us. The grasses rustled and fluttered to some vague music of nature, the sound slithery and serpent-like altogether. But that was just my anxious mind. In truth the grasses were beautiful and the sound soft, insistent and quite pleasant.

The forests I remembered from my childhood, thick and almost impenetrable swathes, had diminished considerably but many small copses of trees draped over the watery landscape, covering fen violets in bands of shadow. The oatmeal-coloured grasses that now shielded us had been playgrounds for children. Not for me the fear of legendary waterwights, that they would leap from the depths and devour any child that set a toe on the banks. The water had been a source of enjoyment and I had grown with the sound of snipe, bittern and lapwing piping and flapping. I was as comfortable in river-craft as I was mounted in a creaking saddle on a good horse.

The modest sight of Walsocam appeared through the waving banners of the tallest grasses. A small place, it was marked by an inn, a severe church in the Norman style and a smithy's from where a hammer knocked rhythmically against an anvil. Smoke curled into the pale sky from a dozen or more dwellings and a few bleached grey punts attached to the riverbank by worn mooring lines.

'I know this place.' I spoke it quietly, in fear of being overheard.

'Of course,' Guy responded. 'It's Walsocam. We are a day or less from Moncrieff.'

Again my stomach tilted. Perhaps my nerves were becoming overly delicate but I pulled my horse sharply to a halt occasioning a twist of a disapproving mouth from my companion.

'I do not wish to stay at the inn, Guy. I'm not sure it is safe and would rather sleep rough if I have to.'

Since we had left Saint Eadgyth's we had conversed little, both locked in our own thoughts. Once we spoke of my father's self-styled library. It appeared to contain less than a dozen manuscripts – some Norman, an Irish Book of Hours. But the centerpiece and one that might be worth a King's ransom was a Saracen's book of poetry. Guy's eyes lit up. 'It is beautiful, Ysabel. Written in the Arab tongue by a skilled scribe. The poems are illustrated delicately and depict their way of life and it is bound in an ancient style. But its value is not in its content, but rather its covers. They are made of wood, the back rubbed smooth as silk and the front heavily inlaid. Not with other woods, but with gems. With large rubies, pearls and emeralds in a pleasing design laced with gold filigree.'

'How did my father come across such a book? And how could *he* afford to pay a King's ransom?'

Even I could detect the bitterness in my voice.

Guy refused to be drawn and I guessed straight away.

'Oh my Lord, he won it in a game of chance, didn't he?' I slapped my palm on the pommel and swore. 'Do you gamble like my father, Guy? Do you fritter away your hard-earned monies on paltry entertainments?'

His face barely moved, the master of inscrutability.

'With what would I gamble? I am but a steward. Besides, the book may just save you, Ysabel, think on that.'

'If my father hadn't gambled at all, I wouldn't be in the position of *having* to save myself.'

We lapsed into an uneasy silence and continued to the grassy outskirts of Walsocam where I had whispered '*I know this place.*'

'I think we should seek a barn on the outskirts. There must be one somewhere amongst the steadings. And...'

Guy listened, no comment, no expression.

'... I don't think we should continue on horseback, we should take to the water. I know the fens well and I am familiar with backwaters that are secret and we can follow them to Moncrieff.'

His profound silence had the capacity to make me doubt my thoughts but then he shrugged.

'As you wish Lady Ysabel...'

Lady? Have I touched a nerve somewhere, how so?

'But,' he continued, 'we shall have to leave the horses.'

'Then we shall,' I replied. 'The money we lose is immaterial. Better to be secure on the water.'

Unkind Ysabel.

I knew it. He had paid for the mounts himself and I dismissed the fiscal loss as if it were nothing.

Unthinking.

We spent time circling Walsocam surreptiously, leading the horses, and eventually a barn, a pile of logs and daub with a roof, was revealed alongside a poor sort of dwelling. No smoke, light nor movement indicated habitation. 'We must stay here,' I said. 'It's empty.'

'Does it not concern you that it may be an empty dwelling because of illness?' Guy seemed reluctant.

'If it were a contagion they would have burned it. No, it is empty for other reasons.'

Witchery, revolt, the family dying out, forced off; I cared not. To hide was paramount.

When did I become the decision-maker? When did it become right to reduce Gisborne to the position of a mere employee?

I *knew* I was behaving like a shrew, acting with fear lapping at my legs, but I could barely control it.

So much yet to lose.

We crept into the barn, our horses' hooves muffled by the eons of grasses and leaves that were piled into the structure. We placed the animals in tumbled stalls that were laced with spider-webs and a search for feed revealed a stook of oaten hay, somewhat denuded of its goodness but not mouldy. Water of course was close by – a rivulet sluggishly pulsing behind the barn; a ubiquitous punt, elderly and careworn, pulled onto a sandy defile.

The sun had begun to slide as we finished watering the horses to return them to their stalls. In the muffled distance we could still hear the smithy at work and the occasional sound of a small community, voices light on the spasmodic breeze that rippled the rivulet.

We had secured the animals and were venturing out of the barn when Guy grabbed me back, holding me against the walls. He put his fingers to his lips and lifted two fingers to his eyes and then pointed out and I swiveled to peer through the crumbling walls. A punt drifted past with two men, the smell of a pile of eels drifting toward us. They were laughing as they poled away, unaware of the fugitives behind them.

I exhaled.

'You see,' I said. 'It's that easy to be noticed. I thank you for your quick wits.'

He nodded. 'We need food. Stay here and I'll search the dwelling.'

I let him go. I was tired and he was a man after all. Let him provide for me.

He was back in a short time with an insubstantial pile of goods.

'A bit of wheaten flour but we need to pick out the weevils. Some stale ale fermented enough to blow the doors off the barn and some almost dry honey.'

'Can we risk a fire?'

'If we don't, we starve.'

'Then if we do it in the barn, the smoke won't be noticeable.' I said.

'True.'

He had tipped the flour onto his cloak and was sifting through, lifting the tiny cream grubs and squashing them between thumb and forefinger.

'Well then?'

'Better to wait till night and light it outside. The smoke won't be seen and if these folk are as superstitious as I suspect, they won't go near the water in the dark. We have a lot to thank legend for.'

I guessed he was right, the likes of the waterwights held great sway in peasant minds.

I made up a mixture in a cracked earthenware flask. Some flour and a little sour ale to wet it, some scrapings of the honey crystals. I stirred it with a stick and when night had settled a dark cloth across the sky and eery threads of mist crept toward us from the water, Guy stroked a spark onto the neat pile of tinder. We built the fire and then let it burn to hot coals, placing a stone over them to heat and then dripping the mixture upon it and making flattish cakes. We flipped them with a piece of flint from the yard. They tasted of nothing but old flour, stale ale and a wistful memory of honey but they bulked our bellies and it was better than nothing.

We poured water on the coals, then some sand from the defile. On the morrow, Guy said we would spread it and it would look as if no one had been there. The horses we would turn loose – it would serve.

I hope.

In the barn I had just enough energy to yank my hood off and shake out tightly coiled hair. I ran my fingers through, pushed my head back and stretched it to each side.

Two hands slipped onto my shoulders and I froze, knowing with unerring instinct the hands that had loved me rested there. I stood so still, my breath held and then I rubbed the side of my head against his knuckles. He turned me round, tipped my chin and our lips met so lightly there was barely sensation. And again, and yet again.

His hands eased under the surcoat, lifting it, sliding it over my head and I watched as he pulled off his own. Our bodies touched.

We made love in silence again, not a word spoken, moving in a rhythm that was as driven by desperation as it was by affection. As if both of us needed to defray the tension of what approached, maybe even to hold it at bay. Afterward we lay in the damp and fusty hay, my eyes heavy, Guy's body around mine like the sheath that protects a knife and I slept.

Much later the slightest movement woke me, as light as a mouse's tread. I saw him leave and the word 'trust' grinned at me like some Devil's sprite, taunting me, defying me. I dragged on my clothes, slid out the door following his shadow – a drifting shade in the dark. A guardian angel sat at my shoulder that night. Not once as he and I moved in our separate spaces, did I tread on twig or dry leaf. Not once did I startle a night creature into revealing my presence. In single file and far enough apart, we progressed into Walsocam and my heart crashed as loud as a thunderclap.

What draws you from our shared bed, Gisborne? Who?

The answer when it presented itself was so obvious I almost laughed with the bitterness of its revelation.

Halsham waited outside the inn.

The two cousins talked and money clinked in the night as a bag was passed over.

I didn't wait. I reversed the way I had come, quickly passing dark dwellings as a lone cur barked, edging through sedge and reed, once disturbing a water fowl that clacked and flapped, but reaching the bank where lay the punts. With speed and as quiet as I had ever been in my life, I stepped in, pushing off with the pole and drifting into the slow current that would take me to my secret byways and to Moncrieff.

Without Guy of Gisborne.

Be calm. Think. My heart raced as the vessel humoured me, allowing me to slip along in the current, barely making a ripple. But the darkness suffocated. Swathes of giant grasses lined the banks like serried rows of pike-men in some army. Huge trees towered above the grasses and I fancied they resembled trebuchets. The air itself, hardly moving in the night, was moist and laden with the odour of mud and weed. As Walsocam drained into the rivulet there were other smells as well – excrement, the bloated remains of a butchered sheep, dead cats and rats.

But the current slipped me past and presently the air was sweeter, less of man and more of the watery fens. Nothing awoke to my passage and I pushed the pole into the mud and held it there to track my journey.

Landmarks, I need landmarks. Mary Mother, help me.

The shapes around me blended into the shadows of midnight as I swung myself in a circle.

River. Walsocam that way. Trees. Willows. Three oaks.

I could define the shape of the leaves as they leaned down over the rivulet and the occasional acorn dropped in the water with a subtle plop.

Three oaks!

I poled the punt toward the sentinel trees and pulled myself back and forth amongst the grasses, the noise a shifting, crackling sound.

There! There it is.

A disused opening to a channel that seemed deep and navigable but overgrown and unseen. This was the secret backwater – this was the way to Moncrieff.

I pushed through the reeds, allowing them to close over the punt, meshing fast like a portcullis slamming down. The darkness was total. So overgrown were the sedges they leaned right across my head. Spider-webs feathered across my face and I rubbed at them with the crook of my elbow. I hated spiders.

Don't think on them, keep going. Breathe.

The water flowed sluggishly away toward Moncrieff and I realized if I sat down low in the punt the current could do the work. As long as I reached home before dawn.

Riding the roads, Guy and I would have taken a day to reach Moncrieff, but in full view of any who might look. By these discreet channels it would be safer but maybe longer and it could take an unknown time – I didn't know what obstacles I might find. Fallen trees, mud, even worse, swathes now drained and used for water meadows. I only knew that I must get home before Guy.

Why?

I couldn't answer my question beyond thinking on the gut reaction at watching that bag change hands. I closed my eyes. All I wanted to see was his face when he delighted in something – an anecdote he related, a book, even something I said.

His face when he said, 'Ysabel...'

I hated him.

I grunted as the punt swung a little in the dark. My back and belly ached with a vengeance and I thought I detected a faint warmth between my legs with no cloth to staunch it.

Hope for a slow arrival of my courses until Cecilia meets me...

I blamed such discomfort on Gisborne. What he had put me through on this whole journey.

He? Was it not Papa's actions that had reduced my life to a travesty?

I shook my head. This wretched voice of conscience tried repeatedly to gainsay me, to upset my conclusions and I would not listen. I travelled on through the tunnel. A water rat flopped from the bank, too close for comfort and occasioning a squeak from a tight throat. So much of sneaking rats and rats' eyes reminded me of Halsham.

What of Guy? What does he remind me of?

A snake.

Remember the snake in the Garden of Eden, hissing its tempting words.

But a snake has black, gimlet eyes. Guy's eyes seared like the blue of summer in Aquitaine.

Time snapped at me. All the while I was conscious of night flitting by and dawn approaching too rapidly. The current meandered and finally I could stand it no longer and stood with the pole to push myself on faster. We skimmed along and a feeling of success lightened my anxiety and just as I sighed with relief at the increased speed, the bow hit something and I crashed forward. My head collided with the gunwales as I went down and there was a brief pain and then nothing.

I opened my eyes to a paler dark, to the snipe of a lone bird somewhere and as I tried to sit up, aware of dawn beginning to break, blood trickled down my face, the bottom of the punt leering up at me. I sank onto stiff buttocks.

God, why? Mary Mother, tell Him!

I held my arm to whatever contusion was in my hair, feeling the egg-sized lump as I sopped the ooze and moaned.

Ysabel, cease your wailing and get moving. Watery sentiment is for later.

I hung my legs over the bow, feeling with cold toes to see what the punt had hit. A spit of sandy mud blocked the way and I trod forward to determine how much further the bank would prevent my passage. In the strengthening light, it was possible to see the channel stretched on, splitting to flow around an islet. I leaped back into the punt, poling in reverse and then heading for the left hand side; sliding into a space the width of my craft, poling, pushing, grasses dragging against me, light gaining, my breath puffing and blood dripping onto the tunic.

The current seemed to strengthen beyond the spit, almost as if it had its own agenda and I let the boat float on as I tried to staunch the bleeding. I had no care for the depth of the wound, nor anything other than the need to enter Moncrieff by my secret way before full daylight.

The marshes were tipped in pearl light and a dove-grey mist rose off the water, the colours blurred and the banks almost featureless. But the palate of the place, so lately in my thought as something of welcome, a tender memory, was now merely camouflage and subterfuge. I chafed to find the secret entrance to the tunnel that curled through the bulwark of home.

Then, drifting on the morning air, the sound of baying hounds followed by men shouting and then hooves, a dozen or so horses hammering the paths close by. A voice I didn't know. 'She's at Saint Eadgyth's. We'll find her there.'

How can they know? Seriously, Ysabel. You wonder?

The water opened out into a broad sweep the colour of iron. The lake that my family had conceived by judicious building of weirs and walls pooled around the castle structure and I took a breath to make the last dash across the water – nothing to hide behind or under until I reached the rushes around the castle foundations.

I pushed away, kneeling low, using the pole as quietly as I could. I glanced up expecting to see soldiers pacing the battlements but it was as barren and bare of life as a graveyard. Not even the Moncrieff pennant flew and that thought delivered bile onto my tongue.

The punt slid against the wall, the sides scraping against the rock, the sound like someone drawing an axe over a stone. I pulled myself along until I reached a tumble of boulders I knew well and tugged at some draping reeds, dragging the punt deep into the undergrowth. I heard horses gallop across the drawbridge, heard nothing but shouts and only knew that before my heart stopped completely, I needed to get closer.

The punt was too much of a liability and I nudged it hard under the sedge so that it could rot there for eternity, and without care for anything other than reaching my home, I slid into the cold water.

My home? Betrayal.

I could still feel his hands on my shoulders. On my lips I could feel his... I spat out a small mouthful of river water as the grille that covered the secret entrance appeared to my right.

Dear God, have mercy.

I was almost there, almost to the grille and something whined past my ear from high up, feathers flashing past my cheek. My shoulder burned and a voice shouted.

'Ere, what do you do?'

Another voice. 'Thought I saw a big water rat.'

'Halsham'll have your guts for wasting arrows. Put up now and just keep watch. Save the arrows for when they're needed.'

Thea's little string bracelet hung limply from my wet wrist as I hauled the grille open just enough to pull up and slip over the ledge. I flopped like a half-dead pike onto the beaten earth floor that was the very foundation of Moncrieff.

Dear Lord.

Water dribbled down to the dirt, the stain of blood spreading across the shoulder – an arrow graze.

Better a graze than a piercing.

I could hear nothing in these bowels, nothing but a dripping silence and it suited me. Moncrieff's layout was tattooed on my heart and mind. I stepped from the chamber, looking to the left and to the...

A hand slid over my mouth, and I was pulled back hard against someone. They held tight, so that I could almost feel the bones of the fingers, my lips numb with the pressure.

A voice spoke, a disconcerting sound that raised goosebumps.

'Ysabel,' Gisborne whispered. 'Why did you run away?'

I could smell his hand and struggled, squirming and pulling against him, realizing I could never call for help.

To whom? De Courcey's men?

I tried to kick backward...

'Stop it,' he hissed. 'Do you wish to reveal yourself?' Every muscle in my body tightened with fury as he continued. 'If I take my hand away, shall you be sensible?'

Sensible? I'll kill you!

I breathed hard; irregular snorts like a cornered horse and then closing my eyes I nodded. The pressure of his hands eased and I whirled around.

'You betrayed me, you *betrayed* me!'

His face glowered in the dawn shadows of the chamber, sarcasm slapping at the walls.

'You say?'

'You exchanged money with Halsham. I saw you.'

Mary Mother but the anger lay inside me like a cornered wolf. I wanted to bite, to scratch.

There beat one moment. An inexorable moment where the hand of Fate slid back and forth deciding to weight the proceedings one way or the other.

Finally, 'You didn't wait long enough to see me hand it back,' he said.

Another moment and then I lifted my hands and slapped them so hard into his chest that the noise echoed around the chamber and I almost knocked him off balance.

'*What* do you think I am, Gisborne? Some sort of fool? Why else would you meet your cousin but for money? You told him I approached Moncrieff. By the Blood of Christ, you traitor! Why *else* do they look for me this instant?'

'They look for you,' he snarled, 'as they have ever done because they know you are in England, that you set sail from Calais, that you were dropped somewhere on the coast…'

'With you!' I interjected. 'Their own efficient information source.'

'In the name of God!' He ran his fingers through his hair. 'In the name of your mother…'

'Holy Mary! How *dare* you invoke my mother's name…'

'I *dare* woman, because if I don't you will not listen and her last words to me will mean nothing.'

Silence, but for the hoarse breathing in the damp space. The light mellowed as the sun moved round the edge of the castle walls, sifting itself though the bars of the grille.

'What – words?' I glared at him, my face tight with hate and disbelief.

'*"Protect my Ysabel, Guy. Find her, keep her safe from her father's misguided behaviour."*

'Oh.'

My anger deflated in a whisper, my mother's words striking my heart and piercing it so that I shook my head and walked to the grille, rubbing my hands over the damp stone of this castle that should have been an inheritance. But my mood was sombre for less than a moment.

'And why, Gisborne, would you pay heed to my mother's words? You barely knew her. You were a mere steward.' I emphasized the word 'steward' as if it was as dirty as peasant's feet, the lowest of the low.

'We had respect for each other. She trusted me.'

'How fortuitous.'

I wanted to strike him where it hurt, my tone almost a sneer.

'By God, you bitch. Rot here then with your bleeding head and shoulder. Try and avoid De Courcey. But as his net closes about, remember I could have helped.'

He took a step back.

But I needed to have the last word.

'Gisborne! How did you get here before me?'

The question hung in the air like the sword of Damocles.

He shook his head, a marginal shake, barely there. 'I know every inch of the demesnes. Every track, every swift and secret way. I broke the horse galloping here and the beleaguered animal is even now hidden in a coppice. His saddlery is thrown in a bog and he sweats as if he is ill. If he is found, there are no saddlemarks amongst the froth of his exertions. I made sure.'

He had an answer for everything. As cold as a winter wind, not a sign that he tried hard to convince me although others would say he merely told truths.

'What about the castle? How did you know about the grille?'

'I told you, I know every inch of this place, the domain *and* the castle.'

'And sold the plan to De Courcey for a recommendation to moneyed knighthood, no doubt.'

Our whole conversation had been uttered in wrenched tones and he replied in a strangled whisper.

'Cecilia showed me because your mother was too ill. Over time I was able to ascertain that the bailiff was unaware. If your father betrayed any of the secrets of the castle to any other of his staff then you can be sure De Courcey will know by now. Methinks however, that if they knew about this, they would be here with a guard and they are not. Cecilia trusted me to use the secrets for safety should I ever need to.'

Cecilia!

He disappeared out the door leaving me a beaten woman and I stood there for less than a heartbeat. I ran after him as he disappeared up a narrow snaking stair.

'Where is she?'

Guy stopped, a darker shadow against the unlit walls. I could decipher nothing in his expression as he turned back. He was alarmingly neutral.

Got her, he must be thinking.

And poor unfortunate me, I had no choice but to let him.

'She's been placed…'

'Placed?' I interrupted, visions of cells and dungeons looming large.

'In your mother's chamber, the Lady Chamber. We can go via the passage.'

But of course I knew that and pushed past him to hurry away. I heard the scrape of flint and there was a flare of light and a flame followed me. Straight ahead I forged. Then up, up again, curling around the tower. My legs ached as I hauled them step after step, climbing all the time until I reached the heights of Moncrieff. The secret passage was narrow – fine for someone of my breadth but Guy's shoulders scuffed against the stone behind me.

'Ysabel, slow down. She may have a guard with her.'

I stopped and turned toward him, the flames casting jumping shadows across us both.' 'Why would she be guarded? What has happened here? Does De Courcey hold the castle outright now, with none of Moncrieff's men about?'

My breath came in ragged spurts.

'It would appear so.' Guy leaned against the wall, the torch flaring in the secret air.

'And my father?'

'I haven't been here long enough to locate him. We must rely on Cecilia.' Guy pushed past me, the flame brightening and then fading as he turned a corner. 'Only a little further, come on.'

A couple more bends and we stopped just as the flame gutted, leaving us in a dank and close darkness. My breath sucked in. Within seconds, the claustrophobic walls pressed on me from all sides, my heartbeat stalled and the heat of panic steamed through my body.

I will not give in…

I quieted, breathing more slowly and the darkness eased so it was possible to discern light around a narrow aperture. Guy shuffled toward the infinitesimal gap, pressing his ear against it.

'We'll have to wait. She's not alone,' he whispered and his fingers squeezed. 'Did you hear that?'

I thought I did – a rumble of voices, a door opening and then closing. 'They've gone.'

Guy shouldered his way through the aperture that had been concealed by a yielding cover; a heavy rug that hung on the wall. My mother's chamber was uniquely situated on the first floor in a round tower and was well lit by four commanding windows. At enormous cost, my father had shipped panels of glass from Normandy. Despite being distorted and thick, with bubbles of air trapped within the viscous layers, sun streamed in and it was possible to find thin, clear spots through which to gaze on a world below. Through these strange little viewpoints, one could observe the verdant beauty of Moncrieff – woods crisscrossed with ribands of narrow waterways for miles hence.

The remaining chamber walls were softened by a number of unusual carpets – massive, knotted rugs my mother purchased from itinerants when they passed through Aquitaine from across the Middle Sea. One of the rugs concealed an entrance to a secret passage – the slimmest opening. Wide enough for a man unafraid to compress his body to the thickness of a wafer and where lesser men might balk at the thought of being permanently stuck to wither and moulder through the centuries.

From inside the chamber all seven carpets hung innocently, betraying no secrets. No weaving looked any different to another except in the patterning and unless one had prior knowledge of the labyrinthine secret of Moncrieff, such deception would always remain undiscovered.

Cecilia was standing at the fire and when she heard movement behind her, she swung around, a small knife whipped from her sleeve. Her grey eyes widened and she almost shouted as her eyes settled on us.

But momentarily I did not see her. Instead I saw my mother seated at her tapestry frame, a needle trailing a flare of wool. She laughed at something a rambunctious eleven year old girl said as the child twirled around in a lined and embroidered cloak of her mother's, tripping on the folds.

'Ysabel,' my mother had a honeyed voice of great subtlety. 'You shall never be a lady if I don't send you to Cazenay.'

'When?' cried the girl who was almost a woman, kicking the folds of the cloak out of the way.

'Oh immediately,' said Lady Alaïs. 'When you reach twelve years of age.'

'But that's tomorrow.' The girl stood still, eyes widening. 'Can we leave for Cazenay tomorrow?'

'Not tomorrow, my daughter. We shall have a celebration here first. But we leave at the end of the week. In four more days.'

I saw the excitement in the younger Ysabel's eyes, the anticipation. She could barely wait to leave Moncrieff.

How I wish she had not.

Cecilia leaped forward, an expression halfway between joy and terror whilst I stood stockstill, frozen with memories. Her arms clasped me and she whispered but I could not hear. Only my mother's voice, her Occitán accent, and all I could see was her lovely hair coiled and deliberately uncovered. My beautiful mother…

'Ysabel,' Cecilia spoke by my ear. 'You risk your life.'

She pushed me back behind the rug, staying in the room herself as she cast a worried glance at the door of the chamber.

It was then that I focused on my mother's companion, my godmother. She had grown gaunt and drawn, her hair covered by a wimple not unlike Thea's, her *bliaut* dark-grey and unembellished. But the fine white linen of her chemise and the heavily wrought silver of her girdle betrayed her nobility. That and the rings upon her fingers – a twisted marriage band of gold and silver and a plain silver band studded with a ruby the size of a quail's egg. It was so heavy that it fell to her finger joint, rattling there and looking out of place, the more so because Cecilia had been a widow for at least the twenty years of *my* life. Her husband, Sir Hugh Fineux of Upton, had been killed in some battle or other and as a child I couldn't care despite that fact that I looked at my godmother now and wished I had.

Cobwebbed wrinkles fanned from the corners of her eyes and worry had ploughed two deep trenches between her fine eyebrows. In fact my mother's friend had aged beyond belief and yet she held the knife in her hand with strength and familiarity. It was that above all else that brought the harsh message thudding home; Moncrieff *was* in a state of siege.

'Cecilia,' I could barely speak as the memories crushed my throat. I wanted to collapse into her arms in the belief that all would be well. 'Where is she?'

'She is in the chapel. Your father commissioned a sculpted tomb but...' She grabbed my arm. 'You must *not* go near because De Courcey has men everywhere.'

I hated that he was here as if he had the right. That he was in control.

Gisborne's voice echoed my concern.

'How many men?'

Cecilia clasped him like a mother with a son.

'Lord but I am glad you are both safe,' she said. 'Well done, Guy. I knew I could trust you to bring her back. But things have happened between times and she is not safe now and we must conceive a plan.'

'Lady Cecilia, I thank you for your belief in me...'

Your belief in me? Is this some kind of lesson, Gisborne?

He continued, '... but what has happened and how many men?'

'De Courcey has taken over the castle, his now by law. A full garrison of a hundred men guarding the castle and Moncrieff village.'

A hundred men! It's a King's army! What has happened to Moncrieff's tiny force?

'By what right does he take what is not his? Where does he get the men?' I was shocked.

But they ignored me. Gisborne swore, the language of the soldier's camp betraying his surprise and fury that we should be so curtailed.

'And the Baron?'

Cecilia sighed, her tongue clicking in a brusque 'tsk'.

'I know not,' she said. 'My own lack of freedom prevents me from knowing much at all.'

I broke in for it was as though they had forgotten I stood inches away inside the wall.

'You didn't answer me, Cecilia. By what right is he here? Where does De Courcey get these men that presumably guard my father as if he were a threat to King and country.'

The look she gave me was filled with sadness.

'Moncrieff is his, my love. It was ceded to pay debts and that is the law. The men are De Courcey's own; an army of Free Lancers who march across borders for money. Currently they are in England at the King's behest...'

I turned away. All I could see was Halsham's face above the livery of his Free Lancers surcoat.

CHAPTER TEN

'Listen to me,' she said. 'You must hide because they will be in and out with food and I am taunted by De Courcey and his officers as if they think to use me as bait.'

She reached again for my hand and gave it a little shake.

'They know you stepped off near Great Yarmouth so they are on your tail. You know where you would hide up the stair in the hole as a child? You must go there and stay now, both of you, until I am able to talk with you. It will be late at night when they tend to leave me alone.'

I opened my mouth to question her but she interrupted.

'In the hole there is a cover and cushion, for I hoped you would come.'

She hurried to a salver and grabbed early apples and some cheese and thrust the food into my hands.

'I shall get some bread and…' she reached for a stoppered leather bottle and threw it into Gisborne's hands. 'There, watered wine. Go quickly.'

She pushed at us and we had little option but to let her, allowing the thick tapestry to fall behind us.

'Go!' she whispered.

I headed toward the footsteps of my childhood. Ever upward, where darkness shut out today and touch focused on yesterday. The cheese was squashed to my chest together with the apples, and the smell of the orchard raised a dozen memories and threatened to stop me in my tracks.

But I kept stepping up, aware of Gisborne close behind.

'Here,' I muttered, turning into the slim space.

Gisborne hovered, aware of the lack of room.

'Oh for God's sake, just come and sit where you can.'

An arrow loop bled a measure of light onto the floor upon which lay a rolled blanket and a tapestry-covered pillow. Perfect for one person. I flopped to the floor, exhaustion beginning to bite at my legs.

'Have some fruit and cheese,' I offered as he folded his height half in and out of the space. I threw an apple to him and he took his knife and sliced pieces, doing the same with the cheese. I ate because my stomach demanded it but in truth food mattered little as my mind went over and over the scenario outside the walls.

'What are you thinking?' he said after sucking on the leather bottle.

'You don't know?'

I hunched back against the wall, sighing and resting the back of my head against the cold stone. The light through the arrow slit lay on my toes, a measure of comfort.

'De Courcey has the place,' he said, mirroring my thoughts. 'You wonder how it has happened so quickly. You wonder if you are safe; if Cecilia is safe. How you shall find your father. What you shall discover *when* you find your father.' He held his knife between his hands, the point and haft pressing against the balls of two fingers, bridging a gap over no-man's land.

'Do go on. You have all the answers.'

'If I tell you what I think, you must accept that I know a little more than you and that I have tried to prepare you for this eventuality all through our journey.'

There was an earnestness about him that dismantled my anger just a fraction.

'I think your father has been imprisoned by De Courcey, Ysabel. Perhaps he hasn't paid his gaming debts in full and De Courcey is angered. As to your role in this, I think he plans to have you as well. I believe he sees it as a neat way to tie up Moncrieff. Marriage takes the taint of robber-Baron away.'

Blood pounded in my ears.

'Good God, how can this man get away with what he has done? I will go to King Richard, I will…'

'I suspect that De Courcey has supporters. Supporters who may have the King's ear and there is little you can do.'

'No. You're wrong, my father was gulled.'

'You and I know this but to others it would seem your father gambled away his estates in full knowledge of what he was doing.'

'No one who gambles is in their right minds. Besides, you said they would get him blind drunk on their sorties. Is that not coercion?'

'And how would you prove it?'

'I…' I threw a piece of apple at the wall.

'Truth?' He looked neither smug nor righteous. 'You cannot. Not when someone has proved himself invaluable to the King. Have no doubt, Ysabel, the mercenaries that De Courcey fields are earning the King's notice and gratitude.'

I barely debated my next comment. I really didn't care if I offended anyone right now. I wanted to kick out and kick hard.

'And you think to be a Free Lancer? With De Courcey and Halsham as your senior officers? Your sense of purpose and self-preservation does you credit when your integrity does not.'

His expression did not change, his voice did not harden, but his fingers gripped the haft of his knife until the knuckles showed bone-white.

'I have been charged with your safety. I must protect your interests and those of Cecilia, even if Moncrieff is beyond my care at this point.'

I dipped my head in mock deference.

'Then we must thank you, my dear Gisborne, for such *perceived* loyalty.'

He stood up, the apple cores and cheese rind falling at my feet, and clipped away down the stair. I heard his boots tapping and his shoulders scraping the walls well past the entrance to my mother's chamber. I wondered if he left me to cool his anger or whether he departed the castle and any further involvement with the Moncrieffs. Or if he left to sign up with De Courcey and divulge my whereabouts.

Whichever was the case he was gone and I was alone.

The sun drifted past the arrow loop and I lay down as I did as a child and peered through. In those far off days, I would pretend I was a bird on a sill about to take flight and I would gaze across the view imagining it from the bird's eye… over the lake, trees and fields. Villeins working my father's lands… tilling, seeding, weeding, scything, gathering in the harvest – colours changing from brown to acid green, to pale gold and to brown again – like some beautifully illuminated Book of Hours right before my eyes.

Now the fields were tinted bright green as the seeded crops grew to maturity. After harvest they would plough them again and then let them lie fallow until the spring thaw when the men, women and children would seed the soil with barley or oats. My childish memory recalled the rime-edged furrows, the crows swooping in flocks to feed when the fields were seeded and the children lined up with stones to keep the birds away until the crop struck.

A noise far below dragged at my attention, horses clattering out over the drawbridge… a cohort of a dozen men on thickset rounceys with powerful quarters. Their quilted saddle cloths carried the Free Lancer's colours – De Courcey's own it would appear. My fingers balled into fists as I watched them scatter a group of Moncrieff folk across the stony road, a child falling into a ditch and crying as they swept by.

The place had all the appearance of a military encampment. How the people of Moncrieff would hate this regime. Under my mother's care and with my father's wealth, they had wanted for very little – they were never hungry, they were allowed to cook their own bread instead of paying the lord of the manor for the privilege and they were paid in coin for any service they rendered Moncrieff. They had a chance to better themselves and to become free men but now a fool could see all that had changed when my mother died.

I lay my head on the tapestried cushion, my hand underneath it to lift it a little higher off the cold stone. I pulled the blanket over me, thoughts darting everywhere and then slowing, drifting…

'Ysabel, wake you.' Cecilia's voice gently prised me from a place of dreams where exhaustion was salved and worry smothered. 'You poor young thing, you're washed out.'

Her hand smoothed over my head. A faint flickering light glowed behind her, giving her the appearance of a religious vision in my sleepy state.

'Ysabel,' she asked. 'Where is Guy?'

I growled as I sat up, pulling the rucked surcoat down over my back, noting the candle further down the stair.

'I know not nor care. He is untrustworthy.'

Cecilia looked at me, her eyes dark circles in a face marked by shadowy lines. 'You say? Then you misjudge him to be sure.'

'He's Halsham's cousin, Ceci, and the man himself dogged our footsteps from Cazenay to Moncrieff.'

'I know he's Halsham's cousin but he is cut from different cloth I can assure you.'

'You think? He plans to join the Free Lancers as soon as we are safe. How can you trust someone who wishes to work under De Courcey's banner?'

'Ysabel, this is hardly the time to dispute Guy's future. When he has delivered you safely far from De Courcey, what he chooses to do with his life is none of our business. What matters is that you are alive and free.'

'Ceci', I snorted. 'I am in the lion's den. He has brought me straight into a lair from which I may not escape.

'That is untrue, Ysabel,' Gisborne's voice broke in. In the heat of argument, I had missed the sound of his footfall as he climbed the stair. 'If you had stayed in Walsocam where I left you, I would have taken you far from here where you could get to Wales or Ireland safely. But as always you acted impulsively and ill-advisedly.'

'*Lady* Ysabel…' I muttered.

'*Lady* Ysabel,' he sneered.

'Stop it,' hissed Cecilia. 'This serves neither of you. Ysabel, Guy is right. You should not have left Walsocam so precipitately.'

'But I needed to … my mother, you, my father…'

'Your father is of little use to your situation. In fact he could make it worse.'

My heart skipped as her words sank in. 'What do you mean, *of little use?*'

The church bells began to peel in the village and I realized they marked Vespers. Such a long dark night yet to follow…

'He is very frail, Ysabel. Immediately after Guy left to retrieve you from Cazenay, he and De Courcey had an argument. Everyone inside the Hall and out heard it. De Courcey wanted the debt paid in full; for his ownership of Moncrieff to be acknowledged in writing and that any valuables within your father's possession be handed over. Your father declared that he must retain something as the dowry for his daughter, that it was only right and proper and that she should not be condemned to penury because of her father's sore actions. He argued the demesnes of Moncrieff, including the castle, paid the debt. De Courcey objected, showing your father a paper that calculated each loss your father had made at dice, chess, even cockfighting and horse-races.'

Papa, you didn't forget me.

I could not help a choke in my throat. 'But why did he…'

Cecilia reached over and touched my hand, squeezing gently.

'Ysabel, he was bereft; a parlous grief that settled on him so that he seemed to know and feel nothing else. Common men would have been called mad.'

'Truly?'

'I think so. You must remember his adoration of your mother, almost an obsession. His heart broke when she died and he replaced one obsession with others. Drinking and gaming blotted his pain. It was only after he lost Moncrieff and after I chided him that reality began to set in. He tried to ignore De Courcey but the man is choleric and that last day in the Hall was frightful. He roared at your father, even drew his sword on him and your father screamed back. He was livid. I tell you, I have never ever seen Joffrey so incensed. I expect the anger was with himself more than anything, that he could treat Moncrieff with such lack of respect. I am sure he thought he cast dirt on your mother's memory.'

'What happened?'

I had an ugly image of my father shaking with disgust and distress, De Courcey's face ruddy, his bullish bulk rearing over the diminished form of Joffrey.

'Your father was gesticulating wildly and of a sudden he had a seizure. He fell straight down, awake but insensible. The infirmarian from the abbey diagnosed an apoplexy. Your father lost the power of speech, his face collapsed sideways and he lost the ability to walk or hold things in his hands. De Courcey allowed him to be taken to the Master Chamber and I have nursed him since, but he can barely eat, chokes even on liquids and is fading away. He is incoherent and yet I would swear there is recognition in his eyes when he looks at me … oh Ysabel…'

Tears ran down my cheeks as I remembered my sweet, detached father who had, all of his life, worshipped at the altar that was Lady Alaïs. This was a man who wrote poetry and I couldn't imagine him never being able to speak it aloud.

'He is dying,' I said.

I looked up at her and she met me with a steady, honest gaze.

'I think so. He is not yet quite ready to die but it will be no more than a month.'

'Do you think De Courcey knows that he is dying,' I asked.

Cecilia shrugged and sighed.

'Till yesterday I nursed him and would report only good things to the man, as it suited me to see him discomforted. I do not want him to think that all is going his way. I had hoped that you would return and that … well … that things might return to normal but it is a fool's dream, my dear. Your father is dying, Moncrieff is lost and for your own safety, you must leave. It was not what I intended but it is surely what must happen now. You must get away.'

'I *must* see him, Cecilia. I *must* let him know I came home.'

'Ysabel, they took me away from him and locked me in your mother's chamber and for all I know he might be…'

'He has been moved.' Gisborne butted in. 'When I left earlier, I searched all those parts of the castle I could get to and he is no longer in his chamber. It is De Courcey's own…'

Cecilia sucked in her breath.

'You were not seen?'

'I think not. But that De Courcey has taken the chamber is obvious. His accoutrements are everywhere.'

'You see, Ysabel?' Cecilia reached for my hand. 'It is pointless. We do not even know where…'

'I have found him. He is in one of the cells.'

Cecilia and I both spoke together.

'No! Did you…'

'Is he…'

'He is wrapped in a fur over a wadding of straw. I did not speak to him, merely saw him through the spyhole.'

I grabbed Cecilia's arm. My father deserved my care, he had not forsaken me after all and for that I was glad. I had no doubt he suffered terribly for his weakness, existing in some dark place where he was unable even to scream or cry with grief.

'Ceci, he will starve with no one to feed him. And what about water? De Courcey is a murderer! I must see my father.'

Cecilia jumped up.

'Not now, Ysabel, you must stay here and I must return to the Lady Chamber, but I will come again before Matins. Please Guy, watch her. She must not go to the cells.'

She grabbed the folds of her *bliaut* and threaded back down the stair, whispering as she left, 'We will plan when I return.'

The candle flame jumped as she passed and then settled as silence filled the space.

'You *must* leave, Ysabel. Without seeing your father.' Gisborne shifted on the stair and lowered himself to sit above me.

I shook my head. If I thought back, I could see that the moment I opened that fated packet in Cazenay I released a plague of curses. I was Pandora. Every step of my journey home had been filled with deepening distrait.

'I can't leave Papa to die alone. No matter what mistakes he has made, no matter that I should hate him and want him to fester and rot in a dungeon, I cannot. Others might say let him fade in the knowledge of what he has done, let him suffer the pain. But I cannot.'

I looked toward that tiny jumping flame that defied the shifting air within the passage, standing strong and lighting dark corners. Somewhere I could hear dripping water and wondered if it rained outside. It often rained in the fens, it was a childhood memory.

'My father is *in* my heart.' The words came out softly. 'My mother is a *part* of my heart and so is Moncrieff, and yet you and Cecilia ask me to abandon everything after coaxing me on this journey anyway. Why did I bother acceding to your wishes? It would have been safer to remain in Cazenay. What was the point of bringing me home? You *must* have known things had changed. Halsham knew for a surety.'

'He did not. He was returning from the Holy Land with the Free Lancers…'

'The Holy Land.' I gave a low, disbelieving grunt.

'Yes, the Holy Land. If you remember when you first met him. That aside,' Gisborne's deep tones floated down the stair. 'Whatever he knew until he reached Calais would have been old news; no more than I knew. In Calais of course, that changed when De Courcey arrived.'

'And what was the old news, Gisborne? That his employer had taken over Moncrieff?'

'No. But that he desired the estate, yes.'

'Was *I* part of the estate?'

'Not immediately.'

'When?'

'Halsham told me in Walsocam that De Courcey wanted you, that what I predicted had indeed happened. That by having you as his bride he would be fit to appear in the court of Richard as the son-in-law of Baron Moncrieff.'

I huffed out a disgusted breath.

'Ysabel, it gives me no pleasure to tell you any of this. It never has. But the final thing I will tell you is that I was offered money, a great deal, if I handed you over at Walsocam. I told Halsham that it was not possible as I had left you at Saint Eadgyth's by your choice. That we had disagreed over a personal issue and that you chose to stay within the priory for the moment.'

'And he believed you? I can't imagine he would be so ingenuous. Besides, how did he know you would be at Walsocam? That was a little fortuitous, surely?'

'It was a mistake on my part. He was passing through the village on his return to Moncrieff and saw me at the inn. I had almost purchased food enough for two, the words almost out of my mouth. It was luck on a grand scale that I had not spoken.'

'Luck?'

'Yes. Luck. The point is that I hoped to have returned you to Cecilia before any of this latest transpired. When you could perhaps have helped your father in his anguish and prevented his losses from accruing.'

'So you say.'

I stared at my hands – dirty hands with grimy fingernails. Nothing of the lady hung about me anymore.

'You do not believe me.'

Something in his tone made me look up. I could barely see anything of him, just a broad shadow blocking the stair, but for one brief moment I thought I detected defeat in his voice and it seemed so very wrong in such a man. I wished I could see his eyes but I could not. Instead I said the first thing that sped into my mind – my torn-apart, ill-guarded mind.

'I cannot see into your heart, Guy.'

The trite sentence was all I could think of to explain my ongoing disquiet and his reply was so cool my skin prickled.

'And yet, my *lady*, I have never allowed any harm to befall you. It seems to me that heart notwithstanding, I have fulfilled the task I was given. I saw you to Moncrieff and I can yet see you safely away. Remember I said I owed you my life? I will honour that.'

He shifted in the dark silence. His leather surcoat creaked and I heard something clink against stone – the dagger in his belt.

'You may not see heart in such a vow,' he continued. 'But then perhaps that is really not my problem. It is yours.'

He went to stand, as if to move past me – a gesture of dismissal, and I felt chastened. Part of me wanted to be angry at being made to feel so ungrateful and thus so petty. Because no matter what – jeweled girdles, pers-tinted *bliauts*, shelter and sustenance – all that aside, he had indeed seen me safe, had honoured his self-styled debt. Whether I approved of his manner of doing so was immaterial. I was in Moncrieff with Cecilia, and De Courcey had no idea.

A masterful stroke.

I shivered. The wind had strengthened outside, buffeting the tower. It sent a foraging party through the arrow loop where the fingers of the nasty draught tunneled and bit into my body. I pulled the clothing tighter and shuffled away from the opening.

'You are cold,' Gisborne observed.

'Cold, afraid, confused, desperate. All of those,' I muttered as my teeth clenched to stop an emerging shudder.

He stepped down, sitting between myself and the slit so that his presence warmed me. Just the feel of a body close to mine, a broad one that blocked the breeze was enough but I couldn't deny other things.

'Ysabel, you can see, can't you?' He took my hands and rubbed them between his own, chafing warmth into the tips. 'Very soon they will know that you are not within the priory. They will begin the hunt. I say you have just hours to leave. After that, it will be too late. We can follow the secret channels to the river and then head west, but it will be long before we are safe away from De Courcey's net and we shall have to hide in the forests like outlaws.'

'My father…'

'He will not know you even if you do see him.'

I sat weighing the danger.

'I agree then, I shall let you help me. But I must be allowed to farewell my father.'

'Ysabel…'

'Please.'

I turned to him and in the light of that tiny flame I could see the face of the man who had cared for me.

He leaned forward and kissed my forehead and it was as if the sun shone. I had put my faith in him and it seemed meet and right that he should touch me like a benediction. I lifted my face to his and our lips joined.

We made love with urgency, as if for the last time. There was a harshness to it. A rawness, flesh on stone, quick breaths. I laid my head on his chest as we regained our breath and whispered.

'Sir Gisborne, I did not want to but it seems I…' I stopped and cleared my throat.

Do not say it! Do not, Ysabel.

'I owe you an apology,' I prevaricated. 'You have been stalwart.'

His voice rumbled through his ribcage like once before.

'Then Ysabel, you must surely be able to see into my heart after all and know that I…'

We heard footsteps and hastily rearranged our clothes in time for Cecilia to appear and for us to act as if nothing had happened. But she barely looked at us.

'The castle is in uproar. The Baron rode in not long since – did you hear? – and ordered me taken to the Great Hall, demanding I tell him why you should choose sanctuary at Saint Eadgyth's Priory. I had no idea – it was the truth. Guy, have you set a false trail? Good for you, my dear, if you have.' She didn't wait for a reply. 'Whatever the case, he almost reduced me to ashes with the heat of his temper and left immediately. He has gone to Saint Eadgyth's to see for himself. A party had been sent much earlier by Halsham so you must go now, while they are occupied elsewhere. Hell will descend when he returns without you.'

'She understands, Cecilia.' Guy's hand pressed my waist from behind, 'and has agreed to leave.'

'Aah.' Ceci gave a relieved sigh. 'I am so glad, child.' She placed a small drawstring bag in my palm, curling my hand over it and squeezing. 'Your mother's comb, a necklet – the one you loved when you were small, do you remember? The rest I shall keep hidden until you can … until you are safe. But I have this – you must take it now.'

She passed over an object about the size of a man's palm.

'God's breath, Cecilia. How did you get it? I wanted to retrieve it from the Baron's room but with De Courcey taking the chamber for himself it was a risk.'

'I searched for it when I was nursing Joffrey. I had such a feeling about Moncrieff, that De Courcey would strip it bare to the bones, leaving nothing for Ysabel. It was in a coffer that was filled with Joffrey's clothing. It seemed like nothing should anyone have looked… a scrap of d'Aumiers silk. It could have been spare fabric to mend his chemises.'

'What is it?' I reminded them I was still there, sitting with the object in my palm.

'It's the book, Ysabel; the Saracen book.'

I unwrapped it swiftly for time was running away. As the silk slithered off I could feel the irregular surface of the cover and then it lay boldly in my hands in the dull light of the candle. An oval ruby nestled in the cover, as smooth as a wren's egg and surrounded by irregular shaped pearls. Gold filigree laced in and around so that the remarkable cover looked like a tile from an Arabian palace.

Lovely, delicate.

I opened it, the cover creaking, and there lay the unknown text, illustrated on every second leaf with a detailed miniature of Saracen life. It smacked of wealth, of privilege, as if it had fallen into the hands of thieves who were brazen enough to climb a sheikh's walls to secure it. Worse, it could have been Christian knights who pillaged some bastion in the Holy Land and then gamed it away to my father.

'It's worth a King's treasury, Ysabel.' Cecilia said.

'Indeed,' Gisborne added. 'And may be needed to pay your way. Now quickly, pack it and let us leave.'

I rolled it with haste and pushed it into the drawstring bag, shoving the latter down the front of my surcoat where a belt held it at my waist and prevented it from falling. 'My father,' I said as I jerked the belt tighter.

'Ysabel…' Cecilia frowned.

'No. I will go only when I have seen him.'

'Ysabel, he will be unable to speak to you and he may not even know you.'

Cecilia made no bones about my choice but I didn't care if Papa didn't know me or that he couldn't speak. It was to satisfy myself that I did this, to know that I had been daughterly. That I hadn't just run with my tail jammed between my legs like a frightened cur.

Briefly I wondered if I was delivering some sort of perverse message to Gisborne; saying see, this is how one fulfil's one's obligations to one's parent no matter what the parent has done. He had chosen to slice his father from his life with an incision deep into the heart. There was no room for compassion or care for a man who had left he and his mother to the whim of the Knights Templar.

But no, why would I be so specious? I was doing this for my mother and for me, no other reason; to satisfy the corner inside *my* soul that Lady Alaïs inhabited, not to win a point over my escort. Guy of Gisborne had lost his heritage, his mother and his father; so had I. And yet for some obscure reason, a reason I couldn't rationalize, I felt in my heart that his loss was worse than mine.

Was it because my mother had died in a richly appointed home provided by her loving husband? And that my home and heritage were only lost after my father became insane with grief? Gisborne had lost his mother in awful circumstances on the road, and penniless after his father, without a thought for their future, had followed his obsessive ambition. Thoughtless, selfish, cruel. But had my father been any less thoughtless?

I could hear my mother's voice.

'Ysabel,' she would say. 'Your father is just a man who lost his way. And by the very depth and breadth of his mistake I can measure how lost he is – a lovable fool who lives now in his own Purgatory. Is that not enough punishment?'

Oh yes, I thought, enough punishment.

'But Mama,' I would counter, 'is Gisborne's situation any different? His father gambled with his son's future. He trusted the wrong people to protect his family whilst he fought in the Holy Land. Ultimately his price was to contract leprosy and die. My father has an apoplexy and is dying by starvation. In each case, the fathers' children lost their inheritance. I think it is the same, what say you?'

'Perhaps the issues *are* no different,' Mama might say. 'But *you* can only do what gives you a form of inner peace at this time. Master Gisborne has acted in a way that was enabling for him. It is not for you to say what is right and what is wrong. This man after all, is trying to see you safe.'

And so I took Cecilia in my arms and hugged her.

'Ceci, place some flowers on her tomb. And do whatever you must to keep safe.'

I could not say I would be back for in truth I had no idea. But with no other word I pushed past her and leaped down the stair as if the devil licked my heels, passing the Lady Chamber and entering the unlit ways of Moncrieff's secret labyrinth.

I could hear Gisborne's steps behind me, close enough for him to touch my shoulder, to pull me back, to say *Don't do this. I know what fathers are like, you are a passionate fool.'* But no, instead he let me go on and I chose to believe he accompanied me because he must, because he would see me safe. The part of me that wanted to believe that he trod behind me because he might care for me was pushed away. This was not the moment to reflect on the progressions of our intimacy or our divergent attitudes. Being safe, keeping safe was the focus.

Moncrieff's passages were concealed in only one of its four towers. My grandfather had built the castle around a square bailey, furnishing each corner with a semicircular tower in the style of Saracen defensive structures. Such knowledge returned with the men of the First Crusade and my grandfather had used it, along with the men and the labour. A secret passage, concealed wall within wall, showing great foresight should Moncrieff ever be breached – *such* a secret that it lived and died within my family.

I wondered what had happened to those builders – the masons and carpenters. Their mouths must have been shut in some way or other for the passages to remain so concealed. I preferred not to think on the possible legacy of brutality that might line the stairwell, instead I thanked

God that it existed at all and that we, Guy and I, had a chance to leave the poisonous place that Moncrieff had become.

'Slow down, Ysabel. Hold,' Guy hissed.

I jumped.

Guy touched my shoulder. 'Just beware. Do not assume we are inviolable.' He pushed in front of me, taking my hand as he passed and I wanted him to keep holding because if I felt brave it was merely bluff and I wanted reassurance.

We progressed down the stair, Gisborne's candle flickering and almost gutting a dozen times but at the foot of the passage, he huffed the candle out and we were plunged into gloom, our eyes adjusting to seek darker shade on light; we proceeded slowly, he leading me like a child until we halted.

Hands cupped each of my shoulders, more softly on the arrow graze, and I looked up and saw the whites of his eyes. I dare say he hoped I might have reconsidered my decision on the downward flight but it was not to be. I nodded my head at him, my hand reaching up to lay over his knuckles.

'You must prepare yourself,' he whispered, and turned me toward the spy-hole.

I climbed onto a block of stone that had been positioned below the hole. The hard, chiseled walls chilled my body as I leaned into them, a freeze that hovered like a death wish. I positioned my eye over the hole and blinked to focus.

The cell was lit with a vague dancing flame from a cresset. The high window, barred and barred again made me wonder not for the first time just who my grandfather might have kept prisoner here because for sure they would never have escaped. I thought of the engineer who had designed the castle fortifications, of the labourers.

No.

As to my father ... he would never have imprisoned anyone and it seemed more than cruel irony that a chamber built by my grandfather should imprison his dying son.

Because he *was* dying. The rasping breath was a sure sign.

A month, Ceci? God's breath, it will be a day or less.

Fluids bubbled with each breath and I could envisage the flood in his chest as he struggled. There was no evidence of De Courcey's guard, the spy-hole looking straight to the door.

Papa lay huddled under a fur, a shrunken, wizened shape, no sign of the handsome husband and father. His skeletal face was shaded with stubble, an indication that Cecilia was no longer his nurse. His face had indeed slipped sideways, his mouth twisted and open and a shine in the light of the flame indicating he dribbled. His hair lay about him, filled with bits of straw.

Mama, how you would hate this! You would attack De Courcey with dogs and a pike for this wretched treatment of your husband ... you would hang the man's remains...

Joffrey began to cough – a wet, choking sound and it horrified me. Gisborne's hand slid up my back and I straightened a spine that had begun to sag.

'Father,' I called. Gisborne's fingers curled to a fist. 'Father!'

'Ysabel!' He went to pull me down.

'No! Just let me speak to him.'

I pushed him away and looked back into the cell. My father had stopped coughing and gone very still.

'Papa...'

What could I say? What would matter to him as he lay dying?

'Mama waits, Papa. She waits and all will be well. All manner of things will be well.'

Did he hear me? How could he show me? He could not, of course, beyond his breathing which had quieted, his chest ceasing its frenzied rise, slowing and calming. There was a rattle of metal and footsteps and I looked to the door. Keys rattled in the lock and a guard pulled the entry open.

'Give 'im the rites, priest. 'Ee needs 'em fast.'

'He should not even be here. It is a disgrace in the eyes of God,' the priest barked as he walked into the cell.

'Baron De Courcey wanted 'im 'ere. 'E don't care if the chap's dyin'. Not sure it matters to the chap either. 'E'd 'ardly know if 'e was in 'eaven, 'ell or in between.'

Anger began to boil inside me but Gisborne's bunched fist tapped twice against my back reminding me of the need for caution. I cast an anguished look at him but he just shook his head, his mouth a thin, uncompromising line.

'I am distraught that this must be,' said the priest. 'Leave us.'

The guard, an older man whose face I didn't recognize, turned away. 'Won't lock the door then. 'E 'aint goin' anywhere.'

'As you wish…' the priest muttered, seating himself by Papa's side.

This man I did know. Brother John, our family's dear friend from the tiny church of Saint Agatha in the village and who had seen many births, deaths and marriages within the domain. I recalled how he had become a part of our family. He was found sleeping in the old hermit's hut and had been invited to take food in our Hall. It transpired that as penance for a perceived transgression, Brother John had left the monastery to which he belonged to walk the length of England, begging for food and shelter. My father asked him what he had done that was so bad he cast himself adrift from his religious brothers.

'I lusted after my work,' Brother John replied.

'What work?'

My father had been intrigued, the priest's educated voice a sign of something more than a mere monk working in a monastery garden.

'I was in charge of our scriptorium, I was considered by many to be a gifted scribe. In time, my humility was overtaken by my ego and I began to work for my own satisfaction rather than for God.' He laughed, a rueful sound. 'Hubris. Suffice to say, Baron, I lost my way. To walk is my personal penance. I have been walking for many months now.'

Brother John however, walked no further than Moncrieff. I was born whilst he ate in the Hall and he stayed to christen me in the miniature church that was Saint Agatha's. Easter followed and a number of village weddings and burials occurred. In time, there was always something, some soul to be helped, a kind word to be spoken and Brother John became part of the fabric of our lives. Watching him now, I thanked God. This man was my father's friend.

'Dear Joffrey,' I heard him say as he reached for my father's hand. 'My dear, dear man…'

I sucked in a breath to call to him but Gisborne's hand slid over my mouth.

'No. Don't confound the issue further. The less who know of us the better.'

I shook my head violently.

'Ysabel, enough. *Now* you do as *I* say.' He tugged me down off the stone. 'You saw your father and God help us, you spoke to him. Now we go or your freedom is forfeit.'

I pulled away from his grasp but he was tenacious.

'*Now,* Ysabel!'

A hoar frost could have sprung from his tone and of course he was right, so I allowed him to tow me back to the fork in the passage and the grille, my heart weighing heavy on my toes. He lifted the iron frame and looked out and I realised how much I owed him for who else would have made sure that it was greased well enough not to squeak should we need to use it.

'Into the reeds and wait.'

He legged me up over the sill and I flopped into the sedge, crouching until he joined me so quietly I would swear he had magicked through the walls.

Moncrieff connected to the lakeside by a causeway – stacked stone creating a track to the shore and at the end abutting the castle a portcullis and barbican to protect from incursion. The causeway had been known to flood at times of high-water, rendering Moncrieff a solitary islet – a place redolent of myth and legend I would think when I was younger, as mists rolled across the water.

I looked out at the moonless surrounds now and the self-same ribbons of mist twined tendrils up into the air, strands drifting around sedge and reed to thicken and thin. In its very opacity lay our safety and we edged forward, feeling our way around the walls. Occasionally a foot would slip on the greasy rocks and slide under the water but if there were ripples they were concealed and we barely made a sound.

We reached the causeway and moved underneath the planks of the drawbridge where we could sit and take stock. The nightlife piped and splashed spasmodically and from within the castle there was but the bark of a dog, a door slamming shut, some heavy footsteps and a murmur of voices.

Guy once again pulled at me and we began to move beneath the bridge, easing onto the side of the causeway. The water level was low enough for us to tread with dry feet – it had obviously been a dry winter and spring and I wondered at the future harvest with such conditions and what the drinking water would be like, because Moncrieff folk mattered.

We only had to wade through water once and in a matter of moments we had broached the shore. The bell of Saint Agatha's rang out for Matins and it cut through me like a knife for I believed it was tolling not just as a farewell to my father but to me.

'We must move away from the road,' Guy no longer whispered and it was like a shout after the night of secrets. 'We need horses. Without them…'

Without them we are easy prey.

We slipped into the fog, wraiths of the darkling hours, the air moist and heavy. I lost all sense of direction and followed dutifully behind like a faithful hound, Gisborne's tall body a mere shadow. We walked for perhaps twenty turns of Thea's bracelet, pushing through shrubs and under trees. I fingered the quaint knotted string out of a desperate need for blessings and jumped when Guy broke the silence, my mind far from the lake and by the side of my father with Brother John.

'Here,' Guy indicated ahead.

A squat shape emerged through the fog and I recognised Brother John's hermit's hut. Decrepit walls and roof still stood although it was much lower to the ground. Of any door there was no sign – if there had ever been one.

Guy stepped aside to allow me to enter, having brushed cobwebs from the doorframe. The mist had thinned enough for a paling night sky to be observed. We had been lucky, a league or two away from Moncrieff and in the last moments of night.

'We rest,' Guy folded onto the ground and I joined him. He dug into the pouch at his waist and pulled out a crust of bread, passing it to me. I broke it in half and handed back the largest piece.

'What now?' I fingered the dry bread.

'Horses,' he replied, chewing. 'I will have to steal them and hope we are well into the forest before the alarm is raised. De Courcey will know it is you after he discovers your absence at Saint Eadgyth's.'

'And you, Gisborne? Why should he not think it is you on the second horse?'

He looked back at me; a steady gaze.

'Oh of course,' I raised an eyebrow. 'You told Halsham a falsehood. Wither do *you* journey, Sir Gisborne?'

He swallowed the bread. 'To London.'

'Really?' I felt sick, my stomach curling. 'And the second horse?'

'You have a guide – a fellow you hired at Great Yarmouth. The Sisters at Saint Eadgyth's will confirm it.'

My mouth had filled with a sour taste.

'You think of everything.'

And as he went to reply, I bolted to the door to throw up what little I had eaten at Moncrieff, puking until all I expelled was foul yellow froth. I groaned and wiping my mouth with some grass, walked to the other side of the clearing, my arms wrapped around my middle.

'Father's dead.'

I stared at the unfurling leaves on an oak tree. Ironic that it symbolized a rebirth whilst my father died.

'Yes.' Gisborne spoke gently.

'Do you think he knew I was there?'

In my own heart, I thought he did. The way his breathing changed, and the way he became so still, but I was afraid to enunciate the idea to Gisborne in case it was repudiated. It seemed important to hold onto such a feeling.

'I think so – he grew very quiet,' he replied.

'You sensed that?'

'His breathing was laboured before you spoke.'

'Perhaps he just moved closer to death.'

'Perhaps ... but I think not.'

His words were balm even though he might be saying what he thought I needed to hear. Whatever the case, it was kind.

'I've lost everything. My mother, my father and my heritage and as quickly as a lightning strike.'

'It gets a little better over time, Ysabel.'

'You think?' I spun round. 'Enlighten me. How?'

The anger rang out, the bile in my belly as vicious as the acid that tainted my words. And then I understood.

'I'm sorry. Of course you know. That was stupid of me.'

He passed me a sprig of greenery.

'Wild mint. Chew a leaf and then spit it out. It will make your mouth feel fresher.'

The mint revived me. If there had been honey as well, a paste of the two would have been even better.

'Where did you find it?'

He indicated either side of the door.

'Our hermits obviously knew the value of herbs. There are others ... rosemary, rue, borage, thyme. Maybe more.'

'Guy, I'm sorry I was so tactless.'

The light grew brighter with each passing moment and I marked the exhaustion in his face, guessing my own was little better. His hair was tangled and stubble threatened to become a black beard. His eyes crinkled at the edges.

'It is of no account. But...' he added wickedly. 'We are now equals, my lady.'

He bowed over my hand.

A smile stretched on my own face, coming from God knows where on this day of death and realization.

'Indeed, Sir Gisborne. Equals.'

'Come, Ysabel.' He took my hand in his own and it felt as normal as if I were his wife. 'We need to hide. Are you a little eased?'

My stomach had ceased its up and down motion and I thought I could manage to sit in the dark shelter without racing outside again and so I nodded and let him draw me within.

He passed me watered wine in the stoppered flask Cecilia had given us.

'Was it worth it, do you think? Seeing your father?'

I needed no time to ponder.

'God, yes. I was so rancorous. I hated him and yet when I saw him I could forgive him everything. He suffered his own indignity and pain – it was obvious. I can't blame him for what happened any more than one can blame a maladjusted fool for opening a hen house and letting the fowl fly. Father was maladjusted, Guy. My mother's death had tipped him over the edge of reason and he was a lost cause. What he did, if you can believe it, came from loving someone *too* much. So I can forgive him that. I can imagine one could love someone too much. Do you agree?'

Gisborne raised an eyebrow.

'I am not sure I would know.'

No, of course. Why would you?

'Why would I hate him? It is not going to give me back Moncrieff, is it?'

'No...'

I thought on his own situation.

'Do you think you might have forgiven your own father in time if you had seen him?'

He sucked down a huge mouthful of the watered wine and I suspect he wished it were something far stronger.

'On the contrary. If I had seen him, it would have been all I could do not to...'

'Guy!'

'No. Think on it, Ysabel. *My* father did nothing out of love. Least of all provide his wife and child with surety. He was a man I did not admire. He was cruel to my mother, even though she brought a huge dowry to their marriage. Sometimes both she and I wondered if that was the sole reason he married her, because Gisborne was hardly a monied estate when the marriage contract was drawn up. My lady mother had no say in the matter as her father, a lesser noble, saw the marriage as an expediency. My father was highly regarded by Henry when he was younger and my Angevin grandfather liked the idea that such nobility should sit around his own family. But in truth, my father got me upon my mother and then lost interest. He was pleased he had an heir but she never conceived again and I could ask any number of questions about *that.'*

Gisborne had never been so open, not without me soliciting, and I watched him closely as he spoke. His face sharpened, the planes slicing to a knife-edge in the emerging dawn light; a face writ large with dislike. His voice dipped and rose with a hard then soft timbre depending on whether he spoke of his father or mother. I began to see the many layers beneath that hard outer skin and relished that he shed them with me. Did that not bespeak some sort of trust between us?

'He removed himself from me, his son. I was left to my mother to educate. She organized for the priest to teach me letters. It's where I learned to love books, a rare enough thing to be sure. She organized for the steward to teach me to ride, for our master-at-arms to teach me the bow and arrow, to wrestle, to throw a knife. It was as well he had travelled and fought across the Middle Sea. He knew much and but for the fact that he had lost half an arm, would never have come our way. I thank the Lord he did. Edwin was more of a father than mine ever was.'

'Then what happened to Edwin when the Templars took Gisborne?'

'They employed Edwin, realising full well that he *was* the estate, far more so than my father. He wept the day my mother and I were turned off.'

He shook his head and looked down at his hands.

'Ah Ysabel, so much to regret. So much to ha...'

'Hate? Is that what you would say?'

I lay my own hand on his.

He didn't reply.

'My word, Sir Gisborne,' I chastised. 'I should not like to be someone you hate. You hate for life I should think.'

'My father is owed such, Ysabel, I thought you would understand.'

I grabbed at the fraying closeness about us.

'I do, Guy. I swear.'

Just don't hate me the same way.

He flipped his palm up and closed his fingers around my wrist, pulling me toward him and I hoped I smelled of mint and nothing else.

'Ysabel ... you are the kind of young woman my mother would have l ... liked.'

Is that your way of saying something else, Gisborne? Do you grow fond of me or am I still someone who is like a horsefly, driving you to distraction?

'When I was at Saint Eadgyth's, they told me of her. I would have liked her, I am sure,' I said.

He leaned forward then and pressed his chin against my forehead. We sat very still, his hands over mine. He brushed his lips over my eyebrows and sat back.

'Ysabel, I must try and find horses. I beg of you, do not move. Do not leave the hut. No matter what.'

He stooped under the sagging doorframe and I followed, leaning there as he walked across the clearing, his shoulders carrying my whole life upon them. He turned at the edge of the coppice and lifted his arm, the smallest smile playing around his lips.

Ah yes, Gisborne. For better or worse.

CHAPTER ELEVEN

Loneliness is an uncomfortable thing. It burrows into one's awareness like a tick, creating discomfort to begin with and then a larger and larger pain. I sat as the daylight strengthened, initially glad of the solitude. With Guy gone, I could drop my defenses. Cry if I wanted, reminisce, or better, think of nothing. The trouble is I could not think of nothing.

I wept for my mother and father and then for myself, but outside birds were chirping and forest creatures moved about. In the gloom of this crumpled hideaway, it was easy to allow the sorrows of the past to tunnel in further and so I moved to sit against the doorframe in a beam of weak sun, allowing its mediocre warmth to carry me to better places.

I set thoughts on my family and my loss aside, watching a small brown wren hopping across the glade and flirting with shadow. She chirruped and I dug into the small belt purse for the remains of the crust. I tossed the crumbs and she moved closer, bright-eyed and confident and I wanted to assume at least part of her joy of life.

'Where is your partner, little wren?' I asked. She gave no sign of having heard me, just bobbed here and there, scooping up the crumbs with dainty dexterity.

My partner has gone and left me, little bird. But he says he will return and it won't be too soon, I confess.

Till now, Gisborne had eased my fears. I might have laid claim to a certain amount of bravado but in essence I was a coward; such a spoiled young woman who had suddenly been confronted with a destiny that terrified her and would not admit to her weakness, instead lashing out at others. I think he understood my fears because at some point he had experienced that same trepidation.

But there is a difference, Ysabel. He uses hate to propel him on. Shall you do the same?

Who could I hate, I wondered? I had forgiven my father, so that left De Courcey and Halsham but I could do nothing about either except flee. Perhaps it was hate that propelled me so earnestly but in a moment of bleak honesty I thought it was fear. I wondered what happened to Guy's venomous hatred for his father now the man was dead. Who would he focus on?

That traitorous voice in my head whispered: *For sure, it won't be De Courcey and Halsham...*

The sun had moved swiftly and hung overhead, still pale and winsome – the kind from which a fine drizzle is sure to emerge, especially here in the fens. The wren took precipitous flight at my feet as if something had disturbed her ... gone in a moment. I sat very still. All around had grown quiet, it seemed as though every living thing held its breath.

And then I heard the sound in the distance, not a league away; the baying of lymers and I could feel the blood racing from my face to pump through my heart. Lymers could sniff out anything. My father had used them to drive quarry toward the hunters. He loved the grand dogs, proud of their ability to seek and drive a hind to the kill. He had a pair of alaunts as well, ferocious beasts that he used for boar hunting. But I was sure the sounds I could hear, the baying that ripped through the forest were lymers and if I had a choice I would rather the lymers hunted me than to have my throat shredded by the alaunts.

I jumped up, the small book slipping to one side under my tunic.

'I beg of you, do not move. Do not leave the hut. No matter what.' Guy's words tugged at me, holding me back. The dogs' baying echoed across the forest. If I stayed, I would be caught. If I ran I would have a fighting chance... if I could make it to a stream where my trail could be hidden.

I am sorry, Gisborne.

I began to run.

The daylight had shifted the forgotten puzzle that was Moncrieff's green ways back into clear focus. If I ran *that* way, past the oak, and kept straight on, I knew I would meet a stream and I set off, fleet of foot, hoping I would meet Gisborne, that I could leap on a horse and we could gallop far beyond the hunting pack.

I ducked under branches, tripped over roots, moving quickly, trying to be mindful of my surroundings and then I glimpsed the rivulet, saw the dull sheen of its surface in the watery light. I pushed along its banks, running ever upstream, looking behind with every second stride but heading west and realizing with a sinking heart that Gisborne might not find me, that I was alone and must save myself this time.

I climbed over tree roots that sank themselves deep into the river edge and noticed a large fallen willow whose branches lay well out into the water and thought if I could move along the trunk to drop into the river and swim upstream for a distance, the lymers might lose my scent.

I edged along the riverbank, pushing through sedge. One more bole of an enormous beech to skirt around and I was...

'Lady Ysabel of Moncrieff!'

An iron grip fastened on my arm as someone growled and a blade was held to my throat.

No, no, no!

'Are you running away? What *will* Baron De Courcey think?'

I hated that voice. Hated it beyond belief. Hate was here, by my side. It was my friend; it would support me. I struggled and the point of the dagger nicked my throat.

'Enough.'

Both my arms were grasped and twisted behind my back.

'Cedric, give me rope!'

Rope was passed and my wrists were tied and I was turned toward my captor.

Robert Halsham grinned at me.

'Hello,' he said, his voice falsely friendly. 'I'll wager you didn't expect to meet me here.'

I deigned not to reply.

'Oh come now, Ysabel. You can't play the high and mighty lady now. You're trussed and ready to be dispatched to the Baron. Time to step down off your high horse.'

Still I refused to be drawn.

'I have to say the Baron will like your dutiful silence. He hates opinionated women.'

How did you find me? How did you know?

He walked around me, still grinning and I recalled once again that painted image of Beelzebub.

'Do you wonder how I found you? How I knew where you were?'

I closed my eyes and turned away but he grabbed me and twitched me back.

'You'll like this, Ysabel. I ran into Gisborne. I gave him a last chance, blood being thicker than water. I said to him that if he told me where you were, I would allow him to ride away on a mount provided by me, with money provided by me to a position provided by me. If he did not then I would make sure the Baron knew of his perfidy and his attempted murder upon myself. And that dear Cuz, says I, will be the end of your onward and upward journey, end of everything.'

The bastard grinned at me before continuing.

'He debated for the time it takes to lengthen a stirrup leather. As he did exactly that, he told me about you and then left for London with a bag full of money tucked in his belt and a spot of duty as one of the King's best.'

Gisborne, you did not. Please God, no.

My heart cracked but I would not give Halsham the pleasure of seeing me so hurt. I drew myself up and sneered at him.

'Gisborne is cut from the same cloth as you, Halsham. What you say is no surprise. It is why I have been running. I knew he would betray me. It was a given and I knew I must get away.'

'You say.' Halsham's sarcasm stripped bark off trees. 'Horses, Cedric,' he called.

A horse was led up and I was bundled into the saddle, feet thrust through stirrups. As I had been thrust up and over, the hood covering my knotted hair fell off and the horse's hooves shifted and ground it into the muddy riverbank. Halsham grabbed the reins, passing them to Cedric who was not a Moncrieff man that I remembered and for a mere moment I wondered what my father's men thought of this new situation or if they had cleverly vanished into the backdrop of village life, subtly withdrawing their services from men that they surely could never respect. Suddenly the thought that there might be a hidden group of dissenters who might help me gave me strength.

'Lead her,' Halsham ordered. 'I shall follow behind.'

Cedric clicked his tongue and jerked the reins and the horse tossed his head, following irritably.

I gripped with my knees, my balance wrong with hands tied behind, an ignominious position that began to fuel something nasty. Fury began to flow like spring sap. At Halsham. At God.

How can You allow this? Whatever have I done to deserve such things as You have delivered?

Brother John had always spoken of the magnitude of God's love, of how we, His sheep, were cared for and protected by the majesty of such affection. I swore. If God loved me, He'd never have allowed my parents to die or Moncrieff to be lost. Such 'majesty' would never have allowed a lamb to fall foul of wolves like Halsham or De Courcey.

'You're the very picture of a woman scorned, Lady Ysabel,' Halsham mocked. 'Do you fret for the loss of Gisborne?'

Gisborne. The traitor

'You are wrong,' I straightened my shoulders until they were as rigid as an axe handle. 'I do not pine over the loss of men like Gisborne, just as I would not fret over your loss should it happen. There are some things simply not worth *fretting* over. My freedom and property are entirely different.'

'Your freedom is in De Courcey's hands and I for one would not fuss myself if he uses those hands to induce a change in your manner.'

Halsham's voice betrayed such arrogance, it was all I could do not to rant. But his next comment stepped on the burning wick of my temper.

'As to your property, as you say, that is another thing entirely.'

I tried to turn but could only glimpse his horse's nose on my hindquarter. 'What say you, Halsham? Your comment is tiresomely oblique.'

He laughed.

'By God De Courcey's in for some sport with you.' He kicked his horse up by my side. 'I mean simply that you need not be concerned about your position.'

I had learned in a short space of time to hide any expression from this loathsome boil and replied in a barely interested manner. 'You say. Really,' shifting my body away from him as we rode.

'Indeed, Lady Ysabel. I *do* say. And whilst I would that I could tell you more, I must not. The Baron and your father will make it clear to you…'

My father! Halsham doesn't know! He doesn't yet know my father is dead.

He also seemed unaware I had been within the castle. Not unless Gisborne had held forth and it seemed he had not.

As if it mattered.

We had regained the road to Moncrieff by now and its ramparts loomed ahead. The sky had darkened still further and dampness began to eat into my clothes. Mizzle drifted down like a veil, blurring the outlines of my home, of the place where lay my parents. I cursed Fate and Guy of Gisborne. I cursed God.

By now, I should be galloping on horseback through the woods and westward, ever further from the home that wasn't mine anymore. We clattered along the stony way, the hooves beating a dirge, until the sound changed and we moved onto the wooden bridge so lately passed beneath. Moncrieff's pale stone appeared grey and uncompromising and its foursquare shape with rounded corner towers, so dearly loved in the past, now threatened another sort of life.

We walked under the raised portcullis, men gathering as we halted. All were in the hated black surcoats of the Free Lancers and I could see no familiar face, not one, my heart sinking as I gazed at the rough cut henchmen before me.

Cedric dismounted and held my horse. Halsham threw his legs over his horse's wither and slid down, approaching me with a knife in his hands, reaching up to cut the bonds that had begun to chafe.

'Is the Baron returned?' he asked as he took me by the arm and helped me dismount.

'No sir.' Some lackey who held a saddled horse, spoke up. 'None are back yet.'

'God's blood, Ysabel. He's going to be livid when he finds he has ridden to Saint Eadgyth's for nothing.'

He held my arm tightly as if he thought I should make a break for the bridge and freedom.

'Aidan, to horse man, and get onto the road to Saint Eadgyth's and inform the Baron that Lady Ysabel has joined us at Moncrieff.'

At that, a low burble filled the courtyard as men eyed me curiously. Some nudged each other and lewd comment bandied about.

'Enough!' yelled Halsham. 'Show the lady the respect she deserves as chatelaine of the castle in her departed mother's place. Aidan, get you gone! Did you not hear the order? The rest of you to your posts. And lower the portcullis until the Baron returns.'

He pulled me after him and all I could hear were the hoof beats of the departing mount, the grinding of the gear that lowered the portcullis and men shifting to their duties. No children running to and fro, no banter and laughter, no poultry and dogs, no women, nothing of Moncrieff life as I remembered. This was now a stronghold, a place where armies met and melded and I shook my head as we climbed from the bailey to Moncrieff's Great Hall on the first floor.

Each step took me back one year and then another. By the time we had passed through what my father called the Triumphal Arch, I was revisiting all the memories of a childhood. The arch was my father's folly – carved and fluted as if it were an entrance to a great Norman cathedral. He added it to the Hall on marrying the Lady Alaïs because he believed bringing her home to Moncrieff was tantamount to a triumph. But it was a pretension that arch, like so much of my father's life.

Even after so long away, I found the Hall glowing with light. My mother was a creature of the sun, and unaccustomed to the subtle light of England and the fens in particular, she had the walls of all the chambers within the castle whitewashed. She hated the rushes strewn across other halls and would require the staff to wash the timbered surfaces daily. She burned dried herbs in the giant hearth, insisting that aromatic wood be used to ameliorate the smell of bodies and food. She banned dogs from the Hall and expected a degree of manners and behavior at her table. In all she gave Moncrieff an air of sophistication and gentility that it may never have had otherwise.

Sadly that is where her legacy now ended … with the whitewashed walls. The floors reeked of rancid food and waste and no one had cleaned them for some time. The tables were littered with the remains of God knows how many previous meals and the hearth was filled with a detritus of cold embers, no fire having been laid. Mercifully, the walls seemed clean, the giant shutters hanging wide, the opaque glass my father had insisted be fitted to each and every casement in the Hall shining dully.

Beyond the Hall was a passage not unlike a cloister, vaulted by simple stone arches and leading to two chambers; one was the lord's room, the Master Chamber and the other, the Lady Chamber. Halsham led me to my mother's door and I prayed that Cecilia, no doubt still immured there, would not give away my secrets.

'There is a friend of your late mother's in residence, the Lady Cecilia Fineux of Upton. She stayed on after your mother died to help your father.'

'But not enough to prevent your garrison from soiling Moncrieff's Hall, obviously.' Tart rhetoric was bound to find its way out sooner or later. 'Or is it that the Baron will not let her maintain my mother's high standards. Then again, perhaps the Baron and his cohorts are unsophisticated and would not know the difference between a dog's kennel and a clean Hall.'

Halsham flushed red.

'Be careful, Lady Ysabel. You tread on thin ice.'

He ordered the armed man at the door to turn the key and I was pushed inside, the door locking behind me.

Cecilia sat at the window, an embroidery frame on her lap and she turned as I stumbled into the room. That the door was shut was a mercy because her face collapsed and she whispered 'No!'

She ran to gather me into her arms and hold me tight. I had thought I would cry but in fact another sensation began to climb from my toes. I could feel it hardening blood in my veins, choking emotion, almost strangling life. I became an ice maiden in those few short moments in Cecilia's arms. Not because of her – not at all. If not for her, I would have had no chance. She kept a tiny corner of the ice-maid's heart warm – just a miniscule patch of life that would sustain me when there was nothing else.

She rocked me back and forth and hummed a beautiful melody that rose and fell with her movement. Finally I held her away and moved to look out the window into the bailey. It was indeed home to a garrison. Men passed before my sight, all in livery, all busy, leading horses, carrying saddlery and armour, carting water and fodder. A small group lined up and faced an archery butt, shooting with long bows that they handled like the kings' archers they were.

As I watched them, I recalled Harry's murder, the arrows shrieking through the air to pierce his body. I turned around.

'The man is wily.'

'De Courcey?'

'No. Halsham. De Courcey I do not know. But Halsham is a born traitor. He will sell half his soul to the Devil and half to God and then bankrupt them both.'

'Strong words, my dear, and I confess you might be right.' She moved to the fire and kicked at a smouldering log. 'But tell me, I was resting in the knowledge that you were safe and free. How came you to be caught and where is Guy?'

'Huh,' an empty laughed echoed from my corner. 'Halsham's cousin, the Gisborne, sold me out. For a bag of money and a position of note in London.'

Her veined hand flew to her chest, rings clinking against each other.

'I do *not* believe you.'

'It is true. Halsham took immense pleasure in expanding on the detail and as you know the Devil is in *that*. Halsham found me west of the hermit's hut and no one but Gisborne knew I was there. Not even you.'

The floor tilted at that moment and I reached back to one of the hanging carpets. Its dense pile cushioned fingers that clutched in despair.

'God but I am tired, Ceci. Tired of everything.' I plopped onto a coffer against the wall, hanging my head in my hands. 'I am done for. There is no way out now. De Courcey will have his way and I am powerless.'

I had not heard Cecilia move close and her hands ran through my hair. The tender brushing should have succoured me but instead it raised images of Gisborne and I making love and I knew in that minute that my heart had been completely shattered.

Broken into a thousand pieces.

'Enough for now,' she said. 'A bath, food and sleep and then we shall talk. I shall not let De Courcey near until you are ready.'

I nodded my head; no words, just dryness on my palate like the ashes of a long dead fire, all flames and warmth quenched and done for now.

'But Ysabel,' Ceci took my chin in her hand, raising it so that I must look her in the eye. 'You are wrong. Whatever *you* might think, Guy did not betray you.'

She let my chin go to move to the door and shout for a bath.

He did, Ceci, and I know hate now. Such hate. It shall stand me in good stead.

The bath cleaned me if nothing else. Cecilia washed my hair before I stepped in, lathering it in a herbal essence that gathered away the oil and sweat, and then I sank into the bath water feeling neither warmth nor succour, merely indifference. She tactfully left me alone to wash myself, dry and dress – retiring to another part of the chamber with distaff and a basket of wool, humming that same ethereal melody. It reminded me of the cantos in one or other of the religious establishments on my journey. Thoughts racketed immediately to Gisborne and hate brought forth a warm flush, a force to be reckoned with, a wild beast smelling blood, a madman seeking murder.

God!

'The clothes,' I slid my hands over soft woolen folds the colour of honey. 'Where did they come from?' The words raised memories of an inn and a midnight tinted gown and I shivered. I placed a woven girdle around, a knotted silk thing, and it reminded me of Thea's bracelet which hung abjectly damp on my wrist.

'Your mother.' Cecilia dropped the spindle into the basket with the hank of wool she had spun and looked at me, assessing my body, grey eyes running up and down. 'You are of a size. Now come to the fire and let me comb out your hair.'

As she combed, so I smoothed fingers over the folds of the gown, looking down at feet shod in embroidered kid slippers.

I walk in your shoes, my mother, and I need you to guide my steps.

Cecilia plaited the now dry hair, leaving it to hang down my back, placing a light linen veil over my head with a twisted filet of linen to hold it in place. She had left me to my thoughts as she worked and I was grateful because I had no wish to talk. Odd, because I wanted to tell her Father had died, wanted to talk about my mother. And most traitorously, I wanted to talk about Gisborne, to tell her that he had broken my heart and destroyed my faith.

The door rattled and a guard entered with a platter of food and I recognized the smell of frumenty and fresh griddle cakes and there was a jug of watered wine. The guard was dressed in the livery of the Free Lancers and as he bent to put the platter on a table, I noticed he was a fresh young man, pleasant of face, and it seemed strange because I expected every man in this place to be rough cut, to mirror Gisborne's opinion of De Courcey … the *'moneyed thug.'*

'Get help and carry the bath away,' Cecilia ordered. 'Do it swiftly. The Lady Ysabel would like to eat and then sleep and is unable to do that if the chamber is prone to people walking in and out as if this were the bailey.'

'Yes milady,' he backed out, somewhat tremulously I felt, and I laughed.

'You have a way, Ceci. Even mercenaries are scared of your tongue.'

She smiled but slid the expression away and replaced it with a gorgon's scowl as the fellow hurried back in with an older man. In moments the bath had gone, a little water slopped here and there, and the door locked once more.

'You ordered food for me.'

I touched the top of the frumenty and a skin slipped along as I dragged my finger across the surface.

'No, I didn't.'

Not De Courcey, not yet.

'No,' she knew what I was thinking. 'Not him. It can only be Halsham. Perhaps he sees you need nourishing, Ysabel.'

'I would need no nourishing if he and his lord hadn't chased me across France and half of England and stolen my home.'

My voice could have cut meat with its sharpness.

'Eat the food, my dear. You are in need.'

My stomach could take very little but welcomed what I did eat. The frumenty comforted, sliding down easily, honey sweetening it. Cecilia poured wine from her own flagon, no water, better than most I had tasted lately and as I drank, the door rattled, the key turned and Ceci swung round with a vast sigh of exasperation.

The guard, my food deliverer, stepped gingerly into the room but before he could speak, she hammered him with her wrath. Come more from my situation, I thought, than the fellow's apparent ineptitude.

'I asked you all to leave the Lady Ysabel to sleep. She is ill and must rest undisturbed. Are you dumb as well as deaf that you don't understand?'

He flushed. 'I beg your pardon, my Lady Cecily…'

'Lady *Cecilia.*'

He flushed.

'Lady Cecilia, I'm sorry. But Sir Robert wishes you to join him in the Hall momentarily to discuss meal requirements for the castle.'

'Well! I would be of a mind to say no if I wasn't so sick and tired of being immured in here for the last few days. His manners are inexorable of course. He should have come himself.'

A weak smile traced across the guard's face, discomforted and ill at ease with the termagant that was Cecilia. He indicated the passage.

'My lady.'

'At least Lady Ysabel can sleep undisturbed now, can she not, young man?'

He nodded. 'Yes, my lady.'

Ceci called over her shoulder.

'Ysabel, rest if you can. You are weaker than you think and I would that you had strength about you when the Baron returns.'

She swept out ahead of the guard, her manner regal, her rings clashing like a pair of swords, the folds of her grey gown undulating around her like a battle pennant.

The door closed, the key turned and I sat in my mother's chamber making much of memories. Cecilia was right. Weakness unlocked every muscle in my body and I folded onto the bed, my head on a goose-down pillow. I pulled up a woven coverlet, listening to the pop and crackle of the fire. My eyelids drooped with exhaustion, weighted as if God's hands rested there.

It might have been a breathing moment or a few bells, I don't know, but a strange sense of unease woke me – a feeling that I was no longer alone and that it wasn't Cecilia or silence that was present in the Lady Chamber.

I forbore to move, instead searching every part of the room with my eyes – reaching one of the windows where stood a man whose dark hair lay against his neck and who looked at me with distaste.

'How dare you come in here after what you have done!'

I threw the coverlet back and leaped from the bed, my fists balled tight, hatred filling every secret niche of my body.

'What *I* have done? My lady, you jest surely.'

He almost sneered as he looked at me. His eyes were dead, nothing of his soul was reflected. Flat – as empty as his voice. *This* Guy was almost magick, so different and yet similar did he appear. He could change in an instant and with apparent ease to suit the moment. All the while I looked at him my body vibrated like a drum that had been struck – the resonance articulating hate in its echo.

Despite that, I wanted to rush to him, grab hold of his hands, look into those eyes and defy him not to admit he cared as much for me as I did for him. Part of me wanted to drag him to the bed and seduce him. But such thoughts fired self-disgust and anger to the point of violence. Had a dagger been close by, I'd have pitched it.

'Jest, jest? Goddamn you to hell, Gisborne. *Why* did you sell me? After so long, after so much effort to escape.'

He laughed, *laughed,* at my unease.

'Madame, I made no secret of what it was that I sought for my life to move onward. It happened that after your father's death I realized I *had* no loyalties to concern me. I was free to make a choice. To deliver you to freedom might have been good for my soul but to sell you was so much better for my purse and my purpose.'

'I hate you! You are despicable!' I could hardly bear to step closer and yet I did, wanting to gouge his face. 'You might have status but you have no honour.'

'Oh come now, Ysabel.' He walked to the fire and poked a log, occasioning a flare and a skein of red sparks lifting toward the cavernous chimney space. 'What *is* honour? One man's honour is another man's treachery. Quite simply I pick the men I deal with.'

I could feel myself splitting in two as deceit and damnation piled on me. I could barely believe that this was the same man who had made love to me not long since. He appeared no different.

Except for his eyes.

'Guy,' I pleaded. 'You took my heart, my soul. Mary Mother, you took *me.*'

He played with the smouldering log, his back half-turned.

'When cherries are offered on a platter, why should one deny oneself? I took a cherry that you offered. My gain, your loss. As to your heart and soul, Madame, you always said you knew which way the game would be played.'

The man in front of me looked like Guy of Gisborne and yet his words were the kind I imagined De Courcey might use. I picked up the nearest flagon and pitched it at him and hearing me grunt he turned in time for the hard-edged lip to strike him above the eye.

Immediately blood flowed and I gasped. He said nothing, didn't even staunch the wound, just headed for the niche behind the carpet and left.

I whispered after him, 'I asked you not to regret us. I did.'

I threw myself on the bed, lying with my head buried in the pillow. I didn't give way to tears because the core that had begun to harden was now rock-solid. I just lay there, thinking of everything and then nothing until I slept.

I stirred much, much later – curtains had been pulled to enclose the bed end of the room and the space was made for nestling, soft and warm. I felt safe behind the draped folds and it was easy to lie comfortably. But voices sounded through the shielding screen.

'She has slept near a whole day, sir…'

A day!

'… and that must surely indicate to you that she is unwell,' Cecilia hissed.

For a moment I wondered if I were in the castle passage again. At the memory, I truly knew pain. Almost enough to elicit a groan, but nascent cunning saw me silent – listening for the identity of the man to whom she spoke with such annoyance.

'Lady Cecilia…'

De Courcey.

His was a voice roughened by shouting for attention – a voice that stripped and flayed.

'It is only your relationship with the King that gives you any rights in this place. That is all, nothing else,' he continued. 'However, if you say she is unwell then she is unwell, in which case I shall send the field-surgeon to look at her.'

'You shall do no such thing! At the very least, sir, you might send for the Abbey infirmarian who attends her father, but no *field*-surgeon will touch Lady Ysabel. Whilst you remember *my* relationship with the King, it may serve you to remember the Lady's own standing with the King's mother before you order a *field*-surgeon's hands upon her.'

'By God, woman,' De Courcey made no pretence at quiet now. 'You push too hard. What relationship?'

Cecilia gave an empty laugh. 'Huh, you do not know? Then tread carefully Baron, for whilst I might be a godmother to the King, the Lady Ysabel's mother was Queen Eleanor's cousin which makes Ysabel the King's cousin. Eleanor is also the young woman's godmother and Ysabel remains loved by mother and son. If you hurt her, be sure the royal household shall hear of it.'

Footsteps moved, spurs jingling and I thought the Baron prepared to leave the chamber. But no.

'You threaten me, Cecilia Fineux, and I shall remember, be warned. And be careful.'

'Sir,' she said. I could imagine her drawing herself up to her fully diminutive height. 'I believe it is *you* who must be careful.'

He left then. Two heavy strides and the door groaned a little as he pulled it open.

It nearly fell off its hinges as he slammed it shut.

I jumped up and wrenched the folds apart.

'Cecilia! You are beyond brave.'

'Pah, he is a common ruffian. It was time he learned of your connection to the Royal family. I am staggered gossip hasn't already informed him. He was shocked I can tell you. He flushed red and then paled like he was being bled. Such a connection to Richard can only be to your benefit, my love. Now, do you feel better?'

Cecilia's face had been ruddy with anger from her confrontation with De Courcey but her colour receded as she bustled around stoking fires and filling a bowl with warmed water.

'Here. Wash your face and I shall order some f…'

'No,' I took the small cloth she handed me and bent over the bowl. 'I am not hungry. Hearing De Courcey has made me quite queasy and I will wait until dinner.'

'It is almost that time now,' She gave me an assessing glance. 'You know, if you are able, I feel it may throw the Baron completely off balance if you can attend table in the Hall. Pre-empt him if you can. It might give you the position of power you need to be able negotiate your father's release to our care.'

I rubbed at my face. Such tiredness.

'My father is dead.'

I dried my face on a piece of linen, wondering where my mother's little mirror was. It was about the size of my father's hand, beaten metal and surrounded by a carved oak frame wrought with ivy leaves. I had loved looking at myself as a child. Such innocent vanity. Then it had reflected unguarded joy but I could imagine with little difficulty what I would see now. Eyes dull and as empty as Gisborne's had been, hair escaping from Ceci's braid, shadows looping from eye-sockets to mid cheekbones and a pallor to rival the colour of Ghislaine of Gisborne's headstone.

I held my hands out over the bowl, hoping Cecilia would not notice that I checked to see if they trembled. They did not and satisfied, I wiped them dry and met her stare.

'Ysabel,' she gasped. 'Do not say such a thing.'

'Since it is true it is best acknowledged.'

I folded the linen cloth and laid it by the bowl.

'But how do you know this?'

Cecilia moved forward, her gown swishing in an agitated rush about her feet. A log split in the fire and the broken pieces collapsed with a crack, sparks fizzing.

I turned to her, no tears filling my eyes, no lump in the throat. Hard. It would serve to survive.

Survive for what, Ysabel?

'I saw him die. I watched through the spy-hole and I spoke to him, Cecilia. He was feverish and restless and I told him all would be well and he quieted. Then Brother John arrived to give him his rites, unaware that I was so close, and as he blessed my father, he just slipped away.'

'Oh God bless poor Joffrey.' Cecilia bought her hands to her face and then quickly crossed herself.

'So you see,' my voice had the crispness of winter about it. 'If De Courcey uses my father's *life* against me, I have a winning move and I shall play it, trust me.'

Cecilia must have noticed my eyes glittering with intent because she shook her head.

'May I advise that you do not go charging like a knight into battle? I propose you check the lie of the land first.'

'Meanwhile my father lies dead, rotting unburied in the bowels of Moncrieff.'

Cecilia slumped onto a seat by the fire.

'I mean, Ysabel, don't play your piece at the beginning. Play it at the end and have him at checkmate. And might I say play it with your father's benefit in mind. It may be that it's your own benefit as well.'

I nodded and she took up the brush and quickly braided and looped my hair at the nape, grabbing a veil and filet and within minutes some semblance of the noblewoman began to take shape. She pinched my cheeks for colour and with an enquiring glance, hammered on the door to ask for the guard.

As the door swung wide for us to leave, a wave of noise surged from the Hall – men in their cups, in the throes of ribaldry and gaming. Loud braying, shouting, dogs barking. In days gone now, the noise would have been gentler – perhaps the plucked chords of a lute and a chanson in a sweet tenor voice. Modified laughter and my father's mellow voice reciting poetry for he liked nothing better than to play to an appreciative audience.

He has no audience now.

I grabbed the forgiving folds of mother's robe, not unsurprised to find my palms were sticky but intending in no way to be threatened by the man I was to meet. I already hated him, nothing could be worse. *Hate.* In the space of less than two months, my life had become overloaded with hate like some foul cessbucket overloaded with excrescence. The difficulty being that no one would empty this one into a stream or moat. It would just lie, the filth becoming worse with age. I almost gagged.

As we passed into the passage Cecilia whispered to me. 'Ysabel, the book. Where is it? It could not find it amongst your clothes.'

My eyes grew wide as I thought back. No it was not, nor my mother's comb and necklet. When I began to run, I had forgotten about the book and bag in my tunic. It would have fallen out as I leaped over twig and root and now I was as penniless as I had been before Gisborne delivered me to Cecilia. There was the faintest hope that with the book I had a means to some form of independence. If I had escaped to Ireland or Wales, it would have funded me. If I were forced to stay here then perhaps it might have funded entry to a religious house. But now?

I looked at Cecilia, my hands turned out, empty of anything and she just shook her head, her lips compressed.

We pushed to the end of the corridor and entered the Hall and the noise, enough to make me shake my own head, rolled away like an ebb tide. Everyone turned and I felt eyes rake me from top to toe.

De Courcey sat in my father's chair, Halsham in my mother's. The Baron pulled himself upright; tense as he took stock of the daughter of the house. Halsham lounged against one side of Alaïs' chair, fingers to his cheek as if he expected some pert amusement to head his way. I wanted to smash the look off his face.

'My ladies.' De Courcey bowed his head in an exaggerated attempt at manners. 'How ... delightful that you should join us. You are feeling more yourself I hope, Lady Ysabel? No longer at Death's door as Lady Cecilia would have us believe?'

'Time moves us all a little closer to Death's door, Baron. Some sooner than others.'

I felt the folds of my gown tugged at the rear and knew Cecilia was warning me. De Courcey's eyes closed to slits as I continued.

'I am always myself, sir. I have merely been tired. It has been an arduous journey from Cazenay. We seem to have been chased and it was disturbing.'

'Chased you say. And by whom do you think?'

De Courcey dared to look around the men in the room and they dared to chuckle.

Sycophants.

'By unprincipled felons who care little about honesty, I imagine. Perhaps by those who thought to improve their own lives by bartering mine.'

I heard Ceci sigh and Halsham's eyebrows rose for the skies.

De Courcey flushed and his fingers closed hard on the haft of the dagger he had used to cut his meal.

'But, Lady Ysabel, it seems you have survived to tell the tale. You were obviously well protected on your journey. Where *is* the redoubtable Gisborne?'

'My father's steward? I shouldn't have any idea but his cousin might. Is that not right, Sir Robert?'

At that De Courcey's glance shifted with speed to Halsham and I had a moment where I wondered if the Baron had not known his second in command was related to Gisborne. Either way, I had little care. I only wanted to tip snakes in amongst the fowl.

Cecilia slipped her arm around my waist.

'A fine gathering of knights you have here, De Courcey – none of you with the manners to so much as stand when a lady enters the chamber, nor to offer her a seat, nor food. Come, Ysabel. We shall do better in the kitchen.'

'Wait,' De Courcey's sharp retort rattled round the Hall. 'My men and I forget ourselves. We have not had women in our ambit for some time.'

Someone sniggered to his left but he ignored them, pushing a flagon and the knife out of the way as he levered himself to stand.

'Men, you heard. Where are your manners?'

He moved to shift one of his men off the chair on his other side and glared at Halsham who jumped up and pulled my mother's chair out.

'Lady Ysabel,' De Courcey said with mock gallantry. 'Please take Halsham's seat and Lady Cecilia you must sit on my other side. Men, pass the wine, and Halsham, tell the kitchens to send in some food for our guests.'

'Your guests?'

My fingers curled around a goblet of wine and I hastily took a sip, then a large swallow. I wasn't at all afraid, just dry and crackling with anger.

'Baron, this is still my home until my father tells me otherwise. Do you think I wish to assume the role of *guest* here? What would my mother say? Indeed, what would my *father* say? In fact where *is* my father? I am surprised that you have not bought him to my mother's chamber so that he may see for himself that I am come and that I am unharmed from my hazards.'

'You will see him anon, my lady. He is somewhat indisposed just now.'

A flush began in my chest and I could imagine it creeping up my neck to gush forth in vituperative from my mouth, but as I looked at De Courcey, hating him afresh, I could see Ceci lean forward and give the most infinitesimal shake of her head.

If you say, Cecilia, not yet. Except…

'Then if he is unwell, I must see him immediately.'

I went to stand and the Baron's hand, a broad rough hand with a dusting of auburn hair and wide fingernails, reached for my own and pulled me down. He squeezed quite hard and our eyes met – two assailants engaged on the battlefield. I was challenging him and he knew it. One could almost hear the clash of blades.

'That is unwise, Lady Ysabel. He is sleeping. It is for the best.'

'You say.'

'I do. Ah, here is the food. Please eat, and we even have music for your pleasure. Halsham, find the performers.' He turned away from me to Cecilia. 'They are a travelling troupe, I have no idea of their skill but it may serve on this night to welcome Moncrieff's daughter back to the fold.'

De Courcey obviously suffered no economies in feeding his men. I picked my way around a platter of creamed fish, nibbling at the edges like a mouse. The pike had been prepared the way my mother would have instructed – boiled, flaked and placed in an almond meal sauce with a little saffron and ginger. There had obviously been other fish courses as the detritus lay around the table. When the men went on to eat a roasted pig, I picked at baked quince, apple with honey and pear in spices. I ate some cocket, thinking that wheat must be in poor supply else we would have had far better bread.

Since returning to Moncrieff, my appetite had deserted me as my resolve had hardened. I would not go down to De Courcey without a fight and if I crossed Halsham on the way, it would be even better. As for Gisborne, if he so much as placed a toe over my path, he would lose it and much else besides. I felt strangely euphoric in my thinking. I had nothing to lose and when one has nothing to lose, it makes the odds so much better.

On the edge of my consciousness, I heard the musicians' melody. The plucked notes of a lute threaded between the lighter melody from a flute, a deeper, insistent rhythm emerging from the skin of a tabor whilst a rich voice sang the lyrics. But my thoughts tumbled and turned, drowning out any words other than my own as I moved through a dozen likely confrontations with Baron De Courcey. And yet the melody was insistent, recalling a distant past here and a more recent past at Cazenay and it served to induce a sadness which had its own power and for that I was grateful.

The meal had not long to last and I was glad that we had entered almost at its end. Outside the windows the day had progressed and De Courcey expected his men to make the most of the remaining light. He nodded at Halsham who stood and the rumble of talk, conversation that Cecilia and I appeared to have dampened by our presence, ceased altogether as Halsham ordered the men to follow him to the bailey. There was a shuffling, dogs whining and the rattling of sword sheath against trestle. My mother would never have let a man come armed to her table and I watched these men leave, their eyes daring to meet mine, some curious, some lascivious, all grinning. I doubted there was a mannered one amongst them.

Cecilia waited until the Hall had emptied of dog and man and then stood herself, preparing to return to our room. She surveyed the mess at the table and I could almost see her nose twitch with disgust as she breathed in the smell of fish bone and stock.

Clearing his throat, De Courcey rose and bowed a little more deferentially than when we had entered the Hall.

'Lady Cecilia, I would speak with Lady Ysabel alone. You will return with Cedric to the Lady Chamber.'

This time the nose twitched mightily as she drew in an offended breath.

'I shall not, my lord. It is most improper for my god daughter to be alone with a man she barely knows.'

'And yet I understand she travelled from Tours to Moncrieff with Guy of Gisborne and no chaperone. Lesser people than myself could draw some particularly colourful conclusions.'

'How dare you!'

Cecilia clenched the edge of the table.

'I dare because I can,' he replied with insouciance. 'Now shall you leave or shall I get Cedric to manhandle you?"

Cecilia's eyes hardened to the colour of pewter as she prepared to whip the man with her tongue but I broke in.

'Cecilia, I shall be quite safe I am sure. Baron De Courcey knows that I am connected with his liege lord. I doubt he would damage his status by harming me.' I threw the full force of a cool smile upon the Baron. 'Am I not right, my lord?'

He studied me hard but there was no reply, just the beginnings of that flush that presaged a temper I knew lurked beneath the facade. Cecilia left unwillingly, Cedric pushing closely behind. I gave her a confident smile and turned back to my gaoler, for he *was* that.

'What is it that is so important you must keep me separate from my godmother?'

For all that he was not as tall as Gisborne, De Courcey was powerfully put together – stocky with knotted muscle lying beneath the linen and fine wool and a strong face that some women might find deeply attractive. His hair skimmed his collar in a wave and was a curious red wine shade. His suntanned skin colour complimented the unique tint and oddly he had a smattering of boyish freckles upon his nose. In any other, it might be assumed an engaging person was housed inside that framework. Instead, it was like looking at a thundery sky – russet and umber clouded with black intent.

His eyes glinted and he walked back and forth as he began to speak.

'Lady Ysabel, it grieves me to confirm something you obviously already know – that this castle and the whole Moncrieff domain have been ceded to myself by law for gaming debts sustained by your father.'

Perhaps he hoped to give me the impression he was uncomfortable with this disturbing outcome and he studied me for some sort of reaction. All *I* could think was how fortunate it was Gisborne had forewarned me because it was easier to appear unconcerned, to show no visible emotion.

His brows creased fractionally and he poured himself a wine, pausing to quaff a substantial mouthful.

'Your father staked everything…'

'Even my mother's possessions? I am surprised my father did not think of *me* at all in this time and keep something of hers for his daughter.'

I sat upright, my fingers toying with the stem of my pewter goblet, rolling it and rolling again.

'He lost everything, madame. Daily he would play at any type of game, staking more and more until there was nothing left.'

I had a vision of my weak father, drunk and incapable, being pushed around a circle of bullies, back and forth until his purse had been well and truly picked and *he* dizzy and confused.

'Daily sir, he would ride out with his *cronies*,' disgust laced my words, 'who lubricated him until he lost all sense and reason.'

De Courcey laughed, a gravelly sound, and replied with a trace of mockery.

'And you think he was an unwilling playfellow? I fear you are wrong, my dear.'

'Oh, I dare say he was as willing as any man who has lost his most adored wife and his reason. But it strikes me that other men, *friends* shall we say, would have extricated my father from the sticky bog into which he had cast himself rather than pushing him deeper.'

De Courcey's eyes had darkened as I spoke, anger rippling his brow. He strode to the table and ripped out a chair to sit directly opposite and we sat like two opponents in a chess game.

'Pray continue, my lady. What is it you infer?'

His voice was as soft as swansdown, such a contrast to the visible energy that emanated from his very fingertips.

'I *infer* sir, that you manipulated my father so that he lost the very thing you coveted. How convenient for you.'

Careful, Ysabel.

The square face had hardened, cheeks flooding with colour. He slammed his hand on the table, the flagon of wine crashing to the floor. I blinked as it hit the stone flags but would not be cowed.

'*Don't* push your position. You are not above my discipline.' He leaned close and I smelled wine and food on his breath. 'Don't ever tell me what I should and should not have done, Lady Ysabel. Your father was an incompetent fool and as for you ... by the saints madame, you watch yourself.'

'Or what, sir? What shall you do to Richard Plantagent's family?'

He smiled and that was when my heart sank to my boots. Something about his expression, about the innate confidence, made my stomach turn up.

'Ah, to be sure we shall find out. I have written to my liege lord explaining your predicament and asking what are his wishes in respect of your wardship.'

I stood, my self-discipline flying out the window on the wings of full-blown anger.

'Wardship? How dare you? Did you know then, when you wrote to the King, that my father had in fact died? Did you? And if you knew that my father was dead, why did *you* not have the decency to inform me the minute this conversation ... hah, *conversation! What conversation?'* I yelled at him. 'Why did you not inform me with what little grace you appear to possess that my father was indeed dead?'

He went to speak but I slammed *my* hand on the table, shouting him down and leaning forward.

'Do not, Baron. Do not speak! The fact is that my father has been dead these two days and is lying rotting in the dungeons and with each minute that passes as his corpse disintegrates, I shall blame you for the most appalling care of a man who deserves so much better. And before you castigate your men for revealing such a truth, know that I was aware how dangerously ill he was. Daughters do. I felt it here…' I wrapped my chest hard.'

'Sit!' he roared, face filled with ire. 'Hold your tongue! Your father is indeed rotting beneath the soles of our feet, but he brought it on himself and you know it. We shall bury him tomorrow…'

'*With* my mother. They must lie side by side. And then Lady Fineux and myself shall leave you to your spoils.'

I turned for the door but my wrist was grabbed and I was spun around.

His voice sank low and I knew it presaged something unpalatable.

'You and the Lady of Upton go nowhere. Not until we receive word from the King.'

'How dare you!'

'You, Lady Ysabel, haven't seen a quarter of what I dare. Now…' he called for Cedric and the man pushed the door ajar. De Courcey lowered his voice, his words laced with poison.

'Take the lady to her chamber and lock the door.'

CHAPTER TWELVE

'Ysabel!' Cecilia rushed to me as the door slammed shut behind. 'What happened?'

Perhaps I looked pale that she should react so. But inside I felt hot, blazing – as if the most stupendous fever raged. But it was hate, anger and so many other insidious emotions besides. 'He admitted Father is dead and has agreed he shall be buried tomorrow. That's all.' I turned to the window and stood with my forehead pressed against the cool, cool stone of the embrasure.

How has all this happened? I am sinking into the bowels of some sort of Hell.

'That's *not* all. Not by a long stretch.' Cecilia stayed by the hearth, the fire as dead as I felt inside.

Ashes, dust.

'Tell me,' she sighed.

'He has written to the King asking what Richard would wish for my wardship.'

'But that's preposterous! I am your godmother, it is perfectly natural that you would live with me at Upton.'

'And yet that is not what he would have. He waits in some delight for something else. It would seem he might want me.'

'Hell and damnation! I worried about this, my dear. He has Moncrieff and I hoped it would be enough. If all he wants is to dip his wick, lord knows there are plenty of noblewomen who would oblige a man as wealthy as he. But…'

'Cecilia, I know what you will say. You call him an illbred ruffian. Everyone is no doubt aware of his nature – the man who runs a mercenary army, the man who is loyal as long as the monies last. He has a disreputable reputation. How could he remove such a taint from his person? How could he lift himself further in Richard's eyes? For sure, he has already provided the manpower but it is the trust and recognition he craves and what better way of earning it than to claim he cares for the future of the daughter of Joffrey of Moncrieff, lately deceased. You and I both know that Richard will offer my hand to one of the men *he* most needs to support him in *his* endeavours. It is a plan made in Richard's and De Courcey's version of heaven.'

'Oh my love. Hell, more like! We must write to your royal godmother.'

'Eleanor, as ever, is involved in her own machinations, Ceci. You know and I know what she is like. And by the time a plea arrived, I fear the King's answer would be in De Courcey's hands and the decree expedited.'

'Then you must get away. Use the secret passage again.'

'To what endeavour? Do you not think he would find me as easily as I was found this last time? No, Cecilia. I cannot see a way out of this. And to be frank, I just want to bury my father and then…' I rubbed a forehead that ached with foul intensity. 'God knows.'

The morning of my father's burial arrived with a flash of wind-driven cloud across the window. Outside the tower that housed the Lady Chamber, the wind moaned – a dirge to match the spirit of the day. Once again my back ached with such ferocity I thought I should have to lie down, nauseous with the pain.

I hoped Cecilia was unaware that I nibbled at my food and I wondered at how thin I must be as I felt my belly and hipbones. Food was more than I could stomach on this day of emotional torment. I wondered if I would be allowed to speak with Brother John and at least have some say in the progression my father's burial should take. But it was obviously not to be as the hours passed.

I had dressed in a midnight wool *bliaut* of my mother's. It reminded me of the sable-edged cloak that had once been mine in another place; a place where I had discovered something of the truth that lay in wait for me at Moncrieff. Cecilia braided my hair into a plait and I let it hang down my back, refusing a veil. Instead, we went through all the chests in the room, eventually unearthing a false bottom in a coffer. Secreted away was a filet of silver, twisted and turned delicately like a wreath of flowers and as I lowered it over my forehead there was something of the gesture of a queen and I wondered if I was pretending to assume an authority I just did not possess. There was also a sapphire studded cross on a chain … the round sapphire as smooth and deeply coloured as the ocean. It had been my Cazenay grandmother's and as it slipped over my head I thought it may be worth something should I be in need.

You will be, Ysabel, you will be.

I grunted.

Cecilia and I examined the few possessions left in the room. It was so obvious that Lady Alaïs' jewels had been taken – all bar the filet and the cross. But her small looking glass lay amongst creams and simples and we found her Book of Hours in amongst wool and pieces of incomplete embroidery. Her frame lay against a wall and it was this unfinished piece – a design of a maid and a unicorn – to which I turned to while away the moments until we would be called for my father's farewell.

'You would think he would at least have let Brother John come to give me comfort or to discuss a prayer, a hymn … something. The man is such a piece, Ceci. Poison! I'll wager he won't even open my mother's tomb, that he will cause my father to be buried at the side of Saint Agatha's with the rest of Moncrieff. Can you imagine how my father must have longed to be laid with Alaïs? It would have been the one warm moment for him, that soon he would lie by the side of his heart's love.'

I didn't cry as I spoke. I suspected that any tears had evaporated in the blaze that had lit my body the previous night.

'We must hope that some honour may be shown, my dear.' She tutted and sighed. 'I wish we had heard from Gisborne.'

'Well I do not and we shan't. He betrayed me, Cecilia, I have told you. Halsham paid him with coin and a career. I am where I am right now because Gisborne is as tainted as the rest and nothing, *nothing* you say will make me think any differently. I shall tell you, once in our journey he said to me that status is power and put me under no illusion that his plan was to seek such status and thereafter have the power he craved. I think the side you saw and the side I saw were two different beings.'

Cecilia sat calmly stitching.

'On the contrary my dear. I think the side you saw on your journey was exactly the side I saw. I'd venture to say that you are falling into Halsham's net, believing what he wants you to believe.'

'Ceci! They are cousins. Have you not heard that blood is thicker than water.'

'Be that as it may, Ysabel, I think you are wrong. Now, let us not dispute. We must stick close together and to be honest, today is a day where we truly shall need each other. It is an awful thing to have to bury one's dear ones.'

I knew full well she talked of her own loved husband and the baby son that died two days beyond his birth. And that she talked of Alaïs as well. She and my mother were like sister-friends and as I thought about them I wished I had a sister or a friend like Cecilia Fineux of Upton.

But I have. There she sits, calmly pushing a needle and thread through fabric.

I jumped up, letting my own frame fall, and went to throw my arms about her and kiss her cheek.

'Goodness, what are you doing, my love? I'll needs unpick my work.'

'I thank God I have you, Cecilia. I really do.'

I squeezed her shoulder and walked back to my seat, picking up the frame and re-threading my needle.

'By what other name is the man called? I have yet to hear him referred to as anything other than the Baron or De Courcey.'

'You do not know? God's blood, I thought it was common knowledge. He is called Benedict; such a lovely name for such an unlovely man.'

I snorted, staring out the window at the clouds that fled across the sky still, as if the Devil were behind.

Benedict. Blessed. And De Courcey a corruption of the meaning.

Saint Agatha's bell had just rung for None when keys rattled in the door and it swung open. The familiar guard from previously entered and dipped his head.

How is that you are trapped in this spider's web? You have a look that I think I could like.

He was perhaps my age or a little younger and I felt a curious comfort when he glanced my way, the way one feels in the company of a friend or a favourite cousin.

'My ladies, it is time for the burial. If you would follow me.'

He stood back and Cecilia and I dropped our frames and went to the door.

'My lady,' he said, as I passed. 'I am sorry for your loss.'

I stopped. His mouth widened in an attempt at kindness and I responded by touching his arm.

'Thankyou. I am grateful. What is your name?'

'Ulric of Camden, my lady.'

'Ulric of Camden,' my hand still lay lightly on his arm. 'You are most kind.'

'Young man.' Cecilia at her most imperious swung back to Ulric as she began to walk along the passage. 'Do we go to the chapel or the church?'

'The chapel, my lady. The Baron has caused Lady Alaïs' tomb to be opened and the d … deceased will be interred with his wife.'

'Huh,' was all Cecilia said but for myself I sighed in relief. My mother deserved to have her husband by her side. For his part Joffrey had surely paid for his own foolery and could at last rest with her.

The chapel sat in another of Moncrieff's four towers, its one arched window sitting high in the wall and facing out to the lake. The chapel had no pretensions to grandeur – humble and cold, a small altar with a brass cross and two large smoking candles. The embroidered altar cloth my mother had made was missing.

'There were flowers when your mother was buried, masses of them,' Cecilia whispered.

My mother's tomb, set inside the door to the left, lay open and I was glad we were by the door because the smell was overpowering. Brother John rushed up and took my hands and squeezed, his own roughened ones a welcome feeling. De Courcey was nowhere in sight and so John spoke quickly and without fear.

'It's a bad thing, Ysabel. A bad thing. All of this.'

He threw his hands around to indicate my mother's tomb, Moncrieff and life, I suspect.

I waved my hand under my nose and Ceci thrust a strip of linen filled with cloves into my palm and I sucked in the aroma greedily.

'I will make this as brief a service as I can by the grace of God. Do you understand?'

I nodded. I hadn't yet glanced inside my mother's tomb. I was afraid my memories would be shattered.

Behind us I heard feet shuffling and turned to see four men with a shrouded shape on their shoulders, a look of distaste on their faces. De Courcey led the way and nodded at me. 'Lady Ysabel.'

'Why is my father not dressed in his finest accoutrements? Why a ragged shroud?'

Even I knew the formula for a nobleman.

'Because I would expect no man to deal with the smell that has become your father's remains.'

'That is yours and Halsham's fault. If you had acted when he died, he would have been accorded the respect he is due.'

De Courcey's straight lips twisted.

'The respect he is getting is hardly his due, my lady. He deserves even less, in my opinion. Be glad that he shall be interred with your mother and not in a pauper's grave out there.'

He waved his arms to indicate the Moncrieff walls.

I could say nothing in reply. What was there to say? My father *was* a pauper and besides, in this instance I had no energy to fight. I watched the men lay my father none too gently in the tomb, noting that in his own grief, he had obviously given instruction the tomb be broad enough for he and my mother to lie side by side. I glanced toward her, grateful to note that she was dressed in a most magnificent gown and her face, God be praised, was covered in a dark veil.

Brother John began the obsequies, quickly passing through an abbreviated service, flicking holy water across the corpse. I sniffed at the cloves and was surprised to find moistness on my cheeks and yet I had nothing of the tightness of tears in my chest. In what seemed minutes it was done, the tomb closed, the vast slab of stone pushed and manouvred until it clicked into place. And for the first time, I heaved a great sigh of relief.

It drew a line in my life. Whatever I did now, I would be moving forward. My only concern was to what? De Courcey stood leaning against the chapel door, not a vestige of sympathy or etiquette about him. It seemed he'd been appraising me as I stood listening to Brother John.

'Baron, when did you send to the King? How long until there shall be an answer?'

He pushed away from the doorjamb and walked toward me.

'When I returned from Saint Eadgyth's. If I had known you were connected with my liege at that point, I may have phrased the letter differently. As it was…'

'What did you say?'

'That is between my liege and I, my lady, but in answer to your earlier question, I envisage a reply in a space of seven days. Perhaps seven more, but no longer.'

Seven days!

'So I am locked up for that time? A prisoner?'

He tipped his head to the side and pursed his lips.

'What do you propose?'

'I should like to visit the Moncrieff villagers at the very least.'

I wanted to talk to someone else familiar, someone who knew me from a time when my parents lived and Moncrieff was blessed. I wanted something to ameliorate a fate that sped toward me like a herd of wild horses.

'I am not inclined…'

Brother John pushed next to me, his wiry body reminding me of his asceticism, his scalp gleaming in the darkening light of the afternoon.

'If I could interrupt, my lord.'

'What is it, priest?'

'I would take responsibility for the lady and you could appoint a guard of your choice.'

'I could.'

De Courcey looked at his fingernails and then lifted his gaze to me, another assessment.

'But shall you be trusted I wonder? Let us see, shall we? Ulric,' he called to my door-guard and the fellow shifted through the men that surrounded us and stood in front of the Baron.

'You shall guard the lady, and yours and Brother John's lives shall be forfeit if anything should happen.'

Ulric swallowed but John just smiled and said quite equably, 'Then there shall be no problem, shall there?'

Lightness filled me; relief I thought, but then I fell forward as that odd feeling in my head became an overwhelming blackness and I knew nothing more.

Strong arms laid me on something soft. I opened my eyes and found De Courcey's face disturbingly close to my own as I observed the hangings of the bed in the Lady Chamber. He smelled of something fresh but I could not place it.

'Lady Ysabel.'

His voice seemed a little thick; if I were less awry, I would have said something about our closeness stirred him.

He was pushed aside and Cecilia bustled next to me and laid a cold cloth on my forehead.

'You see, Baron, it is as I said. She is not well after her journey and now the burial. I do wish you would try to understand.'

'I do,' he growled. 'Credit me with some sense, madam. I see that she is moved by grief, that she is tired and that she is under duress wondering what her future shall be. I just wish *she* realized she is not to be thrown out of Moncrieff.'

'It's perhaps what she *will* be retained for that upsets her,' Cecilia muttered.

If De Courcey heard he did not respond.

Instead he said, 'I am sure you shall care for her and I have no doubt she will be well. I am to leave now as I have business away and shall return in a few days, by which time...' he pushed in beside Cecilia and ran a hand down my cheek as our eyes met. He barely smiled.

'By which time I suspect she will be up and about and visiting the Moncrieff domain. Take care, my lady.'

This last was said as he pushed my lips hard with a finger.

You dare!

I shut my eyes and turned my head away, hearing the door close more quietly with his exit than it had in the past.

'Well!' Cecilia humphed. 'He is a cunning piece.'

She turned the cloth over so that the cool could do its work.

'Ysabel, what is wrong? Are you sure there is nothing we need concern ourselves with?'

Her grey eyes were filled with concern.

'It's just my back,' I replied, shifting on the bed. 'It hurts so often. Very low and it comes round into my belly. I had to ride a warhorse you see, for many miles and the horse was tall and so very wide and I think I may have done some damage. If I could just rest comfortably ... but it seems I rarely get the chance.'

The door rattled and Brother John walked in, his robes swinging, and I was reminded of Sister Thea.

How I long to be in that sanctuary.

'My dear girl! What *shall* we do with you?'

'She says it's a back injury and tiredness and one might agree but...' Cecilia frowned.

'Then I shall get the infirmarian at the abbey to make up some pain relief and a tonic and we will have you up and about in no time.'

I smiled.

'Thankyou, Brother John, I am so very grateful you were there for my father at the end.'

His brow creased as if I spoke of something of which I could not be aware so I hurried on.

'They told me you were with him in his last moments. And I know you would have done as much as it was possible to do to ameliorate my father's state of mind. You were always his friend.'

'I was that. Even though he continued to beat me at chess until he lost interest.' He seemed to look at a past reminiscence but then folded it away. 'But now you are come and we shall walk, visit folk. Maybe you could ride. No? Well then, I shall take you in the punt and we shall fish. You used to love that once.'

He chattered on and each memory he bought forth was like a sparkling jewel and I could feel my heart begin to brighten as he set gems in it and polished and polished again.

Eventually I became sleepy and Cecilia and he moved to the fire and sat murmuring. I could not hear and sank into a healing sleep.

The next few days passed in such a fashion – calmly and without the threat of De Courcey. I had no interest in enquiring what he had disappeared for. He had left a skeleton force and the whole place quieted in consequence, so much so that I felt well enough to walk each day. Eventually I felt strong enough to venture beyond the walls and summoned Ulric who in turn called Brother John. Before we left, cloaks wrapped around in an unkind wind, I asked Cecilia if she had found a small purse on the belt of my steward's attire.

'In fact yes.' She delved into her own purse which hung from a twisted leather girdle, revealing my leather pouch and passing it over.

I opened the cord to withdraw locks of hair. 'Wilfred's and Harry's.' The memories scalded more than I expected. 'They were killed as we traveled.'

'Oh no!' Cecilia's hands flew to her mouth.

'Jesu,' said John, his fingers flying as crossed himself.

Ulric remained silent, staring at the curls as if he could see the story they told.

'Give me your arm if you please, Ulric,' I asked. 'We shall visit their families first.'

Cecilia and John led the way, Ceci leaning on John and with a staff in her other hand. I rested my hand in the crook of Ulric's arm and he seemed embarrassed as we left by the castle gates, his face flushing as the other men whistled and called.

'The men are illmannered. Take no notice,' I said. 'You do me a service, Ulric, for I am still weak.'

In truth I was not but it served to have him believe he was most necessary to me. Something about his gentility and deference made me wonder if he *could* be a friend because I needed to build a force of loyal supporters. He was politely quiet when we met with Wilf's and Harry's families and I relayed the dreadful story, telling them how brave were the men.

'Were they braver than those soldiers?'

One of the children pointed to the castle.

'Much braver.'

As I spoke I silently begged for Ulric's forgiveness, wanting him to see that I mended children's broken hearts and nothing else. I would not have him lumped in with the disreputable men that comprised the Baron's army.

'Were they knightly?'

'Mary mother, of course! The most knightly you can imagine. They saved my life as they lost their own, fought like heroes and will always be remembered as such.'

'That Baron's not a real knight.'

The younger children were outspoken as children often are.

'I fear he is,' I said. 'It is best you do not speak thus or his wrath may strike at your families. Will you do that for me? Keep silent? You see the King has deemed him a knight and you must show him respect. You know you can't gainsay your King.'

'I hate the Baron. He takes grain that is ours and we have no bread.'

'Then I shall make sure you have grain back. Don't fret.'

Ulric listened to all of this and spoke as we returned to the castle.

'My lady, you might be able to give them grain whilst the Baron is gone but he shall find out and may penalize them.'

'Ulric is right, Ysabel,' said Ceci and Brother John nodded his head. 'You should not promise what you may not be able to give.'

'I will tell the Baron myself. If he has a complaint it shall be with me. Ulric, when we return, please make sure that one bag of grain for each household is taken from the granary. The village is not so big, and I'll wager the castle granary can afford it. The people are not to starve until the harvest.'

'Are you not afraid?' Ulric helped me step over a puddle.

'Not now but I shall probably tremble when I confront the Baron.'

'You are quite a surprise, my lady.'

'How so?'

I turned and gave him my full attention. His blonde hair gleamed in the dull light of an insipid sun and his blue eyes stared beyond me to my lake.

My lake?

'He is…' he seemed to struggle with his words.

'Yes?'

'Be careful, my lady.' His gaze switched to my face and became intense. 'His temper is… well known.'

So, he uses his hands, does he?

'Consider me warned, Ulric, and thankyou.'

The villeins received their grain and life continued in a placid fashion as the leaves thickened and the late spring promised better weather to come. Brother John and I went fishing, caught some pike and talked – at least I talked and he listened. Occasionally his mouth would tighten but he let me empty of my thoughts and hurts.

Finally, 'I think Cecilia is right about Guy and that you see it wrong, Ysabel. He was more than honest here and was highly thought of by noble and serf alike. I can't see the man you talk of at all. It will be proved ultimately, I am sure.'

'You do not convince me, Brother John. And in any case, it is too late.'

'I know. But time will tell. What's that?'

We heard a voice shouting from the banks and Ulric waved his cap in the air. Brother John poled us over and Ulric's face glimmered and flushed as if something was awry.

'Ulric?' I asked.

'The Baron is returned. The letter from the King has arrived. He wishes you and the Lady Cecilia to attend him in the Hall. Brother John as well.'

My time of calm had ended, my heart speeding up. But I would not let the others see and so I hopped to the shore, grasping Ulric's hand, holding the folds of my *bliaut* high.

'Then let us discover what Richard Plantagenet would do with me. Come on!' I chastened them. 'I would not have us suffer the Baron's wrath so soon.'

We hurried over the causeway with our fish, tossing the catch to a kitchen-hand and continuing to the Hall where the Baron lounged against my father's chair, his back to us as he played with a thick packet. He turned around as we clattered in, resplendent in a scarlet surcoat. His hair blended with the rich autumnal tints of his clothes and if it wasn't Benedict De Courcey, one might have been impressed with the figure he cut.

He glanced at the fish stains on my gown, at my hair blown away from its plait.

'Jesu, there is little of the lady about you now. I shall forgive you because I see you have colour in your cheeks at last and your eyes are clearer.'

It is not for you to forgive anything.

I dropped to a curtsy, my head bowed. Might as well start with the pleasantries.

'I am much improved, thank you.'

'If I didn't want to know immediately what the King shall say, I would ask you to wash and change and return in a state fit to hear what is your future. As it is…' he passed the packet to Brother John. 'Open it, priest, and apprise us of the royal wishes.'

Brother John slipped his finger under the thick royal seal and fragments of red wax fell to the paving stones like drops of blood.

An execution warrant. Nothing less.

The parchment crackled and I waited, an out of body experience, cursing my head for its lightness, holding onto Ulric's arm as to a lifeline. His fingers crept to my hand and squeezed.

'Courage, madam,' he seemed to say.

Finally Brother John unfolded the letter and began to read.

'*Richard by the grace of God King of England, Duke of Normandy and Aquitaine and Count of Anjou, to my Lord Baron De Courcey, greetings. We were saddened to hear of the straitened circumstance of Our cousin, Lady Ysabel of Moncrieff and owe you gratitude for thinking of her care. Our mother Eleanor by that same grace Dowager Queen of England, has let it be known that She would welcome Our cousin to Her court but that She has no purpose for her. As you indicate, Our own Godmother Lady Cecilia Fineux of Upton is also the Lady Ysabel's godmother and but for her increasing age would have offered fine care of Our cousin. It seems thus that the Lady Ysabel can best be provided for by marriage...*'

I gasped. My future turned and looked at my present and shattered into a million pieces.

'*...by marriage,*' Brother John repeated. '*And it would please Us that a man We respect and admire can offer his hand and his beneficence. We therefore propose and approve the betrothal of Lady Ysabel of Moncrieff to Baron Benedict De Courcey...*' in the silence, Brother John finished the message. '*... of Moncrieff.*' He looked up. 'It is of course signed and dated by Richard Plantagenet.'

I closed my eyes to prevent the world spinning but it continued to spin anyway and I began to pool in fishy folds at Ulric's feet.

'This is becoming a habit, Lady Cecilia. What ails her?'

'Shock, Baron. What think you? That she is happy to marry a man she barely knows?'

'Other women have done it as a matter of politics since Time began and she maintains a position in her familial home. It should be enough. Not many would want her, penniless as she is and with a reputation.'

'A reputation? *What* do you say?'

Cecilia's ire crept into my brain and sharpened my dulled wits.

'They say she may not be the maid she pretends after weeks alone with Gisborne.'

My eyes closed with the memories.

Foolish, naïve Ysabel. Virginity lost. And how you shall pay!

'Have you asked Gisborne?'

'In fact I did and we came to blows, he denying he should want her at all and that I was disparaging *his* reputation. He also said he had an idea she would be very poor and it did not suit him. I laughed at that.'

Snake, Gisborne, snake!

My back ached but I kept quiet.

'Fix her, Lady Cecilia. We shall be married by week's end. The King cannot be present but a few of my friends shall attend. It shall be a small occasion.'

'Do you not want to shout it from the rooftops to all England, my lord Baron?'

The sarcasm in Cecilia's tone was as ripe as well-aged game.

'It is enough that the daughter of Moncrieff shall be my wife. And may I say enjoy the next few days with your god daughter because at the end of the marriage banquet, there will be no need of you here any longer.'

No!

I heard his boots tap over the floor, spurs jingling and then the door shut.

Wife, wife, wife!

But in truth I was not sure what hurt the most; that I should be this man's wife and consort, that Cecilia was to be banished or that Guy of Gisborne had said he did not want me at all, that I did not suit his reputation and that I was poor. *He* had said that about *me*. My back stabbed, the pain convulsing around to my loins and I grunted. Hearing the noise, Cecilia was instantly at my side.

'Huh, you are awake. I think, my dear, that it is time you and I had a little talk.'

'Cecilia, he is sending you away!' I held her hand tightly, her rings cutting into my palm. 'I cannot lose you. I cannot survive without you.'

'Hush, we shall not talk of this yet, although I could have gelded the bastard when he spoke.'

Her hand closed to a fist beneath mine and I could imagine her grabbing his organs and squeezing before delivering a sharp cut and oh how I would have helped!

'Tell me about this pain of yours,' she continued. 'Where is it exactly?'

I pointed at my lower back and my belly.

'And you are faint and lacking in appetite and I dare say you are nauseous daily. Tell me, when did you last have your courses?'

Of course I knew. Perhaps I had known all along but in typical Ysabel fashion chose to deny the truth.

'I am with child,' I whispered.

Cecilia nodded, her wimple straining against her chin.

I pushed off the bed and went to the window to stare out, seeing a man with black hair flying off his collar as he strode away. I tried to speak but nothing emerged and so I just shrugged my shoulders. What does one say?

A crow flew past the window and then back, dipping and soaring on the eddies that circled the tower. I longed for his freedom but I shivered because crows hung about with legend ... death, witches, all things unpalatable.

'He will kill me when I produce another man's child.'

'Most likely.'

Cecilia, never one to gild a lily, said it like it was, determined to make me face some truths. The fire crackled and then more un-gilded and surprising words reached me from where she stood on the far side of the room.

'*If* you tell him.'

'I should think it will be obvious when my stomach begins to strain like a cow with bloat.'

'But he needn't know it is not his child. It is you and the babe we must think on presently, my dear, because you *are* in trouble, that cannot be gainsaid. I think it is as well the Baron is marrying you this week. There is time for him to do what he must and then you can claim he is to be a father and for the next few months he will accept your changing form as a product of his manly seed.'

'Cecilia, please!'

The thought of opening my legs to De Courcey filled me with horror and not just because I now carried a child who belonged to another.

'Face the facts, my girl. Surely when you allowed Gisborne to dip his wick you realized this might be an outcome? This is no time for shyness.'

Did I? I don't think I gave it a thought. Even more naivety, Ysabel.

But I could never tell Cecilia. I just looked out the window again. I decided to trust myself to her hands because the one thing I knew about her was that she was indomitable, that problems existed to be solved and that the inevitable might as well be accepted as fought against. I also learned that many little wins could lead to a mighty big win. This was the legend that was Cecilia Fineux of Upton and I was to lose her ... just as I had lost all who loved me. Another one...

'How far along are you? That is the key.'

'My courses were last at Cazenay the week before Gisborne arrived.'

'Well then, give or take a week, you must be almost two months which means you shall have to claim an early birth. Mary Mother but I hope he is away when you deliver.'

The so-called marriage, for all that it would be officiated by Brother John, took a lesser position in my mind as I pondered hour after hour about this child I was brewing. That it was Gisborne's created a dichotomy of emotions; on the one hand a type of fury that the man who had spurned me had got a child upon me. On the other, the vague belief that if he knew of my condition, he might spirit the babe and myself away from all that was inglorious.

But Ysabel, he has a life plan. A man who wants status and power does not desire a penniless wife who can bring nothing remarkable to his table, child or no. And besides, you have no trust in the man and do not forget it.

But it seems I would forget a lot to escape the approach of my personal apocalypse. I would ask myself repeatedly why De Courcey was so set on marrying *me* the penniless bride, and that would remind me of the wedding and I would quickly turn my thoughts back to the babe again.

But the hours of night are long and there was many a moment that I lay wondering why Guy of Gisborne, a man apparently on the rise, should find my situation so repugnant when De Courcey did not. And all I could deduce was the oft mentioned fact that by marrying a noblewoman connected with royalty, De Courcey was giving himself prestige he would never have had otherwise whereas Gisborne was already from an ancient and noble family and needed no woman's antecedents to give him such gravitas. He only required wealth and that he could earn without the inevitable ties.

De Courcey's history was a rough one. Ulric told it to me in that week before the marriage, as we sat watching the blacksmith shoe horses.

'He comes from a small estate – family of little importance. He left his home when his father and mother died of a pox and the manor and its roughshod lands reverted to the lord of the time. It was a none too fine estate on the southeastern coast, a place called Rickham. It had no pretension to anything, least of all grandeur and no monies either. De Courcey did not care for the bucolic life and chose to develop what were his real skills – bullying.'

'Ulric! Hush, you shall be heard and...'

He looked around but we were alone and the noise of the blacksmith's anvil muffled our words.

'My lady, I am surprised you have not been made aware of your soon-to-be-husband's background. It is important you know, as it is part of the man. He hired himself out to bigger estates, gaining a reputation for fighting skills and tactical wherewithal and he was soon in Henry's eye after he began to put a small force together. He received his titles as an inducement to stand behind Henry in any engagement and in fact helped Henry resume Cumberland, Northumbria and West Moreland. In addition, he was an exceptionally young man at that time which stood in his favour. But he is a man with an eye to the future and has played both sides with great ability. He had a small force with Barbarossa in Northern Italy and as well, Venice has had their eye upon him. Thus he is as rich as Croesus because when he fights he fights with dirty cunning and when he plays, he plays to win. But he is what he is, a common bully.'

'And yet you...'

'It seems odd, my lady. But I am adept at languages and I can write...'

'Ulric, I did not know.'

'He uses me to draft secret code that is taken across the Middle Sea to Italy, Constantinople, to wherever his private forces are at work.'

'But...'

'It is money. I am paid. My mother shall not starve.'

'But ethics? Morals?'

'Are for those who have the liberties of life, my lady, not for those whose families may be *in extremis*.' He looked down at hands that I noticed were ink-stained. 'You know why he marries you?' He took a giant breath and muttered as if to another part of himself. 'I should not be saying this but

I like you and you remind me of my sister who died. I would you were forewarned because forewarned as they say, is forearmed.'

'Ulric, whilst you scare me a little, I am aware he is a dangerous man. But tell me and have done. Why *is* he marrying me, the penniless daughter of Moncrieff?'

Ulric looked into the distance beyond the blacksmith. I noticed it was a habit he had when relaying words of heavy weight, as if he couldn't bear the response he might find on a person's face.

'He took Moncrieff by force. Not by the kind of force you expect, but an uglier more insidious one. There have been rumblings of disgust through the nobility, perceived un-knightly behaviour. By taking you, the daughter of the estate as his wife, he nips that in the bud. Richard Plantagenet has blessed it after all and thus all is right with the Baron's world.'

And so Ulric, bastard son of a knight of Camden who had been killed in a drunken brawl somewhere between Acre and Famagusta, had turned from guarding me *for* De Courcey, to guarding me against De Courcey. All in a week, and I was glad because I was moving closer to the day I would lose not only my life, but my godmother and it seemed to me I needed such support.

I asked myself if it was my hand on Ulric's arm that did it or was he merely a genuine friend just when I needed one. In any case I spoke carefully, hand on his arm again.

'Ulric, you put yourself in grave danger by speaking thus.'

'Not to be cocky, my lady, but I am the only one he can rely on to create and decipher code. He will not rid himself of me in a hurry.'

So was any of what Ulric had revealed any different to what I had thought or what Gisborne had said? Not at all. But it confirmed a belief and in that there was some relief because it allowed me to accept what was happening and to guard against the inevitable hurt that would go with it. Ulric hovered on the edge of my existence like a quiet dog, Cecilia waded right in like an alaunt, snapping and keeping everyone away and Brother John just wafted between the opposing forces of good and evil, as I had come to think of De Courcey's side and mine, like a guardian angel.

De Courcey had disappeared again, Ulric said to Ely and part of me hoped that he would be delayed or attacked on the road – something, anything, to change my fate. But if it didn't change, I just hoped he would disappear as frequently after our marriage.

Each day passed with odd guests arriving and being billeted around the castle. All men. Not a solitary woman amongst them and I thought what a ghastly wedding feast this would be. So different from what I had imagined for myself as Khazia and I journeyed along the highway two months before.

The guests were noblemen of a high order, evidenced by their embroidered robes, by the number of their retainers, by the deference that was paid by De Courcey's own men. To feed and house such an increase in our population must be costing my future husband a fortune, but I cared not. I was merely pleased that these new arrivals had about them a mode of etiquette and that they respected my family home. It seemed to quieten De Courcey's own men by consequence.

I wondered if these were the nobles who had disapproved of De Courcey and whether they came because they must, because this marriage had a royal seal upon it. Whatever the case, the castle ran smoothly under the bailiff's and Cecilia's care. I preferred not to be involved, enough time for that later. I watched from the window and when I did venture out, it was through the kitchens and as inconspicuously as I could manage.

Once Brother John and I went to the punt, me dressed in monk's robes, and he poled me far to the other side of the lake. It was a calm, summer's day. The lazy damp wind had died and everything was still. We could hear the guests challenging each other to archery contests, or riding out with the falcons and if one forgot they were connected in any way with De Courcey, it was a pleasant enough sound. The osiers had cast a few unwanted leafsprouts into the lake and a dainty flotilla of yellow-tinted leaves floated around the water's edge. The birds piped, quacked and chirruped and somewhere a fox barked and it was hard to imagine that my world was shifting, that it would never be the same again.

'I suspect he will leave you alone for long periods, Ysabel,' Brother John said as he stuck the pole in the mud to hold us steady.

'I have no doubt. But it is the time he shall not that worries me. He is rough they say and I am but a woman.'

'Surely he would not dare to hurt the King's god-sister, or the mother of a child.'

'Time will tell, Brother John. But I tell you, it is all I can do not to run right now and get as far as I can. If I didn't think he would have the lymers on my scent and me baled up like a fox in a hole, I would do it.'

'What has stopped you?' Brother John looped a worn rope around the pole and held us still.

'Perhaps the quieter I am and the less fuss I make the better. And I have the Moncrieff folk to care for and who will care for me in return. That makes it bearable.'

'If it gets too hard, rest assured Richard shall know.'

'I am not sure Richard would care. A force to add to his own army is more important than a mere woman so distantly connected.'

Brother John didn't reply, just pointed to an empty bird's nest strung between reeds and laced in sunlit cobwebs.

I cherished this time of day. The sun lay behind the world around us and every minikin thing was illuminated by its subtle beams – bugs and flies, mosquitoes and spiders, motes of dust and seed-heads – busy but beautiful to behold.

'I love Moncrieff,' I said, as if that made everything acceptable.

The day before the wedding, Ulric walked in loaded with a heavily wrapped bundle. 'The Baron has sent this to you, Lady Ysabel. He has just ridden in and is accompanied by Sir Robert and two others. All the guests have arrived now.'

Halsham. My cup runneth over.

'And not a woman in sight, Ulric. Are none of these knights married? I feel at a disadvantage.'

'Then it as well you have me.' Cecilia was not in a good mood and her manner lacked her customary brightness. 'If only for one more day.'

'Do not say it. I find it easier to bear if we do not speak of it, Ceci. But I tell you this – he will have to let you return when he hears of my condition, I will make sure.'

She swung quickly to me, her brows creased and her mouth in a flat line, but already I realised I had revealed something within Ulric's hearing that perhaps I should not. Both Ceci and I looked at him at the same time.

His eyes were wide and his mouth had formed a small 'o'.

I took the bundle from him.

'Thank you, it feels like clothing. And yes, now you know I am with child. But not to the Baron. If you feel you must tell him, there is nothing I can do to stop you. But please Ulric, think on the babe, if not on me.'

He shook his head and began a circumnavigation of the Lady Chamber. He did not ring his hands but the intimation was there.

'Lady Ysabel, I would not dare tell him.' He walked past my secret passage, the rug lying snug and flat against the wall. 'I know I should but I will not. Not just for the babe's sake, but for your own. The father is…' He stopped. 'I would say it is a pity the father does not know. It would be all to the good if he did.'

'Ah,' I said. 'I wish you were right but you are so very wrong. This babe's father has no interest in saddling himself with a mother and child. So we must play-act, Ulric. This must be the Baron's child that I bake, do you see?'

'I do and you must not fear that I shall reveal anything else, my lady.'

Ceci had watched this and said nothing so that it was a surprise to Ulric when she clasped him in her thin arms and hugged.

'Mary Mother but you are a good boy, Ulric of Camden. I would be proud to call you my son and I shall be more content now, knowing you care for my godchild. She needs someone like you.'

Ulric blushed, the stain spreading into his blonde thatch. He smiled and then turned, saying over his shoulder.

'The Baron wishes you to dine in the Hall tonight with his guests. He asks that you wear the blue one.'

He shut the door, as ever, quietly behind him.

The parcel fell open to reveal velvets and damasks from across the Middle Sea, of a quality I had never seen, not even at Cazenay. On the top lay a deep rose damask woven with gold thread through the warp and weft and edged in a roll of velvet the same colour. I had no doubt this was to be my wedding gown as De Courcey had a predilection for the autumnal shades. A soft veil sat atop. But the gown beneath caught my breath in my throat.

Pers tinted, its shade and texture raised memories that threatened to crush me. I held the fold of velvet in my hand. Thicker than the wool of Gisborne's gown, it nevertheless felt as soft. The hem was padded and the sleeves were tight – a beautiful blue *bliaut,* but I didn't care.

This was the gown I must wear to dine with our guests because De Courcey wanted everyone to see that his future wife wore the colour of faith and love. *I* would have moved heaven and earth never to wear a *pers* tint again.

The noise from the Hall was more ordered, a deep resonance, the occasional burst of masculine laughter but what I called a sophisticated sound. I stood rather in awe of these guests who had wrought such change in so short a space of time. I had already decided they must be some of Richard's finest and that they had been sent by their monarch to mark this occasion rather than coming of their own volition.

I would be interested to see how they engaged with my questionable husband-to-be. This perhaps, was Richard's gift to a man with a private army... to sweeten him by giving him the respect he craved. The only thing that could have made more of a mark was the King's own presence but he was deep in the construction of his kingship in London.

Cecilia tugged at my folds and patted down loose curls.

'The blue suits you, it echoes your eyes but I worry that you knotted your hair instead of plaiting it. And the veil, do you not think the Baron might be angered when you arrive with your head uncovered?'

'Let him be angry. I do not care. And let others see that Ysabel Moncrieff has her own mind.'

Ceci 'tsked' and I knew she thought I pushed my boat too far and probably into muddy waters. But it mattered little to me because it was difficult enough to attend this function, let alone wear the blue gown and present myself as the precious 'bride'. After tomorrow, I should be obliged by convention to wear veils and wimples like a nun in a convent, so why not taste freedom whilst I could?

'You do realize that your condition is placing a bloom upon you that many might see as the excitement of love and marriage, my dear. It is ironic that another man's child should make you look so perfect for the man who professes to make you his wife on the morrow.'

We had almost reached the Hall and I swung to Cecilia.

'If I bloom then I could almost hate the babe for making it so and yet the babe itself is the only thing that makes my future worthwhile and so I shall love it instead.'

I gave her a small smile that barely curled my lips and reached forward and kissed her smooth cheek, letting my lips linger with affection and gratitude in a gesture I doubted De Courcey would allow me to make later. She held me hard in her arms for a tiny moment only and then gave me a smart push to Brother John's side so he could escort me to the table.

The Hall quieted as we entered and I walked on, glancing at no one, seeing my chair waiting for me. I knew I was being assessed and measured and I wondered if they approved of the future partnership. Could they see in the rigidity of my body and the stiffness of my face that I despised the man who stood as I walked closer?

His auburn hair sat on a thick rolled collar and a long blue velvet tunic fell away to his toes. A gilded girdle hung low on his hips and he emanated vivacity. His eyes sparkled with ownership and he glanced quickly away to calculate the effect of my arrival. In that moment, I noticed Halsham stand and bow his head with much irony in his stance. He moved slightly to allow the guest on his other side to push his own chair back and stand and my gaze shifted to the tall man who towered over him.

Now I understood his irony.

Clad in black velvet and with no jewelry and cold eyes, Gisborne watched me approach.

It was like walking toward the devil.

Chapter Thirteen

It takes a moment to place one foot in front of another and in that time I studied every loved and hated detail of his face, the minutae of his surcoat which was edged in even darker ebony embroidery so thick it weighted the garment against his frame. His gaze caught mine and burned into my soul.

One step only and all that happened in the blink of an eye.

I flushed, the heat of it warming my cheeks. Quickly I glanced back to the Baron to see if he had noticed my attention engaged far from him but he was only just turning his head back. Worse was the look that Halsham gave me. A satanic grin and then a wink.

One day…

'My lords,' if the Baron had been a rooster he would have crowed. 'May I present my betrothed, the Lady Ysabel Moncrieff, god-daughter of Queen Eleanor, god-sister of King Richard. May I also present the Lady Cecilia Fineux, ladywife of the late Sir Hugh Fineux and chatelaine of Upton.'

What liberties you take with the noble names, sir.

Hate roared through the blood vessels.

The assembled guests stood and a polite round of applause greeted Ceci and I as we were seated, the high backed chairs shifted so as we were comfortable.

'Whilst you are standing my lords, may I ask you to toast my future bride.' The Baron raised a wrought pewter goblet. 'The Lady Ysabel.'

My name echoed around the Hall and emptied goblets were placed on the tables as the noise of pulled seats filled the space. A hand movement from De Courcey indicated that food be bought to the tables.

Nausea filled my gullet. I could barely stand the sight of the rich courses of game that were placed in front of us. I sat between my future husband and Halsham; Cecilia sat on the other side of the Baron with Brother John at the very end of the head table.

A happy little family.

Only one person, Halsham, sat between my babe's father and myself and that gentleman an insult to the word 'knight'. If there were a tangible connection between the infant's father and me, I imagined it would feel like touching a vibrating metal thread. Something that could drill into the core of one's very being.

I played with dish after dish.

'My Lady Moncrieff, you do not eat?'

Halsham leaned toward me whilst the Baron called across Ceci to one of the distinguished guests.

'Perhaps it is the excitement of your forthcoming nuptials.'

'Perhaps it is, Halsham.' I spoke between gritted teeth.

'Isn't it fortuitous that I met up with my cuz in London and that he could be persuaded to attend your wedding?'

'I am surprised he wanted to.' At that point, I lifted my eyes to Gisborne, daring him to ignore me. 'But no doubt he thought it worth his while.'

Gisborne said nothing, but his expression iced over and his shoulders angled away as if he were bored.

'You *are* a sharp little thing, aren't you, my lady? Of *course*, it's worth his while.' Halsham slapped the blade of his dagger against Gisborne's arm. 'Isn't it, cuz? Look around. Half the men who mean anything in Richard's court are here.'

'Then if the other half are in London, sir, surely as much would have been gained by staying there, without the inevitable discomfort of travel.'

Gisborne spoke then and his voice sent a thrill through me and I wished I could throw myself onto his memory and mercy.

'You do not wish me to attend your nuptials, Lady Ysabel?'

No.

'I have no say in who attends, sir. It is entirely up to my lord Baron who shall attend. Obviously he wishes you to be here.'

To rub your nose in his doings. To make you realize he is my husband, my liege-lord, my owner.

How unnecessary it all was. Surely even De Courcey could see that a man who sold my whereabouts cared little for me at all.

And then something jumped out and winded me. I coughed on my wine.

'What ails you, my love?'

De Courcey was so honey sweet it should have galled me but I just shook my head, gasping as I lifted the wine to my mouth again.

For what had sucked the breath from my body was Gisborne's face.

There was no injury. No scar. No mark to show that I had hit him with a flagon and wounded him enough for a great blood-letting when I woke to find him in the Lady Chamber two weeks before.

'Ysabel?'

Cecilia called out and broke me from my trance. I raised my eyebrows and quirked my lips almost as if all was right with the world. But it was not. Not really. I had no doubt dreamed that ugly confrontation and confusion filled my head with aches and tension as I wondered if it really mattered.

But why would it? Because tomorrow I marry the man to whom I was sold.

It would never have been a normal wedding, even if my father had been alive to place my hand in my future husband's. The day was hardly a normal summer's day – the sky so low it touched the flagpole now resplendent with De Courcey's flapping colours. The wind whined around the stones of Moncrieff and small white wavelets snapped at the breeze as it bullied its way across the surface of the lake.

The swan flotilla had disappeared and there was something of bitterness in the air – a reminder that in six more weeks, autumn would turn the world to russet and bronze. Jesu, how De Courcey would love it. I wished he would don his autumnal colour and get irredeemably lost in the falling leaves.

The rose damask cascaded to the ground and Cecilia laced it. It made a shivering sound as I moved, as if it were telling me things I should know about being the wife in the marriage bed. But I ignored it because it spoke out of turn, instead giving my attention to my hair. I should have let the curls and strands fall in an unbound swathe, glorying in its unfettered status for the last time. Instead, I had Ceci plait a long tight braid that hung down my back. The rose veil lay atop with my mother's twisted filet holding it in place. Like the damask, the veil spoke – a whispering admonition to behave and make my betrothed proud.

I couldn't bear Cecilia to say a word. Not 'courage' or 'I love you, my dear' or even 'I shall say my farewells now'. I held my fingers up, shook my head and in this silent mode, walked on the longest yet shortest journey of my life to the church of Saint Agatha outside the walls of the castle as the bells rang for Tierce. Or perhaps they rang to celebrate marriage, except that Brother John knew my state of mind and I doubt he would wish to underline my agony.

Cecilia walked behind me holding up the dragging hem of the gown. I could hear her praying to the Virgin Mother, asking for protection for me. The villagers had gathered to cheer, calling blessings. Obviously their liege-lord had declared a holiday in order to honour the marriage but I doubted they approved of the nuptials – not the villagers I remembered.

The church was filled with rows of men. A smell hung low underneath the arched beams of the modest building – of leather and candle, incense and body odour. Nothing had been done to soften and improve the church's harsh interior and its dour stone merely glowered.

Finish this. Have it done!

Inside, my soul shrieked.

I do not want this.

As I paced forward, I searched for Gisborne's face, wanting not to find him and yet relieved when he turned as I passed. He looked but did not see.

Help me, cried my soul.

I hate you, condemned my mind.

I cannot remember the form of prayer, the actions of Brother John, my responses nor those of my husband. A torpour pervaded as I placed myself far from the situation. Far from what could hurt me – a place of little sensation and no thought.

It was only as a door clicked that my actual being clicked in response.

The nuptials were over. I was wedded. Without me being aware, the Baron De Courcey and his lady had walked back through the crowd of cheering villagers, had walked across the causeway, under the portcullis, through the bailey and into the Hall. From there, Cecilia had guided me into the Lady Chamber and she had quietly shut the door.

I turned at that clicking sound.

'It is done then.'

'Well yes, my dear, though you were like the walking dead. I am glad you are back with us. Such an odd thing but then you never would do things in the accepted manner.'

Odd? Perhaps. Convenient? Of course.

'I put myself in a better place, Cecilia. It made it easier to bear.'

'You are such an unusual girl and yet I can imagine following the same path myself if I had to marry such a man. Honestly, one wonders what sort of conscience the King really has. That said; the Baron seemed barely to notice your abstraction so you are lucky. Only those of us who know and love you would have seen any difference. Jesu, De Courcey is so full of himself – so arrogant. He struts like a cock. And my girl, they wait to begin the festivity. Do you intend to put yourself in your faraway place or do you plan to join them?'

Sadness tinged Cecilia's comment as she, like me, counted the moments until her mount was saddled and she and her small retinue left for Upton – a definitive dismissal by my husband. I hugged her.

'Oh Ceci, how shall I survive? When it is time to declare my condition, I shall *demand* you return and he *must* agree out of concern for his child.'

'I confess I worry for you, Ysabel. I have heard so many things. Thank God you have Ulric. He is such a good boy.'

I smiled as I changed my boots for a daintier pair of slippers, remembering how Cecilia had flayed poor Ulric with her manner when I had first arrived. How things had changed.

Please let Ulric protect me. I am so frightened but cannot tell Cecilia.

'I presume we must go then.'

I linked my arms with hers and we opened the door where Ulric waited to take us to the so-called festivities.

Course followed course and I picked around the edges, managing to quaff quite enough unwatered wine to soften my outlook. I almost disappeared to that place far on the other side of my soul until my heavy-lidded eyes spotted Gisborne. His black-clad frame leaned in toward another man, the intensity of their discussion arousing interest.

To others it might seem they debated the lute the other man held as he turned it over for Gisborne's inspection, the latter reaching out and stroking the bowl with gentle fingers. But I had a different view of what they did. Gisborne's nature, his subtle fact-gathering ability, caused me to wonder if he sought and stored information.

The man was middling height and slim with shining, blond hair that fell to his shoulders in a wave. He had a sensitive face, even and attractive, and his manner was neither bullish nor forward. His eyes were dark and framed by sculpted eyebrows that a woman would envy and in fact there was much about the fine appearance of the man that many a woman would covet. He trod a fine line between male and female.

'I see you looking at the King's favourite,' the odious Halsham whispered in my ear.

'Already a favourite and in the King's presence for such a short time.' My words were weighted.

'You think I mean Gisborne? Ah, but of course you do. My lady, you must try harder to hide your interest or your husband shall find out.'

My teeth snapped together and I quickly switched my attention to the pustule before me.

'You forget yourself, Sir Robert. You must learn to show the Lady De Courcey more respect.'

He bowed his head with his hand on his chest.

'My apologies, my lady, of course you are right. I just remember his arm round your waist when you were so charmingly dressed as a boy. Ha! It is of no account. But talking of boys ... the perennial youth who speaks with Gisborne is the King's favourite. He is the troubadour De Nesle, and whom the King lovingly calls Blondel and would you believe the Plantagenet has sent him to sing a song to celebrate your wedding and your beauty? What a highly regarded person you must be.'

I wanted to slap his insolent face but instead turned away just as my husband called to Blondel to urge him to sing.

'You are honoured, my love,' De Courcey picked up my hand and kissed the fingertips, his hand squeezing to the point of pain. 'To have Blondel fête you is a miracle most women would die for.'

'Then I *am* honoured, husband, as you say. I would hate to die before my time.' I spoke quietly and smiled at Blondel de Nesle.

He sat on a coffer by Moncrieff's enormous hearth and as he tuned his lute, humming, the noise of the Hall gradually subsided and looking directly at me, he began.

'Your beauty lady-fair,
None views without delight;
But still so cold an air
No passion can excite;
Yet this I patient see
While all are shunned like me.'

There were more verses to follow, each identifying an apparent coolness in my manner and the power and pain of unrequited love. My boorish husband squirmed in his chair; how he would love to have stopped the song and consigned Blondel to a punishment – but he could not. This man was the King's favourite and a gift into the bargain. De Courcey must endure and I silently begged de Nesle to change tack and introduce a song that might laud my husband's good fortune at marrying me.

He began another chanson; a more gentle, less pointed one…

'This is what joy is all about.
To love sincerely
And when the moment comes
Give generously…'

At which De Courcey began to subside and I thanked the Lord. Other chansons followed. Less courtly, more rustic and bawdy with rebec, tabor and flute joining in and presently the Hall rang to many male voices in lusty choruses. Ceci signaled to me and I leaned toward De Courcey to beg his indulgence to retire and when his gaze met mine as he licked his lips, I shivered.

Guy of Gisborne loved gently and with consideration. That at least I would admit. A virgin found herself carried carefully along an unknown road so the journey was memorable for many wonderful reasons of discovery.

But I now had a point of comparison in an otherwise limited experience.

Benedict De Courcey took what he wanted on *his* journey with brutal violence, plundering the landscape and leaving a welter of scratches and bruising behind, fulfilling my fears and concerns. But I cared most deeply for the safety of my babe and that required submission to such treatment; for in so doing I protected the infant and myself for another few months. I turned my head to the side at one point as he cut and thrust and saw his strong hand pinioning my own, the auburn hairs catching the candlelight and mocking me with their softly silken look.

A tiny splinter of bone was all that was needed to create the trail of the blood required to fool De Courcey into thinking he tupped a virgin wife. Reeking of wine and ale, he collapsed to snore loudly and it was a matter of a quick prick and drag to paint the picture and to then throw the bone into the blazing fire. The rest I would leave to his imagination, if he remembered anything at all.

But he did remember and the next morning rolled me over to examine the stain of blood between my thighs and on the bed. He smiled, took me again and as he imprisoned me once more, said in menacing tones.

'Mine now, little Moncrieff. Defy me and you shall be punished. I am your liege-lord.'

He finished and wiped himself, washed and changed and left the room without a backward glance. No glance at the face of his wife which was swollen and bruised and was a reminder to her to love and obey.

Ulric gasped when he entered at my call.

'Lady Ysabel…'

I shook my head.

'Let it be, Ulric. It is the way of it. But procure some arnica please; it might help. Did I hear a departure?'

'Yes, milady. The Baron has left with a force of men for London.'

God be praised.

'For how long?'

'Until after the coronation.'

'And our guests?'

'Departed with him.'

'All?'

His expression could have sweetened honey.

'Guy of Gisborne rode out in the company of Blondel de Nesle and Halsham.'

'Ulric, I…'

'Madame, I know Gisborne is the father of your child. You are no profligate and seeing you now, I wish that he knew.'

'He must not. Ulric, he must not. I beg of you.'

'I will not tell him, even if I disagree with what you say but...'

'Just the arnica, Ulric. And the Lady Cecilia?'

'Was provided with a guard and left after you had retired.'

I stood at the window, the door closing quietly, and wanted to cry for the injustices and for my grim future. But it would be no good for the babe and so I sponged my face, scrubbed my body to erase the scent of De Courcey and threw the wedding gown and veil on the fire. I opened a chest and unfolded another of my mother's gowns. A pale grey wool *bliaut* embroidered with a filigree of silver and I pulled it over a fine linen chemise. And because there was no one but myself and a few men and the servants I knew and trusted from former days within the castle, I left my hair in plaits. Convention meant nothing because this was no meaningful marriage and I'd be damned if I'd pretend it was.

Ulric returned with the arnica and bless him, sat holding a looking glass whilst I smoothed the ointment onto the contusions. Nothing would scar, it could be worse. And the consolation was a month alone without the presence of a violent man.

'Lady Ysabel?'

'Yes?'

'I have something to tell you.'

I looked up. Ulric's expression was heavy with concern.

'I am ordered by the Baron to travel to London and stay with his men. Half of the legion he took is to head to Cyprus after the coronation and I am to provide the necessary cipher for messages to and fro.'

No!

'Ulric.'

I reached out and grabbed his hand.

'I have told Brother John and he will be even more stalwart and I believe you will find the villagers loyal to Moncrieff's daughter. They know what you did for Wilfred and Harry and that you saved Gisborne's life.'

'How can they care about Gisborne? He is full of cunning...'

'He served them well as your father's steward and they remember.'

'Ulric,' I whispered. 'He sold me.'

'I think you are wrong but it is of little matter, you have said what you feel. All I am saying is that there are people who will care for you and you have only to send for Dame Cecily...'

'Lady Cecilia,' I corrected without real care.

'Lady Cecilia,' he added, not at all chastened. 'I have had an idea for which I may needs beg your pardon because it transgresses our separate positions in life.'

I shrugged my shoulders indicating he continue. I was intrigued after all.

'You and I seem to get on well,' he explained. 'You know I don't like my lord but that I am in need of coin so I shall stay in his employ. But should you ever need me you have only to send a note.'

'What if the Baron sees it?'

'I have an easy code for you to use and I can reply in that same code. You can send a commonplace message and I can interpret it for my purpose and you likewise. You won't be so alone.'

I looked up from the explanatory parchment he pressed into my hands and found his image swam.

'Thank you,' I whispered again. 'I *would* like to know how you get on and when the Baron might return. You can give me warning. And...'

No, silly woman. Do not.

I sucked in a breath to swallow the tears that stuck in my throat.

'I should like to know how my child's father does, Ulric.'

He said nothing, just reached over my hands with his ink-stained, bony writer's fingers and patted me as if I were a little lapdog that is loved and cared for.

Thus did my married life become an odd one shared with a growing unborn babe, the villagers of Moncrieff who seemed to see something of Alaïs in their new lady of the manor, and with the remaining legion of De Courcey's army, fifty men in total and who gradually became approachable, deferring to me, even laughing with me. A more relaxed existence to be sure.

After three weeks, I saw fit to send a message of my condition to De Courcey and received back a long chain to wear around my waist and which was studded with topaz the colour of the leaves that were beginning to tint the Moncrieff forests. Rather apt, I thought ... the chain and the autumnal stones, but I chose not to wear it, it was ugly and cumbersome.

I received a message from Ulric and took delight in sitting in the Lady Chamber to decode it. I had taken possession of a puppy, a hound with pretensions to a gracefully long body and even longer legs. At this point it was sturdy and comfortable, showing little of the type it would grow to and sat on my lap chewing the edge of the parchment on which I worked.

I had also employed a girl from the village whom I was training to be my maid and companion. She was friendly and a pretty, intelligent child with strong Saxon traits and who was already betrothed to the blacksmith's son. Gwen idolized me and it had its benefits. She sat on the other side of the chamber folding laundry and laying it in the chests with bunches of lavender as I read and deciphered Ulric's note.

'*Court, royal attention,*' by which I knew he meant the babe's father. And then something that bore into my heart. '*Sicily.*'

And it was then I knew that Guy of Gisborne was irrevocably lost to his child and that he truly had succeeded in his search for status and power. He was patently to leave for the Middle Sea for King Richard. What I could not understand was why it should matter to me? Why else would I ask Ulric to inform me of his doings? Whilst consciously I believed he was as cunning as Halsham, unconsciously the tiny doubt that I was wrong sustained me. Now, with the news that he left for Sicily, I felt he was well beyond his child and myself and it pained me so that I threw Ulric's note in the fire and cuddled Sorcia the pup close.

The following week, on the third of September, 1189 Anno Domini Iesu Christi at Westminster, Richard was crowned King of England. To celebrate, my villagers had a day of feasting and bonfires, Brother John holding a service of blessing and Saint Agatha's bell ringing cheerfully on and off throughout the day. I wandered in and out of the small crowd wishing Ceci was with me, that we could share the roasted pig, fresh cooked fish and the eel pies with each other and with Ulric, that we could laugh at the children playing hide-a-seek and we could huff on the hot crisp pastry of an apple pie. Instead I was accompanied by Gwen dressed in a cut down *bliaut* of my mother's, and who cast blushing glances at Peter, the blacksmith's son.

I watched with envy and interest, wondering why my own parents had not betrothed me to some ordinary but acceptable noble at an early age, thus avoiding this terrible heartache. Pointless to wonder. I was married to a Baron who held the King's ear. Short of him dying in an unforeseen circumstance, I could only watch Gwen vicariously.

A week or more after, an encoded note arrived from Ulric, telling me of a dreadful event in London at the coronation banquet. It seemed that a number of the nobility were superstitious of the Jewish merchants who came to do homage to their new monarch. Whisper and accusation spread like a plague and within a short space of time, Jews within Old Jewry were attacked and burned in their homes. Ulric made mention of the lack of punishment for the offenders and I remembered what Gisborne had said about De Courcey, that he would commit murder and go to a banquet afterward and I knew without fear of correction that my erstwhile Baron had been at the forefront of such appalling misdeeds in the knowledge that he would be entirely protected by the King's goodwill. The despair that I should be connected with such a brute darkened the day. The fear that came with it darkened the night.

Not so many days after the sickening note, horses, shouting and a horn could be heard approaching the lake. The early autumn day was beset with mists and drizzle and the light was half-hearted. I ran to the window with Gwen to see who approached and grasped my small bulge as I saw the De Courcey pennants. My husband led a group of a dozen men across the causeway and into the bailey and my heart jumped and dived. I sat on the edge of my seat composing myself, draping the folds of the brown *bliaut* in such a way as to camouflage the size of the bump.

'Gwen, the chain!'

Ulric, why did you not tell me he was coming?

Gwen dug in the coffer by the window, the chain rattling like a spectre's warning, and I hastily thrust it round my body just below breasts that were becoming full and motherly. The topaz gems sat over the folds, a display that would surely please the Baron and give me a moment's reprieve.

The door crashed open and he strode in, his colouring fire and brimstone and tinged with a harsh ruddy flush.

'How now, Ysabel, mother of my child...' He grabbed me and pulled me up. 'Lord but you are expanding.'

He ran his hand over the front of the gown in a proprietorial way and I gritted my teeth, thinking of hands that had lit fires in London.

'But damned if you don't look good with it.'

'It often happens that a woman grows rapidly. Then again, perhaps I brew two babes. There are twins in Cazenay. And yes, I am well although prone to decrepit tiredness and the odd pain. I hope it will pass.'

There were of course no twins in my family but I was becoming an accomplished liar and he was so full of his prowess at siring a child in a mere strike or two that I could see he would listen to anything. I just hoped he would not be violent, not again, and I tried hard not to upset him.

'One child ha, maybe two! These are my *heirs*.' Initial joy lasted but a moment as his eyes hardened. 'By the Saints, wife, if I do not hear that you mind yourself or that the staff do not mind you, there shall be a price to pay.'

'Then it is as well that I am cared for. The servants, your men included, have been pillars of support. The demesnes runs well. The harvest has been got in. So you see my Lord De Courcey, I wonder why you are come? I had thought the King required your services elsewhere.'

'He does and I have already served him well. I am here to see my wife and to gather the rest of the men. Richard is to begin seeking funds for a crusade and we are to bolster his forces.'

'You think he shall need force amongst his own people?'

'He is unsure how his Barons will react and believes the Free Lancers shall be an incentive.'

Force?

'For how long shall you be here? I will make sure the food supplies are adequate.'

I moved to leave but he grabbed my hand, his eyes filled with a look I had grown to despise.

'A night and a day only – enough time for the rest of the force to arm and prepare. I have told the bailiff to organize food for us.' He pulled me into his arms roughly, his fingers pinching. 'By the saints, Ysabel, I want you.' I could feel his manhood hard against my stomach and begged God to help me. 'But…' he pushed me away. 'It seems I must not. I shall have sons madame, I am sure, and nothing, not even my rights, shall threaten their being. They shall be the sons of a kingmaker.'

He spoke with sickening grandeur and for one ghastly moment I had a window into a frightening future.

Kingmaker.

It was what I had thought so long ago.

Kingmaker, kingbreaker.

Gwen shifted in the corner, Sorcia squirming out of her arms and running to me. I bent and picked her up and De Courcey glanced at her.

'A hound, Ysabel, and like to be huge. Hardly the dog for a Lady Chamber.'

'She is a good bitch from Eodmund's litter and will add fine blood to your own.'

But his eyes had drifted from the dog to Gwen and the glance was filled with thickly scented interest.

'And this is?'

'Gwen. Since you sent Cecilia back to Upton, I have felt in need of help. A girl from the village will suit my needs as the months move on.'

'Gwen.' He walked around her, his eyes on her young breasts and formative hips. 'Your father?'

'Died protecting the Lady Ysabel in Anjou, my lord.'

You angel child! You lie as well as me.

Gwen knew, I could tell. More worldly wise than me at the same age, of course she knew what her liege-lord was about and sought to placate him.

'Then you are welcome in my house, Gwen.'

His voice had softened to silk and I hoped Gwen would use her wits. If not, placating him could take a whole other course entirely.

'Oh!' I grabbed at my lower back and sank onto a settle.

De Courcey turned back, his eyes dark with something nasty.

'What ails you?'

Untruths!

'Back pain. Gwen, run to your mother and ask her to come to me with her herbals. When she leaves, you must take the youngsters to your aunt's.'

She bobbed and dashed out. There was no aunt nor siblings and I prayed for sharp little Gwen to go where she could not be found. I prayed also that a good meal and plenty of ale and wine might dull the Baron's excesses. And there were always Gwen's mother's herbs.

I drugged him.

The herbs for my so-called back-pain were nothing but the extract of poppy. Brother John had directed me to Gwen's mother on witnessing my post-marital bruising, saying she had experience with herbs and had helped the sick and needy at times.

'She will give you a drug to feed into his drink when you want to avoid him, my child. I will not see the daughter of Joffrey so treated. He is an animal.'

And so I placed the drops in his ale and by the end of the meal, he lay with his head on a half eaten trencher. I ordered two of the brawny men I had come to know to carry him to the Master Chamber and I passed a more comfortable night in the knowledge Gwen and I would be left alone.

He departed in a foul temper next day. He snarled at me to mind his heirs, squeezing my arm, and I bit my tongue so as not give him pleasure in my pain. He almost kicked Sorcia but I grabbed her as his booted foot was drawn back. He knocked his squire down when a chainmail vest was misplaced, the fellow hitting his head and bleeding. He yelled to the bailiff that the bushel yield from the harvest had better exceed last year's else his position would be forfeit. And when his horse reared on being mounted, he raked his spurs along the animal's sides leaving bloody scores.

Moncrieff seethed as the men mingled and mounted, forming into lines. They clattered out two by two leaving the castle with a guard of six men-at-arms and peace.

I watched until the noise of horses and men faded on the air. Till the honk of bird and bleat of sheep sounded, until harshness was replaced with poultry pecking at worms disturbed in the bailey's soil, Sorcia barking at a cat, children chasing the pigeons that flew up with a flacking of wings to settle on the corbels of the walls. It was then I finally took a breath of wonder as my child quickened inside me, a butterfly touch so that I rubbed the mound and thanked God and the Saints that we were left behind and that De Courcey, God rot his soul, was heading in the opposite direction.

Straight away I hurried to my chamber and wrote two notes – one to Cecilia begging her to come. The other to my despised husband saying that in view of my apparent discomfort and his interest in the care of the mother of his offspring, it seemed sensible to secure the cosseting companionship of my godmother.

Thus the months passed – Cecilia, young Gwen and Brother John ... my triumvirate. All guarded by an alarmingly large Sorcia. There was enough barley and wheat harvested to be distributed amongst the villagers and by judicious numbering of the bushels in the records De Courcey would never know. Livestock fattened through the summer was butchered and salted for the winter, autumn fruits provided just enough to sweeten our appetites. We had no real need of complaint. Apart from my name, my condition, and the introduction of the six men-at-arms, it seemed Gwen said, as if nothing had changed at Moncrieff in years.

Cecilia's company was a boon beyond all expectation as the cold set in and snow fell. We walked, our feet in pattens and Ceci holding me tightly in case I should fall. I met the villagers, visiting in an ox and cart, and sat quietly talking to Ceci about Alaïs and Joffrey, paying respect to them once weekly and laying wreaths on their tomb. I told Cecilia about Ulric's code, and his notes continued to arrive by devious means – a relic pedlar, a pilgrim, a returned soldier travelling west.

But I knew the day a thick encoded packet arrived, that it contained something vital.

Cecilia was looking at me as someone knocked at the chamber door.

'Ysabel, you are so big and the child hangs so low, it's as well that excuse for a Baron is not here. You are fit to burst, my child.'

'My legs and back ache with the weight of it, Ceci, and if I am right I think I only have days to go and us yet with no plan.' I arched my back and called 'Come.'

The fire flared as the door opened, the flames dipping and diving.

Gwen slipped in.

'My lady, a merchant has passed this to you. He is even now with Brother John.'

'Then let us hope Brother John shall thaw out the poor man's feet and prevail upon him to put aside his wretched travels until the snow clears. It is a God forsaken freeze outside.'

Cecilia growled. She hated the cold, her bones aching and her blood sluggish; another reason to be away from Upton which lay on a bleak hill in the middle of wind-scoured moorland.

I held the heavy packet in my hand, gazing at how it was folded upon itself and I thought back to the very advent of the turn my life had taken and the package of death that I had opened on that day ... the hours before I met Guy of Gisborne.

We all of us lose family – it is the natural course of life, but I think I had ached with it for months now, grieving in fits and starts. Just once I would have liked to cry and be heart-sore without pretensions to strength. I don't even recall flinging myself into Ceci's arms and wailing when I saw her that day Gisborne and I slipped from the passage, nothing but the odd quiet tear and an unconscious urge to dig deep for something to anchor me. I think it was the child that sustained me now – that giant bulge that put pressure on my spine and made me realize I *had* a supporting backbone.

My finger slipped under the fold held down by the hated De Courcey seal, flicking the crumbling wax apart. The parchment trembled, as there was something of the troubadour's Death Roll in the air. De Courcey's death or Gisborne's, my heart quailed for alternate reasons. I watched the wax segments crack and flutter to the floor like aged petals.

'It is from Ulric,' I breathed with relief. 'Shall I read it?'

'Of course, Ysabel, and for God's sake sit, you're quite pale.'

I subsided onto a coffer. 'It will take me time to decipher, so have patience.' I spoke more to give myself a moment than anything.

'He has a good hand and should surely be an excellent steward for someone so much more noble than De Courcey. He begins with the usual...' I tapped the page, skipping over the opening pleasantries. 'He says... *You would find the costumes of court a wonder to behold in winter, my lady. I have never seen such thick velvets nor so many extravagant furs but the women are ugly and as pale as a hardboiled egg and the men strut like cockerels ... perfect company for my lord Baron. It is however impossible not to be awed by His Majesty. He is as golden and perfect as you would expect a child of Eleanor of Aquitaine to be. Prince John is like a black spider next to a wondrous butterfly by comparison and such an odious man to whom our lord Baron appears to be tying himself.*

An inner circle of very different men surrounds the King though. Master Gisborne is one; although he comes and goes...'

My cheeks flushed as I realized he was no longer in Sicily and I was glad I sat by the fire so that Cecilia needn't employ her dry wit.

'*However he is no longer Master,*' I continued reading Ulric's words aloud. *'He is knighted and has had estates gifted, a favourite you see, and the Baron chafes to see it is so. The Baron however has been ordered to ready his men for a departure. He is to take his men as an advance cohort to the Middle Sea and they shall billet in a location that must remain undisclosed. I can inform you of nothing more except that the King plans the crusade for July and of course we are now in January.*

The Baron returns to Moncrieff on the morrow to see yourself and to issue instructions for the estate for the next few months. Keep you safe, my lady and beware. I wish you... and so on, signed *Ulric of Camden.'* I looked up. 'He has dated it. A week ago, Ceci. The Baron must be ... argh!'

I dropped the parchment and grabbed at my stomach as a wave of pain clutched it and squeezed. At the same time, warmth ran down my legs and I glanced floor-ward to see a trickle emerge under my gown and soak the edges of the letter. Another pain as I reached to throw the document in the fire. I held to the stone surrounds.

'Cecilia, the child! Gwen, get your mother!'

It seemed that a whirlwind of activity occurred but I withdrew into a small space defined by the scope of my pain. I walked, I cried, I screamed and swore. I sweated and eventually allowed myself to be stripped to the chemise and laid on the bed.

'The plan, Cecilia. We have no plan.'

I grabbed her hand, my voice husky with exertion.

'Hush, just save your breath.'

But her expression was grim.

'Madame,' Gwen's mother, Brigid, spoke to Cecilia as I writhed. She wiped my face with a damp cloth and took my hand.

'Listen to me. I can see the head right now and it's covered in black hair which aint goin' ter please the Baron too much.'

I groaned.

'Milady, you listen. I've a sister in Wales and as I'm on me own, I was thinkin' I would as like to live with her as here. I'd take Gwen too if you'd allow, as I think she's unsafe when the Baron's here. I remember yer face, milady, beggin' yer pardon. Shush, you jus breathe. Nice an' easy. There. Now rest. Next one'll be a big un.'

'Well for God's sake, Brigid,' Cecilia wrung out another cloth and passed it to the villager. 'What's your idea? Lady Ysabel's life is forfeit if we have no plan.'

'I'm sayin' I take the babe to Wales as soon as it is born. I can suckle it with goat's milk as it's too dangerous to have a wet-nurse and you jus tell the Baron the babe died.'

She looked at Cecilia and for a moment I held my breath, storing my energies for the last purge.

'Gwen, get Brother John.'

Cecilia's voice took on such a tone that I knew she saw this as the only way the child could live.

'Put it around that there is a sickly babe like to die and that the Lady Ysabel is weak and it's in God's hands as to whether she or the babe survives or neither. You, Brigid, deliver this infant and then you will leave undercover of night with Gwen and the child. I don't know how you will get to Wales but it is the only plan and better this child lives than dies.'

My breathing began to build to a roaring crescendo and I pushed with every bit of strength left. There was a slithering sensation between my legs but I just lay in a pool of exhaustion, letting it drag me to an oblivion I craved.

'Ysabel,' my cheek was slapped. 'Hold your child! He's a fine boy.'

Brigid lay something over me and I opened my eyes to see a waxy face and scrunched eyes and little fists crunched tight. My hand crept to his back and he arched under my touch and then his fist opened to the tiniest star and lay upon my flesh. He snuffled and sniffed and at one stage gave a tiny yawn which ended in slight cry, but in essence it was as if he knew the need for secrecy.

He was indeed his father's son.

'William,' I croaked, lifting my head to kiss him. 'His name is William.'

Cecilia took him away to a bowl and washed him and wrapped him in a cloth of fine wool as the afterbirth slithered out. Brigid cleaned me and wadded some cloths to soak up the blood and Cecilia, the infant in one arm, passed me a warm, spiced wine.

Brother John hussled in with plain swaddling in his arms and gave me a kiss.

'Well, Cecilia. And what skullduggery do we pursue now? Lord I hope I am forgiven for all this.'

'Rubbish, you silly man,' Cecilia thrust William into his arms. 'You dote on the subterfuge. *Your* God will forgive *you*, of course he will. De Courcey's might not. Bless him and name him and intercede with God for him because he must leave immediately.'

He tickled the babe under the chin. 'And I suppose I am burying a phantom babe on the morrow?'

'What a clever priest you are.'

Brother John laughed softly and I felt the warmth of relief. My son, named and blessed, to be delivered beyond De Courcey's wrath.

All will be well.

I slept through his naming, the Latin words sonorous and soft and fading in and out of my hearing. And then he was wrapped like a dead child.

'We go, Ysabel,' the priest whispered to me. 'Our visiting merchant is an old friend and heads toward the Welsh border. He will take Gwen, Brigid and William as far as he can. Rest easy now.'

I heard the door click and even then the fact that I had lost my child didn't register. I just imagined the little rescue-party as I dozed – Brother John carrying the 'stillborn' babe with a measured tread, Gwen and Brigid following with the piles of bloody laundry, all of them knowing they would meet in Saint Agatha's later.

The next day I woke with an ache in my belly.

Cecilia sat next to me and looked up from her spindle when I stirred.

'You have slept long, my love.'

'Will…' I went to ask.

'They are gone. Leagues hence by now. Peter, the blacksmith's son, has gone as well. He would not let Gwen leave without him and Brigid said she will send word when she is safely in Wales.'

She 'tsk-ed'.

'How we shall interpret the loss of *three* of De Courcey's villagers, I am unsure. There will be hell to pay.'

Hell.

'I have no child, Ceci.'

'Now, now. You do, but just not in your arms. Better he lives far and safe than here and doomed. I trust Brigid and Gwen to care for him. They love you and are loyal.'

'But my child sustained me.'

'Well you shall have Sorcia to sustain you instead. She has laid her head on your bed through all of yesterday. Ysabel,' Cecilia said in her matter-of-fact way, 'Brother John buries the 'babe' later today. I shall go to Saint Agatha's but the lie would be enhanced if you stay abed.'

I turned my head away but Sorcia burrowed under my fingers and I loved her warmth and succour.

The 'child' was buried and Cecilia ordered a small stone slab to be laid, with the name William De Courcey chiseled into the stone and the date. Not many days later and with his habitual angst, De Courcey galloped across the causeway and into the bailey. I heard him and lay back, weak and anxious. The door slammed open and he stood there aflame with wrath.

'Leave,' he hissed at Cecilia.

'How dare…' Cecilia began to steam.

'Ceci, go,' I grabbed her hand. 'And take Sorcia.'

She frowned but grabbed Sorcia by the collar and skirted around the Baron's figure. He slammed the door after her and walked to the wine flask to pour.

'So wife, you birthed an heir. They say he is dead.'

'He lived long enough to be christened…'

'Weakling…' he roared and threw the goblet against the wall. 'What does it take to birth a live babe, Ysabel? If pigs and sheep can do it, what is it that prevents you? You're a mewling imitation of your father.'

I jumped from the bed shouting like a shrew, feeling the sweat of weakness trickle between my breasts.

'How dare you! I carried that child. Do you think, sir, that I take joy in not being able to hold it in my arms? God's Blood, you know nothing. A quick rut and your responsibility is done.'

The hem of the linen chemise fell around me as its folds untangled and a warmth ran down my inner thigh. I noticed the blood, as did De Courcey and I dove in for the kill.

'Yes Baron, look you. It is blood from the birth, a birth that was timed by every bell that rang through the day. It split me in half and even now bleeds and bleeds.'

He took a step back and for the first time ever was speechless and I tell you I gloried in it as he turned and left, slamming the door so hard I swear the stones trembled.

I heard the horses' hooves clattering back over the causeway and for the horses' sakes some part of me hoped he'd changed mounts before leaving. If he went to Saint Agatha's I'd have been surprised and yet Brother John informed me later that he had done so. He'd stared at the tiny slab.

'William?' His voice rose with each syllable. 'God damn her to perdition! Why William? Strike the name, priest, get rid of it. He was to have been John if the bitch had asked, after Prince John. Strike this name I say because the child is nothing. There shall be no name. Do you hear me? No name!'

Chapter Fourteen

If I had been a great *trovairitz,* I would have composed a ballad the like of which had never been sung, about Ysabel De Courcey lately Moncrieff, about this young woman of the winsome face and hair the colour of a Canterbury-minted silver penny. The men might have sighed and the women cried at the words of love and loss that took place over a year. How she had become an orphan and then a mother who held her own babe but once.

There would have been verses about what might have been but now would never be, words that tore into the heartstrings of the nobles who listened in rapt attention. And at the end, those same nobles would have dried each other's tears and nodded sagely about her courage, determination and forthright nature as Fate played its hand.

Ah yes, that's what I would have sung about this woman I barely recognized as myself. But what I would not have sung is how she began to concoct a plan, an idea that when the crusaders left for the Holy Land she could re-shape her life and shrug off what she was and become something new and altogether unrecognizable.

And yet maybe part of that new story may have had the nobles sitting on the edge of their seats; the women in awe, the men perplexed that a fair maid should have such outrageous courage.

I counted each bell that marked each hour of each passing day as the date of that holy departure grew closer. None the wiser on the fate of those of meaning in my life, William of Nowhere and Ulric of Camden, I refused on any account to succumb to more grief. To be sure, I cried in secret when Cecilia or Brother John could not see me for I am not made of stone, but that hard streak inside me had deepened and widened to give me strength when I might have had none.

I sat against the sun-warmed stone of Alaïs' garden, admiring the freshly weeded paths between beds of herbs and fruit trees heavy with spring blossom. A garden seat corrugated my bottom and I noticed dirty knee marks on the green gown. I brushed at them and spread the stain further.

Bees buzzed around the blue flowers of borage and rosemary and I wondered why they so liked blue flowers when there were other brighter colours – saffron, ivory and yellow. They bumbled heavily back to the woven willow bee bothies and I thought it would be a good honey harvest.

Cecilia entered the garden behind a leaping Sorcia who punched her head under my arm, leaving a further stain on a chemise that had unrolled its dagged sleeve to where it was fair game for a dog.

'There you are,' Cecilia puffed. 'Lord but I have looked for you everywhere.' She wiped a hand across her wimpled head. 'I'm getting too old, Ysabel. I should be sitting in a solar, stitching pretty threads. Now listen. I must away to Upton for a week. It seems there is tension between my bailiff and a tenant over dues to be paid and it requires a sorting. I am assuming you are enough yourself these days not to need me to prop you up?'

Ever the plain speaker, she put me quickly in my place so that I wondered if my new strength was really so self-made after all.

There had come a point one night between the bell for Compline and the bell for Matins that I had decided I could no longer be rolled back and forth like a twig in an ebb tide. Life had the capacity to end when one least expected and be damned if I was going to waste any more days. That was my epiphany.

With a faintly snoring Ceci on the other side of my parents' bed, I nodded at the darkness.

A new day.

A new Ysabel.

A plan.

'Of course I shall be perfectly well. Have you not noticed I take my role as the Lady Ysabel quite seriously? And with much loved charm?' I mocked.

She snorted.

'Yes. Well. I shall be back before you can get yourself into trouble because I can see you are brewing something. We shall talk when I return.'

No we shan't, Ceci. But I love you anyway.

Cecilia and two Upton retainers left immediately, rattling over the causeway, and were barely gone for two bells when a clattering of horses sounded back the other way. I took little notice because horses came and went and the bailiff would send for me if I was needed.

I stood naked before a bowl of water, washing away the exertions of the morning, my dirty laundry piled high. Sorcia slept curled in a dark shadow, almost hidden. I undid my hair and reveled in the silken swish as it slid down my back, running a comb through and then I reached for a fresh chemise…

The door crashed open, my head flew up and De Courcey, hated husband, burst in upon his wife as if she were *in flagrante delicto.*

'Now that is what I call a homecoming, wife!'

His unbuckled sword and scabbard crashed to the floor.

I backed away holding my chemise against me as he advanced, ripping a travel-stained surcoat over his head, a chemise following. I stared at the powerful torso where the auburn hair sat lightly, his chest rising and falling with excited breath. He managed to pull his *chausses, braies* and boots away and still move with animal grace toward me, his manhood purple with intent. The stones bit into my back and my small oratory, the cushion littered with parchment, quills and a quill-sharpening blade, prevented a sideways step.

His hand reached out and grabbed me.

'Great minds, wife, that you should so prepare yourself for my quick homecoming. You knew I would want to sire an heir before I left for the crusade, didn't you?'

He ran a hand over my breasts and it was at that very minute that the new streak inside me spread to my heart, pumping the final dark syrup through my veins.

He nudged my legs apart.

'You do not speak to me, Ysabel. Are you not glad I am home to wish you a touching farewell?'

His hands moved to wrap into my hair and he tugged brutally. I cried out and heard an answering growl from Sorcia in the corner.

I twisted my head away from his lips and he grasped my arms to shove me hard up against the wall, pushing inside, thrusting against an unwilling entrance.

'Open to me, you bitch. Open to the new seed of my heir else you shall suffer.'

He began to grunt furiously and with each grunt I was slammed against the stone and a base streak exploded in my head as his hot breath filled my face.

I will kill him.

'Open to me!'

His hand hit my face with bone-jarring force, my head whipping so that the heavy stone sill bit into the flesh near my eyebrow. Blood ran down my cheek and I could taste it on my lips and tongue as I fell sideways against the oratory with him on top, glued to me like a rutting dog. My fingers closed over something sharp as black, insistent words filled my mind.

I am Ysabel of Moncrieff and you shall not!

I shrieked and Sorcia came running, launching herself into his back at full-force. Enough to knock him out of me to roll onto the floor where his head hit the wooden frame of the oratory and where my hand rose and fell.

He lay still, his eyes closed and the quill sharpening blade sunk deep into his left breast.

Sorcia stood over the body of my husband. In the bailey, men's voices shouted, a cock crowed, horses neighed and a dog barked, Sorcia rumbling deep in her throat in reply.

'Shush,' I whispered.

A dark shape flew past the window, its threatening shadow swooping over De Courcey's inanimate frame. I shivered.

Think.

I grabbed my chemise, tugging it on.

Think!

I rubbed the blood from my face, wincing at the bruise left by his palm and gingerly patting around my eye. It felt fleshy and broken beneath the tentative fingers.

Think Ysabel!

De Courcey lay in a pool of his own blood, Sorcia reaching to smell it and then backing away.

The plan…

I raced to a chest filled with embroidery accoutrements, digging beneath to extract the youth's clothes from a year before, pulling them on, dragging hair back to stuff under a hood, wadding a kerchief to staunch the still flowing blood. I pushed my mother's comb and the small Book of Hours into the purse at my waist with one hand and thought how I would have killed to possess the Saracen book as a form of insurance.

Would have killed? Ysabel…

'Sorcia, come!'

I hushed the order, one frantic glance at the prone form of my husband, then leaped for the secret way, making sure the large tapestry hung back cleanly behind us.

We had no light but we raced round and down – Sorcia by animal instinct and me by memory. Reaching the grille, I heaved it up. Outside, dusk cast long shadows.

'Sorcia, hup, good girl.'

I dragged myself after her and we hunkered in the sedge, she sniffing the damp air of a spring evening, me holding her collar with one hand whilst pressing my face with the bloodied cloth.

Think.

We waited till it was fully dark and as I began to move across the stones and through the sedge, Sorcia padding by my side, I heard a shout from the bailey.

'Sound the alarm!'

They've found him.

We ran over the boulders, across the causeway to the far side of the lake. In the village, Saint Agatha's bell rang for Vespers and we sped to the church, meeting no one. I slipped inside, Sorcia's and my feet silent on the paved floor. The priest stood at the altar, a taper in his hand.

'Brother John,' I whispered, wiping at the blood.

He turned quickly, the taper flaring.

'Who goes?'

'Ssh. It is me.'

'Ysa...'

'Hush,' I glanced back over my shoulder. 'I need help.'

He said nothing more, snuffing out the altar candle and the taper, the smell of tallow heavy on the air. He ushered me out the door and into the small stone and thatch dwelling that was his quarters.

Then, 'I need to see to your face...' He looked closely. 'Jesu, Ysabel, it's opened almost to the bone. It's a wonder you still have an eye.'

'I've killed him. Listen, they raise the alarm.'

From the castle, the sound of shouts, horns and alaunts started a stormfront of shivers down my spine.

He lit a candle and stirred the fire, filling a bowl from the kettle that hung over the coals. He gently peeled my hood back and grabbing a clean piece of linen, began to bathe the wound.

'Curse the man for the devil spawn that he is, he has really done some damage this time.'

I jerked away as he probed the flesh.

'I need to see there are no bone splinters there, Ysabel, be brave.'

He poured some wine onto another cloth and blotted away and I sucked in my breath as it stung and I wished he'd hurry. The noise from the castle had freshened and then drifted away as if the search party had left in another direction entirely but I knew they'd be back.

'I need to cobble this together Ysabel, else it'll never heal.'

Cobble together?

'You mean sew?'

He threaded a bone needle with a piece of thread and as he reached for my skull, I jerked my head away.

'Have you done this before?'

'Yes, many times to the villagers when there was no time to get to the infirmarian.'

'I did not know you were a barber-surgeon, Brother John.'

The first piercing of the needle through my face was like a branding iron.

'We are all of us many things other than what we seem to be, Ysabel.'
He dug in again and tugged and I moaned. 'People have had wounds
stitched together since before Time and whilst I am not trained like some
from the Middle Sea countries, I am competent enough.' Tug and tug
again, stitch after stitch. 'That said, my child, I am afraid you will most
likely have a big scar.' He tsked and pulled once more.

'There.' He cut the thread with a sharp dagger and picked up a small
stone bowl. 'I shall apply a paste of honey, it helps the healing, and I shall
wrap your head with this linen. Lord knows who you shall get to remove
the stitches when it is time.'

'How long?'

'Half a month.'

'I shall find someone. Just help me get away, I had thought I might
have time but I don't...'

'Time? What say you? Ah but of course! You planned to run away
to Wales, didn't you? Well run you shall. I'll not see you stay here to be
convicted of a brute's death. But Sorcia must stay behind because she will
indentify you too well.'

'No...'

But I knew he was right, my most perfect man of God. How many
such priests would there be who would help someone guilty of murder?

I knelt and hugged her.

'Stay, Sorcia, and I shall not be long. Sit. Good girl.'

She sank onto the floor and tilted her head as Brother John guided me out
the door and I resolutely tried not to turn back to look at the dog that had
taken the place of my child, the dog who was my shadow in so many ways.

My head ached and I longed to wait till the throbbing passed but there
was no time. We pressed against the outside wall, listening for noise but
the alaunts howled from far away and I breathed out.

'I shall keep Sorcia hidden until this is over,' my dear monk said, 'and
then give her to Lady Cecilia when she returns. She will be well cared for,
do not fret.'

I knew this to be true and had no fear for my giant hound. I would miss
her but there was no time to indulge in such grief. I had made a promise
with myself on the night of the epiphany and nothing would change it.

Brother John continued. 'And there's one thing you can be grateful to the Baron for, Ysabel. He left a mere six men … even if they use the villagers, none will help willingly. It is to your benefit!'

We walked swiftly through the dark, our feet finding neither obstruction nor bulwark to hinder us. I thought we headed west away from Moncrieff and I felt nothing as it disappeared behind my back; nothing but fear that I might be found and elation that I might escape. The moon shadows dimmed as we entered the heavily wooded ways of the forest and for a moment I was confused.

'Where are we?'

I touched my head as a sharp pain pulsed around eye and ear. Underneath the bandage the wound snaked from eyebrow to cheekbone and into the hairline.

Bigger than I thought.

'Brother John? Tell me where we are.'

'We are well into the Moncrieff woods heading northwest in the direction of Lincoln. I will leave you with an old friend of Moncrieff's and she will take you further. She is adept at finding her way hither and yon through the forest without being seen. She's a rare creature.'

'Who is she?'

I tripped on a root, the jolt hurting my head and I sucked in a breath.

'Nearly there, Ysabel, not too far.' Brother John's hand took hold of my arm and steadied me. 'She is called Frida. But tell me, is he really dead?'

'I … yes. I struck him near to the heart.'

'Why?'

Such a direct question and I wonder you have not already guessed the answer.

'He was raping me, Brother John. I am sorry to talk of such things but he wanted an heir begun before he leaves for the Holy Land and he t… he…'

'No more of it, leave it behind. He is in the Devil's hands now.'

He helped me over another root, the larger trees creating undulations on the forest floor with their spreading foundations.

'What makes you think he is dead?'

'Sorcia knocked him down and he hit his head on the wooden edge of my oratory. There was a lot of blood and I struck him with my quill knife. I plunged it in.'

'To his heart you think?'

'Aye. It stayed upright…'

I shuddered as a cold sweat crept over me, bile ascending into my throat. I began to vomit.

'What do you do to the poor young boy, monk?'

A hoarse voice with the tinge of a Saxon accent spoke from the shadows.

'Frida! We search for you…'

'In the dark with no flame? It must be odd business then.'

'Dangerous business, Frida. This young person needs help to escape far from here.'

'Why? What is the deed?'

'Murder. Baron De Courcey.'

Frida spat.

'Huh, no loss then. So that was the noise across the forest; they've raised an alarm.'

I struggled to make out Frida's features in the shadow as I lifted my head and wiped my mouth with a wad of grass.

'This is the Baron's wife, Frida. Alaïs' daughter. She has been sorely used and fought to protect herself.'

'*She!* Aah! Oh aye, I can see blood staining her hood.'

'He hit her and broke open her eye and cheek.'

I was sick of them talking over the top of me.

'Can we sit while we talk? I feel a trifle weak.'

Frida stepped from under the tree canopy and into a moonbeam that filtered through branches. She was as wrinkled as a dried up apple-skin, her eyes dark and expressionless, her face unreadable.

'She's pale, Brother John,' she said. 'Needs to rest a few hours to settle that head wound.'

'I don't *have* a few hours.' I sighed.

'You have as long as needs be,' Brother John rejoined. 'She can hide you and you must do as she says.'

'I'm hardly in a position to do otherwise. I'm a fugitive like to be strangled and burned if caught. Or worse.'

'Dead's dead, my lady.' Frida laughed. 'Doesn't matter if it's by hanging, or any other of the ways they have to finish a person off. Come, let's get you to where none shall find you. You can leave her in my care, priest. She'll be looked after.'

'I have no doubt,' said Brother John, reaching to grasp me in a hug as I stood. 'Ysabel, take care, don't take risks. Get to Wales safely and send word to Cecilia or myself. We must know you are well.'

He clasped me like a father clasps a daughter and momentarily my eyes prickled but the epiphany loomed large.

'I shall beware, Brother John. God bless you for being like a father to me.'

'You shall always be my daughter, as you are God's own. I loved your mother and father and I have loved you, their child, since I first entered Moncrieff. I shall pray for you.'

'Then pray frequently and often, priest.' Frida took my arm. 'She'll need it to get to Wales. She must cover a lot of ground.'

She tugged for me to follow and I hurried after her, glancing back at the dark cowled shape that was my family's priest, waving but seeing no arm waving back. It seemed I left another part of my life behind as I paced in Frida's steps but all I wanted was to escape; leaving a life behind meant little.

Running.

It's all I had done for a year.

Running toward an unwanted destiny.

Running alongside someone I had thought was my champion.

Running away from a terrible fate.

Frida walked with assurance in the dark and I tripped and fell after her until we fetched up against a rocky bank. Where it lay and if it were concealed by foliage was impossible to discern as clouds drifted in uncompromising grey bands across the moon. I looked up. A halo of diffuse light surrounded what little I could see of it.

'It'll rain tomorrow,' said Frida. 'See how there is veiled ring around the moon? Good for you; wash your smell away. Give you time to plan.'

More clouds and we were in the dark again. I heard the swish of leafy branches and then my hand was grabbed and I was dragged into a dry, comforting cave that wrapped round me like a womb round a babe.

For two days I stayed. Frida fed me, dressed my wound and the rain poured down and not once did we hear a search party close by. She told me how my mother would come to her for rare herbs and medicaments and how she was fond of Alaïs.

'A sad day,' was all she said of my mother's death.

But then she spoke of other things as her hand wove stems of hazel or she crushed leaves and petals.

'You know, she did a good thing the day she employed young Gisborne as your father's steward.'

My attention was hooked like a fish on a line.

'He was a good man.' She stirred the honey for my wound, warming it over the flame. 'Pity he left.'

He left to find me *and finding me, realised that status and power were more important.*

Frida wasn't the most verbose person but she waxed lyrical for quite a long moment about Guy of Gisborne.

'I was tending my traps one day and I looked up and he sat on his horse watching me from the other side of a copse, must have seen me stuff a rabbit in my sack. He sat as still as a statue. Could've ridden me down and dragged me to justice but he didn't. Just sat there, a small smile on his face and then he touched his forehead in a salute and rode off.'

Damn him and damn you, Frida. Don't.

But it was the only time she spoke of herself or Gisborne.

'You need to get to Locksley. The abbess there is a good woman. She'll see you safe.'

Locklsey. Beyond Nottingham, closer to Wales.

Frida dressed my wound daily.

'Priest did a good job of his needlework. It's a pity it's like it is – it'll drag your brow down and you'll have a ridge across to your hair. Spoil your pretty face.'

She was readying a new paste and as she eased the old bandage off, hair stuck to the seepage.

'Ow!'

'Damn your hair, girl! Lies in the honey and ooze.'

'Cut it off.'

'Eh?'

'Cut it off. Now. Before I think on it.'

'You sure?'

'Yes.'

I passed her a sharp knife.

She raised her eyebrows, shook her head and in a series of sawing motions, cut my hair to chin-length; a style favoured by squires like Ulric. I fingered the silvery largesse that lay in my lap.

'Can you dye it?'

'Dye?' Frida flicked the knife onto a table.

'Yes, I might as well change my appearance completely since the Baron half changed it for me.'

She stood with her head on the side, her own grey hair writhing like Medusa's coils in a faint breeze that edged around the cave's bends.

'I think brown, easier to manage. Won't show so much as it grows. Bit of mulberry wood steeped with a drop or two of oak gall, maybe a blot of henna. Yes, I think I can.'

And so I lost my crowning glory and became nutbrown-coloured sometime between Tierce and Sext. Bells drifted intermittently on the rainsoaked breeze but I forbore to ask from where. At dawn on the third day, Frida passed me a bag filled with some bread, apples and nuts. Underneath was a chemise and faded brown *bliaut* not unlike a nun's habit.

'I'll take you to the northwest edge of the forest. You'll meet the road to Nottingham and you can skirt the town if you want and move on to Locksley. If I were you, I'd stayed dressed as a boy till you get to Nottingham and then change back to the woman's clothes in the sack. The more changes you make the harder to track you down for there's a price on your head, lovey, mark my words. De Courcey's a favourite of King and prince.'

It took a day to reach the Nottingham Road and Frida sat with me as we ate bread and cheese.

'I'll stay till suitable company comes past.'

She wrapped herself in a heavy cloak in front of the small fire, snoring almost immediately but I just lay sleepless, watching the stars break out across a clearing nightsky.

Frida amused and awed me. She was afraid of nothing. She shifted from shadow to light as if she were fey, she handled a dagger, bow and trap like the best hunter, she had the skill of an apothecary, the tender hands of an infirmarian and the grounded nature of a religieuse. Age left its mark on her knotted fingers, her hair and her wrinkled skin but her eyes were as clear as a child's, as uncompromising as a King's, and as inscrutable as an ancient's.

But now she slept the sleep of a babe whilst I sat twisted around in tangles with anxiety. Not long after dawn we had the company of four merchants and their wives travelling to Nottingham in two carts and with two men-at-arms. They obligingly took me aboard and as I turned to wave to Frida, she had gone – drifting like a shadow amongst tree and leaf.

As I walked down the muddy alleys of Nottingham much later, I thought on likely talents.

I was able in the house and fields. I could handle dogs, horses, even sheep and fowl.

I looked down at my hands.

I can embroider. Even shoot an arrow and wield a knife.

But the hands that had held a needle and dragged gold thread through silk were roughened by life and the faded clothes gave no inkling I had once followed gentler pursuits.

I walked through the gates, people staring at my wounded face. My dearest hope was that none knew of the injury Lady De Courcey had suffered. The less attention I drew the better and when I left the noise and crowds well behind, I dug in to Frida's bag and pulled out Alaïs' comb and Frida's crumpled linens which proved to be a wimple and veil. Pulling the hair back under the wimple, I made sure the headdress sat low on the forehead, covering as much of the hideous wound as possible.

To be sure I felt the drag of eyebrow toward cheek but when I fingered around the edge of the linen, I could see much was concealed. The veil knotted at the base of my skull and I knew without doubt that I looked like a peasant. If found on the road, I would be questioned smartly as to why I was far from where I might belong. The lie, if it were needed, was not so far from the truth. My husband had died. I had no tenure of our home and thus I returned close to the Welsh border in the north, to my aunt and uncle who were in need of extra hands.

Locksley was no more than a day or so's ride from Nottingham, but I was not used to walking on foot. Every step throbbed and my soles wore thin. When I came to a large stone manor house, I went to a door in the yard and spoke to the maid who carried slops.

'Work?' I asked.

'Here?' She looked not unlike a pig, turned up nose, bristled hair that curled from an unwieldy knot and a body that indicated the pigs wouldn't get everything in the bucket.

'You'd have to be strong in mind and body to work here.'

I sighed, fingering the wimple.

'I am.'

'See the bailiff. Extra hands'd do round here for sure.'

I became a laundry maid within minutes in this house of pretension, for I could see the tapestry hangings and the pewter and silver. My instruction was to go to the lord's chamber and collect his clothing and proceed to wash and mend anything that needed it.

The house was unloved and contained a capacious Hall alongside which stood an incongruous tower that held a solid stairway. Four separate doors lay along a first floor corridor which sat heavily atop the Hall like a minstrels' gallery. No doubt the doors led to private quarters.

I knocked on the door of the closest.

'Enter,' a muffled voice called.

I pushed the door ajar, bobbing a faint curtsy and feeling for the veil and wimple – that they concealed as much of me as possible.

'Your laundry, sir, I am to take it.'

'It lies on the bed.'

I looked up quickly at the sound of that voice – a voice that chimed within memory, a visceral rumble, one that I had felt against my cheek as it lay on his chest.

No...

I walked swiftly around the room, away from his half-naked form, my back to him, collecting linen and fine cotton, my heart pounding.

'Thank you,' I strained my voice in order to change it. 'I am sorry to disturb you.'

He stood at the door as I left and I was diminished by his height. As I pushed past him I knew his eyes followed me. His clothes lay in my arms, my memories soaring back over the last year, the fragrance from his unwashed surcoat, *braies, chausses,* reminding me of the night we had seeded a child. My mind screamed at me to leave, to run, but like a bee near pollen I hovered and knew I would rue the day.

'Take care, take no risks.'

Brother John's words snapped at my heels.

That first night I was so exhausted I could barely find a bed. I removed myself as far from Guy of Gisborne's staff as I could and found a warm corner in a stall in the stables, pilfering a heavy caparison in which to wrap myself for warmth and to protect my body from the scratching straw. But in truth I was so strung out it wouldn't have mattered if I had slept naked in a field of stubble as I went over and over the reasons why I should leave and over again why I wanted to stay.

For a week I avoided him, speaking to no one if I could help it, inviting no questions and asking none.

A week, Ysabel. Foolish girl!

Always reason chanted in my head but what is reason next to emotion? It stood no chance.

I earned my food and keep, if you could call my lodgings 'keep'. The food was often the gravy, crusts and remains of Gisborne's table and I decided it was no wonder the kitchen maid ate the pigswill. But food and keep was not enough, I needed coin because I knew I must leave and soonest. Finally that voice had shouted loud enough to be heard.

Gisborne is part of De Courcey's circle, Ysabel. Part of the King's circle. How tight do you want the executioner's hands to be?

The day had been windy and I washed everything I could lay my chafed hands upon, manhandling bulk onto a line I had one of the black clad men-at-arms hang for me. As the linens flicked and flacked, I noticed a tear in a fine shirt. Sewing above all gave me peace and comfort in times of loss, even though my water-roughened skin caught on the fabric with a rip-like sound as I pushed folds around. Despite the fact it could be considered work, I took pleasure in mundane mending and had no doubt the men of this manor were surprised when they found only two armholes in a chemise and not three.

This evening, I had the torn shirt with me to mend by the light of a candle. The work I did was meticulous, the stitching tiny and I was careful to fold it and blow out the flame before I settled for the night, sleep descending on me like an avalanche of stone.

I vaguely heard a voice later, a voice which became an ugly growl.

'Wake up!'

Something was grabbed from near my head and then there was another explosion of sound.

'Thief!'

The caparison was whipped away, leaving me lying in my own ragged linen with its scuffed edge. I jumped up, wrapping my hands around with desperate modesty.

'You!'

His eyes drifted over my form.

I sighed, reaching for the brown *bliaut* and holding it against me.

'Yes, my lord.'

I pulled the garment on and was glad it slid to my toes as I grabbed the loose girdle. Tying it, I scrabbled at rough-cut hair, letting it fall close to my face and forehead, my head hanging.

'Sir, I sleep in the stables as far from the rabble that is your staff as I can, and I did not steal your shirt. I mended it. It had a fray in the seam under the arm.'

A quick glance revealed discomfort but he retorted anyway.

'As I remember, *you* are part of the staff you call a rabble. And what would you know of good or bad staff anyway?'

'Enough.'

I turned away and picked up my cloak for I doubted I'd be working here at dawn.

'So you have been in noble houses?'

'I have.'

'Is that how you managed to secure a chemise of good linen?'

Damn Frida's shift.

'A gift from my previous employer.'

He grinned and with a sarcastic edge, asked, 'For services rendered?'

I knew that tone of voice. It was the one that had frightened me, as if he would explode and leave me by the side of an Angevin road.

'In fact, yes. I ran the household for the mistress and was given such things.'

'You say,' he drawled. 'And where is this fine house?'

'Far away sir, and belongs to another now and I return to my family as my husband is dead.'

True enough.

He stroked the neck of the horse in the stall. The animal had been my only friend and companion since I took up residence in this dangerous house. She was a quiet old mare whose time was no doubt running out. As was mine.

'What are you called?'

'Linette, sir. Linette…'

Gisborne's eyes did not so much graze over my face, they positively ploughed every line as though he searched for something.

'You are well spoken and I believe there is a history behind you that you are loathe to tell. I should ask you more about your husband, your family, but … I shall not. Nobles are accompanying Prince John to this estate in a week for some hunting. I need someone to organise the domestic issues within my house as my bailiff has little idea. If you do it, I shall forget your transgressions this night.'

My transgressions? *I who ran a castle and served meals to nobles? If only you knew. Ah yes, I know of your lineage and your reputation but you shall never know mine. Not now.*

'To satisfy your curiosity sir, I have no home and no money because my husband was a drunkard, and am returning to family in the northwest. As to your house, I shall do it…'

Ysabel!

'… as long as you make it clear to your staff that I am working to your orders.'

He was sour in reply.

'What a way you have, Linette from who knows where. Quite the Lady High and Mighty, aren't you?'

Guy elevated me to a position of mild authority in a heartbeat. That he had no thought for anyone's interests but his own was a surety – son of a Crusader, a noble whose heritage was subsumed by greedier men. This was a bitter man tied to the apron strings of the Realm. And for what?

Elevation, estates and entitlement; all in a year.

I knew I should not be near him; that there was too much history. I could not believe he did not recognise me. My fingers crept to the wimple and touched the scar.

Am I so changed and disfigured?

In days I knew I would have to find someone to remove Brother John's embroideries and then I wondered what Gisborne might see.

I had known him when he was on an upward path through life whereas I had done the reverse. I had not meant to find work near him, let alone *for* him. And yet the Fates played other games. To work for him was to risk my life. He and Halsham were close and I knew I was a marked woman and yet to get to Wales I needed his monies and a pathetic part of me craved his nearness. Or perhaps it craved revenge. I *was* a craven woman.

I ordered his house the first day in my new position. I walked the interior, made notes of dirt and dust, of tapestries and carpets to be beaten, of pewter to be polished, of linens to be washed and folded with fresh herbs and beds prepared. I left the kitchen management to the bailiff, the ordering of food, wines and ale. Interesting that he should ask my advice on the feasts to be served and which he did with ill grace. But I told him it was his choice, he knew his master better than I. I sensed an enemy to be made if I played the game wrong. But I had no intention of staying and hoped to make few ripples as the pennies filled the purse at my waist. I wanted that money. It was all I could offer a babe of less than a year who waited for his mother. The chance must be taken.

The first day of my new position passed and my list was long, but already the wood was cut and stacked and the lines were full of ever more washing, fires being laid in chambers. Baskets of lavender were trimmed from the surprisingly well-stocked potager and I placed large bunches under bedding and hanging from the rafters in the one garde-robe that graced the manor. I saw nothing of Gisborne which was fortuitous as I found myself discommoded by his presence. I wasn't scared of what he had become and what he might say, but I was afraid of what he had been in his past and what he had been in mine.

Late in the evening I entered the stable and spoke to the mare that nickered in welcome, nosing my hand as I offered her an apple. Briefly, very briefly, I thought back to Khazia and wondered whether she was happy. But it was pointless rumination, so I looked at the caparison hanging from the rafters and moved to pull it down for my bedding.

'If you take it again, I would have to charge you with theft.'

My heart stopped and my mouth dried. I spoke without turning.

'Then it would be your loss, Sir Guy.'

I heard a chuckle.

'I believe it would be, Linette. Already my household quails at your lists.'

'Your manor will be the better for it. Now sir, I have a big day on the morrow. I would appreciate it if you left me alone with the mare so that I may sleep.'

'Sleep you will, but not here. There is a small chamber on the first floor you may use.'

'The first floor is for family…'

'I have no family,' he snapped 'and I am lord of the manor and can give sleeping quarters to whom I want when I want. Don't be churlish.'

Me churlish? I turned and dropped a curtsy.

'My apologies, Sir Guy.'

I spoke to the floor.

'Say it again.'

'My apol…'

'Not that… my name.'

I looked up then and his dark blue eyes had frozen, fists clenched at his sides. Even the mare had laid her ears back and snorted.

Don't remember.

'Again,' he said, threateningly soft.

I lifted my voice an octave. 'Sir Guy.'

I couldn't bear to look at him in case a key turned in the lock of his memory. He was silent and still but then he moved close, grasping my arm and pulling me behind.

I followed in his long strides. Four of mine to one of his. Strides that seemed impelled with anger. We met no one awake in the Hall and he pulled me up the stair, caring little if I stumbled – along the passage, past cressets where flame jumped in our wake. He thrust a door open and pushed me through it and I stood and stared, sensing his body behind me, close to my back, my arm still throbbing where he had grasped it. I knew if I leaned back even a fraction, our bodies would touch. Instead I focused on what the miniscule room contained. There was a cot, blankets, and a candle lit so the tiny space glowed. Across the cot lay a gown… a *bliaut* of deepest sapphire.

Not blue. Please not blue.

A plain shift of ordinary quality lay folded and a girdle of plain homespun embroidered with field flowers draped across the gown. I closed my eyes at the generosity, telling myself it suited him to have a housekeeper dressed to her station in his house.

I thanked him, turning toward the intimidatory silence.

But he had gone and with him the fear of my past.

I barred the door.

I was glad Gisborne was gone frequently because when he was around, it was like an intimation of a thunderstorm and the house whispers elucidated on the damage such storms could cause.

I remembered this about him – this volatility. But could he be as thoughtless and cruel as those I had left? Did Halsham still have a hold on him? None of this sat well with me and I condemned him righteously whilst sighing for what had been between us.

But then I reminded myself that I too was doing almost anything for money. By working in his house, was I not condoning what he did by smoothing the ruffles of what had been a rough household – a silk purse from a sow's ear?

The afternoon before his guests arrived, I heard shouting and horses, and lifting my head from the herb garden where I picked borage and rosemary, I noticed a cavalcade gallop past with Gisborne at the head.

The men were armed and the hated Free Lancers' black and red pennant streamed behind.

I returned to the house, the basket of herbs on my hip, dirt falling on the folds of the old brown *bliaut*. Laying the herbs on the table, I cut the boughs of elder I had collected earlier, my purpose to arrange two large churns in the Hall. The waxy cream elder flowers would look pleasant against the bitter blue of the borage and I was hoping the rosemary and whatever herbs I could find to throw on the fire would conceal the smell of men. My mother had… ah, but there was little use dwelling on that.

The cook clicked her tongue against her teeth behind me, sighing and then clicking again. I turned, knowing she wanted to talk.

'Ellen, is there ought wrong?'

I touched her hand. She had a heart did Ellen, more than the rest of this house.

'Oh Linette. It's Owen, my nephew…' she sucked in a breath.

'Go on?'

'They ride to arrest him.'

The words gushed out, all a-tremble, almost as if she would cry.

'Why?'

What could be so bad that Gisborne should arrest someone?

'He stole a sheep. He has five children and three are poorly. Their barley crop failed and their little savings were taken in place of their tax-share and Owen was distraught. He stole one of Sir Guy's sheep for food and you know what that means.'

A theft punishable by hanging. My stomach flipped over as Ellen turned a pallid face toward me.

Gisborne … what are you become?

Much, much later I placed the last churn on the other side of the hearth and stood back. I should have been pleased. In a short time, this dour, heartless place so redolent of its tenant, had transformed. I'd wager even Halsham would be jealous. And frankly who cared, if it brought down wrath upon this stinking manor.

'You know your job.'

The voice spoke from behind me.

Always he comes at me from secret places.

I needed two seconds to think and then answered back.

'As you appear to know yours.'

I turned and he was leaning against the entrance to the stairwell, blocking my exit and with his arms crossed over his chest.

'Meaning…' his voice was low and if he'd been a dog, I'd have seen his hackles rise.

'A starving man and his family, Sir Guy. You should sleep well.'

He was across the floor in two strides, an arm lifted, but I stood my ground and stared him down, forgetting my face. The arm dropped but the sound of his breathing was enough to ruffle any feathers. Finally I pushed past him.

'Excuse me, *my lord*,' the sarcasm dropped from my lips, 'I go to the abbey.'

'The abbey? You think to become a religieuse?' he mocked.

Do you remember how I said I should fail in the Church?

I turned, wondering if I should see something familiar but the shadows of the chamber masked his face and I could see nothing.

'No, my lord. I go to pray for lost souls. Yours and Owen's.'

I left apace but not quick enough to avoid the sound of pewter hitting a wall.

CHAPTER FIFTEEN

The abbey's soaring, vaulted roof and its handsome wooden pews should have sustained me but as I knelt for ages, my hands knotted together, no vestige of relief came. Only a biting cold that soon had me shivering.

As well that I shiver.

It approximated the incipient fear that was beginning to stir. How dangerous it would be to work in a house that would entertain the highborn of far and wide and who would know of my husband.

Peril, Ysabel.

'My child,' a hand grasped my shoulder and I jumped. 'You have been on your knees longer than it takes to ask God for assistance and I can feel you are as cold as ice. My abbey is a marvel of construction but men forget that warmth is as much one of God's blessings. Come with me.'

I turned to look at the woman who spoke and met steady eyes and a tranquil face of some age. By the white of her veil I knew her to be the Mother Superior, Beatrice of Locksley, and one whom I should have sought out long since.

'Thank you, Reverend Mother, I *am* chilled.'

Later, in front of a warming fire and with bread, cheese and spiced wine in my belly, Beatrice had inveigled my distress from me. My disgust of Gisborne, my fear of incoming nobles, my desperate need for coin.

'My dear, we are not able to pay what Guy has promised you, but you would be welcome to stay here and work in the gardens. The infirmarian needs help with the herbs, they have got away from her and she is so very busy here and in the village.'

I listened to the silence, surprised at how familiar the Reverend Mother was with his name. The only sounds were the crackling flame, the occasional swish as a nun entered the chamber and then left. There was order and calm and it sustained me like nothing else had for weeks.

But it was not part of my plan.

'Reverend Mother, I thank you, but I will fulfill my obligations to Sir Guy. By then I will have enough monies to reach Wales. If I can travel with traders or pilgrims, I shall consider myself fortunate. My fear at the moment is my anger toward Gisborne. He never used...'

My words were halted by the tolling of the Abbey bell.

'Tis Matins and I must hasten.' Beatrice of Locklsey stood. 'I can see you are exhausted and must not return to the manor this night. There is a cot in the dorter that you may use. One of the lay sisters will direct you and you must break your fast with us in the morning. Perhaps you might attend Lauds and pray for guidance as well?'

Whilst Mother Superior couched this last as a question, I knew in fact it was a polite order. I thanked her as she moved away and not long after, a lay sister called Matilda led me to the dorter. Although stone and severely plain, it had a glowing brazier and was warm enough and even though no one else slept in the other cots, I cared not, wrapping myself in my cloak and the blanket provided and falling into a deep oblivion.

It was only moments later, I swear, and Matilda was shaking my shoulder. The room was dark, still and cold and her breath blew over me like a fog.

'Lady, wake you. The bell for Lauds is ringing.'

I groaned, remembering Thea, thrusting fingers through my hair and scrubbing at my scratchy eyes. As Matilda hurried me through the cloister, I spotted a fountain and quickly rinsed my face.

Nuns passed in pairs like shades, their feet soundless, their veils brushing my arms, their heads bent in presumed contemplation. Matilda led me into a small Lady Chapel and we sat with the other lay workers, all women, whilst the nuns seated themselves behind a carved screen and began the hymnal. Under any other circumstances, I would have been transported by the purity of the women's voices but already I felt the familiar tug: go, stay, go, stay.

I needed to be paid, that much was obvious. After that…

A ruckus arose at the abbey doors and the voices dwindled as booted and spurred feet could be heard approaching the Lady Chapel. The portress jumped up from behind the screen and hastened to the abbey proper, Reverend Mother following, pulling a further screen across the entrance to our chapel and sealing the nuns and lay sisters from view.

'Where is she?' I could not mistake the voice. 'Is my housekeeper here? Answer me, goddamn it!'

'Sir Guy!' The Mother Superior's voice lifted briefly and then lowered again. 'How dare you raise your voice in God's House and how dare you disturb the Sisters at Lauds. I must ask you to show respect and remove yourself.'

I could see his face in my mind, the painful effort of self-control.

'Reverend Mother, at least tell me this. Is she here or must I drag the river or send searchers into the forest?'

Why would you do that?

'She is here, sir. There is no need to be precipitate. She is safe within the Abbey confines and I expect she will return to the manor when she is ready.'

Oh Reverend Mother, thank you.

'Then tell her my guests arrive at Sext. If she wants to be paid in full, she must see their stay through to their departure on the morrow. If she does not return, she will receive nothing.'

'That is not the act of a god-fearing man, Sir Guy. Has she not already ordered your house fit for princes? You owe her for that at the very least.'

I heard a breath suck in and turned as Matilda whispered. 'Mary, Mother of God, but she's a brave one.'

The Obedientary shushed us from her screen-concealed corner as Gisborne answered.

'Half her pay then, Beatrice.'

'You may not be able to bargain with God so easily, my son. Now please depart the abbey in the manner of the knight you purport to be.'

Her tone slapped at his heels good and hard and I felt a smile blooming in the sunless cold of the Lady Chapel.

'Go in peace, Sir Guy,' she added.

He said nothing and she slid the screen open just enough to slip through. But nevertheless, his glance caught mine and in that fraction of a moment, I imagined the whole church must have stopped breathing.

But then he turned and as I dropped my head in relief, all I could hear were the jingling of his spurs and the sound of his boots in the nave as the Sisters' voices sang the end of Lauds.

'Gisborne arrived in Locksley with papers from King Richard endowing him with the manor and domain.'

We walked across the abbey's carefully tended potager where the laywomen dug and weeded. The abbess led the way to the dulcet quiet of the hedged infirmary garden, where weeds had far outstripped the medicinal plants.

'You see it needs some work. But Sister Catherine is frantic making her simples and caring for the villagers and cannot spare the time. We haven't enough lay workers and I worry that ultimately our medicine supply will suffer.'

'Can you not ask Gisborne for a woman from an outlying village?'

'I could but I choose not to. From the outset,' she continued, her hands folded neatly into her capacious sleeves, 'I determined to be a friend with Gisborne but certainly not a dependent. It is better that way.'

'I see.'

Independence.

I sighed. 'Gisborne is about to hang someone, Reverend Mother. Did you know that?'

She laughed. 'I think not.'

'But he arrested Owen for theft.'

'Guy is not what he seems, my child.'

I heard Brother John then… *'We are all of us many things other than what we seem to be, Ysabel.'*

'He greases his own way,' I scoffed.

'Not at all,' said Beatrice. 'His arrival here was a good thing for the people of Locksley, my dear. I can assure you, God would view him kindly.'

'You say? When he is about to hang a starving man?'

'Guy of Gisborne hangs no one. Whatever his secrets are, Ysabel, I would say they prompt him to keep the balance sheets very clean in his own domain. He is a fair individual and Owen is well known as a simpleton and a recalcitrant poacher into the bargain. If he had any sense and his family were hungry, he had only to to approach the bailiff or myself and help could have been arranged. But he is, God forgive me, one of God's idiots. No my dear, never fear, Owen will not hang. He will be punished but he will not hang.'

'Punished for trying to feed hungry children? Then your Gisborne is neither fair nor decent, Reverend Mother. There are extenuating circumstances for Owen.'

'Which I am sure will be taken into account.'

'I cannot see fair nor decent in Gisborne. I am sorry.'

'As I said, my dear, Sir Guy hangs no one. He makes arrests and arranges surreptitious escapes.'

I laughed, but her expression halted my mockery.

'Truly?'

I fingered my stitches, aware my voice still displayed disbelief. For a moment I was quiet and then, 'Why, it's ... it's rebellious, treasonous. If the Sheriff or other nobles should find out...'

'But then who would tell? I will not.'

'This is unbelievable,' I shook my head, finding it hard to reconcile my newfound knowledge with my most recent observations.

I subsided onto a stone bench under the boughs of an almond tree. Beatrice reposed beside me.

'You tell me this for a reason, don't you?' I said.

'You seem to have a memory of him from the past.'

I sat up straight.

'You knew him once, did you not?' she asked.

The question was posed softly but it none-the-less skewered me like a dagger. How could I tell this woman of God that I had born a child to Guy of Gisborne?

'I did, Reverend Mother . . .' my hands twisted.

She laid her own over them and said gently. 'I can listen, dear girl. It will go no further and you may find a burden lifts.'

Two tears drifted down my cheeks. In a moment I was in Cazenay, surrounded by all that was familiar and on the brink of a tempestuous affair from which I don't believe I ever recovered. I lapsed into quiet on the stone bench in the Infirmary Garden. Beatrice of Locksley played with the folds of her habit, and all was silence but for the birds that filled the almond and fig trees.

'Reverend Mother, it was a short time but makes a long story...'

'I would not have you upset, my child. I would like to know your connection with Sir Guy as I can see it turns you awry even now but perhaps it is not the time. Rather you need to decide if you shall return to the manor or whether you should proceed on your way. I can give you coin to get you to the next town if you wish, but there are just two things I would say.' I watched her fingers press hard together. 'You have told me some truths today. And whilst I realize there is a lot more to tell, I owe you more of the story I related.'

She stood and began to pace back and forth, her robes swishing, her crucifix swaying as she flung herself about to walk back. 'I was ... expeditious with the truth for which I must ask God and yourself for forgiveness, but it seemed to me that you disliked Guy unjustly and I sought to remedy that. What I should have explained was that when he arrived, he appeared every bit as dark as you seem to think he is even now. That odious Halsham forever dropped in and out and one drew conclusions. He and that godless man, De Courcey ... Devil's consorts!'

My heart began its freeze again and I despaired – as if my life stretched before me as a dank and muddy road with nary a sunbeam in sight. 'And what changed?' I dared to ask. 'What made Gisborne different in the eyes of Beatrice of Locksley?'

Beatrice sat down. 'He is an enigma...'

'An enigma? Huh.' I remarked emptily and then sighed. 'Reverend Mother, even if any view I might have of him changed, it is better if he does not know me.'

Her brows drew together as if something I said displeased her, but as quickly smoothed out again. 'Do you think he recognises you?'

I could not help the bitterness in my reply. 'I am different now. Very different,' I said gesturing to my wound and my hair. 'And in truth I have been at pains to change my voice as well.'

'Would it really matter if he remembered? It might be what God wants for you both.'

I gave a small laugh, acrid and dry. 'Reverend Mother, it is not what *I* want.'

Isn't it?

A bell tolled. 'Sext. I must get back to the manor. Mother, I would speak with you again before I leave. May I see you on the morrow? It will be after Vespers.'

'Of course dear child, I think we have much more to say. But can I ask you to go back to the manor with an open mind and an open heart?'

'I'm not sure I can do either, Reverend Mother.'

The time for an open heart ended when he sold me and I wished only to find my way out of England and into Wales to find my son but it was not for Beatrice to know this, not yet. I knelt and kissed her fingers and felt her hand on my head as she offered a quick blessing.

'Go into the kitchens and calm the cook.' His voice barked at me.

'Good day to you too, Sir Guy,' I muttered without even looking at him.

He grabbed my wrist as I pushed past.

'If you'd been here, the house would have been calm and the kitchen under control.'

'If you hadn't arrested Owen, the cook wouldn't need soothing,' I retaliated, jerking my hand away.

I slid by him, knowing it was an unjust comment, that if Reverend Mother was to be believed, Owen was probably already a man on the run far from here.

Ellen seemed lost, leaning against the wall with a cloth to her eyes. I took her by the elbow and led her outside into the yard, conscious that Gisborne had followed me and even now, was watching from a distance.

I turned Ellen aside, my arm around her, and whispered, 'Pull yourself together. Owen's life depends on it. He will live but it is our secret.' She tried to pull away, surprise and shock in her action, but I held tight. 'Tell no one what I have told you. Remember it is his life.'

She dabbed her eyes and nodded and I pushed her toward the kitchen. 'Cook, Ellen, better than you have ever done.'

She bobbed a curtsy at Guy as she squeezed by him whereas I just strode on unconcerned to the hall where long trestles had been set. The head table had prodigiously carved chairs as well as a fine embroidered linen cloth I had pilfered from what looked like Church accoutrements. It had been in a chest in Gisborne's chamber and I thought nothing of purloining it for un-ecclesiastical use.

He had said he wanted platters and not trenchers and so I found a collection of pewter, enough for the noblemen who would sit with Prince

John. The rest of the guests would be seated down the long sides of the Hall. Behind the high table hung banners in Prince John's and colours and my flowers bloomed in their churns.

The walls were hung with more pennants and the manor's men-at-arms were clean and polished. I thought that whilst I languished at the Abbey, Gisborne had been a very busy man. I ordered the huge hall fire lit and the flagons on the tables to be filled. I spoke to servants and gave them orders, Gisborne having brought in extra villagers, cleaning them up for this occasion. Indeed I wondered why he needed me at all as everything seemed to be proceeding smoothly. But I remembered Ellen in the kitchen and hurried back to find her once more well in control of the food. I encouraged her with a smile and decided it was time to wash and change into clothing more suited to the proceedings.

The water pitcher and bowl stood where they had been left yesterday and it was a matter of moment to strip to my skin. As I did so, I heard horns and horses, barking and much shouting and knew the regal party was arriving and wished I could curl up on the cot and think my dilemmas through. I was almost there, so close, and by this night's end I would have earned enough pennies and would be able to leave with no fuss.

No fuss?

The chemise slid down my frame softly and the fine wool of the *bliaut* clung to curves I'd forgotten existed. The girdle encircled the folds – it really was excellent embroidery – and I took Alaïs' ivory comb causing a small chamois bag to fall to the floor with a clink. Picking it up and pulling it open, silver pennies were revealed and I realized Gisborne had been into the room and left my wages – a gesture no doubt urged by Beatrice together with a belief that I would stay as long as required.

Dangerous, Gisborne.

But I wondered if I meant his confidence was misplaced or if I was in danger by thinking thus.

Thoughts ran over what I had related to the abbess as I worked at tangles in the hair until the shortened length hung smooth. How wonderful it would be if life could be dealt with so easily I thought, a sheet of brown hair slipped over my eyes. It smacked of carefree youth and I snorted, quickly dragging it away and searching for a veil in the small chest on which stood the candle. There were a few feminine things concealed inside, a little aged and crumpled – a kerchief and a folded veil that I set upon my head, wondering how to secure it. But at the bottom of the chest was a filet of twisted linen and perversely I wished for a beaten looking glass. But such things were not for housekeepers and this room was merely a servant's cupboard, the chest contents merely remnants of a previous occupant. Besides, such things as wounds might not warrant detailed investigation.

By now the first floor noise had disappeared down the stairwell and I could here a muffled hub-bub in the Hall, bursts of laughter, a cheer as Prince John no doubt took his seat and then a murmuring quiet as Gisborne gave his welcome. Knowing I should be in the shadows, discreetly checking for knots in the fabric of my early endeavours, I thrust open my door and clipped down the stair, noting cressets that needed to be lit and braziers that would need lighting later.

The Hall hummed with the burble of guests. Men and women from the adjoining demesnes and swathed in richly trimmed robes had taken their seats whilst the royal table oversaw the mélange from a dais. I kept to the darkened walls noting Ellen's food was being delivered and devoured and pleased that she had kept her word. I slipped into the kitchen without raising any notice and found the cook sweaty and tired as she ordered the hirelings around.

'Good job, Ellen. Good job indeed,' I complimented.

She looked up from dismembering a roasted sheep carcass.

'I trust you, Linette. It's all that matters.'

And the word 'trust' lit a trail of bonfires through my mind and illuminated a past that I never wished to countenance.

A hand touched my shoulder and I turned. Our eyes met and I could read nothing in his, as I hoped he could read nothing in mine and yet his hand lying on my shoulder did more to stoke those bonfires than anything.

'You look…' he appeared to struggle.

I modulated my voice, altering the tone, attempting to confuse.

'Clean and serviceable as your housekeeper should, for which I must thank you.'

'I was going to say lovely,' he snapped. 'But have it your way.'

I closed my eyes. 'I'm sorry. I am tired.'

'All that praying, no doubt.'

'Perhaps,' I replied, my lips twitching.

We stood in the passage, servants squeezing past with giant platters of meats and breads and flagons of wines. But for a brief second, we were alone and his fingers touched my cheek near the stitches and I felt as if a *misericorde* scored a well-worn track.

'How did you…' his voice cracked slightly.

'Gisborne!' A depised voice yelled from the hall. 'Get yourself here, Gisborne.'

Sir Guy's midnight eyes shuttered again and his hand, so lately gentle, clenched. He turned, rigid and withdrawn.

'Thank you,' he threw over his shoulder.

Halsham!

Bile gorged into my belly, swirling around as I thought of vipers and the bloody body of Baron De Courcey.

Another trail of food marched to the Hall on the shoulders of the hirelings and I followed with trepidation, managing to secure a place in the darkest corner, almost concealed by a long hanging. From this secret place, I could watch the proceedings and assess any problems for the household.

Or myself.

Prince John sat sideways in his chair, a leg carelessly thrown over the arm, his hand dancing up and down which I assumed was from boredom. From such negligence, only potential trouble could come and from his flushed face and sparkling eyes, I could see he was filled with the grape and I feared for any who crossed him. He was indeed the swarthy Plantagenet son, unlike his brother Richard who was golden haired and tall. John had none of Eleanor's nor Henry's looks and I suspected he could almost have been a changeling if one believed in the fey. Halsham whispered in his ear and it was like watching one snake coiling around another.

'Gisborne,' Halsham's voice had the drawl of a man in his cups. 'His Highness tells me Baron De Courcey is absent for personal reasons. Did you know?'

I grabbed the colours to hold myself up, my knees folding as De Courcey's name pierced my soul. In a vacillating distance, I heard Sir Guy answer with cool remove.

'I did not. What say you, Sire?'

'It is a laugh,' responded Prince John. 'De Courcey has woman troubles.'

He sucked on a leg bone and followed it with a draught of wine, waiting until all in the Hall had turned to hear his wit and words.

'Not long since, Lady De Courcey stabbed him and ran away. The Baron has searched for her ever since. Murderous bitch! She missed his heart by an inch they say. If I found her, despite her pleasing countenance I'd beat her to a pulp, have her strangled and hang her body from the castle ramparts.' He slapped the table and laughed and the inebriated Court joined in. 'He is a loyal subject and We have placed a price on the slattern's head. Gold and much thereof shall be the reward. No one dares harm a favourite of the Prince's.'

I turned to go, lightheaded with fear but I caught someone watching.

Gisborne stood as if he were carved from stone and I knew by his expression that my life was in his hands.

CHAPTER SIXTEEN

He remembers. He remembers me.

I hurried against the tide of servants, through the kitchens and outside. My freedom was at stake and I had fought for it too savagely. I found the external door of the tower which I knew gave onto the stair, opening it to slip through, hurrying up to the little chamber. In minutes I had packed my small possessions inside Frida's old clothes, secreting Gisborne's wage at my waist, flinging a cloak over the lot.

The noise from the Hall was louder and musicians had begun to play. It suited my needs, giving me cover to escape to the stable where the old mare waited. She was equable and friendly, alert to the fact that she was at last to leave the stables and journey forth. I mounted the horse astride, gown hitched high, the cloak maintaining decorum, and within minutes we were at the gate of the yard, the guard circling like an animal in rut. His hands reached for the reins and his voice was thick with ale and ill manners.

'What's a lass like you think you're doin'?'

'Let me through. Lady Demaze has been taken ill with labour pains and I am to fetch the *wortwyf.*'

'That old witch! Better to fetch the butcher.'

'I'm sure I will have to if you don't let me through, and on your head be it. Sir Guy and Prince John himself will be livid if their favourite damsel loses her child and I shall watch your punishment with interest. Open the gate!'

I knew Lady Demaze was with child, it had been mentioned, but not anywhere near as advanced as I portrayed. But it suited me to lie and the brute looked crushed by the mention of his superiors, heaving the gate open. I dug my heels into the mare and we cantered down the road, heading toward the Abbey.

The portress opened the main gate for the mare and myself, the horse taken to the Abbey's barn. It was almost Compline and the sisters had moved to the chapel early for quiet meditation so the portress lit my way along the cloisters to the Reverend Mother's chamber. I could not sit and whilst I knew Beatrice would finish the devotion before she attended to my temporal needs, I paced back and forth, my hand worrying at my forehead and then at stitches that prickled.

Guy's fingers.

Oh yes, I could feel them and part of me longed to go back, to tell him I had given birth to his son, to beg for help. But it was a fool's thought and I sank onto a coffer by the fire and stared into the flames, chafing with anxiety.

Compline had still not ended and so I took a poker and stirred the embers, placing two logs of apple wood on top. The room filled with warmth and scent as I sat nervously, fingers moving to my teeth to be chewed upon, to fiddle with the stitches, to tighten the linen filet. I glanced around the sparsely furnished chamber. Coffers and seats were furnished with cushions whose simple embroidery created a monastic comfort. A small oratory hugged a wall where a crucifix frowned down and a carved wooden statue of the Virgin occupied a corner. An oak table held a tray of wine and goblets but I forbore to pour as it would be an abuse of the Reverend Mother's hospitality.

She glided into the room moments later, a picture of serenity.

'My child,' she said as I kissed her hand, 'I did not expect you this night.'

She listened while I told her of the unfolding of truths at Locksley Manor.

'I can see you must go far from Prince John and Halsham. Although…' she poured us both watered wine. 'Guy would not denounce you, Ysabel. I swear that is not the man he is, and if I read into what you told me yesterday, I would say there is a deep relationship between you that he will remember and want to protect.'

If only you knew.

'You talk about the man *you* know, Reverend Mother but I know an altogether different man who would sell me as quickly as he sells a good mare.'

'And why should he?'

I closed my eyes and all I could see were his arms around me, holding me close. I could even smell the fragrance of leather and freshness that hovered about him.

'It will take all night to tell and my chance of escape will be gone if I stay. Don't you see?'

'I do, but I have a much safer plan. We shall keep the horse here and tell Sir Guy you left it with us and departed with a small group of pilgrims who travel to Compostella. That you plan to leave England and travel as far as Aquitaine with them.'

Aquitaine!

I looked up from studying my clenched hands. If anything might convince Guy...

'But he will know if a group of pilgrims have left here recently.'

'Then it is as well they do. As well that a young woman travels with them.'

'But *I* do not.'

'Ah,' she tapped the side of her nose. 'But another does. It is all that matters.'

'And how shall I escape west?'

'Tomorrow one of our Sisters travels to Blithbury Priory near Stafford to deliver our rarer herbs and medicaments to the Infirmarian. She is travelling with merchants and a priest. But instead of one nun there shall be two, as there should be. You shall be our accompanying Sister: Sister Claire. From Blithbury it is not so many leagues as the crow flies to the Welsh border. By the end of the week, you shall be in Wales.'

I jumped up and hugged her and then stepped away, my cheeks flaming with the impropriety.

'Oh Reverend Mother, I apologise. How remiss...'

'Nonsense. I welcome a good hug and miss it here where there is such a godly code of conduct. Tuh! I shall have to confess to covetousness. Ah well, let she who is without sin cast the first stone. Now! We have all night, you shall tell me the rest of yours and Guy's story.'

Tell her the story I did, every minute of it. I cried and laughed. I walked back and forth with anger. I told her of my time at Saint Eadgyth's and she nodded.

'I know the prioress. She is a redoubtable woman. And Sister Thea, ah, I should like to have her here. She would do well I think.'

The Moncrieff chapter of my life, the Baron, the pain, the birth of my son ... all told. And she cast no aspersions, listened, nodded, leaned forward and rubbed my hands when I needed succour.

'Ah Ysabel, for I will call you that – I think we can leave Linette behind now. My poor dear child, you are so close to Wales.' She rubbed my hands again. 'So let us just concentrate on getting you away from here. Firstly your wound. I shall have Sister Catherine look at it for I think the stitches could be removed.'

She reached for a handbell and when a nun opened the chamber door, she asked that the Infirmarian come immediately with wound dressings. It seemed sleeping was something the nuns paid little attention to, whereas my eyes ached with tiredness.

Beatrice reached forward and ran her fingers lightly across Brother John's stitching and I shivered as I remembered another's fingers but the door flew open and Sister Catherine dashed in, robes flying, a leather sack held close to her chest.

As the Infirmarian picked away at my stitches, all I could think of was fast-approaching freedom and the chance to hold my son – to see him grow. The fact I had no idea of his location was something I refused to countenance.

'It is a big scar you have, madame, and it drags at your brow and eye. Livid red with it too but it may settle. Rub it with this – it's coltsfoot and comfrey mixed to a paste. It will aid in the healing.'

Her fingers were infinitely gentle as she eased the stitching away. After, she dabbed the area with a piece of linen and smoothed some of the paste into it.

'At the very least you can be glad it has healed clean.'

Ay, I can be glad of that if nothing else, I thought, touching this altered face that was now mine and thanking her. Beatrice bustled in with an armload of clothing as the Infirmarian stowed the tools of her trade in a linen strip and then placed them in the sack. She backed out of the room, a small smile of greeting to her superior.

'Well now,' Beatrice bent to look at the scar. 'Tuh. It looks angry, if clean. Ah well, I see you have Catherine's miracle cure there. Be sure and use it. She has a reputation for mixing helpful creams and potions. Now, here is your habit and there are some men's clothes as well. You must hurry and change. Your companions have almost finished their repast.'

I hastened to assume my new identity, just another one, wondering how these women could wear such rough clothing as I lay Guy's blue gown aside. No time for pointless reflection though, I needed to keep my wits sharp and my eyes wide. As I picked up the roll of men's clothes, I felt something hard and unyielding in the middle, pushed deep into the fabric. My eyes shot up to the abbess's face and I caught her watching me.

'Better to be safe than sorry,' she said with no expression, taking me by the arm out to the entrance where the portress unlocked the door and pulled it back, her keys clinking in the uncommon quiet of the moment.

A cart stood behind two men-at-arms, a group of horses waiting. The carthorse occasionally stretched his neck, stamping his feet and jingling his harness as one of the men-at-arms held the reins. I climbed aboard, quickly thanking Beatrice. She merely inclined her head before slipping her hands inside her sleeves and moving through the gate, a picture of Divine innocence.

The travellers appeared one by one to mount their horses... the merchant with a cloaked woman riding pillion, the priest in his dark habit, his bald head gleaming in the early morning light and finally with a lot of sighs and puffs, Sister Helewys who was to deliver the herbs and ointments to Blithbury. She nodded at me and smiled at the priest... a little mild-mannered zephyr blowing into our midst.

'Where is our other merchant friend?' she asked.

The mounted merchant called over, 'He had to have a quick word with the abbess, Sister. He'll be but a moment.'

The portress pulled open the gate again and our merchant-driver rushed through, clambering up next to me, taking the reins from the men-at-arms. My head drained of everything, a wind whistling through and I almost slipped sideways in a faint.

His hand grabbed me.

'Sister, take care, the wagon is high above the road.'

He looked at me, wimpled and veiled and dressed in the course brown habit of a nun. I kept myself in profile so that all he would see was the dragged down eyebrow and the vicious cut snaking underneath the wimple. But even so...

'Lady Ysabel,' Ulric whispered. 'Thank God I have found you.'

I sat mute with horror.

Ulric! How close is your employer?

Sister Helewys sat by her bundles as the cart lurched off in the cavalcade, and began to chat to Ulric, quizzing him on his station and occupation. It appeared he was a wool merchant seeking fleeces near Stafford. No, he wasn't married and yes, he found travelling tiresome but he had seen much of England and had been to Bruges and when's all said and done, he was luckier than some. When he said he was a wool-merchant, my eyes slid to his hands and all I could see were the tell-tale ink stains of De Courcey's skilled secretary.

No more a wool merchant than I am a nun.

Sister Helewys seemed to tire of her inquisition and slipped down amongst the bundles, the cart rocking her to sleep like a baby, the snores that emerged the antithesis of an infant. The horse flicked his ears at the sound as I focused ahead, the merchant-wife's cloak flowing over the rump of her husband's horse. The men-at-arms led the way and I felt there was sufficient distance between us all and that Sister Helewys was in a deep enough sleep for me to quiz my once-trusted friend.

'What are you doing here?' I hissed.

He turned that young-old face toward me and he still looked the same, so kind, not at all a De Courcey man.

'Looking for you.'

'De Courcey sent you out?'

'De Courcey is scouring between Moncrieff and London for you, Lady Ysabel. But word has it that you headed northwest toward Nottingham and so he sends men that way as well. Led of course by the redoubtable Halsham...'

'Ulric, Halsham is only a few miles away with Gisborne and Prince John at Locksley.'

'I know. I saw him.'

'*You* saw him? Did De Courcey send *you* to Locksley? Mary Mother,' I looked behind me. 'This is such a mess.'

'No, he did not. I was there at another's behest. The place was in uproar on your account, especially when one of Halsham's men came with the news that a youth with a bad head wound was seen entering Nottingham and a woman with a similar wound was seen leaving.'

'God!'

My voice lifted and Ulric's hand held my arm.

'Shush, Ysabel. Let me go back a step.' He remained calm and the snores still huffled from the back of the cart. 'De Courcey did not send me. I have not been in his employ since Sicily, when I was seconded to Sir Guy's service because of my skill with codes. I have spent much of my time travelling everywhere, conveying and gathering intelligence as required.'

'You?'

I looked at my mild-mannered friend who would have been happier in cloisters than with codes and ciphers.

'I can see you think me an unlikely agent but it is because I am so ordinary that I can be a dozen different people and no one is any the wiser.'

'I am stunned. Is this why you did not write to me again after that last message.'

He nodded.

'I am sorry. Sir Guy's work fills every minute of my days and nights and in truth I would have found it difficult to get notes to you from where I have been. Besides, what would you have thought when you discovered I worked for another you despise?'

What indeed?

Ulric sat quietly allowing me to digest all that he had said and the air around about was filled with the creak of harness and the rattle of the wooden cart.

'Then tell me, Ulric,' I finally asked. 'What price is there on your own head, now that you make off with the very person the King and Prince John wish to see brought to trial? Surely you play with fire.'

We had crested a rise in the road, emerging from a thickly wooded passage to gaze down over a valley, the trail upon which we journeyed rolling in higgledy fashion down the decline.

Within our sight and less than ten minutes away, a troupe of horses approached.

'Quickly,' said the priest. 'Away you two into the woods and hide.' He leaped from his horse, unsaddled the beast and stowed the saddle beneath Helewys's bundles, swiping at the warm girth marks on the horse and tying it to the back of our cart.

Ulric slid down and helped me jump in my awkward robes. Sister Helewys, woken by the priest's agitation and immediately focusing on danger, took my place by the priest's side, making shooing motions with her hands, Ulric dragging me to a leafy cover as we heard the three-part rhythm of horses cantering uphill.

'There,' whispered Ulric. 'Get down in there.' He pulled me toward a pile of old fallen timber overgrown with ferns. He pushed me in amongst branches to a space between the tumble and followed behind until we were tightly wedged.

We were far enough away from the road not to hear the detail, close enough to observe the troupe halt and the priest's arm lift in greeting.

'He lies for us,' said Ulric. 'They all do.'

'Is this subterfuge then?' I asked as I willed the troupe to move on.

'Yes. Helewys and Brother Dominic were warned there might be trouble and of what type. They are good people and the soldiers are more ingenuous and tractable in the face of devout religion.'

Are they? And yet they work for people like Halsham and my husband. My husband – alive and full of vengeance!

And then Ulric's words sank in.

'What do you mean they were warned of trouble? Who warned them? If it was Beatrice, she is a saint!'

'Beatrice? Oh I daresay she was in on it. For sure she has told Sister Helewys and Brother Dominic you were not a nun nor I a wool merchant.'

So Sister Helewys just played a game in the back of the cart, enjoying the subterfuge.

'Ulric,' I grabbed his arm, 'Tell me!'

'Ssh. Later.'

He nodded towards the road. Brother Dominic was pointing back toward Locksley. A question was asked and Brother Dominic shrugged his shoulders, but then put his finger in the air as if he remembered something.

Within seconds the men set off at a gallop. We stayed where we were until the sound disappeared into forest silence whereupon the priest whistled us back.

We clambered out of our hideout, hurrying back to our companions, the habit catching on twigs as I grabbed at Ulric's arm, 'Tell me who warned them.'

He gave me a look as we rushed back to the cart and I knew.

It wasn't Beatrice.

It was his employer, spy for the royal household and a knight of the realm, master of the estate of Locksley.

It was Sir Guy of Gisborne.

'You were lucky,' the merchant said. 'They believed us.'

'What did you say?' asked Ulric.

'What Sir Guy told us to say. The Lord and Saints protect you from the likes of De Courcey. His reputation from London and Old Jewry has spread.'

The merchant spat on the ground and his wife chided him.

Old Jewry. They know?

I tried to butt in but the merchant continued.

'They asked if we'd seen a woman with a wound to her face. And Brother Dominic shrugged and said no, and that it is surely a shame as a woman who tried to kill her husband deserves the wrath of God.' He looked at me and grinned. 'Forgive me, Lady Ysabel, we were told to lie.'

Sister Helewys spoke up, excitement rampant.

'And Brother Dominic *did* lie. So well! Reverend Mother said it was a lie blessed by God and that we must do what we must for you. So we said we hadn't seen anyone since Locksley, saving themselves.'

'But then I remembered,' Brother Dominic's eyes glinted with irreligious craftiness, ' that there was group of pilgrims who left when we did, heading for Compostella. There was a young woman with a savage cut upon her face travelling with them.'

'And they left,' the merchant added. 'But I tell you, Lady, you must leave us now. Get away while you and our young friend here have a lead.'

I looked at Ulric, my mind jumping everywhere, but mostly that Gisborne had helped me.

Sister Helewys said, 'Lady, Reverend Mother said you have men's clothes.

I think you must change and jump up on the horse behind our wool merchant friend and make haste. This has all happened rather too early.'

My heart clanged.

Too early? This is what it has been like for a year, dear Helewys. If only you knew.

I reached for the clothes bundle in the back of the cart.

Change again? Why not? It was fast becoming a fleet skill I swear I could sell as market entertainment.

The habit rolled into a rough ball and I threw it into the back of the cart as Ulric fastened the girth of Brother Dominic's mount. He leaped up and I climbed onto the back of the cart and slipped over the horse's rump behind him, aware Reverend Mother's little *misericorde* lay at a handy angle at my belt.

The horse circled, sensing our anxiety.

'Thank you,' I called as Ulric straightened the animal. 'Thank you all!'

But the words fled behind me as Ulric's heels closed on the gelding's sides. Vaguely I heard Helewys's 'God bless!' as we galloped down a track away from the road, heading into a forest that seemed to stretch on and on.

Once again I thanked my father for teaching me to ride a horse in whichever way was needed – astride, pillion, even fashionably sideways. But this ride was fraught, with no saddle and only a bouncing rump to cushion me. I held my legs away from the horse's flanks, unwilling to interfere, wrapping my arms tight about Ulric, my body trying to relax into the horse's stride. Downhill we fled, and I prayed the animal was sure-footed, dreading what might happen to my insecure seat if we must turn hard at a corner. Trees concealed us and as we moved deeper into the forest along that willing track, Ulric slowed until we trotted and then walked, with the horse blowing down its nose. Reaching a fork, the track changed to nothing more than a defile but I had lost all sense of direction in this leafy maze.

'Where do we go, Ulric?'

'Chester, and thence to Mont Hault.'

'Mont Hault?'

'Ay. The Welsh call it *Yr Wyddgrug* and even though it is in English hands,

I can secret you at the priory. There are a small group of Benedictine nuns…'

'Of course there are. I owe my life to nuns,' I muttered. And then louder, 'I appear to owe my life to *God*.'

'You owe your life to God and Sir Guy right now, Lady Ysabel.'

'Sir Guy… so you say, and yet I find it the oddest thing. Tell me how it is that I seem to owe *him* so much.'

'It is not for me to reveal, Madame. It is something between you and he and if not Sir Guy, then with God. Leastways you are alive, you will be free, and little William of Gisborne will reap the benefits.'

William!

'William? You know where he is?

'Aye. He is in Mont Hault, with Gwen and Brigid.'

'My God, Ulric! How have you done this?'

My hands had flown to my cheeks, unlatching from my escort's middle.

'It is my job. Intelligence.'

'Does G…'

As I spoke, the horse shied at a bird flying from a coppice directly in front of us and I slid sideways off the animal, landing in a soft bed of moss and fern.

'My lady!'

Ulric hauled the horse to a halt, jumping down by my side, but I grinned. Then I burst out laughing.

'Ulric, I swear when I saw you this day I thought I was marked, that I would be a pile of ash by the King's command. Now I find you give me hope.'

I wanted to pursue the question of whether Guy knew he had a son and that son in *Yr Wyddgrug*, but it was enough now to know I would see my child anon and I thanked the Heavens and all in it for that chance.

'Lady Ysabel, we have much ground to cover yet and it mayn't be safe, so do not hope for too much. We shall have to creep around Chester, change horses. It won't be easy. Even less so since the Welsh lost Mont Hault back to the English. It means De Courcey and Halsham will have ears and eyes.'

'Damn them, Ulric. I haven't come this far in my life to have them stop me. I will prevail, I assure you. No matter what.' Inside my head, that faint epiphany began to rise like a phoenix. 'We will be travelling for some days then?'

'Oh indeed, Ysabel. Perhaps longer depending on what problems we confront.'

Travelling.

Through forest and by stream, sneaking past villages and where Ulric would surprise me. Leaving me with the horse I had named Dominic after our perjuring priest, he would sneak off into the dark shadows of night or the stripey shades of dusk and he would always return with food of some sort. We made a practice of filling our bellies with fresh clean water when we came across streams far from settlements and I learned to forage like wild boar to keep hunger at bay.

I became dirty, the rigours of travel embedded in the wrinkles of palms and under fingernails. When I slapped at insects, a cloud of dust would rise from my jerkin, and even though we washed in streams the filth became ingrained – a second skin. We neither of us looked the same. Ulric no longer resembled Ulric of Camden, the pleasant-faced young man from Moncrieff and he told me that his Lady Ysabel had vanished long since.

I wondered if he realized how ironic was his choice of words – Lady Ysabel had indeed vanished, quite literally, yet her spirit soared higher and stronger than ever as each league we travelled brought her closer to Chester and closer too to Mont Hault.

Summer days lulled us – the warmth, the blue skies, the abundance of fodder found in the thick forest and rolling hills of the countryside. Our feet need only be cautious of occasional bogs and reed patches, and once a thunderstorm lit the night, Dominic laying back his ears and swishing his tail, but we were dry 'neath a rocky overhang, aware the gates and bridge of Chester waited not far off.

Perhaps summer was too kind, a somnolence born of sun without cloud. Dominic plodded along, me in the saddle, Ulric alongside. A whining shape sped past my ear, my cheek grazed by feathers that burned. I dropped to the horse's neck, the sound of another arrow soaring past my other cheek as I felt for my blade and heard Ulric's sword being drawn – like the sighing of an ill wind.

The two thieves came at us from separate sides of the track, the one on my side reaching for Dominic's reins. But the horse sensed danger, smelled strangers, and threw his head high, dragging the reins free, shying away and stepping down on the man's foot with an iron-shod hoof.

The fellow's anguished howl set up birds and I slashed at his shoulder with the *misericorde* as Ulric grunted with his own sweep and parry. He leaped for the horse, swinging onto its rump and clamping his heels hard against Dominic's flank and we jumped the fallen and bleeding villains, galloping far away until we pulled up on the fringed edges of the Dee hard by Chester, horse's sides heaving, our own matching his breath for breath.

I slipped from the horse, my knees folding so that I almost fell. In a heartbeat I was back amongst the carnage of the Angevin forest with Gisborne. My heart pounded even harder than Dominic's galloping hooves had when we left our erstwhile companions days before. They talk of the cold sweat of fear and that is precisely what coated my filthy palms. Panic horrified and annoyed me all at once. I took a breath, remembering Gisborne holding me, wrapped around me that night and my breath slowing to match his.

As I took command again, I knew the violence of Wilf's and Harry's deaths would haunt me forever and the haunting was entirely dependent on my reaction to it. At that moment, all I wanted was to find quiet and peace with my son and I vowed and declared that I would do everything necessary to make it so.

'Alright?' Ulric whispered, looking at Chester's walls.

'Yes. Yes, I am.'

My hand smoothed Dominic's neck and I wondered if we would have to leave him behind and secure fresh horses. Ulric said no if we rested for a day hidden in the forest. He would buy an extra mount for us and yes, he had coin and then we could make haste to Mont Hault perhaps three or four leagues away if we kept to the byways.

So close!

I waited whilst he walked to the town gates, feeding into a little group of people loaded with goods for the market. The brooding shape of the castle stared across the Dee at me, and I shrank into the trees, wondering how many eyes could see me as the soldiers walked the parapets. Would they have been warned to watch for a woman who had tried to kill one of the King's favourites? One of Prince John's favourites?

I wondered how Ulric would convince anyone that he wasn't merely a filthy villein on the run with stolen pennies in his purse. I daren't think of him being anything other than successful and I daren't think of Gisborne. Not yet. I wanted to, to be sure. I wanted to try and sift through all the information that countered my own experience, but I wouldn't. I dipped further back into the woods, holding Dominic's reins as he grazed on the forest grasses. Eventually he rested, his head hanging, bottom lip dangling, his hoof tilted so that his hip angled like an old man's. I sat against a tree, reins hooked over my arm, tired and hungry.

'Ysabel! Ysabel!'

Ulric's voice woke me and my head jerked up. He threw a small bag in my lap.

'Fine mess you'd be in if it weren't me,' he said from the back of a thickset chestnut mare to which Dominic stretched his neck and whickered. 'I've got bread and two pies. And some cherries which I stole from a handsome tree near the church.' He grinned. 'They're very sweet.'

And so we began a day's rest, secreted deep in the woods around Chester. We ate and chatted about Moncrieff, about Cecilia and Brother John. Of Camden and De Courcey. Oh yes, we talked long about *him*. I avoided nothing in my discourse on my late marriage. How could I? Ulric and I were almost as intimate as an old married couple. I say 'almost' because of course we were not a couple. Would never be.

But he was my friend.

The shade of his current lord and my former lover sat beside us all the while. Despite its presence, we never mentioned Gisborne. I never asked and Ulric never revealed – too much of truth and untruth that would need days to unravel. Besides I had another to think on – a reason to concentrate and stay alive.

William was at Mont Hault and needed his mother at least.

If not his father.

Ulric decided to move us on in the middle of that night. We left as quietly as two horses can and Ulric found his way along tracks with unerring skill. Whatever he had done for De Courcey and Gisborne had given him innate knowledge of hidden ways round the towns and settlements of the country. I remembered him as an apparently callow youth guarding me, and it seemed odd to reconcile that with the sharply attuned man who now rode in front. I realised I may have completely misjudged him. Perhaps I misjudged many.

Even Gisborne.

We didn't talk, just moved doggedly on as far from Chester's walls as we could get before light. Finally dawn lit the pathways and the birds began and I heaved a big sigh.

'Safe now, Ysabel. Far enough away and off the beaten track. I'll wager no one will find us.'

I could hear water chuckling and the chestnut, obviously thirsty, dragged at Ulric's grip to turn toward the sound.

'It's the confluence of the Dee and Afon Alyn. If we follow the tracks along the smaller river, we shall reach Mont Hault in no time.'

'And what is 'no time', Ulric?'

'Oh a bell here, a bell there. You know. Suffice to say, Ysabel, that we are almost there but we must be beyond cautious. I have learned that when the end is in sight is when the worst mistakes are made. Wits, Ysabel, wits.'

He tapped the side of his head.

The rivers joined with a small tussle, a spat of white water as they ran together. The riverbanks fell easily to the water in some parts where shallows were lined with pebbles, steeper banks in others where the water swirled away in a muddy swathe, no sign of clarity. We urged the horses down the decline to the stones and they gratefully drank their fill and we dismounted and washed faces and hands. Ulric offered me wine from our rapidly depleting bladder, worried the water may not be wholesome.

'Ulric, I am so tired of all of this,' I handed him the bladder back. 'Mont Hault and the priory won't come soon enough. I just want to seek peace, sanctuary. De Courcey and Halsham can't touch me if I am under the church's protection.'

'True to a point, Ysabel. But the priory mayn't be one of those that offer asylum in law. Methinks the best way for you to be safe is to be secret. Once William is with you again, we shall find a way of spiriting you and he far into the Welsh deeps where you will never be found.'

'What is the name of this priory?'

'The Priory of Linn. So named because close by, the Alyn runs over a small waterfall. In fact one can hear the water in the chapel. It's a charming place. Only small. A dozen or so Benedictine nuns. But they have an intensive garden and grow for the sister house in Mont Hault.'

It reminded me of Saint Eadgyth's and I said so and then asked how far. Ulric said not far, a day, maybe a little more and for me to be patient.

Patient!

We had a little food left – a bit of stale bread and the crusts of the pies. In the far distance we could see hills that grew to form a barrier between the sky and the land. I liked the look of it, as if nature offered its own protection: a defensive wall. We chewed the food, drank the last of the wine and looked at each other.

'That's it then, Ulric, we *have* to move on. Let's go now and use the daylight and travel through the night as well. Please?'

You do not know what it is to be a mother who has lost her son. Who has run for a twelve month. Whose heartbeat is perpetually startled.

He gave me a long look, mouth in an unhappy line.

'Please!'

'This is ill-advised, Ysabel. Slow and steady.'

'I cannot, I'm close to breaking madness, Ulric. Please!'

Horrified, I felt tears prick my eyes and I blinked.

He stood and tightened the chestnut's girth.

'Alright. But we must be careful. Keep your knife close.'

I thought he stretched the danger, but touched the *misericorde* for assurance after I had mounted.

He led off into the dappled woods that grew beside the Alyn and I allowed the bird and river sounds to calm my nerves. Each time my mind started to race toward imagined disaster, I pulled it back and tried to envisage my little boy. I could feel his hair under my chin, silky and soft. I could smell him – like puppies there is a smell about infants, as if life hasn't polluted their souls yet. And when I looked on him, he grinned. A toothless smile of little relevance really, but a smile none the less.

And that's when I missed the arrow flying past. All I heard was a sharp cry from Ulric as he fell onto the chestnut's neck, an arrow embedded in his shoulder. I spurred Dominic up by his side, grabbing the reins, shouting *hyar* and kicking both horses at a shambling canter toward a dense thicket.

'Ysabel,' Ulric whispered. 'Go. Get you gone. Follow the river. Fly!'

'No. Ulric, it is a mere wounding in your shoulder, let me pull it out…'
I could hear a crashing through the forest behind and my heart leaped as
I grabbed the shaft.

'No! Do not! I order you, go!'

His face had a sheen of sweat atop an awful pallour and I wondered
if the arrow was barbed. I grabbed the shaft and broke it as close to his
shoulder as I could, throwing the rest away.

'There,' I said. You can ride with one hand.'

I noticed a small bow tied to the front of the chestnut's saddle, slashing
at the lash with my blade.

'A bow! Ulric! The arrows, where?'

'Underneath, in the quiver.'

He was close to fainting.

I grabbed one, nocked it and prepared to take on the ambushers as the
noise of shouts grew closer. I loosed the arrow away in panic and heard
a yell but the shouts came on so I nocked another. My hands shook, the
arrow slipping.

'God!' I yelled, drawing back the string, straining it as hard as I could.

Two men burst through the scrub, the horses starting, Ulric dangling
over the chestnut's neck. I loosed again, so close it was impossible to
miss and found a mark, one man screaming and falling with an arrow
embedded in his chest. His companion snarled and leaped forward and I
reached for another arrow but the chestnut shied away with Ulric's arms
hanging down.

No!

The bow was useless and I threw it at the face in front of me. His hair
was long and greasy, his beard tangled, clothing filthy and torn, he had a
tattooed mark on his arm and I watched the tendons slip and slide as he
reached for Dominic's bridle to throw his whole weight on it.

He spoke in the Welsh tongue and his eyes flamed with hatred. I slid
down the other side of Dominic, glad of my male clothes and grabbing
the *misericorde*, ran for the edge of the thicket. But the outlaw followed,
longer legs, faster. He grabbed my surcoat and yanked, flinging me down
hard, my knife grip almost loosening as he reached for my purse.

I lifted my arm to thrust the *misericorde* into his side with every ounce of strength I possessed and it slid through the thin scraps of leather. The felon snarled, his breath foetid, pulling at the blade with one giant maw whilst the tattooed arm reached back and clouted the side of my head brutally, right on the eyebrow. My teeth rattled as I stared at a face that had death carved into every line and I knew my moment had come.

No William.

No freedom.

No life.

And so I closed my eyes, best not to see it coming, as my ears rang with all the bells of an horarium and my head ached with ferocious pain. There was an odd gurgling sound and then a crashing weight fell against my shoulder as I was dragged sideways.

I opened my eyes and stared at the face of death again, his eyes meeting mine. Wide, fixed, the blood from a slit in his neck pooling, some trickling from his mouth and all the while that hideous bubble. Somehow I managed to get to my knees and scramble backward until arms pulled me up and placed me hard against a tree.

'Ysabel,' the voice I would never forget dragged my eyes from the felon.

CHAPTER SEVENTEEN

I looked at Gisborne, seeing but not.

His hand bought a wad to my eyebrow. 'Your scar has opened.'

Nothing to say, no words, just trembles coursing through my body.

But then,

'Ulric!' I pushed from the tree, starting across the glade but his hand held me back.

'By the river with the horses.'

'Alive?'

He nodded.

'Mary Mother!'

I ran then, thrusting him away, afraid of my feelings, of pain and of confrontation – pushing through the thicket away from my dearest dream, my worst nightmare.

'Ulric!'

I found him lying propped against the riverbank, the horses wide-eyed and half-in half-out of the water. His face had paled and he whispered, 'I'm so sorry.'

'For what?'

I knelt and looked at the remains of the arrow still obscenely pricked into his shoulder.

'For not protecting you.'

'You were…'

'He sustained an arrow wound and assumed he would die. Fainted at the sight of blood!'

'As I almost did once.'

'Almost.'

Gisborne knelt by Ulric's side with a broken piece of wood wrapped in a torn strip.

'Bite this,' he shoved it into Ulric's mouth. 'You can be glad the arrow's not barbed or you'd be in a lot more pain. When I pull, don't bring the Welsh down on us, man.'

Ulric's eyes widened to show the whites but he bit anyway. Gisborne grasped what was left of the shaft and pulled, Ulric's moan wretched to hear. Without waiting, Gisborne poured wine in the wound and placed a folded pad of linen over it, blood immediately soaking through.

'We haven't time for more. You need to mount, both of you, and we must move fast. De Courcey and Halsham are on their way to Mont Hault.'

My head throbbed but I managed to speak without slurring.

'Sir Guy, thank you. Now you've discharged your life-debt to me from Anjou, take Ulric and leave. I wish to continue alone to the priory without risking anyone's life but my own.'

As I finished, I took up Dominic's reins, mounted and looked down on them both. Little spots of blood ran down my cheek and dropped onto the hood. 'Ulric, you will ever be my friend, I am grateful beyond belief for your loyalty but please go with your lord now.'

I kicked Dominic and we leaped up the riverbank, cantering along the track by the Alyn, increasing our pace as the track widened.

I could not think. My head was filled with fluffy cloud and the pain with each jolting stride was like hot pincers near my eye. Every now and then, a dizzy blackness would block vision and then clear, enough to see a horse gaining on my near side and a hand reach out to pull steadily on the reins until both horses had jerked to a halt. I shook my head, turning as vision blurred and cleared, blurred and cleared.

Eyes *met mine glance for glance, the air solid and tempestuous, but I recognized something in the expression.* This man *felt compassion for me…*

'Guy,' I whispered and slumped onto Dominic's neck.

Bells.

Every now and then.

Bells that made me feel safe – as if I belonged.

I opened my eyes and a nun smiled at me. 'Ah, awake. Pain?'

'No…'

In truth my head ached, throbbing like a tabor by my temple. I swung my eyes around, a move least like to discommode. A cell, whitewashed walls, monastic simplicity – nothing new then. But the noise, a rushing sound, tumbling, perhaps even roaring if the breeze should change. I turned my head to the window – horn-covered, the strips of flattened animal horn allowing a vaguely translucent light to enter.

'You can hear the waterfall, the *linn* after which our priory is named.' The nun was like an apple, rotund and with red cheeks.

'It's beautiful, tranquil.'

I straightened my head on the pillow.

'My Lady, would you like to bathe? Do you feel strong enough? You are ve…'

'Very dirty, I know. Sister, I am filthy but I need help. Can you … is it an imposition?'

'Not at all, dear child. I will get a bath filled in the lavatorium and I will help you walk there. It's not far.'

As I fell into a doze, I smiled at the way she addressed me as a 'child'. She must have been my age and it was only a moment, I swear, before she was shaking my shoulder gently. 'My lady?' She slipped her arm around my shoulder, levering me up as the world tilted. I put a hand to my temple, then my brow, feeling the linen covered wound.

'We stitched it. It needed to be closed.'

I nodded.

'I realise … thank you, Sister…'

'It's Mercia, Mother Mercia.' She made no comment about my misappellation, just smiled. 'Come now, let's remove the fields from your body. If you haven't actually been ploughing, you look as though you could have *been* the plough!'

Back on the cot, I felt more like a lady, less like a serf. My skin was pink, the light lying across it. My hair, though brown, lay soft and silky on the pillow, the linen bandage removed and the stitching proud. I had been assured it was a clean wound, that the stitching had been fastidious and fine. Mother Mercia had covered me in a rough chemise with longish sleeves and then pulled the blanket over me, propping me with a pillow and my folded and cleaned cloak. She passed me watered wine, a hot griddle cake and a bowl of potage and never had such plain food seemed so good, because whilst I might be wounded I was starving hungry.

But Lord I was tired, the spoon heavier than a broadsword in my fingers.

Mother Mercia noticed and took the bowl from me.

'Sleep now, child.'

'But Mother, I have…'

Questions. My son. His father.

'Not now. Sleep first.'

She left, closing the door as the bell rang for None.

Sleep is a reprieve. No matter the situation. One's mind turns from its dilemmas, one's body regirds. Often as I shifted on the cot, the sound of the waterfall would grow louder and then recede. Normal rhythms reasserted themselves and thus I slept through the night and its bells, waking as Tierce rang out the next day.

I was unsure of my place, where I should go, what I should wear and so I lay watching the dawn light painting patterns across the wall. Listening to the water and the birds' singing and the nuns' chorus adding such a superb descant with a glorious canto.

The door eased open and I turned to smile a welcome to Mother Mercia but the smile died and my hand shot to the stitches, my head turning to hide my face from the person who had entered.

He said nothing immediately, just walked up to me and took my hand in his – he had beautiful hands – very strong, but capable of playing many tunes, not the least on heartstrings.

'Don't cover it. It does not matter.'

His voice … ah, I remembered the tone. Visceral, I had called it.

'It does…'

'No. It is merely a battle scar, that's all.'

He moved away to stand by the window, a tall shape in a black woolen surcoat and dark *chausses* with muddy boots over the top. For the first time I really allowed myself to look upon him. His height and the flowing dark hair that fell around his neck, eyes the blue of a mid-summer's evening.

But, no, no! Eyes like a midnight sky. Remember, Ysabel? The cool remove? The anger?

Even now, he stood rigid, half-turned from me, so alternate to his kindness over the wounding. His face had lost none of its patrician lines in the last year – if anything it had become even sharper. And the stubble lay upon his chin, neither beard nor clean-shaven, as if he shrugged a broad shoulder at both. Perhaps that was the most visible thing of all – Guy of Gisborne was his own man, bending his knee neither to his liege-lord nor anyone-else.

'You are in mortal danger, Ysabel.'

'You think I don't know?'

When I spoke it was barely a murmur and I faced the wall, having turned my awful face from him when our eyes met. The glance breathed air onto the embers of memory – the abbey at Locksley and me behind the screen, the Obedientiary shushing Matilda and myself. Descending the stair in Calais, the blue gown grasping my legs with its folds on the night we made love for the first time. My fingers curled into the rough weave of the coverlet as he continued.

'Your life is forfeit. There is barely need for a trial. Richard has denied *you,* his family, in favour of his mercenary De Courcey. Richard has said you will be strangled, then you will burn, may God forgive him.'

'He does what he must.'

'Jesu, Ysabel! He does what he should *not!*'

That was when the fire that had been smouldering inside me exploded with incendiary force. I whipped round, sitting up and grabbing the cloak from behind the pillow to wrap myself.

'You say he should *not,* you base hypocrite! You, a man who should not have done many things and you dare to stand before me saying that?'

He stepped back further along the wall away from me. When he spoke, it was that growl that made lesser men dive onto their bellies flat on the ground, a sound like the rolling out of a seige engine.

'Meaning…'

'Meaning *Sir* Guy, that you shouldn't have sold me.'

His eyebrows shot heavenward.

'*What?*' He pushed away from the window. '*Sold* you?'

'Halsham said…'

'Halsham,' he mocked.

I stood tall even though he was taller, broader and altogether more intimidating, thinking to myself that fires were difficult to quench.

'Halsham offered you money and position in London and you told him about the hermit's hut. You left me so you could secure the status and power so meaningful to your life. You left me to suffer at De Courcey's hands after all your promises,' I snarled, staring him down. 'Deny it!'

Ferocity burst forth, crashing like a wave about us.

'I *will* deny it,' he shouted. 'Christ above, Ysabel.'

He started pacing but the cell was too small and with the volume of his response, I expected to see the whitewash run, for the horn to fall out from the window, for me to be blown backward by his fury.

'For leagues on our journey, you did nothing but denigrate Halsham. He was a snake, corrupt, the devil spawn. And yet you believe *his* word. God Almighty!'

He pounded the stone sill with his fist and little flakes of whitewash drifted to the floor, the harshness of his words at odds with the gently floating particles.

'You, you…' Unable to phrase anything further, he walked past me but then swung back. 'How can you distrust me so much, Ysabel? What did I do to warrant your lowly opinion of me?'

He stopped in front of me, his hand flexing hard on the hilt of his sword. *What did you do?*

My mouth opened and closed. 'You were…'

His eyebrow rose, a quirk that might have meant humour once, but now…

And what argument did I have that would mean anything? I grabbed at the only thing I could.

'You were secretive always. Prying truths from you was nigh to impossible. Is it any wonder I thought your secrecy was damnable and worse? I could only guess at truths.'

'Secretive. And that is *all?* That is all it took to make you believe I had sold your whereabouts to someone like Halsham or De Courcey? Damn you, Ysabel, I am the King's spymaster. Stealth is implicit but it doesn't

300

mean I am disloyal to those I…' He stopped and shook his head. 'I did not tell Halsham where you were!'

My fires sputtered and died and a hideous flush crept over me as I looked at my actions from his point of view. He had protected me, fed and clothed me, holding me when I grieved about the parlous state of my life. And yet still I believed the absolute worst of him.

'Well if you didn't sell me, if it was pure luck that led Halsham my way, why didn't you seek me out at Moncrieff afterward. Why didn't you return and help me escape?'

He kicked a toe against the brazier, and it rocked as if agitated.

'Gisborne, answer me!'

'I did come back.' He flung round. 'On the eve of your wedding, if you remember. I came back and you looked *at* me, *through* me and *past* me. What message could I garner from that? Surely if you needed to be rescued it would have been evident.'

'Oh Gisborne.' It was my turn to pace. 'By then it was too late. I needed you the day Halsham found me, not the eve of my marriage!'

'Why, Ysabel? Why was it too late?'

His voice had lowered perilously, and I was confused – was he saying something I needed to hear; was there something ulterior in his words?

'Because the King had granted my care and my hand to a mercenary soldier whose forces he needed. There was nothing to be done at that point.'

'Nothing to be done.' He gave an empty laugh. 'You think?'

'Oh for Mary's sake! What? Would you have thrown me over your pommel to gallop away from your hard-won status and power?'

I dared him – so help me as I gazed at that severe face, I dared him. And it seemed as though we clashed close in our duel, our hilts jamming, our breath dragging in and out. He shook off my weapon and felled me with one blow.

'Yes,' he said.

Outside, the waterfall played its tinkling melody as though it was being plucked like a *psaltery*. Footsteps walked along the cloister. Then nothing.

'I don't believe you.'

'Ysabel, if you had given me one sign that you needed help, I would have given up everything and taken you from Moncrieff. But you seemed

301

at peace with your state – as if Richard's decree gave you the freedom to stay at your family home amongst your memories. That it had settled your mind for you. Your face was…'

I thought back to my marriage day, where in fear of my future I had retreated to a faraway place in my mind. Gisborne had seen me progress through the ceremony and the celebration with a veneer of acceptance and calm as if the presence of the man I had once loved mattered not one scrap.

'It was not what you thought.'

'Then if it was not what it appeared to be, can you not grant that I may have misread you? As sadly you appear to have misread me?'

I sat on the cot, the ropes creaking under the straw-stuffed mattress and put my head in my hands. This was a man who was embittered early in his life. Why would he assume anything other than what he saw with his own eyes? Even though he knew De Courcey's history, all he saw was a woman who sat as though becalmed in an ocean. Did she look as if she was affeared? Was she in need? Was there any sort of signal that would be worth him giving up all that he had worked for?

No, of course there wasn't. Why would he make a move that might be met with rejection? He'd faced that with his father and it had left an indelible stain. It was hardly likely he would risk the same thing again. And so I gave birth to his son without him knowing. I suffered rape and assault. And perhaps, just perhaps, it was all my fault.

'Mary Mother,' I whispered.

In the silence of recrimination, the door creaked open and Mother Mercia rolled into the chamber. Despite her rose-red cheeks and her polished apple face, the look she cast upon us both chastised and be-devilled.

'My Lord? My Lady? I trust all is well? Only it seems our walls may not be as thick as we had thought.'

Gisborne turned his shoulder and gazed out the window although Lord knows why as horn reveals nothing of the view beyond. In my turn I flushed, wondering what the world of *Linn* had made of our godless behaviour.

'I apologise, Mother. It was thoughtless and disrespectful.'

'Well then, if you think that things have settled enough – there are visitors waiting.'

The bossy prioress eased the door ajar and a bright face edged in.

'My Lady…' Gwen's pretty face lit with happiness that reflected its light on the space around us.

'Gwen,' I gasped. 'Oh Gwen! Is…'

Behind her and peering over her shoulder, Brigid grinned.

'Lady Ysabel,' she said as Gwen stood aside.

In Brigid's arms lay my son – a sturdy bundle with black hair that tufted over the edges of a shawl. She held him out.

'William,' I whispered.

'Do you not wish to hold him, madame? Come now, open your arms.'

I lifted my arms as if they were not part of my body, as though this experience was a dream or a vision. I had not held my child since his birth and to hold him now, months on, when he was beyond that greasy, newborn state was filled with unreality.

My heart stopped in those moments, as his weight settled and my eyes fixed upon him. I reached a self-conscious finger to his cheek and his eyes opened, the darkest blue gaze staring back. He didn't blink, just observed, then smiled, two outrageously small toothbuds shining back from his bottom gums. My heart started again.

'Biddy, he looks so well. I owe you and Gwen his life.'

In the crowded room, I felt a body push against me, but was too absorbed with my son to pay heed.

'Ah Lady Ysabel, tis not us you owe but Sir Guy. He has made sure young William wanted for nothing, least of all security.

Gisborne?

I swung round but of course Gisborne had been the body slipping past. William's father had left.

'What say you, Brigid?'

William had pulled a dimpled fist free and wrapped it round my finger, dragging it to his mouth as I posed the question.

'Sir Guy, Lady Ysabel. Not long after we fled, we were waylaid and safe-guarded to Mont Hault. We were taken to a modest dwelling with two rooms and a small barn. Peter and our guard, a man called Alfric, slept in the barn and Gwen and I slept in the cottage. It weren't no better nor worse 'n anything we had in the village and we were comfortable. We never wanted for pennies, everything was seen to. Presently Ulric arrived and explained it all.'

Ulric. Of course.

It became clear. Ulric had informed Gisborne of the birth of his heir and by doing so had betrayed my wishes. But did I have the right to abuse him for his disloyalty? Perhaps he had seen beyond my skewed emotions to the reality – which was that William needed support that would be far beyond Moncrieff's villeins to provide.

William stirred, the smile changing as a growl emerged.

'He's hungry, is all. Time for him to break his fast,' Gwen said as she held out her arms.

But Biddy stalled her.

'P'raps you'd care to feed your son, yourself, my lady.'

William had been fed on goat's milk through a cloth until they reached Mont Hault but failing to thrive and desperate at his sinking state, Biddy feared for his life. She had the sense to seek out a wetnurse in the hope he would turn away from a fast approaching demise.

'The little beggar did,' she said. 'Slowly fer sure, but improving nevertheless.'

But he was a desultory feeder and as soon as she thought he was healthy enough to cope, she began again with bread in goat's milk and honey or bread soaked in potage, giving him a little camomile and lemon balm infusion to ease any distrait. He progressed well to the chubby child who sat before me, propped on pillows. I soaked a crust in milk and honey now and enjoyed the gummy smile as he sucked and then experimented with those ridiculous teeth, reaching with a star-shaped hand to hold the crust himself.

After, Gwen and Brigid having gone with Mother Mercia to break their own very late fast, I sat William on the floor on the coverlet, giving him a smooth wooden bracelet Biddy had passed to me. He leaned his body to the side, pushed on his arms and settled himself as if to crawl, rocking back and forth and discussing life in some infantile tongue for which I had no translation. He continued his little *carole,* dancing to his own tune and with some transparent partner, and I took joy in his infancy, feeling awe and love in one.

'You called him William.'

I had not heard him return, so wrapped was I in watching the innocence.

'The name came to me as I gave birth.'

Gisborne sat on a coffer and I looked from he to his son; the likeness was remarkable, even in a child so young, and a perverse part of me was glad that there was no denying the child *was* a Gisborne.

'Why did you not tell me?'

'You had settled to a forward march, Sir Guy. I would not halt you.'

William had somehow manoeuvred himself close by his father and grasped hold of the *chausses* to pull himself up. His hand found the scabbard and he toyed with it.

'This is *my* child,' Gisborne said as his hand slid over the top of William's head. I was surprised to note the pain in his voice.

'I ... as I said, you made your choices, I made mine.'

'Jesu, Ysabel. Then tell me, did you know you were with child when you wedded the Baron?'

The questions! How I hated them.

'Yes.'

'And yet knowing the dire nature of the man, you went ahead and risked not just your life, but my son's!'

William sank to the floor on his belly, his little bottom in the air, falling asleep almost immediately.

'I remind you of the King's decree.'

'Ah yes. The King, your infamous god-brother.'

'And your liegelord, sir. Besides,' I added sourly. 'It was never intended for William to stay at Moncrieff after his birth. Look at him, he is hardly a minted image of the Baron. There was a plan...'

Through the terse discussion, William slept on, obviously to the tension between his parents.

'Ysabel,' Guy's tone changed on an instant. 'What prevents you from acknowledging me on any level?'

Oh yes, Ysabel, what? Pride?

I had not been proud of any answer thus far. Everything smacked of the spoiled child of the nobility that Gisborne was forced to escort from Cazenay a lifetime ago. But I was ever spontaneous in my replies and now was little different. Insecurity wreaks its own response.

'Old Jewry!' I spat. 'And your kinship with Halsham who is De Courcey's man.'

'Old Jewry?'

Again an incredulous tone but his customary body language, that rigidity, was held in check by his son lying at his booted toes.

'You were there. What role did *you* play? Firelighter, murderer?'

I swear if William was not curled on the floor between us, Gisborne might have shaken me till my eyeballs rattled. His fists curled on themselves and I sat straighter, hugging my cloak closer.

'No role beyond challenging your husband to desist before knocking him out with the flat of my sword and ... *disciplining* his men at arms after I had discovered them torching a rabbi's house and with the family inside like bread in an oven. Does that satisfy you perhaps? And then arguing with the King himself that the perpetrators in London and York, of whom a number were De Courcey's own, be tried for murder and hung. But our King ever has his eye on the main chance, and with a Crusade in the offing he needs fighting men.' He took a breath, his voice wrathful. 'Is *that* the answer you wanted?'

All at once I just wanted to give in and so I shrugged and reached down to stroke William's little bottom.

'Ysabel.'

The way he said my name provoked such a bodily surge I felt humiliated it happened within one of God's houses.

'Please. You *must* leave. Take our son. It is more perilous daily.'

Tears began to well but I would not cry. 'It's a mess, is it not?' I said in a trembling voice.

He stood and walked across to me, holding his hand out. I placed my palm in his and the feel of his skin on mine was another memory so that when I stood and raised my eyes to his, I remembered two naked bodies and the making of an heir.

A rap at the door caused an expletive to hiss out as Gwen's face appeared.

'Wondered if you want us to take little Wills, my lady.'

I found that I could laugh, the highly charged moment quenched.

'Wills? Yes, Gwen. You may take Master Wills and see to him but you must bring him to me the minute he wakes. I would not lose any more moments with him.'

We watched our son lifted into willing arms, not a stir from the floppy little soul, and then we were alone.

'If I get some clothes for you, will you walk?'

Clothes? Is it not what you do for me always, Gisborne?

'Why break the habit of a lifetime, Sir Guy?'

I softened the irony with a smile.

One plain dun-coloured *bliaut* and one even plainer girdle later, I was climbing behind Gisborne up the far side of the waterfall the Welsh called *linn* and which was the *psaltery*-sound of the Alyn as it tumbled – a charming place, a pretty resonance, rocks and a tranquil pond up high and further back from the overflow.

Suitable for talking.

'I knew you the moment you walked into my chamber at Locksley.'

I had stripped off boots and hose, rolled the gown to my knees and thrust my legs into the crystalline shallows. The sun shone and it warmed me through as if it were love.

'Then why did you not say?'

'I deal in subterfuge, Ysabel. You worked hard at disguising your voice, you had coloured your hair and you carried a severe wound. I would say you were hiding and wished not to be found. You knew who *I* was. As I said, if you wanted my help, you would surely have indicated it. Thus it was enough to keep a wary eye…'

'But you encouraged me to stay on, knowing the Devil's friends were coming.'

'It was a massive risk. But I could better protect you close by than away.'

All the while he spoke, he sat with distance between us and I could not read him – Jesu, but he was a man of secrets.

'A risk that failed,' I replied.

'Not if you hadn't run. My staff are loyal to a man and would never have betrayed you. Unfortunately you were seen by Halsham's squire as you fetched the mare. It was a matter of moment for them to put everything together. Unfortunately they play the game of secrets almost as well as I.'

'Do they know you help me?'

He didn't answer, but dropped his head and grimaced.

'Oh God! How much could we have avoided by truths? Methinks we might both be at fault.'

I rubbed at the stitches.

'Does it hurt?' He leaned over and eased my fingers away.

I demurred for a moment, then, 'No, but the memory does.'

'Tell me,' he said softly.

So I did. In awful detail, finding I cried a little. He held me, a movement as natural as holding one's child and the water played its odd melody and birds sang and that moment was God-given. One to be cherished.

'Like I said, Ysabel, it is a war wound. A battle with the Devil and you won.' He bent and kissed around the scar. ''Tis like kissing a hedgehog.'

'Then perhaps you kiss the wrong part of me,' I hazarded.

'Perhaps,' he replied.

How does making love happen without one noticing the progressions? A moment and he was kissing my lips. Then we were unclothed and in the water where I could see every part of his lean and muscled frame. His long legs wrapped around me and drew me in, his arms sliding around my back. My hips met his like someone craving water in the desert. His hand gently parted my thighs drawing my legs around him.

They say in Ireland, that the lovers' knot has an unbroken shape, that it simply winds in and out, over and under in perpetuity, and that is forever how I remember the intertwining shape of this day of days as Guy of Gisborne and I, Ysabel of Moncrieff, made love.'

I wondered if making love is any different to loving. Does it mean the same thing? For a man it can be merely one moment's pleasure, but for a woman, the bodily act might signify a lifetime's commitment. Once I said to Gisborne, *'Don't regret this'* and I thought I could say now with a little confidence that he did not. But then would I ever really know what the King's secret servant felt?

We dried in the sun, not worrying about life until I heard William's distant cry, lusty and angry, and dragged on my clothes before Gisborne could react.

'He cries,' I muttered.

'He demands,' Guy laughed pushing away thoughts of the times to come. 'He is my son.'

We hurried back, worries away, but when we spotted Ulric, Peter and Mother Matilda in a tense conclave, it was obvious my past was catching up.

'They are in Mont Hault,' said Ulric.

No!

'And they head to the priory. Money pays for loose tongues.'

Gisborne pushed in from behind me.

'Horses and provisions?'

'Ready,' said Peter as Mother Mercia dashed back through the gates.

'Then get moving.' He turned to me and grabbed my hands. 'We leave, Ysabel. There is a plan so rest easy, but you must ride and keep riding, no matter what.'

'With you?' I held onto his hands tightly as if a thread would snap if I let go and he nodded but turned when he heard Peter and Ulric running back with readied horses that followed willingly, ears pricked, eyes bright.

Gwen and Brigid arrived with Mother Mercia, William crowing with delight at the horses.

'He's fed and happy,' said Brigid unnecessarily. She was a staunch thing, Biddy. She knew we all faced death now and it wasn't written anywhere on her face.

My heart pounded, taking up its old anxious rhythm as we mounted.

'Away!' warned Guy. 'We must make haste to the cover of the trees.'

'Gisborne,' I clicked my horse close to him and reached over, touching my palm to the stubbled cheek. 'Stay close. I would not lose my son's father…'

'My Ysabel,' he said and at that my tears began. 'What I do, I do for you and for William.'

His kiss burned my palm.

I have lost my heart to you, Gisborne. Be careful with it, I beg you.

We rode up the near side of the steep incline by the side of the waterfall. The goat track we used wound in and out of fern and tree. We were never in sight of each other, each turn coming tightly one on top of the other through dense growth. I was conscious of my little family ahead and I trailed second to last with Gisborne close behind. I thanked God he was near.

Almost at the top I looked back, hidden by the trees. Far below, two men, one with russet hair, together with six men at arms were at the priory gates. The bell for Vespers was tolling and the summer light had softened, the gates remaining unopened until De Courcey, for it was he, yelled loud enough to wake the spirits in the barrows.

The gates of the little priory opened and Mother Mercia emerged. De Courcey spoke. I could imagine that choleric face, inflamed by the hatred he held for me, the woman who had emasculated him before his noble peers. How he and Halsham would enjoy watching me strangle and burn. Mother Mercia replied and De Courcey's voice became louder although I could not decipher any detail over the water's plucking and chattering. She bowed her head, tucking her hands into her sleeves and turned to retreat behind her walls, but hated husband mine, he screamed at her, and his men rode to surround her and my hand crept to my mouth in fear for the gentle nun.

I spurred my horse down around the bend, expecting to meet Gisborne, for us to ride to Mother Mercia's defence. But the next turn appeared – empty of my son's father and a horrible expectation began to form in my mind.

A horrific wail broke the air as the priory bell's echo faded. A man in distress, a man who knew there was no hope, who had been caught unawares, who knew the Devil sat behind him.

'Jesu!' I whispered as I watched from that bend.

De Courcey grabbed at his neck. Pierced by an arrow, harsh choking sounds filled the air, as even the waterfall's sound seemed to fade. He was as skewered as a wild pig and I was glad as he slid from his horse, Halsham leaping down to grab at the twitching, bleeding man who was my husband. But De Courcey lay dying, his blood spurting everywhere across the paving stones and I thought of Divine Providence as he gurgled and Halsham became soaked with gore.

The arrow had been a shot from the bow of a master archer and I knew who was the assassin – the man who had trekked behind me on his horse but who like a phantom had vanished and the man who now made my throat close over with fear for him.

'What I do, I do for you and for William.'

'Ysabel, we go *now!*' Ulric rode in behind me, agitated, grabbing my reins and pulling me on.

'*No!*'

I looked down at De Courcey's body as I shouted and Halsham's gaze turned in my direction. Perhaps he could see me, perhaps he could not, but it didn't matter. He knew my voice and I knew the price on my head had doubled in an instant. But it did not signify – not really. I just quailed for William's father.

'He'll flee as far as he can and if necessary seek sanctuary,' Ulric muttered as he grabbed my reins and dragged me after him.

And so we ran far into the dense vales of the Welsh, lost in the trees and tracks unknown to those of Halsham's ilk. William sat astride Biddy's horse, her arms around his baby form as he reveled in this rebellious journey, oblivious to the racking pain of his mother.

Gisborne lived, I knew, for that essential connection remained unbroken, but where he would go and how we should ever find him sent my heart into an altered rhythm each time I thought on it.

And there was no one at all to say to me in this time of separation and loss:
'And all shall be well, and all shall be well,
and all manner of thing shall be well.'

www.ingramcontent.com/pod-product-compliance
Ingram Content Group UK Ltd.
Pitfield, Milton Keynes, MK11 3LW, UK
UKHW021312270125
4312UKWH00020B/89